I0823409

THE TWELVE

THE TWELVE

JOEY GRACEFFA

with

MACKENZIE LYN MARR

HARPER

An Imprint of HarperCollins*Publishers*

HarperCollins Children's Books,
a division of HarperCollins Publishers,
195 Broadway, New York, NY 10007

HarperCollins Publishers, Macken House,
39/40 Mayor Street Upper,
Dublin 1, D01 C9W8, Ireland

The Twelve

harpercollins.com

Library of Congress Control Number: 2025947534

ISBN 978-0-06-333955-2
Typography by David DeWitt
25 26 27 28 29 LBC 5 4 3 2 1
First Edition

For Hecate, Mother of Witches

1

Ophelia

THERE ARE INVISIBLE TIES BINDING US, THIN AS SPIDERWEB but stronger than steel. To have a connection like that with someone, there aren't two people, but one. Two bodies, one soul. Wherever my sister is, the tug of that force connects us. Serena is only on the other side of the orphanage, but she might as well be locked behind fortress walls. I can feel her calling me. For months now, they've kept me from her, unable to reach the other end of that thread. Tonight, though, I'll swallow my fear and do the impossible.

My fingers shake and I breathe in deeply, forcing them to still. Squeezing my eyes closed, I listen to the rain pattering on the dormitory's roof. All day it's tapped against the windowpanes, visiting today on my birthday as it has for sixteen years. Every year, it's like an old friend returning to stir the pool of water splashing within my chest. That pool is always there, rippling gently, but today, it's more alive somehow. Deeper. A single raindrop falls through a crack in the lofted ceiling and, for a moment, it hangs suspended above me.

Tick . . . tick . . . tick . . .

The grandfather clock breaks my focus. The raindrop falls and strikes my cheek, splattering me with cold. Shivers ripple up my arms and legs. All I have is a threadbare blanket, the rough gray wool scratchy against my skin. It's no use against the damp chill clinging to the air, yearning to burrow beneath my skin and nest there forever. Breath hisses in the darkness as the dozen girls in my dormitory snore, sleeping more soundly than I've ever been able to. I barely dare to breathe lest I wake them. One wrong twitch, one squeal of rusty bedsprings, and I'll be caught.

Even the thought is terrifying. As I lie here in the quiet, my palms grow slick with cold, prickling sweat. I'm too aware of every small sound—the whisper of gathering wind outside the windows, the screech of leaves scratching glass, the warped beams moaning, the plaster moldings on the walls cracking. And closer, beside my bed, the skitter of a mouse sneaking along uneven floorboards. A familiar face. On sleepless nights she creeps out, my little friend, whiskers wiggling as she scavenges for crumbs. I like to think she knows me, always stopping by my bed to watch me with clever round eyes.

Growing up here has taught me the most important lesson a mouse must learn in a house full of cats: Don't squeak. Crying, talking back, sneaking food from the dining hall, stepping even one pinky toe out of line only results in bruises. Giving the matrons any reason to notice me is sure to end in smacks from rulers or the sharp pinch of nails. All those punishments pale in comparison to what the night matron will do if I'm caught out of bed at this hour.

Tonight, though, it's worth the risk.

Tick . . . tick . . . tick . . .

I count the ticking of the clock and the beating of my heart. Waiting. Every second seems to grow longer and longer. Eternal.

The more my breath grows shallow and my palms slick, the more the rushing current in my veins surges, ready to flood out of me and wash away every drop of fear.

Midnight is my only chance to reach Serena, when the sound of my footsteps will be covered by the chiming clock.

Bong.

The clang splits the air. I've been waiting for this moment all night, and now that it's here I don't dare move. I don't even dare breathe.

Finally, mercifully, the clock tolls again, loud enough to echo through the entire orphanage. On the third chime, I fling back my flimsy covers. For a moment, they billow, ghostly, in the moonlight streaming through the window. I hang my head over the side of my bed. As a child, I believed in monsters, sharp-toothed creatures waiting to grab my feet and drag me into the dark. But my years here have taught me monsters don't hide under the bed. They hide in plain sight.

After all, there's no place to hide anything in the dormitory, no privacy. We have open shelves rather than drawers, no doors on the bathrooms, no curtains on the showers. The matrons can search our meager possessions with a glance and no one steals anything because none of us have anything worth stealing. But there is one spot, dead center underneath the bed, where no one can see.

It's dark under the bed, but when I push away the limp gold curtain of my hair, it's there.

It's still perfect.

The cupcake is topped with fluffy pink frosting and sprinkled with silver sparkles. The warm vanilla scent brings back a rush of fuzzy memories—images of a time before frigid orphanages. A time of candles and warm hearths, memories that slip through my fingers like smoke.

Bong.

The fourth toll rings through the orphanage, and I don't dare waste any more time on ghosts of memories. Under cover of the clock chimes, I scoop up the cupcake, holding it gingerly so I don't crush it. The squeak of bedsprings as I roll off is lost in the clock's echoing din. I freeze, listening with my head cocked. Tonight, I can't be a mouse. I'm a fox. The night matron is on patrol, lurking, beady eyes searching the darkness. But I have to get to the East Wing, where they're keeping Serena locked up like a prisoner with all the other "troubled" girls.

On the fifth ring I dash between twin rows of sleeping girls, my nightgown tangling between my legs as I hurry on bare tiptoes across the wooden floor. In the silent heartbeat between each ring, I freeze, running again when the sound muffles my steps. I make it out of the dormitory and down the narrow hallway. The walls seem to squeeze in on me, paneled in dark wood with twisting patterns in the grain forming leering faces.

They watch me now, those faces. I'm so close, but the museum still lies between me and my sister. Its rooms once housed the library and ballroom, a parlor and a dining hall. Places once full of life and knowledge and light, long ago when this place was a proper mansion. Now the rooms separating the West Wing from the East might as well be full of ghosts. Once-bright oil paintings have faded to sepia, enormous vases that never hold flowers sit in the corners, rusty suits of armor cast shadows on the floor like phantoms waiting to raise their swords and slay me. I pick at the skin around my thumbnail. We're not allowed in the museum except to clean. To keep it pristine for visitors who see polished antiques, crystal clear glass, and shining brass hardware, rather than girls who work their fingers raw to keep everything spotless.

I long to linger in the shadows, watching, listening, judging if the way is safe. I don't have long, though. Taking a shuddering breath, I wait for the next chime and run through the shadows. I force myself not to look at the wingback chairs poised like serpents waiting to strike or the antique dolls demonically smiling. They reach for me, whispering my name on the wind: *Ophelia, Ophelia.*

When the chime fades, I skid to a stop, panting. I'm nearly to the East Wing, and I have only a moment to take in the low fire burning in a hearth to my right. A high-backed chair stands before it. My heart thunders in my ears as the eighth chime sounds, but I freeze. There's someone in the chair, unmoving, face hidden in the darkness.

The night matron.

My legs tremble until I fear they'll give out, and I clap my hand over my mouth to stifle my shaking breath. I wait for her to lurch up and strike me, and I clutch the cupcake so tightly it starts to crumple. The blow never arrives. Instead, a low guttural sound echoes through the museum. I clamp my hand tighter over my lips to hold in the laugh burbling to the surface as I make out her form, sprawled comfortably with her mouth hanging open. Snoring.

Leaving the sleeping matron behind, I reach the East Wing door on the next chime and slip inside. I hold my breath as the door snicks shut under cover of the final chimes. A shudder racks my body in the dark hall, silence seeping into my skin. As my eyes adjust, I half feel my way forward. In all my years here, I've never been in the East Wing before. There are so many doors, all closed, and I have no idea which one is Serena's dormitory. I trail my hand along the wall, letting my fingers play over every chilly brass doorknob. The invisible thread in my chest gives a tug and pulls me up short. I'm close. I step back to the door I just passed and touch the doorknob. Something yanks on that tether again. This has to be the one. Biting my lip, I turn the knob painfully slowly so it doesn't creak, and step inside.

The dormitory is dark, save for the pale streaks of moonlight striping the floor through the swaying curtains at the far end. The rain has stopped, but tree branches still scrape against the rows of windows on either side of the room. It's nearly identical to my own dormitory in the West Wing, except for the aching sense of dread churning in my stomach.

No one wants to be in this orphanage at all, but the East Wing girls . . . they're different. They're kept here, for their own safety and for ours. At least, that's what the matrons claim. Serena isn't dangerous, though. She's not a criminal or a monster. She doesn't belong here.

When I don't see her right away, my heart swan dives into my stomach. Moving her to the East Wing was bad enough; what if they got rid of her altogether? Maybe she pushed them too far and they sent her to another orphanage, or worse. I slink between the beds, checking every sleeping face. I recognize some, girls who were in the West Wing before they were sent here. At the end of the row, familiar dark hair splays across a white pillow like spilled ink. The knot between my shoulders loosens and my heartbeat steadies. Her chest rises and falls in a slow, steady pattern, and the scowl usually stamped across her face is relaxed in sleep.

Of course they put her in the very last bed, the one nearest the window, closest to the draft and the scrape of branches trying to claw their way inside. It should be a bed for the worst girls, the ones who spit vitriol through pearly smiles, who steal dessert from the littlest orphans, who know how to make others feel small and hurt without leaving bruises.

"Serena," I breathe.

Her eyes snap open, instantly alert. A surge of panic radiates from her, then stills when she sees me. Green irises like dark woodland ponds meet mine. They're so unlike my own blue ones, though the shape is the same as the ones I see in the cloudy bathroom mirror every day: large, round eyes that tilt with mischief at the corners.

"Ophelia?" Her fingers circle my wrist, squeezing like she's trying to make sure I'm real. I smile, and then she's smiling back with the same wide, full mouth that curls at the corners even when she's furious. She tugs me down into a tight hug, which I struggle to return one-armed while concealing my surprise behind my back.

When she pulls away, Serena's smile fades into a scowl. "You're not supposed to be here. You'll get in trouble."

I bite back my retort that getting caught might not be so bad if they put me here in the East Wing as punishment. At least we'd be together again.

Instead, I bring out the cupcake and Serena gasps, all admonishment gone. "Where did you get that?" It's a little squashed, the icing applied in an imperfect swirl, but to us it's perfect. "Quick, get in before somebody sees." She throws back the coverlet and I crawl onto the bed beside her. We sit knee to knee, making a tent out of the blanket with our bodies. Under here, we're as close as we were inside the womb. My limbs loosen, tension melting away like I'm made whole again when we're together.

"I had kitchen duty," I say. "Cook made these for the board's visit." The board members come in occasionally for photo ops, posing with the most photogenic orphans before making another tax write-off donation.

Serena frowns at me, brow furrowing. "Won't they know you took one?"

"Cook made a baker's dozen. The matrons will never know. And I found the candle in the trash after Cook's birthday a few months ago. I hid it in a crack between the floorboards under my bed."

"But I didn't get you anything yesterday for yours," Serena says.

"It's for both of us." I nudge her knee with my own. We always celebrate together, even though we were *technically* born on different days. Twins, born on either side of midnight. I hold the candle out to her. "Will you light it?"

Serena bites her lip, considering, as she stares at the unlit wick with a hollow gaze. I sense the churning reluctance flowing through her, holding her back. Fear of getting caught, not for her own sake—never for her own sake—but for mine. It might be risky, but Serena deserves a proper birthday wish. We both do.

She runs her fingers through a strand of night-dark hair and sighs. "Okay. I'll try."

I press the candle into her hand. We sit together in the darkness, waiting. Concentration twists her face as she stares at the charred wick. Then her hair lifts, full of static. The hair on her arms stands on end and buzzing fills my ears like a fly at the windowpane, a crackling electric sizzle until a flame jumps to life. It's tiny and pale gold, but it flickers and illuminates the fort we've made beneath the blanket.

I gasp. "You're amazing." Her answering smile glows brighter than the flame. Our heads bend over the candle, our hair hanging down and mingling, gold mixed with black. Light and dark, forever intertwined.

"Happy birthday to you," I sing in a whisper.

"Happy birthday to you," Serena answers in a thick, broken voice.

"Happy birthday, dear us," we sing together.

"Make a wish," I say, my breath making the candle flicker.

She winces. "You know what I wish. But it's impossible."

"Wish it anyway, just in case."

Serena purses her lips and blows out the candle. Smoke curls in thin wisps between us. Then she gives a sly smile as the candle relights with less effort this time.

I breathe in, ready to make my own wish, but the blanket rips away from us and the flame winks out. Cold air hits my skin and chills lick up my spine, tickling the back of my neck. Serena's jaw tightens and she hisses not with fear but fury. I force myself to turn, to face the woman standing at the foot of the bed. Lead sinks in my stomach—I should have sensed her coming.

The night matron.

She looms over us with eyes as piercing and golden as a hawk who's found its prey. Two little field mice, shaking the grass.

"Caught you," she rasps.

2

Serena

THE CUPCAKE TOPPLES OUT OF MY HAND, STREAKING FLUFFY pink frosting across the dusty floorboards.

The matron cocks her head like she's snared a mouse in a trap. But I'm not a mouse—I'm a snake. My muscles coil tight, ready to strike. To defend my sister. She folds herself against my side and trembles hard enough to shake the bed.

"I told you to stay away from her," the matron snarls at Ophelia. Like I'm poison. A danger to my own sister. To everyone. Buzzing hums in my head, constant and incessant, pounding against the inside of my skull.

I grab Ophelia's hand. Her fingers are too frail, too frigid. "It's not her fault," I say as I swallow hard against the steady drone in my mind. She's only here tonight to see me. The months we've spent apart have felt like an eternity. There's been a gaping hole in my chest, and now that missing piece has finally slotted into place. It should have been a comfort, but instead her eyes meet mine, wide with terror, and I can't breathe.

The matron seizes Ophelia by the elbow and hauls her off the bed like she weighs no more than a rag doll. I hold on to her, even as the matron's yanking makes the small muscles in my wrist yelp in pain. I won't let them keep us apart anymore.

Crack.

I hear the blow before I feel it. The matron's stinging slap is hard enough that my hand rips from Ophelia's. Rusty mattress springs creak and my temple slams into the metal bed frame. Pain lances through my head as I fight against the stars that swim in my vision, blurring the rafters high above. I grit my teeth, force the world back into focus. She can't take Ophelia. I won't let her. I roll off the bed, the frozen floorboards biting into the soles of my bare feet. Dust and dirt stick to my skin, rubbing between my toes.

The other girls stir now, watching groggily with mussed hair and open mouths, but I don't care. I can't look away from the matron. Standing in the aisle with my bed separating us, she clutches Ophelia against her.

"Leave her alone," I say. The matron clamps a hand over Ophelia's mouth to stop her screaming, though it doesn't keep the tears from streaming silently down her cheeks.

"Take a good long look," the matron says. Ophelia thrashes, long golden hair falling in tangled wisps around her face. Still, the matron holds her firmly. "Because you're never going to see your sister again."

The childlike whimper that breaks free of Ophelia's lips cracks something in my chest. Her red-rimmed eyes frantically scan the room with a terror she doesn't deserve. And neither do I. Not one of these girls, huddled on the rows of beds beneath threadbare blankets, deserves what they've done to us. What they will never stop doing to us if I don't get out of this place.

Sparks crackle in my veins, burning and pressing beneath my

skin. Magic howls at me to let it out, but I don't know how. With a pop, the round light bulbs hanging overhead pulse to life.

"Let her go." Still, the heat in my chest surges, pressure building and building. Threatening to burst out of me. Or swallow me whole. Overhead, the golden lights flicker, casting shadows across the matron's wrinkled face.

"I do not take orders from nasty, insubordinate girls." The matron's lips twist in a sick imitation of a smile.

I dare a step toward them, the humming in my head growing louder by the second. I push back against it, and *pop*. One of the bulbs shatters. The light fizzles and blinks out. One by one, the twin rows of bulbs explode. *Pop, pop, pop*. Sparks and shards of glass erupt, showering around us in a storm of razor-sharp raindrops.

I shield my face from the flashes of light and bits of glass, but . . . did I do that? The sparks in my chest grow hotter, the kernel of magic that has always existed there starting to wake, so much greater and wilder than the measly flickering flames I've been able to conjure since childhood.

Shrieking fills the room as the other girls cover their heads with their hands. The matron doesn't stop them when they rush out. They push and shove, fighting their way to the door. To get away from the real monster—me.

Good.

Let them be afraid of me.

Maybe the matron is right. Maybe I'm a poison, a danger, a curse. Well, if I'm a curse, she's the one I'll hex. Tonight, I wished for one thing—me and my sister together, anywhere but here. This might be my chance to make that wish come true.

I don't know what to do with the lightning beneath my skin, but it's too hot. Burning my insides. I have to get it out before it roasts me alive. The buzzing in my head grows to a roar I can't think around.

Something white-hot bursts from the electrical sockets on the walls. Flames. My fingers curl into sweaty fists. My breath wavers like the plumes of smoke rising at the edges of the room. The matron stumbles backward, pulling Ophelia with her. For a moment, her gaze flicks to my fingertips, like she can see the heat there, begging me to let it burn the whole world to the ground.

Her face blanches.

"Let Ophelia go." I only want my sister. No one else has to get caught in the crosshairs, and even after all the matron has done, I don't want to hurt her. The matron doesn't loosen her grip. Instead, a slow, sickly sweet smile creeps across her face. Her hoarse laugh scrapes along my skin and I shudder at the shiver rippling up my arms. Through her smile, I swear I catch a glimpse of pointed teeth. I rub my eye with the heel of my hand. Am I seeing things?

My chest grows too tight, my heart slamming itself against my ribs like it can escape and fly free. Pressure builds in my veins, squeezing until I can't breathe. *Out, out, out,* it seems to wail. I don't know how, though, and even if I did, the matron is using Ophelia as a shield.

I meet Ophelia's eyes and beg her to understand what I'm asking. She has to fight. And as always, Ophelia understands, like she can read my mind. The matron curses and jerks her hand away from Ophelia's mouth. Blood stains Ophelia's lips from using the only weapon she has.

Her teeth.

The matron swears and flings her with inhuman strength. Ophelia's feet lift off the ground and then she's hurtling across the room. Before I can muster a scream, she crashes into the wall behind my bed and slides to the floor with a high whine.

"No!" I shout, far too late. I grab hold of every scrap of electricity cracking in my veins and shove my hands forward like I can force it out of me. A thin streak of lightning shoots from my fingertips, energy bursting out of me and releasing some of the pressure building beneath my sternum. The bolt slams into the matron's chest and throws her roughly backward. She hurtles through the air, landing in a heap by the door.

When she doesn't rise, I rush to Ophelia's side. *Please be okay, please be okay*, I beg silently. I fall to the floor beside her, ignoring the stinging shards of glass digging into my knees. Acrid flames spread along the walls. The fire reaches scarlet fingers toward her, so I heft her bony shoulders beneath my hands and drag her away from them.

I brush wisps of hair from her face, and they open. A sob of relief bursts from my throat.

Blood dribbles from shallow cuts on her palms and forearms where her paper-thin skin has been split by landing in broken glass, but she seems otherwise all right. I take her hands and help her rise to her knees. "We have to go," I say.

Tendrils of fire creep up the old wood-paneled walls and drops of sweat bead on my brow. Ophelia coughs from the thick smoke already burning my nose. I pull her to her feet when glass crunches behind me and the hair on the back of my neck prickles.

Not with sweat—someone's watching.

Ophelia's eyes go wide, fixated on something over my shoulder. Dread sinks like a stone in my stomach. When I turn, the matron is standing, like the blow that crumpled her moments ago had no effect on her.

Color leeches from her mousy brown hair, strand after strand going white. Her pupils grow until they gobble up the whites of her eyes. Until they are nothing but black pits, so dark and deep they threaten to devour every ounce of light in the room. What's happening to her? I stagger back a step, away from the monster standing before me. She stands to her full height, several inches taller than the matron ever stood. Her hair is ice white, and she would have been beautiful if it weren't for the soulless black voids of her eyes, her lips pulled back into a smile of pointed teeth, sharp as daggers.

"Who are you?" I breathe. Or rather, *what* are you?

"Give in to your emotions, Serena," she says in the matron's gravelly voice, as if I'm a wild animal she can coax into submission. I blink rapidly, trying to drive the dark creature from my vision, but it's no trick of the eye. Her sharp-tipped claws glint in the firelight.

I step sideways to keep Ophelia behind me. "Let us go."

The flames inch higher now, climbing the walls like the vines on the orphanage's ancient stone facade. They hiss and crackle, rabid wolves snapping their jaws. How long will it be until they clamp down on my neck?

"Harness your anger," the matron says.

"Shut up." The buzzing, the smoke, the flames both inside and out, they're all squeezing in on me.

"Let it fill you."

"Shut up, shut up, shut up!" I don't know what she's talking about. I only know I have to get us as far from this place as possible.

This time, when magic sizzles in my veins, I know what to do with it.

I feed it.

I give it every drop of fear, anger, and emptiness in my dusty soul until it explodes out of my fingers in a lightning strike heading straight for the matron.

She steps sideways. The lightning whizzes past her and hits the wall with a sharp buzz. The matron shakes her head, silky white locks swaying.

Ophelia slinks farther behind me. "Run," I growl.

"I'm not leaving you," she says, even as her voice breaks.

Now isn't the time to be brave. I have this power surging through my blood. She has nothing but a nightgown and her own wits. "I'll be right behind you."

I just need to hold the matron off and buy Ophelia time to get past her. The flames are devouring the floorboards now, extending hungry fingers for the rows of beds, racing to engulf the already rotting rafter beams.

I try again, shooting another bolt of electricity that hits a wide beam overhead instead. There's not a hint of fear in the matron's unblinking dark gaze. "Keep trying all you want." She throws her arms out wide. "You don't have enough control to fight me."

My blood boils in the pit of my stomach, and I force all the heat from my body out in sharp zaps. The blinding lightning bursts from me in an electrical storm that sears the air on every side of me until the matron cackles through pointed teeth. With every flash, my insides grow hotter, not just from the blaze threatening to overwhelm the room, but from somewhere deep within.

Not one of my shots lands. The matron is right: I don't know how to control my aim. "Go!" I yell again, and this time Ophelia listens. She takes off on wobbling legs along the row of empty beds, leaping over flames. I expect the matron to go after her, but she keeps her soulless, unblinking eyes on me.

"You're almost there, Serena," the matron says.

What does she want from me? I don't want this lightning in my veins, the entire world going up in smoke around me. And yet she stands there smiling with those awful razor-sharp teeth.

Ophelia is almost to the door, right behind the matron, when the moan of splintering wood splits the air like a gunshot. I throw myself sideways just before a beam crashes down in a rain of ash and smoke. It smashes through the floor where I was standing mere moments ago. The building's ancient bones shudder and groan as the beam plummets through the level below and hits the ground two floors below us. My knees sting, ripped open where I've fallen. Something sticky and warm prickles down my shin but I haul myself to my feet.

A gaping hole separates me from Ophelia and the matron. My vision swims as I peer down through it. The floor is so far below that my stomach plummets. There's no way out on this side of the bedroom—I'm stuck here between the wall and the drop.

"Go," I bark through a hacking cough, but the matron seizes Ophelia's arm and yanks her toward the hole.

"Want her back?" The matron's long, sharp nails dig into Ophelia's arms. Ophelia winces as blood blooms and rushes down her pale skin.

"Don't you dare hurt her."

Ophelia bites her lower lip, trying not to whimper. Her face is flushed and sweaty, and she stumbles as the matron pushes her toward the massive hole in the floor. She digs in her heels, but the matron lifts her with ease and dangles her by one bleeding arm over the dizzying drop. Ophelia goes deathly still, hanging limp over the precipice. I can feel her fear, the certainty that the smallest movement will send her careening to her end.

"Please don't." The hoarse words barely come out of my cracked lips. I don't know if my voice breaks from the smoke or from the fear sliding through my stomach. The sweat slicking every inch of my skin is from more than the unbearable heat. *"Please."*

I'll get us out of this somehow. I'm supposed to protect her, but now . . . I can't reach her. I'm too far, too weak, too helpless. There's nothing between her and the floor except open air, and I'm trapped. Hot tears press behind my eyes, but I blink them back. What good is this pit of crackling embers inside me if I'm not even strong enough to save my own sister?

"I told you that you would never see her again," the matron says. "You never were a good listener."

The matron lets go, and for a moment, Ophelia hangs in the air, wide eyes locked on mine.

Then she plummets.

"Ophelia!" I shout.

I barely hear her terrified scream over the roaring in my ears. I squeeze my eyes shut, not wanting to hear the crunch of bones, but I can't hear anything over the snapping flames and the humming, buzzing, zapping that won't leave my head.

"What have you done?" I clutch at my chest, trying to keep the pieces of myself from shattering, but nothing can stop the pain tearing at every inch of my skin until I can't breathe. I stop fighting the flames. I can't hold on to them any longer, so I let them smother and choke me until I sink into the magic that's always been there, curled up, asleep.

I unleash myself.

White light bursts from my body, engulfing the dormitory in a radiant flash.

I drop down and down and down into a well of molten lava within myself I never knew existed. Warmth floods through me and every inch of my skin tingles with power. I'm a living firebolt, and the sparks crackling in my veins aren't burning me alive. They're protecting me. They're mine to wield, to bend to my will, to make this monster pay. I thought the magic I knew for sixteen years, magic to light candles and make the fire burn just a little brighter, was all

I had, but it is nothing compared to what's awoken inside me now, in the way a distant thunderclap can't compare to a lightning storm.

As the white light fades, the electrical storm pulses through me and this time when lightning rises to my fingertips, it obeys me. It pounds into the matron's stomach and sends her sprawling backward. My chest rises and falls in shallow pants.

"Very good, Serena," the matron croons as she staggers upright, licking her lips like she wants to sink her teeth into my flesh. "All that power, and now it's my turn for a taste."

A shudder racks my body. Power flows through me, vibrating through my bones, tasting of burnt sugar on my tongue. It doesn't matter if she wants to kill or consume me. None of it matters.

I was too late.

My throat aches from the thick smoke choking the air as I rush to the edge of the drop. I don't want to look. I don't want to see her broken and bleeding on the floor. I have to, though—she would look if it were me. She didn't leave me when we were separated by only a building. I owe it to her not to leave her in death.

Gritting my teeth, I peer over the edge of the broken floorboards, and my thundering heart stumbles. Where there should be a shattered girl on the ground, there's nothing.

"Ophelia!"

The matron laughs. I lift my head to find her black pits of eyes on me. "What have you done with my sister?" I hiss.

The well inside my chest opens up, and I let every ounce of heat barrel through my body until sparks burn my palms and singe my fingertips.

If this orphanage burns to the ground, I'm going to make damn sure she burns with it.

3

Ophelia

THE WORLD IS ENGULFED IN FLAME. SMOKE STINGS MY EYES, sweat runs in rivulets down my skin, and the floor . . . the floor is so terribly far below. Nothing but open air separates me from certain death.

My stomach lurches as the matron holds me with inhuman strength above the hole in the floorboards. Sharp claws dig into my skin. Is this a nightmare? The matron transformed into a monster, a creature with talons and fangs. I dare not squirm for fear of the dizzying drop, but I can't help how my pulse races in my throat and my arms and legs tremble, trying to find something to grab onto to keep me from the ground below.

"Serena," I try to say, but no sound comes out. I meet her eyes, finding none of her determination, her fire, her certainty. Only cold terror.

She can't save me.

If these are my last moments, I should give her some pretty speech about sisterhood. I should tell her I forgive her for not being able to help me. But as the matron releases me, my limbs flail helplessly like they might sprout into wings and carry me away. My heart flies into my throat and I drop. I squeeze my eyes shut tight against the floor racing toward me, waiting for the impact that's sure to come in *three . . . two . . . one. . . .*

The ground never comes.

I pry my eyes open. I'm hovering mere feet from the floor, suspended in the air. A girl my age stands with her hands outstretched toward me. She's not from the orphanage, not even from the East Wing. She's dressed in a red-and-black plaid skirt and red turtleneck, not a uniform white nightgown, and her eyes are sharp and determined rather than hollow. Her long hair is a brilliant, burnished copper, save for one stark white streak. She flicks her fingers and I drop the remaining distance to the ground. My elbows bark in pain as I hit the hard floor.

My hands and arms slip in the ash coating the floorboards, and my once-white nightgown is now streaked with charcoal gray. Before I can push myself up, the redhead seizes my elbow and hauls me to my feet. She puts a finger to her lips with a quick lift of her eyebrows above a hard russet glare. Power radiates from her, like the sparks that erupted from Serena upstairs but magnified by a thousand. The magic Serena and I have, this girl has it too. Only, she knows how to wield it. Sweat beads on her brow and I can't hear myself think over the roaring flames above us. I hack a cough so deep I fear my lungs might come right up out of my throat. Smoke billows from the hole high above and the mansion's old wood groans and cracks. It's only a matter of time before another beam collapses and crushes us. Before Serena's flames engulf everything in sight and swallow this place whole. In the distance, the East Wing girls wail, waking the matrons.

"Ophelia!" Serena screams from above.

I open my mouth to yell back that I'm here, but the redhead clamps a calloused hand over my lips. The air pops, and a girl with tawny brown skin, almond eyes, and jet-black hair scraped into a sloppy ponytail appears out of thin air beside me. Like the redhead, there's one white streak in her hair. The redhead's hand over my mouth hides my astonished squeak. Am I dead? Is this a hallucination and I'm broken on the ground, my bones devoured by flames?

I squirm against the redhead's iron grip until she lets me go. "We have to get my sister."

She glares at me. "I think you mean, 'thank you for saving my ass.'"

"Who are you?" I don't know why they're here, but I believe the little voice inside my head that tells me I can trust them. Some part of my magic has always been able to read emotion and intent better than words.

"I'm Leo, this is Sagittarius," says the redhead. "Now shut up and let us do our job."

Sagittarius lunges between us and grabs each of our arms. The air pushes against my bones, like I'm being squeezed through space and time, until I'm no longer standing beneath the hole in the floor. Heat still kisses my skin, but it isn't as present. The smoke no longer claws its way down my throat. I wrap my arms around myself as my stomach roils and my knees wobble. I'm standing in the dining hall among rows of long empty wooden tables, but my insides feel like they've been ripped out and then stuffed back into my body. I suck down breath after breath of cleaner air, though it won't be long until the fire reaches us here on the opposite side of the orphanage.

Sagittarius smirks as I sway on my feet. "You get used to it."

"My sister," I plead. "We can't leave her in there."

Leo inclines her head to Sagittarius like this is a game. How can she be so nonchalant? "Sag will get your sister, but for the love of God, stop whining."

Sagittarius disappears again, blinking away so quickly I wonder if she'd been here at all. In the distance, sirens wail, growing closer and closer to the orphanage. Girls scream, their voices moving farther and farther from the building. Once they're all safely outside, will anyone notice Serena and I are missing?

When Sagittarius slips back through the fabric of reality to my side, Serena is slumped in her arms. I stifle a cry of relief and pull her to me, clutching her by the shoulders as I scan her sweaty, soot-stained face. She leans limply against my shoulder, eyes glazed with exhaustion, but she whispers my name.

"It's okay." I use all my strength to hold her upright. "We're okay."

Leo glances at Sagittarius, who is staring at the ceiling, lips moving wordlessly like she's calculating.

"Grab and go?" says Leo. Something in her fingers glints in the darkness—a dagger. Sagittarius nods. She bounces on the balls of her feet, ready for whatever they're about to do, brave in a way I fear I'll never be.

Sagittarius blows out a long sigh, and this time when she pops in and out of the air, it's with mere seconds in between. She returns with her arms wrapped around the squirming matron's chest. The matron snarls, tossing her pure white hair, and drives her elbow backward into Sagittarius's stomach. Sagittarius yelps as she releases her grip on the matron and stumbles back. The matron whirls on her, but Leo makes an artful swirl of her hands, blade flashing with the motion, and stops the matron in her tracks. The matron thrashes but can't break free of Leo's invisible hold. She's trapped in place. Whatever power Leo possesses to control the world with her mind, she's able to snare the matron like it's easy.

Sagittarius's chest heaves as she retreats to Leo's side, brushing stray strands of dark hair out of her face where they've escaped her ponytail. "Nice work," Leo says with a swift nod, and I realize that retrieving Serena was only practice. To make sure she knew the exact place inside the East Wing to land; to calculate how quickly she could get in and out of the dormitory and grab the matron.

The matron hisses through pointed teeth and I cringe backward, but Leo laughs.

"Not so tough now, are you, old lady?"

"You'll regret this," the matron growls. I can't bear to look into her empty eyes, but I don't dare look away. Not when Serena is so vulnerable, barely able to hold herself up and ease off my shoulder. Leo and Sagittarius seem powerful, but they're all that stands between us and that creature.

"What is she?" I ask, because I'm certain now that the question is not *who* but *what*. That's not the night matron.

"She's a Dark Witch," says Sagittarius. Her eyes never leave the monster ensnared in an invisible trap before us. "A Gemini. There's no telling how long she's been using her shape-shifting powers to impersonate your matron."

Dark Witch. "What does that mean?"

"Later," says Sagittarius.

I bite back my slew of questions. What's a Dark Witch? Why is she here? And what does she want with me? With . . .

"What do you want with my sister?" I blurt, stepping away from Serena, who no longer needs my support to stand. My sudden bravery feels foolish, and I grit my teeth to fight the need to shrink back, to stand behind my sister like I usually do.

The witch cocks her head, and a shudder racks my shoulders, but I don't back down. "Your sister has power. I could taste it before, but now that she's Awoken?" She licks her lips with a low moan.

I shudder, and Leo cuts me a glare. "Ignore her," she snaps. "Where are they?"

The witch spits onto the dusty floorboards. "I don't know who you're talking about."

"Don't lie to me," says Leo. "You know exactly who we're talking about. Stop pretending, and tell us where our friends are."

"It doesn't matter. She has them—you'll never see them again."

Leo bristles and surges forward, but Sagittarius grabs her elbow and pulls her up short. Whoever the Dark Witch took, whoever she hurt, they were clearly important enough that these girls would risk their lives against a deadly witch to find out even the barest scrap of information.

"Leave it, Leo," Sagittarius says. "She's not Dark Twelve, she's a rogue. She won't know anything."

Leo rolls her shoulders and takes a deep breath. She pulls a second dagger from a holster on her thigh and twirls it alongside the first like they're extensions of her arms. If I could do that, if I were that strong and powerful, no matron would ever dare hit me. Serena would never have to save me again.

The witch flashes pointed teeth.

"Fine," says Leo. "Let's end this, then." Her daggers levitate and poise in the air on either side of her, razor-sharp defenders. The cupboards along the dining room walls bang open and an army of deadly sharp knives shoots out. They hang suspended in the air with their glittering points aimed directly at the Dark Witch.

The air around the Dark Witch ripples. Her body contracts and contorts until it's not her standing in front of us but a little girl of no more than seven. Matted blond hair falls just below her shoulders, and she pouts her lower lip. "Please let me go," she says in a child's clear voice.

I blink once. Twice. Shape-shifting, Sagittarius said. How long has she been impersonating the night matron? I shudder. "Leo, don't," I say. She's a little girl, or at least she looks like one. Is any of it real? Is she a terrifying monster or a matron or a child?

Leo doesn't blink. "No more games."

The witch's skin ripples. Her hair grows long and white, and then she's a Dark Witch again. She bares her teeth at Leo. "Do you think I fear death? Death fears me."

"Then let's terrify it."

The knives and Leo's daggers whiz through the air and bury themselves in the witch's chest. I gasp out a whimper at the sickening squelch. Even the witch looks surprised. Staggering, she stares down at the dozen blades protruding from her body, the blood pouring down her front, and touches her hand to her chest. Her fingers come away red. She sways and as her mouth tugs up at the edges, a scarlet bubble burbles on her lips, and she collapses. I fight the urge to bury my face in Serena's shoulder.

Sagittarius rushes forward and drops to her knees beside the witch, two fingers at her neck. I don't need to take her pulse to know if she's still alive. The witch's chest rises in one final great heave. Her gurgling rattle echoes across the dining hall, grating at my ears, and then she goes utterly still. Unmoving on the dusty wood floor. *Dead.*

I force my breathing to steady, but I can't choke down enough air. My body shakes enough that Serena, starting to regain more color in her face, takes a casual step in front of me, and I gratefully shrink behind her. Who are these girls? They killed someone, actually *killed* someone. If it weren't for the blood pouring out of her chest and pooling around her, staining the floor crimson, it would be impossible to tell if she was alive or dead from those unseeing eyes.

Leo yanks another knife from her belt and stalks toward the body.

Sagittarius turns on Leo. "What the hell are you doing? We need to go."

Ignoring her, Leo spins the knife, then drives it into the dead witch's eye. In one sharp twist, she yanks the witch's eye from the socket. It's nothing but an onyx orb, perched on the end of Leo's dagger as she frowns at it. It looks like a brutal crystal ball that, if I gaze into it long enough, might show me how this night went so horribly wrong.

"Cancer might be able to get something from this," says Leo. She takes a handkerchief from her pocket to wrap the eyeball in, and the moment it's out of sight, my chest loosens. Leo scans me and Serena from head to toe. My skin prickles beneath the weight of her fiery gaze and I fight not to slink farther behind Serena, to hide from this girl made of knives and flame. "We got what we came for."

4

Serena

MY HEAD POUNDS AND MY STOMACH ROILS WITH NAUSEA. I squint, trying to make sense of the scene before me. Leo and Sagittarius, in their red plaid skirts and knee-high boots, hold fighting stances. Ophelia in her once-white nightgown, now gray with soot. The dining hall grows hotter by the second. More smoke floods the room, and I choke on a hacking cough. The building's foundations groan; we need to get out of here. I try not to look at the night matron—the Dark Witch—prone and unmoving on the floor. It's dark enough that I can almost convince myself she's just a pile of clothes.

The buzzing in my skull has lessened, as if the magic is soothed now that I've released it from its cage. I scan Ophelia again, still unable to believe she's really in front of me. She's shaking and red-eyed, but she's here and I don't understand how. I saw her fall, I saw her . . . I shake away the panic that rises in my chest and makes my breath too shallow. She's here. Alive. That's all that matters.

Leo swishes her red hair over her shoulder, clicks her tongue, and seizes my wrist. I yank away from her. There's a dead body in front of me and an eyeball in this girl's pocket, and my entire world is quite literally burning to the ground before my eyes. Who does she think she is, grabbing me?

"We don't have time for your little freak-out," she hisses. "You reek of magic; other Dark Witches will smell you."

"Give them a second, Leo," says Sagittarius, although she shifts from foot to foot, fingers twitching like she's itching to leave.

Leo whirls on her. "We don't have a second. I'm not losing anyone else. Not even them."

Sagittarius sets her jaw firmly, but nods. Her hands twitch, making small motions too quick for me to parse. The air ripples and shimmers until I'm looking not at the orphanage but through a door to another world. Before, when she'd moved me, I hadn't had a moment to take in what was going on. I was standing in the burning dormitory, sweat stinging my eyes so badly I could hardly keep them open, and then there was a pop and she appeared. She grabbed me and the next thing I knew, the heat of the flames disappeared and I ended up here. This time though, it's like she's opened a portal. On the other side, there's a plush sitting room with a crackling fireplace.

Leo stomps past me and snaps her fingers. "Keep up—we don't have all day." She steps through the opening like it's any other doorway.

Ophelia catches my hand and the urge to bolt out of the orphanage and into the forest beyond threatens to overtake me. For so long, I've wanted nothing but to be free of this place. To run, and hide, and never be found. If I run, though, the matrons will track us down, and I'd rather face the unknown with these girls than risk going back to the orphanage. And if these strangers are right and other Dark Witches can smell us, I can't put Ophelia in danger like that. So, I step into the portal after Leo, pulling Ophelia through after me.

Immediately, I'm blissfully warm. The floorboards are smooth beneath my feet and the wood-paneled room is lit by candles and the flames crackling in the fireplace. I run my hand across the back of a red velvet sofa. Where are we? The ground shifts beneath my feet and I shake my head, trying to knock off the strange magic.

As Sagittarius steps through, I catch a glimpse of the dining hall collapsing. The whole building, that awful place, crumples in on itself. I should be sad; the place I've known as a home for so many years is nothing but ash and rubble. But it deserves to crumble.

The portal closes the moment Sagittarius is on the other side. It's as if the orphanage, the flames, the smoke-filled dining hall never existed.

Leo sinks into a giant white armchair with a low groan. She places the handkerchief-wrapped eyeball in a gold box on the table beside her. What is she going to do with it? My shoulders tighten. Is it a prize? Some sort of memento for a kill? I assess the room, keeping Ophelia behind me. Sagittarius sits on a chair across from Leo and kicks her muddy boots onto an ottoman. Is this their home?

Sagittarius nods at the couch. "Take a seat and stay awhile."

But what's awhile? An hour, a day . . . forever? I won't be a prisoner anywhere else.

I have only a few seconds to decide, but this room is too stifling. The heat from the fire is too much like the orphanage's flames. It bears down on me like the walls might cave in. I don't know where we are, but Ophelia is my responsibility. I have to get her out of here.

I grip Ophelia's hand tighter and take off toward the door. Somewhere behind me, Leo swears colorfully. Flinging the door open, I race outside. Cool wet air kisses my face. Something roars and rushes in my ears. Gulls squawk and shriek overhead, and mist sends droplets of water spraying onto my cheeks. I don't make it far before I hit a railing and stop.

The endless sea unfurls below me. We're on a boat.

When the ship beneath me rocks, I almost fall flat on my face, but Ophelia grasps my elbow and keeps me upright. My bare feet slap against the smooth wooden planks of the ship and all around us there is nothing but fog and wind. Salty drops of water cling to my skin like a film.

There's water and fog as far as I can see. Nowhere to run. There's only the wooden deck of the ship and the choppy ocean waves. For the first time since Ophelia fell, my heart races. I have no idea where I am or where I'm going. I'm wholly untethered, and this thing that broke loose in my chest and sends crackling embers through my veins threatens to burn any possible threat to cinders. I brush my hair back from my face and find pale white hair entwined in my fingers. My breath catches in my throat as I pull my short hair into my vision. The rest is still dark, but my fingers loop on one white streak. Just like Leo and Sagittarius.

"Serena, where are we?" Ophelia whispers. Her clammy fingers still cling to my elbow. I open my mouth to tell her the truth: I don't know. The words won't come out. I'm always supposed to know. I'm supposed to take care of her. And now . . . I don't know.

Ophelia's fingers tremble against my arm and the buzzing in my head starts again. It presses against my skull as my heart thunders, fast enough that I can't get a full breath. Where are we? I shouldn't have come through the portal. I should have run into the woods when I had the chance and left these girls far behind.

Just when I think I might stop breathing altogether, a pale-skinned girl in a blue sweater and black trench coat descends the stairs from the top of the deck. Even without her presence, the ship's steering wheel moves on its own, like it's controlled by phantom hands. By magic. Her stick-straight brown hair brushes her clavicle, melting into her collar, which is popped up against the wind and the ocean spray. Like the other two, she wears a plaid skirt, black tights, and boots, though her skirt is patterned in shades of blue rather than red.

Her hazel eyes meet mine without blinking and she stands with an ease I'm unused to in girls my age, though she looks a few years older. Despite the rocking ship, her feet are firmly planted, her hands casually in her coat pockets.

"You must be Aries." Her velvety, warm voice eases the tension from my shoulders, and my racing thoughts begin to slow. Calm washes over me like I'm a stone dropped into the ocean that sinks to the bottom and settles into the silt. Ophelia's trembling stops and her breath grows less ragged. "I'm Cancer."

Aries.

"I'm Serena," I say, though the name Aries sends me toppling back through old memories. Words my mother whispered when I was five years old—her face is a hazy blur in my vision, though that name lingers. Stories recounted beside a fire in a cottage far away.

We're special, she told us. We're witches, Pisces and Aries, water and fire.

Cancer smiles, the corners of her eyes crinkling. "You found them," she says to Leo.

Leo rolls her eyes. "Obviously." Cancer grazes Leo's sleeve with her fingertips, but Leo yanks away and stalks to the other side of the ship. With a flourish of her arms, the waves grow higher and the ship moves faster. My stomach churns as the rocking increases, but I force myself to take long, slow breaths through my nose, determined not to get sick in front of strangers.

"Let it go," says Sagittarius at the flash of hurt on Cancer's face. "She's upset the Dark Witch didn't know more about the others."

"I'm not upset," Leo snaps. "I just don't want to get caught by Dark Witches in the middle of the ocean. Is that so hard to understand? We have to get behind the wards before they discover us out here."

"What are Dark Witches?" I blurt.

"And what do you mean you *found* us?" asks Ophelia. She moves smoothly, not staggering and stumbling like I am, to a bench against the railing. She's gone calmer since we set foot on the ship too. Her skin has gotten more color and her head is held high. Being near the water has always been good for her. When I used to imagine us escaping the orphanage, I always dreamed we would go to the sea. Somewhere she belonged.

I follow her lead and sit beside her. I take in a deep breath of salty sea air, realizing that this is the first time either of us has seen the ocean. I wish I could appreciate it more, but right now my head spins with too many questions.

"Will someone please tell us what's going on?" My skin itches with the not knowing. I'm finally free of the orphanage, but I don't know why. I don't know what new horror I might have gotten myself into, what new prison they might be taking us to. I have to know.

Sagittarius and Cancer give each other a long glance, but Leo bursts between them. "Stop being dramatic—we have to tell them eventually. You don't have to baby everyone all the time, Cancer. They're big girls."

I flinch as Cancer rummages in a trunk at the base of the steps. She pulls out two blankets and wraps one around my shoulders and another around Ophelia's. I hug it tighter around me, savoring the thick, soft fabric. At the orphanage, I forgot what it was like to be warm. To have something touch my skin that isn't rough and scratchy and useless. I meet Ophelia's gaze and then drop my eyes to her hands; her fingers stop picking at the angry red skin around her nails.

Cancer leans against the railing of the stairs. Her gaze moves between us like she's monitoring every motion, every bob of a throat, every blink or twitch. "That thing underneath your skin, your magic? It's been there all along, hiding. It pokes its head out on your birthday, when it's strongest, and you can do a few small things with it usually, right? It lies dormant for a while until something happens that heightens our senses and emotions, something we need it to protect us from. Like today. And now it's Awoken—all of it."

I nod slowly. I always knew Ophelia and I had magic, but I never knew it was this much. I certainly never dared say it out loud to anyone else. What would the matrons have done if they knew about our powers? I'm certain they would have tried to carve it out of us.

"How much is 'all of it'?" I swallow hard. How deep does that well inside me go? How much of the world can I burn with it?

"That's for you to find out at the Manor," Sagittarius says from the seat she's taken on the steps. She brushes her pale strand of hair behind her ears and cocks an eyebrow as if in challenge.

"The Manor?" I ask.

"You'll be safe there," says Cancer. "When we arrive, you'll see. Niobe and the rest of us, we'll teach you how to use your powers and control them. So they don't control *you*."

"Why didn't we go there then?"

"There are protective wards around the Isle of Sol. No one can open a portal onto it—not even one of us. This is as close as we can get using Sag's teleportation."

"What about me?" asks Ophelia in a small voice. "Will I be allowed to stay?"

Cancer smiles softly. "Of course you will."

Ophelia chews her lower lip, scanning the other three girls. "And you all have it too? Magic?"

As if in answer, Leo waves her hand and a rope from the rigging overhead comes loose. It slams down onto the deck. A sail unfurls and catches the wind, propelling the ship even faster.

Sagittarius smirks. "We all have different powers. There are twelve of us born every year, one for each sign."

That explains why my power is red-hot and full of electricity, while Ophelia's is a gentle, soothing rush. It rained again on her birthday this year, just as it does every year. Different powers.

"What's yours?" I ask Cancer.

Before she can answer, Sagittarius cuts in and wiggles her fingers. "She's messing with your mind."

Cancer's warm gaze flips into a glare in an instant. "I don't mess with people's minds," she says firmly. "I help them. Emotionally."

I recall our first moments on the ship and the way my fear and panic faded in her presence. She changed my emotions. Maybe I should be more worried about it, but I find that I can't be.

"There's a reason we bring her to talk to newbies," says Sagittarius, though I can't help feeling like my insides are slimy. How can I trust someone if I can't trust that my feelings around them are truly my own?

Cancer eases off the railing and crouches in front of me, like she can read the thoughts in my head. "You're my sister now. I don't use my powers on my sisters unless it's necessary to assist them. You can trust me, I swear it."

Sisters . . . trust . . . the only sister I trust, the only one I need, is sitting right next to me.

"As for your question about finding you," says Sagittarius, "we found you because Niobe wants you. To complete our coven."

"Why?" I ask. "Why us?"

"Because we need you," says Cancer. "If our coven is going to be the best, we need the twelve best witches we can find."

I choke on a laugh. The best? How can Ophelia and I possibly be the best? The power inside me is huge, but I don't know how to use it yet, and Ophelia's hasn't Awoken. How can they know how strong our magic will be?

"That Dark Witch at the orphanage is only the beginning," says Sagittarius. "She was a rogue, on her own. She's nothing compared to the Dark Twelve and their leader."

Leo glowers at me. "They would have made your little fire act look like a baby playing with matches."

Sagittarius ignores her. "The Dark Twelve took our friends. We need your help if we stand any chance of getting them back."

Leo's face falls for a moment, pain clouding her eyes before she blinks it away and replaces it with nothing but hardness. "Two of them. We have to find them."

"The Dark Witches won't stop until they have all of us," says Sagittarius.

"Over my dead body," says Leo.

Cancer puts her hand on Leo's shoulder and this time Leo lets her. The redhead's shoulders ease at the touch. "Not yours alone." Cancer turns again to me and Ophelia. "It's why we train. Our coven is going to kill their leader and stop the Dark Twelve once and for all. Before they can hurt us or anyone else."

"So, you're witches hunting other witches?" I say. "That doesn't sound very sisterly."

"The Dark Twelve aren't our sisters." There's a sharp edge to Leo's voice. "Dark Witches don't feel things like we do. They're not even human anymore."

I swallow hard. Training, and covens, and Dark Witches . . . It sounds like something out of a legend. I'm not a witch, and Ophelia isn't a fighter. For years, I've been told that I should be locked away for everyone else's safety. That I shouldn't even sleep beside my own sister. That I need to be leashed and controlled and stopped.

We sail for so long that Ophelia's head droops onto my shoulder. She doesn't sleep, though. She gazes out over the railing into the dense, soupy fog. Can she see through it somehow, to whatever lies beyond?

Even my eyelids sag, my mind drifting blearily toward sleep, when Sagittarius jumps to her feet. "Take a look."

I wrench my eyes open to find that we're plunged into deeper fog, so thick I can't make out my own hands in front of me. Before I can cry out, though, the fog parts, like curtains sliding open to reveal a dazzling stage and the sunrise kisses my cheekbones. The water is a perfect aquamarine, and the sunlight glitters off it so brightly I have to squint. The rocky shore rises up to form craggy cliffs. I can hear the surf crashing against their faces even from here, white and foaming against the bluffs. Lush green grass carpets the top of the cliffs, peppered with little white dots that must be flowers.

I throw off my blanket and stand to brace my hands against the ship's railing.

"Is this a dream?" I murmur.

Ophelia rises beside me, her eyes the same shade of crushing blue as the waves. "I hope not."

The land itself would be beautiful on its own, more beautiful than any place I've ever seen. But better than the glittering blue water, or the sun, or the grass so green I want to let it cover me, is the mansion perched on top of the Isle of Sol like a jeweled crown. No, not a mansion. The orphanage was a mansion. It was empty and soulless and falling apart. This is a palace. A palace that's calling to me, thrumming with life streaming from its elaborate windows and towers threatening to scrape the low-hanging clouds.

Cancer puts an arm around my shoulders and squeezes gently. "Welcome home."

5

Ophelia

OUR FATHER DIED WHEN WE WERE BABIES, AND I DON'T HAVE many memories of our mother before she passed away when we were six. In my mind's eye she's a warm, hazy figure with a face I can't quite recall. But the one memory I remember best, I cling to like armor. Serena and I would climb onto her bed at night, bleary-eyed but unwilling to let sleep claim us. We'd curl up beside her and she'd stroke our hair and tell us stories until we fell asleep. Safe, warm, and together. They were always stories of heroines, braver than I could ever be. Girls who traveled the world. Girls who sailed the seas and protected each other with magic. Now, with the sunlight scattered across the ocean and the sky so perfectly azure I can't tell the air from the waves, I think I could be one of those girls. The open blue calls to me, like the sky is beckoning and the water longs to wrap its arms around me. No longer do stone walls and stern rules and the severe punishments of matrons cage me. Damp air kisses my face, reminding me with every chilly whitecap spray that we're finally, finally, *finally* free.

Waves lap against the sides of the boat, and my chest aches with the desire to trail my fingers through the water so far below. Serena is green in the face and sways against the rocking of the ship. As we approach the island, her mouth hangs agape.

"Welcome home," Cancer said.

Home.

I'm not sure either of us knows what that word means, but maybe this is it. Someplace we can belong. Here on the water, a quiet weight settles over my body, one that comes from something deeper than Cancer soothing my fears. I don't feel a longing to be somewhere else, a pull toward something far away. It's as close to home as I might ever get.

I lean against Serena's shoulder. "Tell me what you're thinking."

I can see the gears turning in her head, her churning uncertainty. She's too subdued, like the flame in her spirit has gone small. Her fingers flex in and out of fists, though her gaze never leaves the approaching shore. "I don't know about this, O."

"It's beautiful," I say.

"It's perfect. It's too perfect."

Typical Serena. Always suspicious, always peeking around the corner for something to pop out and frighten us.

"Give it a chance. Anywhere is better than the East Wing, right?"

Her throat bobs and her eyes tighten, but she tries to smile. "Right."

In silence, we stand shoulder to shoulder, watching the waves. The steady press of her arm against mine allows my breath to steady and the weight to ease from my shoulders. When we approach the shore, though, my heart sinks. The Manor perches on top of the hill, casting its great shadow across the docks. There's likely food there, and a chance to change into fresh clothes, but I can't help but want to stay right where I am. The rocking waves sing to me, and I long to let them lull me to sleep here on the ship's deck.

Leo strides off the boat without looking back. She gestures over her shoulder to Sagittarius and Cancer. "Get them inside," she barks.

Sagittarius bristles. "Don't give me orders."

Leo whirls and the poisonous glare she gives Sagittarius makes me cringe backward. Short little Sagittarius just squares her shoulders and clenches her jaw, staring Leo down.

"I'm ranked higher than you," says Leo, towering over Sagittarius. "If you don't want to be given orders, be better."

My attention snags on the word *ranked*. Is that what they meant about building the best coven? I pick at the skin around my fingernails. If they rank us, surely I'll be dead last since my powers haven't Awoken like Serena's. She can call a lightning storm. I can barely control a raindrop.

Sagittarius bounces on the balls of her feet and glares at Leo. "I've spent the last hour teleporting your ungrateful ass all over creation. You don't get to act like you're better than me."

"And I've been moving an entire ship, but I don't see you thanking me for that either—"

"Stop it, both of you." Cancer steps between them, arms flung out wide to separate them. Her magic seeps into me as well, a comforting weighted blanket over my senses. Her hand on Sagittarius's shoulder eases her back. Leo flinches away before Cancer can make contact with her.

"Don't," says Leo.

"Take a breath," says Cancer, firmly but not harshly.

"Now who's giving orders?" Leo retorts. She's a walking flame with her copper hair glowing bright in the sun and anger rippling from every inch of her skin, like the living embodiment of the lion that is her namesake.

"Walk it off, Leo," says Cancer.

Leo flicks her hair over her shoulder again, but she takes a deep breath and nods. "I'm reporting to Niobe. See you at dinner." She stomps off the boat and up the path.

Cancer turns to Sagittarius. "You good?"

Sagittarius shakes her head and scoffs. "She's insufferable."

"Good thing we love her, right?"

Sagittarius gives a noncommittal grumble before disappearing with a short pop.

I stare at the spot she occupied mere seconds ago, unsure if I'll ever grow accustomed to seeing her powers in action. I wish I understood the dynamic between them all, the closeness they share, even if it isn't pretty. At the orphanage, there were girls I was friendly with, girls I liked more than others, but no one I shared a real bond with. Will I ever have that with these girls? Somehow, trying to make friends with them seems like I'd be weaseling my way into a bond that's already been forged in magic and blood.

Serena loops her arm through mine as we follow Cancer off the boat and onto the wooden dock, heading toward the Manor. On either side of the path, calf-height grass wafts in the warm breeze. White wildflowers poke their heads through the lush blanket of green, waving hello to us with delicate petals.

"I'm sorry about them." Cancer falls into step beside me. "Things are a bit . . . tense right now." Serena's hand in mine tightens and Cancer's eyes dart to her. "We'll explain it all later. After you've had a chance to rest."

My legs burn as we climb the winding path up the hill. It's worth it, though, for this view. Serena's right—it's too perfect. It's something out of a painting, the kind they kept in the museum, only now it isn't made of oil and turpentine. It's real. The tall grass on either side of the path sways, and now that we're closer, I can make out the daffodils in the field surrounding the Manor smiling at me. To one side of the path, the grass drops away to sheer cliffs and a pebbly beach below. The ocean crashes against the bluffs with great roaring sighs. As we make our way farther up and my lungs heave, the forest spreads out on the other side of the meadow. Dense trees, so green I blink twice to make sure they're not fake, whisper as their branches sway together.

Then there's the Manor itself, in the middle of the verdant field. Ivy crawls up the walls of the three-story stone mansion. On the other side is a tall tower that scrapes against the clouds. In many places, the rooftops are glass, glimmering in the sunlight. The whole place seems to welcome us into its presence, but my skin prickles. There's something beneath the beautiful facade that I can't quite put my finger on. Something that makes my stomach turn with the unease that everything isn't quite right.

Beside the house is a garden with rows of raised beds that look like they grow vegetables and fruits. A girl with light brown skin and a halo of tight auburn curls kneels among the flowers, wearing gardening gloves. She raises her hand, trying to wave despite the bundle of sunflowers in her grasp. Cancer waves back cheerily.

"Home sweet home," says Cancer when we ascend the stone front steps and stop before the ornately carved wooden doors.

"Maybe for you," Serena mumbles.

Cancer pushes open the door and we step into a circular atrium.

The orphanage was huge, but somehow it always felt small and cramped, like it never got enough air or sunlight. Not to mention the fact that we weren't allowed to venture into most of the building, and certainly not alone. Here, though, we're indoors but the air is fresh, not stale.

My gaze is drawn to the ceiling and its lofted rafters, soaring overhead like the vaulted roof of a cathedral. In front of us is a curved double staircase with shining mahogany railings that beg me to slide down the banister like a little kid. Skylights high above send beams of golden sunlight down to a humongous gyroscope floating overhead. Its metal arms, carved with detailed, colorful images of stars and planets, turn gregariously around a citrine crystal the size of a person's head. It catches the rays from the skylights and glows golden, like a miniature sun shining down on us.

It illuminates the marble circle inlaid on the floor at the base of the stairs. In the center of the circle is a sun, a mosaic of every shade of red, orange, yellow, and gold. Around the sun in a perfect wheel are the twelve symbols of the zodiac.

Twelve symbols for twelve witches.

"Beautiful, isn't it?" asks Cancer, noticing my gaze. I nod. "Everything around here runs on magic. That crystal has been there for generations. It holds the wards that protect the Isle of Sol so no Dark Witches can breach the island or sense us here." She pats my shoulder. "Sometimes, when I'm scared, I look at it and remember that there's something keeping us safe."

Safe.

Is that what I'll be here? It doesn't seem real.

I weave my arm out of Serena's and toe at the twin fish and their sparkling blue scales rendered in marble at my feet. Beside it, the ram has mighty horns inlaid with shades of red. Its nostrils flare and its eyes are every bit as fierce as Serena herself. A weight settles in my stomach as I trace the lines. I'm not one of them. I don't have powers yet, and after seeing Serena's, I'm not sure I want them. Her magic is beautiful, but terrible and terrifying. To wield something so great . . . I don't know what I would do with it.

"Come on," says Cancer. "I'll show you to your rooms."

"Rooms?" We've been apart for so long that I don't like the idea of being separated again, and I can tell from the muscle jumping in Serena's jaw, neither does she.

Cancer takes the stairs two at a time and Serena and I trail after her to a second-floor hallway. It's bright here, with floor-to-ceiling windows every few feet overlooking the grass and the forest beyond. On the other side of the hallway there are doors, all of them closed, none of them marked. We follow Cancer around one corner, then another, and another until I lose track of where we are. The Manor is all dark wood paneling, big windows, and plush maroon carpets that are soft and squishy beneath my still-bare feet.

When we come to an open door with a red-and-orange arch of stained glass with the constellation Aries rendered in gold stars over the doorframe, Cancer stops. "This one is you, Aries."

Serena blinks slowly. Her eyes narrow and she looks between me and the door. "Am I required to stay in my room or something?"

Cancer chuckles. "Of course not. But Niobe thought you might want to take a nap or a shower, change clothes, and freshen up before dinner. Everything you need should already be in your room."

"I want to talk to her." Serena's hands clench in and out of fists. "Niobe. Take me to her if she's the one in charge."

Cancer shakes her head. "Please, just relax. You'll meet Niobe and everyone else soon enough."

Serena scowls. She approaches the doorway but doesn't cross the threshold. "What about Ophelia? Can't she stay here with me?"

"The rooms have one bed each. But she'll be around the corner, not far."

"It's okay, Serena," I say, hoping it's true. "I'll see you soon."

Serena nods, but as Cancer shows me the way down the hall, she remains standing in the doorway with her hand braced on the doorframe until I round the corner.

"And this is you," says Cancer when we stop before another bedroom. An arch of stained glass in mixed hues of blue, green, and gold decorates the space above the door. In the middle, the constellation Pisces is made of silver glass stars. As much as I want to see what's inside my room, the hallway ahead of me spans on and on forever and I long to know what happens when I reach the end or find another hallway in this maze of a house. Though my weary eyelids droop and my arms and legs are heavy as lead, I want to fling open every door and uncover all the Manor's secret nooks and crannies. As if she can sense my longing to explore every inch of this place, Cancer says, "Don't rush things. You'll have plenty of time to explore and get to know everyone. Rest for now. I'll come get you when it's time for dinner."

I step inside and she closes the door with a quiet click. Cancer's padded steps disappear down the hallway. The silence in my bedroom is thick and heavy. *My* bedroom. The thought makes my stomach twist; I can't remember the last time I've been properly alone. There are no sounds of other girls shuffling down the halls or snoring in their beds, of the matrons talking about us, not caring if we listen, and even the walls themselves are too quiet. The orphanage was falling apart, full of shadows and phantoms, but at least I always knew what it was.

This place though . . . I can't tell. I don't know what there is to fear, but I know in my bones that there must be something. It's too quiet, like the building is hiding secrets beneath its stones. The back of my neck prickles, and I can't shake the creeping dread that something is wrong.

The moment I take in the room, though, my shoulders ease. The wallpaper is pale blue with a touch of gold, giving the illusion of rippling waves. Bright white curtains, soft and billowy like sea-foam, are open to let sunlight stream in. Through the window, I can see clear out over the ocean, endless blue stretching to a steel-gray horizon. There are dozens of soft watercolor paintings of water lilies and crystalline lakes positioned on the wall above a dresser with gold-handled drawers to match the room's golden curtain rods and gold-and-white lamps on the bedside tables. The dresser is topped with peachy seashells and a statue of a mermaid perched on a rock, her long hair falling to her waist, where violet scales of her tail begin and sea-foam bubbles burble over her fins.

The shaggy white rug is heaven beneath my toes, like walking on a cloud. Most of the room is taken up by a bed, three times the size of the one I used to sleep in. I could spread out as much as I want in this without any risk of toppling off. I press my hand into the mattress and it sinks beneath my touch, ready and waiting for me to dive in. A mountain of fluffy pillows in every shade of blue invites me to curl up on the plush mattress and roll myself up in the soft blanket folded at the edge of the comforter. The wall behind the bed is a mural of the sea, so realistic that I can almost hear the lapping water and the caw of the seagulls swooping over the whitecapped waves. I drag my hand across the blankets, so different from the threadbare excuse for bedding I had just last night.

A fish tank takes up the entire length of the wall across from the window. A dozen fish with iridescent scales of every different color swim leisurely through the water, brushing against waving green plant tendrils as they sail effortlessly.

I cross the room to another door and open it to find a bathroom. All my own, without any need to wait for anyone else to finish bathing. There are no communal showers, no dirty, slippery floor, no cloudy mirror to fight over. I step onto the cool white tile and take in the bathtub, so large I could practically swim in it. On a shelf beside the bath there are numerous glass bottles of soap and shampoo. The face in the mirror catches me by surprise. My cheeks are streaked with soot and my eyes are red, with dark circles beneath them. My hair, matted and tangled, hangs limp to my waist.

As beautiful as this room is, I can't stay here. I have to talk to Serena, but I also don't want to stay in my nightgown. It's dirty and singed, and moreover, it's a reminder of that place and of that horrifying woman—the Dark Witch. I grab a washcloth from the stack of fluffy towels and start on my face first. Once I've washed my face until it's pink and shining, I turn the taps on the bath and water gushes into it. I stick my hand beneath the water to test it and find it deliciously hot. I lose my nightgown and step in. With no one to yell at me for taking too long, no one to look over my shoulder for, I let myself linger beneath the water. It soaks into my skin and eases the tension from my back and shoulders. I open the bottles of soap and shampoo one by one, sniffing at each. Honeyed peach, lemon verbena, apple blossom, and rose, but I choose my favorite, a spicy orange and pine that reminds me of winter. The soap is liquid, not the rough lumps we used to the very last bit at the orphanage. I squeeze it onto my washcloth and drink in the warm scent. I scrub every inch of my skin until I can no longer smell smoke or rotting orphanage air on my skin, and then I close my eyes. I sink down into the water until my head clears and I can finally breathe easily.

When I finish my bath and comb through my hair, I open the dresser and take out a blue-and-black plaid skirt, black tights, and a blue sweater. Each piece is made of soft, thick fabric without a single tear or moth-eaten hole. I get dressed, shove my feet into shiny black loafers without a scratch on them, and take one last glance in the mirror. My hands drift to my cheeks. The girl in the mirror is someone I've never seen before. There's not a speck of dirt on her, her hair is brushed, her clothes are pressed. For the first time, the girl in the mirror isn't an orphan struggling to just make it through the day. Whatever this place is, whatever my life will be now, it will be nothing like anything I've ever known. I smile at myself in the mirror, a real, full smile that dimples my cheeks, and head into the hall to face whatever may come.

Creeping to keep my stiff shoes from squeaking, I tiptoe down the hallway. I'm not sure why my blood thunders in my veins and my stomach flips wildly. I'm not a prisoner. It's the middle of the day, and Cancer said I'm allowed to leave my room. This isn't like the orphanage, where we had to go everywhere two by two in perfect rows, always carefully watched and escorted by a matron. Still, being alone here in the hall—or anywhere at all, really—feels like I'm committing some sort of crime.

I round the corner and stop dead in my tracks, my hand flying to my throat to stifle a startled squeak. A boy leans against the wall, gazing out one of the windows. He has an unruly crop of curls, dark but marked with one streak of white, that graze below his ears, and light golden-brown skin. A smattering of freckles across his cheeks and nose are illuminated by the sun kissing his skin.

"Going somewhere?" he asks in a lilting, musical voice. His smile is so wide I can hear it in his sparkling tone.

"I . . . I didn't know there would be boys here," I mumble. The orphanage was all girls, and I never saw boys except for the occasional kitchen boy or janitor. His white shirtsleeves are rolled neatly to the elbow beneath a black-and-white plaid sweater-vest. He's all crisp lines and clean neutrals in his slate-gray trousers and polished shoes.

"Who says I'm a boy?" His features shift. Where there was short curly hair moments ago, long dark brown curls hang past his shoulders. His facial features soften, cheeks rounder and jawline less angular. Subtle curves sweep up his sides, previously all flat and sharp lines. The girl standing before me smiles and tosses her curly hair over her shoulder.

I jump backward, my palms slick with sweat. That's what that Dark Witch did, changed her face. I ball my hands into fists, not that I know how to defend myself if she comes at me.

She holds up a hand with a smirk that makes my stomach dip. "Whoa, take it easy. I'm not going to hurt you."

I scan her face, trying to sense the energy radiating from her, but my powers can't latch onto any of her emotions or tell truth from lies. Perhaps it's the changing features, the way her cells are able to morph and shift into different configurations. Though if she wanted to kill me, she would have attacked already, here alone in the hallway.

I press my hand to my heart and will it to slow. That Dark Witch is dead; she can't harm me or Serena anymore. "You're . . ."

"Let me stop you there. Not a girl either."

"Who are you?"

"I'm Gemini," they say.

Gemini. The girls on the ship said the Dark Witch was a Gemini too, that must be why they can both shift their features. Gemini extends their right hand but when I hesitate, they lean in to squeeze my shoulder, grip firm yet gentle. When they pull back, their features change again, presenting in the more masculine way they did when I'd first approached. My hand drifts to my cheek. What would it be like to be able to change my face? To slip in and out of bodies like water, become whoever I want to be on a whim. Would it be freedom, or would I forget my own face eventually?

"I'm Oph—" I stop myself. That's not who I am here. "I'm Pisces." The name sticks uncomfortably to my tongue.

Gemini's lips quirk up at the edges. "You'll get used to it."

"I don't know that I'll ever get used to any of this," I admit. I wrap my arms around myself, grasping opposite elbows like I can hug myself so tightly I'll feel safe. I've never felt safe anywhere, not really. But here, I let my shoulders loosen and release my elbows.

Gemini eases off the wall. "I heard you met another Gemini. I hope you believe me when I say we aren't all bloodthirsty and evil. Only the Dark ones." They smirk and my stomach does a dizzying little flip. "I promise if I meet a Dark Pisces, I won't hold it against you."

I try to laugh, but the sound doesn't come out. I look away, hating how my cheeks burn, and shake my head. "So you and everyone else here, your powers have all Awoken already?"

"Yes," says Gemini. "No rush, though. Everyone does it in their own time."

"What about you? How old were you?"

Gemini slides their hands into their pockets and shrugs. "I was eleven."

"Eleven?" I squeak. "How?"

"Robbers attacked me and my mom on the street one day." They shift slightly, tugging a hand through their curls. "They killed my parents and took all our money. They were about to kill me too, but I was so terrified that I popped into a whole different body. Scared the daylights out of the robbers and they ran off without hurting me. Niobe found me not long after and I've been here since."

"So, you've been here for . . ." I eye them, trying to determine their age. Or have they changed their face so much that it might conceal how old they truly are?

"Six years, give or take."

"Years," I muse. I can't fathom being here for more than a few days, let alone years.

"Hey." Gemini steps so close to me that their jasmine-scented cologne fills my nose. When they place their hands on my shoulders, the gentle pressure holds me firmly to the floor. Grounding me. I tilt my head up to look into their warm, golden-brown eyes that sparkle even though their lips are a firm, serious line. "You belong here." Their voice, low and rough, skitters like autumn leaves against my skin and sends gooseflesh rippling down my arms. I breathe deeply, but I don't look away from those eyes that seem to see right through me. Right into the very depths of my soul. "Don't ever doubt that." I nod solemnly and their face breaks into a brilliant smile. They release my shoulders. "Plus, you have to stay here because once your powers are Awoken, I need you to douse Leo in water. She's taking this whole fire-sign thing way too seriously and she's bound to burn the whole place to the ground with her temper alone."

I laugh. "I think my sister is the only one we need to worry about burning anything to the ground."

"Good to know," says Gemini. "I'll be sure to note where the fire extinguishers are when she's around. Until you're ready to be my own personal fire extinguisher, of course."

"What if I have better things to do than be your personal water gun?"

Gemini gasps and clutches dramatically at their heart. "I suppose I'll have to learn to live without my daring Pisces protector."

"Something tells me you can protect yourself well enough," I say. They laugh and my cheeks go too warm. I pull at the skin around my thumbnail with my middle finger. "I . . . um . . . I have to go find my sister."

They step back, sliding their hands into their pockets again. "Right, sorry. I won't keep you." They start to head back down the hallway but stop and catch my hand in theirs.

My breath hitches in my throat at the warm press of their fingers against mine. "Really, though, promise you'll find me if you need anything? Cancer's nice, but she's a goody-goody. I'll show you how to have some actual fun around here."

They wink and my cheeks heat again. I slide my hand away, shuffling from foot to foot. "That depends on how much you change your face. If you show up in a different body, how will I know it's you?"

I don't say that I think I might know them anywhere from their smiling eyes, no matter the shade.

"Once you meet the others, you'll be able to rule people out."

"And until then?"

They wiggle their fingers in a soft wave as they saunter backward down the hall. "Just don't mistake me for Leo and I think you'll be okay."

I watch them disappear down the hall and then I stop in front of Serena's room. I don't bother knocking, just swing open the door to find Serena standing on the other side of it. She gapes at me for a moment and then laughs. "I was about to come find you," she says.

I close the door and take in her space. It's laid out in the same fashion as mine, an expansive bedroom with a bathroom attached, though her furnishings are patterned in shades of red and brown with gold accents. Her window overlooks the gardens behind the Manor, rather than the sea. On one wall, there's a hyperrealistic painting of two rams clashing horns, and the wall behind the bed is a mural of abstract lines that mimic lightning flashing out of steel-gray storm clouds. I flop onto the maroon bedspread and lean back into the pile of fluffy white and charcoal pillows, letting them swallow me.

Serena crawls onto the bed beside me and pillows her head on her arm. I roll onto my side and curl up so we're lying knee to knee. She's dressed identically to me, in a sweater and a plaid skirt, except her skirt is veined with shades of red rather than blue and her sweater is black.

"We should go," she says. "Tonight. We'll sneak out and run. We can go anywhere we want, somewhere far away where no one will ever find us."

"What are you talking about? We can't leave."

We've found somewhere we're taken care of. There's something that gnaws at me, that little voice I know so well telling me that there's more to be discovered, but whatever it is, I'll find it. We're safe here, safer than I can ever remember being, and I'm not ready to give that up yet.

"Why not?" Serena's brow furrows so deeply that her eyebrows threaten to knit into one. "I'm strong now. I can protect us."

I snort. "You barely know how to use your powers. And besides, we teleported onto that boat—we have no idea where we are. We don't have a map, or a ship, or supplies. We wouldn't last more than a day."

"We'll figure it out. We always do."

"No." I shake my head. "I want to stay." There may be a nagging unease clawing at the lining of my stomach, but this is the safest place for now.

"This is just like the orphanage," she says.

I grab a pillow from the mountain at my back and thump her lightly on the shoulder with it. "Yes, because this was the kind of accommodation the orphanage provided."

I've never had my own room, and neither has she. And these rooms seem meant for us—mine soft and soothing like the sea, hers fiery and fierce just like she is.

She snatches the pillow from me with a click of her tongue and hugs it to her chest. "This place might be wrapped up in comfy mattresses and nice uniforms, but that doesn't mean it's any different. We're trapped here, can't you see that?" Her jaw twitches, clenched so hard I worry she might crack a tooth. I recognize that glint in her eye, hard as flint. She's scared, but she's always been too stubborn to ever admit it.

"They can help you with your magic. They can train us, make us strong so that no one can ever force us to be apart again."

All these years, we've discounted our power and thought it was small, usable only on our birthdays. But it's more than just a party trick we keep to ourselves, and if Serena learns how to use that force inside her, maybe we never have to depend on anyone but ourselves again. My magic may not have Awoken yet, but I'm tired of being beaten down and pushed around by people who think I'm less than the dirt beneath their shoes. The white streak of Serena's freshly brushed hair falls forward into her face. Stark against the rest of her dark hair, it's a reminder that she's connected now to these witches here. My stomach churns, but I swallow back the heat that threatens to rise through my chest. I shouldn't be jealous that she has a connection to someone other than me. For so long, it's been just the two of us. That won't change now, not even here.

I tuck the white hair behind her ear. "Please, let's stay. For a few nights, and then we can reevaluate."

She sighs, long and slow, crushing the pillow even harder into a bear hug. "All right," she says. "But just for now. And if anything goes even the least bit sideways, we're getting out of here. Got it?"

I nod. "Got it." I watch her for a moment, so small here, nothing at all like the powerful force of nature she was facing down the Dark Witch. "What was it like? Awakening."

"It was . . . a pressure in my chest," she says, brow wrinkling. "I was so scared and angry. And I-I couldn't help it. It was this . . . white-hot spark inside me that needed to explode out—any way it could. I couldn't stop it; it just burst out of me and it was as if all this power that had been asleep suddenly woke up ready to fight."

I shudder. "That sounds terrifying." I tried reaching for that invisible place inside me where the water in my soul sits, but I haven't been able to find it since yesterday when the clock struck midnight. Even when I can feel it, it's small, a tiny dewdrop that wouldn't be able to help anyone at all. It's like it's stuck in a cage deep within me, waiting for me to find the key and open the bars so it can escape. I'm not sure I want it to, though. Serena's magic burned down a whole building. If I open that cage and that drop of water grows, what will it become? Will the torrent be so great that it will drown me in its depths?

Serena shakes her head against the pillow. "It wasn't scary, it was . . . powerful. I finally didn't have to be afraid of the orphanage or the matrons or anyone at all. I could do anything. But then I couldn't . . ." Her voice cracks; her throat bobs as she swallows hard.

"Couldn't what?" I ask, but her eyes glaze and she blinks quickly.

"I thought you were dead," she whispers. "I've never been so scared in my entire life. Nothing like that is ever happening to you again. I promise."

"I'm right here," I assure her. I can't imagine how that would have felt, though, to think she was dead if our roles were reversed. I'd want to burn the building to the ground too. To burn the whole world to the ground, if Serena were no longer in it. The thought surprises me and I push it away, remind myself that Serena is the strong one. Serena will always be okay.

She must see the fear flicker across my face.

"Whatever happens here, whatever this place is, I'll protect you," she says, voice solid. "Like always."

My heart squeezes, and I blink back the tears pressing behind my eyes before she can see. It's not fair for her to feel that way. She shouldn't have to protect me all the time, like I'm some helpless child. Maybe that would be a good thing about Awakening my powers. She wouldn't have to be burdened with those feelings anymore.

"You can't protect me from everything," I say.

Determination flashes across her face. "Watch me."

We lie beside each other in silence, curled facing one another as we would have in the womb, before we came into the harsh light of a world that wants to do nothing but separate us. I won't let that happen, though. The events of last night and the lack of sleep crash into me. My limbs grow heavy until I can no longer keep my eyelids open and we both drift off to sleep.

Finally together. Finally safe.

6

Serena

I'M SURROUNDED BY SWIRLING FLAMES. ACRID SMOKE FORCES its way down my throat. I can't stop coughing as the flames lick closer. Sweat drips down my skin and an army of Dark Witches prowls closer and closer. There are too many of them to count, blocking my way out, swiping claws at me. I sway and nearly lose my footing as I teeter on the edge of the hole in the floor.

Two stories below, Ophelia is broken on the ground. Blood pools beneath arms and legs all at the wrong angles. Her unseeing eyes stare up at me. Accusing me. I should have saved her. Sharp talons head straight for my throat. The doorways are wreathed in flame. I'm trapped, nowhere to go and no one to run to. Clawed hands swipe at me and I jolt upright, out of my nightmare.

I'm drenched in a cold sweat, but I'm not in the burning orphanage anymore. I'm safe, next to Ophelia. I take long deep breaths through my nose until I stop shaking. The sky beyond the window is a deep, dusky violet and the sun has slipped below the horizon. We've slept the afternoon away. Seagulls caw outside, and if I hold my breath and listen carefully, I can make out the crash of the surf on the Isle of Sol's shore. Beside me, Ophelia sleeps curled in the fetal position with her hands tucked in close to her heart. Her chest rises and falls in slow, steady breaths. Her face is so peaceful; I wish she could stay like this forever. Resting, unbothered. I know it can't last, though. Nothing good ever does.

I don't know how long we stay here, half-asleep, until there's a soft knock on the door. The sound sends me lurching out of bed and my stocking feet hit the floor. I slide my shoes on and search for the heat and pressure of my electricity to find it ready and waiting. Only then do I open the door the barest crack to find Cancer, pin-straight hair brushing her collarbones as she rocks gently from side to side. The tightness in my chest unfurls. My eyes lock onto the white streak marking a small section of the right side of her hair. Marking her, the way I've been marked.

"Ready for dinner?" she asks.

As if in response, my stomach growls and Cancer presses her lips together like she's stifling a laugh. I'd forgotten how long it's been since I've eaten. Since dinner last night, and that wasn't much at all: some crusty brown bread and watery stew with a few meager bits of chewy meat in it. It certainly wasn't chicken, but I never dared ask what we were actually eating at the orphanage. Some things are better left a mystery.

The knot in my stomach eases, though, at Cancer's presence. Is she using her power on me or is she just a familiar face? I shake Ophelia's shoulder gingerly. "Come on, time to get up."

She grumbles and scrubs her hands across her face. "Please tell me there's food," she moans.

"At dinner? Of course not."

She tosses a pillow at me but there's no force behind the throw and it lands on the ground a foot away from me. I grab her hand to pull her upright.

I follow Cancer into the hallway with Ophelia on my heels, and this time we go the opposite direction of the way we came earlier. She leads us down the hall until we reach another set of stairs, this one straight and far less ornate than the one in the Manor's entryway. Cancer practically floats down the steps, moving with easy grace like she's flowing through calm waters.

"How long have you lived here?" I ask. I can't tell if she seems so much older than us because she actually is, or if her powers over everyone else's emotions give her the ability to keep herself calm.

"Ten years," says Cancer.

"Ten?" I balk. "Don't you miss your home?" Is everyone here an orphan like us? Or do they have loving families and warm homes somewhere? Someone to miss.

Cancer pauses. Her brows narrow for a second, and then her soft smile returns. "Some homes aren't worth missing."

I wince. We may have been treated awfully at the orphanage, but at least when the nights were cold and long and so dark I imagined the sun might never actually rise again, at least I still had fuzzy memories of our cottage, a kaleidoscope of broken images to piece together in the dark. Before everything changed.

The moment we step into the dining room, the house's magnanimous quiet is sucked out, replaced with the soft sounds of chatting and laughter. Sagittarius and Leo sit beside each other at a long table, heads bent together as if the hot anger between them earlier today has dissipated. I stop in the doorway, my breath stopping with my body.

"Wow," Ophelia breathes, her gaze not on the girls but up. Massive chandeliers hang from the ceiling and scatter colorful beams of light in every direction, across the rectangular table that takes up most of the room. Everything in here is grand—carved wooden chairs, a cream-colored tablecloth, candles and vases of flowers down the middle of the table, and blue-and-white-patterned place settings with more forks and knives than any one person needs. There's not a speck of dirt on the polished wood floors or the windows, which stretch up to the top of the wall. There are more windows on the ceiling above us, letting the moonlight pour down like I'm standing in a spotlight. A perfectly manicured potted tree sits in the corner and several small potted plants hang from the ceiling in front of the windows, rings of decorative gold spinning around them and glinting in the light.

"The board members don't even get treated this fancy," Ophelia whispers.

Cancer gestures at two empty seats together and then sits across from us beside Sagittarius, smiling encouragingly. There are twelve chairs. Four lack place settings, and the seat at the head of the table hasn't been taken yet.

A tall girl with light brown skin and long curling dark hair saunters through the doorway and Ophelia's short gasp comes out as a choking cough. The girl walks straight up to us and sinks into the seat beside Ophelia, golden-brown eyes trained on her.

"I take it you didn't get lost," the new girl says. Ophelia's face goes so red the color stretches all the way to the tops of her ears.

I kick Ophelia's foot beneath the table and raise an eyebrow at her. Who is this person to make her blush like that? I'm not sure if I should dive between them and separate them or sit back and watch my sister squirm.

Cancer clears her throat and leans across the table. "I see you've already met Gemini."

"Don't worry about them—they're only two-faced on the outside," says Sagittarius.

I didn't think Ophelia could get any redder than she already is, but Gemini winks and somehow the shade deepens to that of a perfectly ripe tomato. Ophelia picks at her fingernails in her lap and quickly looks away, turning to a girl we saw outside earlier who sits on Cancer's other side. Constellations of freckles dance across her amber skin and her auburn curls are pulled into a coiled crown. She has a ball of mustard-yellow yarn in her lap that she's steadily working through with a crochet hook.

"And this is Virgo," says Cancer.

"If Gemini does decide to bite, I'll patch you up," says Virgo. She looks up from crocheting with a shy smile. "You're twins, right?" she asks, and I nod. "You don't look identical."

"We're not," I say. "Technically, we weren't actually born the same day. Ophelia was born on March twentieth before midnight, I was born after midnight on the twenty-first."

The words come out like they're practiced because they are. We've explained it time and time again to every matron and new girl at the orphanage. I try not to let annoyance creep into my voice; she's only being nice.

Virgo looks away quickly. "Sorry, it's just that it's really rare to have two sisters both be witches. Especially twins."

Leo rolls her eyes at Virgo and turns her attention back to me. "Enough of the getting-to-know-you bullshit. We can do fun facts and icebreakers tonight when we have a pillow fight and braid each other's hair. We need to get the others back."

The room falls too quiet. The others look anywhere but at the empty places at the table.

"What happened?" I ask.

"We were on a mission." Leo folds her hands in her lap and states the facts like she's giving a report. There's not a flicker of emotion in her expression. "It was me, Capricorn, and Scorpio. Everything was going according to the plan, and then the Dark Witches showed up. There were too many of them, they were everywhere, and the next thing I knew, they were dragging the others away and I—" Her eyes gutter. "I couldn't do anything."

"You couldn't have saved them on your own," says Sagittarius in a methodical tone.

How many times has she said those words to Leo? I almost feel bad for her, losing her friends like that, not being able to save them. But then she rolls her eyes and says, "No, *you* couldn't have saved them on your own. I should have gone after them."

"You're not responsible for everyone," Cancer says. "You can't carry that weight with you."

"I'm not here for a therapy session," she snarls. Cancer shrugs and exchanges a glance with Virgo.

"That's only two people missing, though," I say. "Who are the others?"

"We haven't found our Libra yet," says Virgo. "Aquarius is out scouting, trying to find her."

"We need her soon," says Leo. "Once we find her and get the others back, we'll have a full coven. Let's just hope that whoever she is, she has a high ranking."

Gemini clears their throat. "But not higher than you, though, right?"

Leo glowers, but Gemini doesn't back down.

"What are the rankings?" I ask. Clearly, they're important to Leo, but from the surreptitious glances from everyone else, I don't know how important they actually are.

"They're cxactly what they sound like," says Sagittarius, leaning back in her chair with her arms folded across her chest. Her hair is neater now, pulled into a slick ponytail without any wispy, falling strands. "You get a number. Tells us whose magic is the most powerful."

She shoves her sleeve back and holds up her wrist to show a tattoo of a bow and arrow with a numeral below it: *XV*. Fifteen.

"What's the point in ranking? There are only twelve of us," I say. Well, eight, judging from the four empty places at the table. It seems like a system meant to antagonize folks with big egos. And Leo's ego might be so large not even the entire Manor can contain it.

"Every witch in the world gets ranked," explains Cancer. "Not just our coven. Niobe is ranked number two."

"Who's number one, then?"

Cancer's lips press into a thin line. "The leader of the Dark Twelve, their Scorpio."

That doesn't sound good. How much stronger are they than we are with the most powerful witch in the world leading them?

"How many witches are there?" asks Ophelia.

Virgo's eyes flick up from her yarn, brightening. "Well, assuming witches live to be eighty or ninety, and there are twelve of us born every year, there should be anywhere between nine hundred and sixty, and one thousand and eighty."

Sagittarius groans and pinches the bridge of her nose between her thumb and forefinger. "Please no math today, Virgo. It hurts my head."

"And considering how many of us the Dark Witches have managed to kill off in the last few decades," says Leo bitterly, "there are around five hundred witches still alive. But none of our coven are ranked that low. The only reason you end up at the bottom of the triple digits is by being old or weak." Ophelia sinks deeper into her chair as Leo scans her slowly up and down. "Or if your powers haven't Awoken yet."

I sit straighter. "So, you think you're better than everyone else or something because you got assigned a stupid number?"

Leo slams her hands on the table. "My *stupid number* is the only single-digit ranking in this coven."

"Aside from Niobe," Gemini points out.

"Yes," Leo says tightly, "but why do you care? I'm still ranked a hell of a lot better than *you*."

Gemini rolls their eyes. "Your rank could be number one and it would still be higher than the number of people who actually like you."

The others giggle and Gemini's face lights up. One moment, they're sitting beside Ophelia. The next, their features flicker and sitting in Gemini's seat is Leo. I gasp, but the others react with a mixture of laughter and half-joking cursing. The real Leo is still sitting across from me, glowering. If I hadn't been watching, I would believe Gemini was her, with long copper hair, sharp cheekbones, and burning russet eyes whose harshness Gemini perfectly imitates.

They flip their red hair over a shoulder and Ophelia laughs, actually *laughs*, as Gemini winks at her. "Hi, my name is Leo and my ranking that I have virtually no control over is the only interesting part of my personality."

Sagittarius snorts a laugh and Leo elbows her. "Take my face off before I slap it off you," she snaps, her glare sharper than the points of her daggers.

In a flash, Gemini shifts back into their own body. "Just get over yourself, Leo, and stop rubbing your rank in our faces every five minutes. It's not important."

"Then why did I find you crying in the bathroom after *your* ranking ceremony?"

"I was eleven years old! And I wasn't crying about my ranking—I was overwhelmed."

"I was younger than that at mine and I didn't have a breakdown," Leo scoffs, waving a hand.

"Well, I wouldn't expect you to understand normal human emotions. Just drop it, Leo. No one cares."

"If no one cares, why don't you tell your new little girlfriend what *your* ranking is?" Leo jerks her head at Ophelia, who puts her head in her hands like she wants to sink beneath the table and disappear. Gemini coughs and looks away.

"Don't bring her into this," I warn.

Leo remains fixated on Ophelia. "She's a whiny, pathetic little girl who will probably be ranked last since she's too scared to Awaken."

I grip the edge of the table until my knuckles go white.

"I'm not scared," Ophelia says in a low but defiant voice.

Leo laughs. "You couldn't even defend yourself from one rogue Dark Witch! You shouldn't be here. You're not one of us. You're just going to be a liability."

"Leave her alone." Sparks dance at my fingertips, singeing the wood beneath them. They can't send her away—I won't allow it. If they do, I'm going with her, though I don't know where we'll go. I want to shield Ophelia, her eyes now glazed with tears, behind me.

Leo's sharp gaze slides back to me, calculating and cold. "Fine, let's talk about you, then." I lean forward. She doesn't frighten me—there's nothing she can say that would be worse than what the matrons told me night after night. I might be worthless and broken and stupid, but at least none of that is news to me. "She might not have powers, but yours are a pathetic excuse for magic. Your powers should be the most powerful today since it's your birthday, but they don't seem powerful to me. You can't control yourself at all. Your aim is shit; you're all flash and no substance. The moment you have the smallest hint of an emotion, you have a complete magical meltdown. How many innocent people did you nearly kill this morning with that electricity stunt?"

The fizzing, buzzing, pressing sensation returns to my body. It slithers against my skull and my fingertips. *Out, out, out*, it yearns. Not yet. I can't set fire to anything else today. I fight it back, but it won't stop coming.

People did almost die today. *Ophelia* almost died today, and it was my fault.

"I don't know why we've been sitting around here waiting to find you all this time." Leo leans farther over the table and Sagittarius murmurs something under her breath that Leo ignores. "This is the best coven in the world, the twelve strongest witches. You're just two little girls who'd rather go run and hide under Mommy's skirts than use any kind of real power."

"You don't know what you're talking about." But that word grates under my skin. *Mommy.* I haven't been able to hide under my mother's skirts in years. Not since she died and we ended up at that orphanage. I close my eyes against the memory of dark frigid night air, screams, someone dragging me by the hand through the forest while Ophelia wailed. The only person I've ever had to hide behind, to rely on for protection, is myself.

A slow, lethal grin spreads across Leo's face and I clench my jaw. She knows she's found her mark. She clicks her tongue and pouts her lower lip out. "Poor baby Aries, can't find your mommy?"

"Shut up."

"She's not around, is she? Well, we don't want you—"

The sparks leave my fingertips before I can pull them back. They shoot straight at Leo and she ducks just in time. A charred piece of red hair falls limply to the tabletop.

The snarl that rips from her is inhuman. She flourishes her hand and a knife floats up from the table, the blade pointed straight at me. I throw myself sideways out of my chair, away from Ophelia. The knife grazes my upper arm and slices through my sweater with a sharp sting.

I reach for my magic, not caring that blood drips down my arm. It seeps through my sweater and patters onto the white tablecloth, staining it crimson. If this is how Leo wants to do things, I'll grant her wish. Let her call me pathetic now.

Go, I silently urge the heat within me. It rushes up through my core, through my arms, into my fingertips, and out. Twin bolts arc over the table, spearing for Leo. Three plates whizz into the air, forming themselves into a shield in front of her. My electricity strikes two of them, cracking them in half, but two more zoom across the table in front of Leo as a fork spears for my head. I dodge to the right, and with a *thwack* and *boing*, the fork embeds itself in the wall.

Sagittarius and Cancer both leap out of the way, swearing, and somewhere to my left I'm aware of gentle laughter. I push it all out and hurl another bolt of electricity at Leo, but my shot goes wide, slamming into a chandelier. Glass shatters. It tinkles to the floor and I'm suddenly back inside the orphanage with broken shards of light bulbs raining down around me.

Ophelia yells my name, but I ignore her. Fire sweeps over me, burning hot from inside my body, and all I want is to burn and burn until it consumes me. A blanket of calm threatens to wash over me, but I thrash, attempting to resist Cancer's emotional straitjacket. I can't stop; I keep flinging bolt after bolt. A drinking glass flies at me and I throw myself to the floor as it shatters against the wall. I struggle to catch my breath and jump up, but as I pull my arm back and attempt to aim, the doors to the dining room bang open.

The ground rumbles beneath my feet, throwing me off balance and sending me toppling to the floor. My elbows slam into the hardwood and vines shoot from the plants across the room and wrap themselves around my wrists to bind them together so tightly that the blood leeches from my fingers. I whimper and struggle upright, more vines wrapping around my waist. A long branch whips out and grabs the leg of my chair. It yanks the chair forward and slams it into me so hard my knees buckle and I fall into the seat. More branches wrap around my legs to bind me to the chair. I struggle against their grasp, but it's no use. Which of the witches is doing this? Ophelia stares at me with wide-eyed confusion, mouth hanging open. Why is no one moving to help me? Or Leo. On the other side of the table, the plants have shoved her into her chair too, her chest heaving behind their grasp.

Ophelia lets out a tiny shriek as into the dining room stalks not a person but a massive panther. It stands three feet tall with golden eyes and great pointed ears that swivel at every small sound. I wait for someone to move to take it down, but the others just dip their heads and return to their seats.

The creature pads silently across the floor, and the closer it gets, the more my legs tremble until I'm shaking so hard, I might fall over. The panther's muscles coil, but instead of leaping, it curls itself into a ball beside the chair at the head of the table, turning to watch the doorway. I follow its gaze.

A woman with ebony skin and a multicolored scarf tied around her hair sweeps into the dining room in forest-green silk robes that swish against the marbled floors. She stalks to the head of the table and rests a fond hand on the cat's head.

"That's enough." Her stern voice booms through the dining room. The glow of the chandeliers casts lights onto her thick gold rings and the golden hoops through her ears. "This is not how the witches of the Manor treat one another. You are a coven. You should know better than to behave in such an abhorrent way." She nods at Leo. "Especially you. Are you trying to get yourself killed? It's Aries's birthday. Her powers are stronger than usual. You're lucky you didn't get electrocuted."

It's the first time I see Leo's fire dim. She bobs her head, red hair falling over her face like she's curtaining off her expression from view. The woman is old enough to be our mother, though she stands straight-backed and proud. Her skin has hardly a wrinkle and she surveys the group before sinking gracefully into her seat.

She snaps her fingers and the branches binding me and Leo release. "I apologize for taking such measures, but I can't bear to have you hurting yourselves or anyone else." I rotate my wrists, wincing as the blood shoots back into them. The woman gives me a warm smile, all of her ire fading. "Welcome, Aries and Pisces. I'm Niobe."

Niobe . . . They spoke of her on the boat. She's the one Leo reported to when we arrived. I press my hand to my heart, trying and failing to catch my breath. Beneath my fingertips, my heart races frantically, and now I feel the pulsating pain from my cut.

"While I consider myself fortunate to be a member of this coven as your Taurus, I am also the Manor's head witch. It is traditional that you call me by my given name, rather than my sign," says Niobe. "I hope that if there's anything you need, you'll make me aware so that I can help you feel comfortable here. But for now"—she raises both hands and claps once, the sound resounding off the walls—"let's eat!"

The moment her clap fades, servers in white-and-black uniforms flood through the doors carrying platters piled high with food. They set down plates of juicy roast chicken; grilled vegetables cooked in butter, garlic, and fresh herbs; fish garnished with bright slices of lemon and dill sauce; mountains of fruit and cheese; baskets of fresh bread with a deep yeasty scent that makes my mouth water. It's the kind of food I've only seen in my dreams, and I immediately start to load up my plate when the cut on my arm stings.

I don't notice Virgo move until she comes around the table and takes the seat beside me. "Let me help," she says, taking my arm. Maybe she has bandages underneath her yarn, but when I give her my arm, I find that she doesn't need them. She pushes up my sleeve and her lips purse in concentration as her fingers dance artfully above the gash in my arm. The blood whisks away like it was never there. My skin tingles and I jolt, but her hand holds my arm fast and I watch in awe as my skin fuses back together. Not a scar in sight: the wound there one moment and gone the next. "Thank you," I say. She smiles, nods, and returns to her seat.

Niobe clinks a small salad fork against her glass. "I nearly forgot! We have something special for today's guest of honor."

One of the servers returns and I can't help my gasp at what he carries: a cake. It has fluffy white frosting and swirls of red and black piped flowers around the bottom. On top, in perfect, looping letters, it reads, "Happy Birthday, Aries!" Sixteen candles surround the words, already lit. The server sets it on the table in front of me and I look at Ophelia, who offers me a soft smile. She should have one too. I know hers was yesterday, but we've always celebrated together.

She taps my hand with a cold finger. "Make a wish."

I don't know what to wish for. Impossibly, I have everything I want. The two of us, together. Away from that horrible orphanage. I'd never imagined a future more than that.

So I slide the cake toward Ophelia. "You make one," I say.

She shakes her head. "It's yours. I can't."

"You didn't get one," I say. "And besides, I already got my wish."

Smiling, she closes her eyes for a long moment, then opens them and blows out the candles. The flames go out, and the witches clap, Sagittarius letting out a whoop despite Leo's eye roll.

Ophelia turns watery eyes to me. "Thank you," she says, so softly only I can hear.

"We are happy to have you here as part of our sisterhood, Aries and Pisces," says Niobe when everyone starts to eat. "I know it won't be long until your powers Awaken as well, Pisces, and you can join us in full. We'll have the ranking ceremony and everything will become official. You're one of us now. Both of you are."

Official. I don't like the sound of that. Official sounds permanent, like something I can't leave. We're safe here for now, and they may have fancy food and birthday cake, but I don't know if I want to enter into a contract I can't back out of. Sisterhood with these witches, this snarling pack of wolves, isn't something I ever asked for. "I don't know that we're going to be here much—"

Ophelia grabs my elbow and squeezes it tightly. "Please excuse my sister," she says. "I know I speak for both of us when I say thank you for having us. We're excited to get to know you all." She glances around the table, meeting each person's eyes in turn—even Leo's. She looks away quickly when she reaches Gemini, though, a blush creeping toward her ears. "I'm sure it'll take us some time to . . . to adjust."

"I certainly hope so." Niobe's voice turns icy. "For your sister's sake."

All my limbs lock into place. My stomach tightens and squirms. "What's that supposed to mean?"

"It means that what you were doing when I walked in was beyond reckless."

"No one got hurt." Though who knows what would have happened if Niobe hadn't intervened. I don't think Leo is the type to give up.

"Not this time. But the road to becoming a Dark Witch is gradual until it isn't. No one gets hurt until someone gets killed."

"I'm not a Dark Witch." I glance between Cancer and Virgo, the only two seemingly sensible ones in this group, but neither will acknowledge me.

"Not yet," says Niobe, and I almost choke on a bite of flaky salmon. "And if you let me teach you and you connect with this coven, then and only then will you be able to slow the process of becoming one."

My heart crashes to a halt. "What do you mean becoming one?"

"The power . . ." Ophelia says, catching on faster than I do. "Does . . . does using it change you? Into that *thing* we saw last night?" She shudders, and I bite back the urge to flip this table over, grab her, and run. Never look back, never touch my magic ever again. But the pressure is still there, bubbling under the surface.

Niobe says in a firm but soft voice, "Dark Witches are not like us. They lose all ability to feel and express emotions; they feed off the energy and power of young witches like you all, like . . ." She blinks once, shakes her head, then continues. "The Darkness turns them into crones. They feed on your magic to stay young and healthy. They care for nothing but power and control. We cannot allow the Dark Twelve to take any more of our own. Not only must they be stopped; it is also imperative that we keep their numbers from growing. They do not currently possess a full coven, and we cannot allow them to reach full ranks."

Leo nods once solemnly and Sagittarius doesn't look up from her plate. Niobe's words are slippery in my mind. They slide through my fingers so I can't quite grasp what she means. I turn to Cancer, hoping for an explanation, but she only smiles softly.

"The Dark Witches *are* us," says Niobe. "By Awakening your magic, you've set foot onto a path. It's the natural progression of all witches: we're born, our magic Awakens, and eventually, we turn Dark."

No. I gape at her, unable to stop the stuttering and stumbling of my heart. We can't turn Dark, that can't be true. It's not possible. There's no way I can become like that Dark Witch at the orphanage, that's not me. It'll *never* be me. The magic in my veins is strong and powerful. It protects me. It isn't supposed to change me into a monster.

"There's no way to stop it?" I ask. None of the other witches have so much as blinked. Have they all just accepted this fate? This isn't right—I didn't get a choice. I was born with this. My powers Awoke on their own. I didn't rouse them. I slam my fork down on the table, trying to gain control of my shaking, shallow breath.

I deserved a choice.

Ophelia deserves a choice.

"It can be slowed but not stopped," says Niobe. "Magic is in our blood. It is a gift we've been given, but it is not without cost. The amount of energy it takes to wield is draining, on our bodies and our souls. It is not unlimited. And if you keep this behavior up without learning to control yourself properly, you're going to race down that path and become a Dark Witch sooner rather than later. There's one way to slow its course: join us. Together, with the power of the whole coven, we can keep each other from exceeding our limits and live our lives as we are for as long as possible."

Ophelia grasps my forearm with shaking fingers, her face so pale I fear she might faint.

"And when I become a Dark Witch"—the words stick on my tongue—"what will you do with me then?"

I catch the barest hint of a wince before Niobe's face smooths again. "When a witch of this coven becomes Dark, we take care of it." She pronounces *take care* with a deadly precision that sends a shudder through my body. "It's our promise to one another, not to allow our fellow witches to live that way."

I barely hear my own voice when I say, "So you kill them."

Her eyes gutter and lose their warmth. "We keep our promises." She shakes her head, and that haunted expression falls away. Niobe tilts her head at me and raises a knowing eyebrow. "Still want to leave and brave the whole wide world on your own?"

I want to run. I want to get as far as I can from these witches who freely admit to planning to kill their own, but I know deep down that if I changed into an emotionless wraith, incapable of any depth or feeling, I wouldn't want to live like that either. Magic thrums through my veins, wild and raging, pounding like a war drum alongside my heartbeat. It begs to be released. It doesn't matter anymore if this place is a prison. My magic is too unruly. If using it improperly is going to turn me into a monster, if it's going to get me and Ophelia killed, I have to learn how to use it and protect Ophelia the right way.

"I'll stay," I say. Ophelia, pale and small, shoulders slumped and caving in on her, squeezes my arm, though I'm not sure if it's a comfort or an admonishment. "We both will."

7

Ophelia

"JOIN US."

Niobe's words echo through my head over and over and over until it's no use trying to sleep. Join them and do what? Be forced to turn Dark? Become a monster like the Dark Witch at the orphanage? I turn over again in bed, kicking my leg out from beneath the layers of blankets. It's too warm. All those nights freezing half to death, shivering so hard the metal frame of my bed rattled and my fingers grew too stiff to move, I never imagined I'd complain of too many blankets. They weigh down on me, though, pressing too closely on my body like they want to suffocate me. It's not just the blankets, though. It's everything. It's fire, and smoke, and ash, and blood, and black eyes, and teeth like daggers, and magic.

My limbs spasm and I lurch upright, flinging the covers off. I need some air or a walk or something other than being utterly alone with my thoughts. I stuff my feet into the simple beige slippers in the bottom of my wardrobe and pull the fluffy white bathrobe on the back of the door over the button-down pajama set I've been trying to sleep in. When I creak open my door and poke my head into the hall, it's silent and deserted. My eyes adjust to the darkness, pitch-black save for the moonlight streaming through the windows in long silver slivers.

I stop at Serena's door. I don't want to wake her, not this late at night. Not when she must be exhausted after expending so much power. If that energy becomes too depleted, I could lose her forever. I told her this place would be good for her, but not if she's going to become a Dark Witch, a creature so terrifying she needs to be put down. I shove away the thought of Serena with white hair and black irises, wrinkles on her face, and walk past her door to the end of the hall. I turn into the next hallway; it's larger and the doors are all open here.

I peek around the first corner into a cushy sitting room with a huge unlit fireplace, lush red curtains drawn shut across the windows, and mismatched yet fine furniture all over the room. Two sofas face each other from either side of the room. The cushions are unevenly worn, like there are certain seats the witches prefer, and blankets are folded over the backs or arms of the sofas and every armchair. On one side of the fireplace, a cluster of chairs has been pushed close together in a makeshift semicircle.

Cancer, Leo, and Sagittarius sit in the chairs, backs to the door. They don't notice me as I press myself into the wall of the hallway and listen, peering around the corner just enough to see them.

"Can you try scrying?" asks Leo. "I know it's been a few hours, but you might still be able to get something from it."

My stomach churns when I see what she extends to Cancer: the eyeball she took from the Dark Witch.

"I don't know, Leo," says Cancer. "I don't think she knew anything about the others."

"Please." Leo's voice is softer than I've heard before, lacking all her metallic bite.

"All right. Let me see it." Cancer stands and cups her hands for Leo to drop the eyeball into her open palms, not even flinching when the gelatinous orb touches her bare skin. Impatience radiates from Leo and her shoulders rise to her ears, but she doesn't speak as Cancer gazes at the eye like it's a crystal ball. The silence grows heavier and heavier as Cancer's brows knit together. Her lips part, and though I can't hear it, I'm certain she lets out a small gasp.

Leo leans forward in her chair. "What is it?"

"Nothing." Cancer quickly drops the eyeball on a side table and shakes her hands with a shudder.

Sagittarius swears roughly. "Are you sure?"

"I'm sure."

I stifle the hitch in my breath: She's lying.

I can sense her deception from here. Her words are filmy, the water in her blood surging, trying to disguise the truth. Why would she lie? What did she see in the eyeball that she would keep from the two of them?

I press myself farther back into the hallway and slink slowly away, trying to keep my footfalls silent. I shouldn't be spying. Leo already doesn't like me or Serena; I don't want to give her any more fuel for her fire if she catches me eavesdropping. So, I leave the other girls and the slimy feeling that seeps into my stomach, and tiptoe down the hall and into the next room. The moment I round the corner, my hand flies to my throat.

It's a library.

The smell of fresh ink and parchment hits me in a wave. Not rotted, or full of mold and mildew. There are walls of books, stretching from the floor to the windows where a second level begins, with rolling ladders on the ends of each shelf to help reach the highest places. A staircase on the left side of the room leads to an upper level hanging over half the room with even more books and round windows at the top, big enough that I can see the stars peppering the clear sky beyond.

With a sigh of contentment, I wander deeper into the library and discover that it's possible to disappear into the stacks of shelves. There are chairs and couches tucked into alcoves the deeper I go, perfect for hiding away and reading without disruption. Approaching a shelf, I draw my finger across the spine of a red leather-bound tome. I've missed reading. Sometimes the orphanage would get donations of books, and I would stay up reading tales of love and adventure until the matrons forced me to go to bed. I'd imagine I was somewhere and someone else, and long after the book was closed, I'd still find myself longing to live in that world. Longing for the friends I loved between each crumbling page.

Serena has never understood it. Books are boring, she would always say, when you could be out having adventures of your own. So, I'd sit on the bed beside her and read her passages of my favorites. She'd lean her head back against the pillows and try to keep her eyes open, pretending she was listening to me. Still, she tried to like them for me. She tried to understand, in that way that we're meant to always understand one another.

Gingerly, like it might crumble in my hands, I pull the book from the shelf and let the weight of it soothe me. Maybe there's something here. In all these books filled with research and knowledge, there must be more information about why we become Dark Witches. Then maybe I can figure out how to stop the transformation and save Serena.

"Looking for something?" someone asks. I jolt, gasping, and

drop the book with a heavy thump on the maroon carpet. I whirl to find Gemini sitting cross-legged on the couch with their skin glowing golden in the light of a lamp on a table beside them. A book lies open in their lap. "Or just having trouble sleeping?"

Clutching my chest, I gulp down deep breaths against my thundering heart. "I might never sleep again if you insist on scaring me like that."

"I wouldn't be able to scare you if you weren't always skulking around." Gemini sticks a torn scrap of paper inside to mark their place, closes the book, and sets it aside.

My cheeks burn. "I'm not skulking. I'm . . . looking."

"Most people look around in the daylight." Their eyes rake up my body until they meet mine. I'm locked into place by that gaze, piercing but full of warmth and laughter.

"What?" I squeak at the smile playing along their lips, their lingering eyes.

A warm silence stretches. "Nice pajamas," they say finally.

I pull my robe tighter around me, aware that Gemini is fully dressed in the same pants and vest I'd seen them wearing earlier. With a quiet chuckle that chases away the unease in my gut, they pat the open seat on the couch beside them, tilting their head in silent invitation.

"If you do need help sleeping," they say after I sit, "I can be extraordinarily boring." Their mouth presses into a serious line, but their eyes twinkle and their lips threaten to creep up at the corners. "I could regale you with the history of witches, or recite the attributes of each sign, or name every constellation I know in alphabetical order. You'll be asleep in no time."

"I think I'll pass for tonight." Though part of me knows their comforting voice would lull me into a secure slumber quickly. "Why are you up so late?"

With a long sigh, they run their fingers through their short hair and leave them there. Bracing their elbow on the arm of the couch, they toy with their curls, twining one around their fingers and tugging lightly. "I'm always up late. Everything is so calm and quiet when everyone else is in bed. I can actually hear my own thoughts. And to be honest, I've never been very good at sleeping."

"Me neither," I admit. "It's like I can't get my mind to shut off—it just goes and goes and I can't get all the thoughts out."

"Anything you want to talk about? To help get the thoughts out?"

I'm about to decline, but they turn sideways on the couch, knees pressing into my leg. I don't shift away. The casual touch is foreign to me, but it's nice. Comforting. So, I say, "It's my sister. I . . . I'm worried about her. I don't want her to change and lose herself and become a . . . a Dark Witch."

I hate even saying the words—Dark Witch. It's such a simple title, and yet the process of becoming one can't be simple. The corruption of the soul cannot possibly be as easy as a shift from light to dark. I imagine it must take time, rotting someone from the inside out until there is nothing left but a husk of the person they used to be.

I shiver so violently the couch shakes and Gemini places a warm hand on my knee. The weight of their touch brings me back, grounding me. I should pull away, but I don't dare move and risk losing that tether.

"You're here now, with us. We can help her. I know what Niobe said is pretty intense, all that stuff about being on a Dark path and needing to be taken care of once we turn, but she loves to be dramatic with that speech. As long as we work together as a coven, the transformation process slows way down."

"But it'll happen eventually—becoming a Dark Witch?"

They nod and my stomach sinks. It's a nice way to say we're all delaying the inevitable, drawing the process out until it becomes more and more painful. And none of the other witches at dinner had so much as flinched when Niobe brought it up.

Gemini pulls away from me, clasps their hands, and tucks them neatly into their lap. They watch me expectantly, waiting for the slew of questions that have popped into my head to pour out.

"How can you be so calm? Why are all of you just okay with this? If what you . . . what *we* have is magic, shouldn't someone be able to, I don't know, snap their fingers and keep this from happening?"

What good is power if it kills you? What good is magic if it can't protect you from yourself?

"It's what we do," Gemini says simply. "We fight the Dark Witches. That's what we were born for. And then one day, we fight so hard that all our energy is depleted and we turn. We become them. It's our duty."

I hug my arms around myself and draw my knees to my chest, curling up tight enough that maybe this problem will miss me purely if it doesn't realize I exist. "What if you just . . . don't? Never use your powers again, don't fight, refuse to destroy yourself?" This is all a choice. There's nothing keeping them or any of us here except *duty.* I've never had a duty before, no responsibilities, no expectations other than to be small and silent and unimportant. Until this moment, I'd never realized that maybe I like things better that way.

"You'll understand once your powers Awaken." They tap their fingers against the arm of the couch. "The power, it calls to us. It's like a siren, constantly singing and begging to be used. And besides, even if it wasn't, I'd keep using it for this coven if it means protecting them. They're my sisters—I owe it to them."

"Even if it turns you into a Dark Witch?"

"It *will* turn me into a Dark Witch. Someday." They say it matter-of-factly, like I'd asked what color the sky is. "Then if I'm lucky, one of my sisters will take me out before I can do anything too horrible."

"And that truly doesn't bother you?"

They shrug. "You learn not to think about it. It's like dying, right?"

"What?" I sputter, launching myself into a fit of coughing, and Gemini thumps me lightly on the back until I catch my breath. Their hand skims down my arm before returning to their lap, leaving a trail of gooseflesh in its wake despite my layers of clothing.

"You have to die one day," they say, like it's simple. "I mean, based on that cough, you might be closer than the rest of us, but everyone does. It's the natural progression of life. You're born, you live, you die. Sometimes you think about it, maybe it scares you, but for the most part, your brain keeps you from looking too closely at it because it's simply reality. There's no point in fighting it. That's what it's like to be a witch. We're all like little caterpillars right now, waiting for our powers to take hold and turn us into butterflies." They flap their hands like mock wings, flying away, but I don't smile.

Instead, I scoff, "Monstrous, tragic butterflies, if you ask me."

Gemini smiles, but it doesn't reach their eyes. "What is life but a monstrous tragedy?"

"That's an awfully cynical way of viewing the world."

"No." They shake their head, curls falling into their face. "I just don't pretend the world is something it isn't. That way the beautiful things can be beautiful, and the harsh things . . ." They huff a quiet laugh and gaze across the library for a moment, the shadows in the lamplight drawing lines across the smooth plane of their cheek. "Well, then the harsh things never have the ability to destroy you."

"Oh." My heart squeezes painfully. Without thinking, I brush their fallen curls back behind their ear. They still beneath my touch and then their expression crumples. For once, the mask of easy smiles and twinkling eyes gives way to furrowed brows and a weary face that appears much younger. This is the face haunted by so many demons that sleep will not come. The face of a person whose nightmares are so difficult to bear that they hide from them in slivers of moonlight, between the pages of a book.

My breath trembles and my knuckles brush against their cheekbone. I expect them to jerk back, but they turn their head toward my hand. Heat floods my stomach, and I look away quickly, praying it's dark enough that Gemini hasn't noticed my blush.

I shift my hand to tug gently at a loose curl. "Tell me about this," I say. "Your magic." In one blink, Gemini is all smiles again. "Leo said everyone goes on missions, so what do you do since you're not all stabby like she is?"

"*Stabby* is an accurate description of Leo." They snort a laugh. "But I can get closer than she can. I can get into places the others can't, just because I can change my face. No one knows who to look for, and I can become as mousy and small and plain looking as possible so no one will notice me." They flash a wicked smile that sends chills up my spine. "Until it's too late."

I try to smile, but I can't force it. "Have you ever . . ." I can't finish the question and shake my head.

"Have I ever what?" Gemini presses after a moment. "Whatever it is, you can ask. I won't be mad."

I take a deep breath. "Have you ever killed someone?"

Gemini stiffens. They uncross their legs and sit upright on the couch now. "Yes. I think all of us have: It's our job to kill Dark Witches."

"What if I don't want to do that?" I stare down at my hands in my lap, unable to meet Gemini's gaze. They'll think I'm a coward. It's bad enough my powers haven't Awoken yet; it's worse that I don't think I want them to.

Warm fingers slide beneath my chin and lift my head. "Listen to me." They lean so close their warm breath kisses my cheek. "You don't have to do anything you don't want to do; no one here can force you. You have a choice. You *always* have a choice."

I nod slowly and they slide their fingers away. "I should go to bed." I force myself not to let my hands slip to my face where the ghost of their touch still prickles against my skin. I doubt I'll be able to sleep, but I should at least try. "Good night, Gemini," I whisper.

"Good night, Pisces," they whisper back. I tiptoe out of the library, but I glance behind me once. They've picked up their book again, but they aren't reading. They twine their hands in their hair, gazing across the library at nothing at all, and as my throat tightens, I realize that the Manor may be much different from the orphanage, but that doesn't mean it isn't also haunted.

8

Serena

THE TRAINING CENTER IS A CIRCULAR ROOM WITH A rounded glass top that lets the sunlight in and sends it bouncing across the gleaming metal weapons hung on the walls on one side of the room. On the other side are racks of weights, punching bags, and targets. The floor is pale hardwood, so different from the carpeted halls. When Ophelia and I enter together after breakfast, sent by Niobe, Sagittarius and Cancer are sparring with wooden practice swords. Sagittarius's sloppy ponytail whips around her face. She feints toward Cancer, but when Cancer raises her sword to parry, Sagittarius blinks out of existence and pops up behind her. She lunges toward Cancer's left shoulder, stumbles, and misses. Sagittarius twirls again, but no matter how many times she tries to get at Cancer, she can't land a hit. Cancer hardly moves, only occasionally raising her sword to block a swipe of Sagittarius's sword.

How is she doing that? Sagittarius leaps after her, all shoulders and gritted teeth, with a primal scream. Ophelia hisses through her teeth and takes a step back, angling herself behind me.

Just as Sagittarius reaches Cancer, though, her face pales and she staggers back. Her eyes go glassy with tears. "Damn you," she chokes out. Cancer smiles sweetly, then steps in and punches her in the gut. Sagittarius lets out a sputtering groan, giving Cancer enough time to sweep a foot behind her ankles and knock her to the floor. She holds the tip of her wooden sword to Sagittarius's throat.

"Do you ever fight fair?" Sagittarius asks.

"Never." Cancer offers her a hand and pulls her to her feet. Sagittarius claps her on the back with a begrudging mumble of praise.

"Stop being useless and grab a target. We have work to do," Leo says as she stomps past us to the weapons wall. Her red hair is pulled into a sleek braid down her back.

"Good morning to you too," I say. If the work she has in mind is going to teach me to do what Cancer just did with her magic, using it to dominate a fight with barely the blink of an eye, I want to do that. When no one else follows her into the room, I ask, "Where's Niobe?"

Leo scoffs. "Niobe doesn't train newbies until they know the basics."

"Why can't one of them train us, then?" I nod toward the others. After yesterday's disastrous dinnertime bout, I'm not eager to step into the ring with Leo.

"Because I'm the best. And you should appreciate that I agreed to do this at all."

"If by *the best,* you mean heartless," says Sagittarius, winking.

Cancer chimes in, "And by *agreed,* you mean that Niobe is making you."

"I hate you both," says Leo. Her sharp gaze flicks to the ceiling and a climbing rope hanging from the rafters slips free.

Sagittarius blips out of sight before the rope can hit her and reappears a few feet away, and Cancer steps sideways, avoiding it with ease. The rope thumps to the ground and Sagittarius grins. "You try harder than that with people you actually hate."

"Admit it," says Cancer, "you like us."

Leo tosses her a rude hand gesture. "Only because you manipulate everyone into liking you."

I wait for them to fight, to throw punches, magical or otherwise, but they both laugh. The sound makes my whole body go rigid. I don't understand how their dynamic works. They throw around insults and call each other out, but they're not angry. When Leo does it to me, though, she isn't joking.

Cancer punches Leo's shoulder and takes up her stance again across from Sagittarius. "No magic this time," she declares. Sagittarius blocks her strike, and together they become a whirlwind of clacking swords and ragged breaths.

"Didn't you hear me?" Leo asks me. "Get a target." She can't tell me what to do. But as much as I don't want to train with her, I want to learn how to do this.

"What about me?" Ophelia asks. When I turn to where she's cowered in my shadow, her lower lip is red from how she's been biting it nervously.

Leo blinks slowly. "Until your powers Awaken, you'll train your body. Like I said last night, you're a liability. What if we're attacked? I'm not about to waste all my energy protecting you, so you'd better learn some fighting skills if you don't want to end up dead."

To her credit, Ophelia flinches but doesn't back away. As much as I hate the idea of her fighting, I have to admit it might be nice if she could hold her own enough that I don't have to constantly worry about her safety.

"Cancer!" Leo calls, and Cancer steps away from sparring with Sagittarius. "See if you can get Pisces to have more muscle mass than a marshmallow, will you?"

Cancer glides over and gives Ophelia an easy smile. "We'll have you in shape in no time." She takes Ophelia by the arm and leads her to a rack of free weights.

In the corner beside the wall of weapons is a stack of round wooden targets with red and white rings. Leo grabs one and flings the other at me with a swish of her wrist. The wind rushes out of me as I barely catch it and am sent stumbling backward. I wrap my arms around it and follow her to the side of the room opposite from Sagittarius and Ophelia. Following Leo's lead, I set up the target.

With a cocky nod, the only thing that approximates approval, and my amazing skill bracing a bullseye against the wall, Leo strides away until she's standing in the middle of the room fifteen feet away. She yanks a dagger from the belt strapped to her leg and levitates it in the air. She bounces on the balls of her feet before going still. She's poised like a statue, back straight, head high, feet slightly apart. She breathes in, breathes out, then flicks her fingers.

Whoosh—the dagger sails through the air and pounds into the bullseye with an echoing *thunk*. With a fist pump, she says, "Your turn."

"I don't have anything to throw." I try to stand tall as I join her in the center of the room.

"Of course you do." Leo rolls her eyes. "I seem to recall you trying to take my head off with a lightning strike last night, remember? Or has all your special birthday magic worn off?"

Right. Of course, I remember. I just have no idea how I managed to do it. Yesterday, the magic was stronger, coursing through me and raging to get out. Today it's still there, but it feels lighter somehow, like it's slippery and hard to grasp. But with everyone watching me—even Ophelia, who is halfway into a push-up position—I guess I can give it a shot. Fixing my gaze on the center of the target, I stretch out my hand and will the electricity to burst out of me the way it did yesterday.

Nothing happens.

"Sometime today," groans Leo. "I don't want to wait another sixteen years for you to do something."

"I'm trying," I growl.

As if in response to my frustration, magic roars through my head, buzzing and rolling in nauseating bursts. Gritting my teeth, I try to tunnel down into the sparks. I imagine grabbing fistfuls of them and yanking them up through my body toward my fingertips as I point a finger at the center of the bullseye.

"No, no, no." She shakes her head impatiently. "Don't point at it. Use your mind."

My mind . . . I have no idea how to aim with my mind. "But *you* use your hands."

"I use my hands to help direct my powers. I don't literally point at where I'm going. That's just telegraphing your intentions to your opponents. Who would want to be that obvious? And besides, our powers are individual; they all work differently. But the base power is the same. Watch." She calls over her shoulder, "Sag, get over here."

Sagittarius stops doing push-ups beside Cancer and Ophelia, who struggles on shaking arms. Sagittarius glances at the empty space beside me, chewing on her lower lip, then disappears.

"See," says Leo when Sagittarius reappears at my side. "She looks where she wants to go, and then makes the jump. She doesn't have to make a big show of pointing."

"What about the portals?" I ask. When she made the one we walked through to get onto the ship, she made twitching motions with her hands.

Sagittarius cracks her knuckles, then brushes her pale strand of hair out of her eyes. She squints, lips moving silently as she sweeps her hands in jerky circles. The air hums and glows, and then I'm looking at the beach. In two steps, I could be on the pebbly shore. I can hear the crashing waves even from here. I step forward, but Sagittarius swipes her hand in the opposite direction and the portal is gone.

"It's all mental," says Sagittarius. "I do that with my hand because it helps me focus and visualize, but there are other Sagittarius witches who don't do it. Like Leo. She doesn't have to flick her fingers all dramatic like that to make things move, but she does because it helps her. And because it looks pretty freaking cool." She winks at Leo, who huffs, but puffs her chest. "And Cancer . . . well, Cancer works best when no one can tell she's doing anything at all.

"So how do I know what to do?" The buzzing in my head presses behind my eyes. It's squeezing my chest. I have to get it out.

"You stop standing around yapping and do it." Leo points at the target.

Heat bubbles in my stomach, but not because of the power. Because of *her*. I want to pound her skull in again. She thinks she knows everything because she has a high ranking and great aim and silky hair that smells like roses.

"I don't know how," I grit out.

"Your power runs through you like a river," says Sagittarius.

"A current," I mumble. I can feel the electricity coursing through my body, but it's not an electrical current; it's a storm. It crashes over me, and I don't know how to force it in any one direction.

"Exactly," says Sagittarius. "Based on what we saw you do last night, you're pretty good at throwing your power around, but you don't have much control yet of where it goes. You have to channel it at what you want."

Channel it. I can do that, can't I?

Extending my hands in front of me, I bend my knees and let my focus narrow until all I can see is the target. The current is too strong and my shot goes wide, toward the weapons wall. It ricochets off a metal shield and bounces back with a deafening crackle. I hit the floor as it shoots red-hot over my head, vaguely aware of someone swearing.

A scorch mark the size of my arm slashes across the wall beside the door and I twist, searching for Ophelia. I breathe a sigh of relief when I see her on her stomach across the room along with Cancer. She's pale and sweating, but unharmed. Sagittarius is right: I have no control. In a fight, I'm as much at risk of hitting Ophelia as I am a Dark Witch.

Behind me, Leo cackles. The sound makes my fingers twitch into fists. I'll give her something to laugh about. I pull myself off the floor and start to turn, but Sagittarius meets my gaze with a sharp lift of her chin. "Ignore her. Try again."

I try again, and this time the shot would have struck Sagittarius square in the chest if she hadn't teleported out of the way. At least I didn't hit Ophelia, now running laps around the training center with Cancer, who hasn't broken a sweat. Leo crosses her arms over her chest and scans me up and down with her lip curling in a way that makes my blood boil. Sparks leap through my veins but I try to force them down.

"You shouldn't be here if you can't control yourself," says Leo. "You're going to destroy yourself and everything around you, and I'm not letting you take out this whole island in the crosshairs."

"I'm trying."

"Try harder, then."

"So teach me." It kills me to say the words. Leo is the last person I want to ask for help, but she's the best witch in the coven, and one of the best zodiac witches in the world if the rankings are accurate. I'd be a fool not to use the resources right in front of me.

She laughs. "Absolutely not. Niobe never should have brought you here. You're too sensitive. We don't need children who let their emotions get the best of them and can't even shoot at a standing target. We're fighting a war—we need warriors."

"Fine," I say too casually. "If you're too scared I'll outrank you, you don't have to."

She goes completely still, flicking her long braid over her shoulder with a glower. "I'm not scared of a baby witch like you."

Shrugging, I try to hide how anger makes every muscle vibrate. "Prove it."

She flicks her hand and two blunted daggers zip off the wall toward her, circling her body in a deadly tornado of metal. Yanking my magic up, I try to funnel it. I imagine plucking off a little piece of light from inside myself and pulling it through my body until it reaches my fingertips.

It crackles in my hand but fizzles out before it can go anywhere.

"God, you're useless," Leo grumbles.

Useless? The sparks fizz and pop in my veins until my vision goes red. I'm not useless. I'm not useless, I'm not worthless, and I'm sure as hell not weak.

Leo tosses me a lazy grin and her eyes flick to Ophelia, standing across the training center with her hands braced on her knees, trying to catch her breath. "But at least you're not as useless as your sister. She couldn't even defend herself from a butter knife."

Before I can tell my feet to move, I'm already in motion. I barrel for Ophelia and knock her onto a crash pad just as Leo's practice knife whizzes above our heads. Ophelia grunts in pain as I pull myself off her and to my feet. Before Ophelia can move, I stand over her, shielding her from Leo's view.

"Leave her out of this," I snarl. She can come for me. She can throw anything she wants at me, but not at my sister.

"Our enemies won't leave her out of this. They'll hunt her down just to get to you, and if you can't stop being so hotheaded it'll be your own fault when they kill her."

This time when I yank up a bolt of electricity, it flares readily, heading straight for Leo's face. She summons a shield from the wall and floats it in front of her in time. She can't redirect my lightning, but she can protect herself from it.

For now.

She can't hide from me forever, though. Lightning ricochets everywhere. Each savage bolt whips for her smug face. She deflects them, but barely, smugness fading. The crackling is so loud it crashes in thunderous bursts. Someone shouts at me, but I can't make it out. There's nothing more important right now than the electricity and the flashing lightning and the storm raging both inside and out. Leo can sit here and say that I'm useless and powerless, but she's wrong. If she doesn't want to help me, she can leave.

There's nothing stopping her. I can't listen to one more moment of her grating scoff or her condescending laugh.

Not at me.

The electricity pours from every inch of my skin, no longer just from my fingertips. My skin is coated in a thick sheen of sweat. It drips into my eyes, stinging, but I can't brush it away with my burning hands. Somewhere behind me, Ophelia screams my name, but I don't turn. I'm protecting her—doesn't she understand?

I don't know where I'm aiming anymore, or what I'm aiming for. I only know that the magic is cascading out of me, and I can't stop it. I don't want to stop it. I don't want to stop until every person who has ever tried to lock me up, and chain me, and cage me like a rabid animal is nothing but dust.

They all deserve to burn.

Warmth hits me, not red-hot like my sparks, but soothing like a summer breeze. It sweeps across me, a blanket muffling my senses.

"No," I cry, because the more the weight of Cancer's calming magic settles over me, the more the sparks quiet and force themselves back inside. I don't want them inside; I want to get them out. I want them to light the world ablaze.

"Don't fight it," says Cancer. "Stop fighting."

Stop fighting? I'm meant to fight. I was born with claws and fangs and razor-sharp teeth. I was born kicking and screaming, thrown into darkness. I push back against the darkness. My sparks surround me until all I can see is a ball of blazing light, cocooning me in its radiance. Until that blanket grows heavier and heavier, and the burning fire inside my chest cools to an ember. It drains from my body, like I'm a sponge being wrung out, until the last drops of anger pool from my fingertips and onto the floor.

The light fades, and I can breathe again. I search for that heat, but it's gone now. Nothing but ashes, deep within my soul.

"You'll have to learn to do that without my help," says Cancer.

I blink, and suddenly I'm seeing the room around me again. There's a light haze of smoke in the air, and through it the other girls watch me warily. Leo glares, Sagittarius stands with her hip cocked and her arms crossed, actually looking impressed, and Cancer is well . . . Cancer. Which is to say, too calm, too reassuring, and too neutral. I try to force my breath to steady, but it's still ragged and burning in my lungs. I can't find my voice; instead, I manage to nod.

I force myself to find Ophelia, still behind me. Her wide eyes are locked onto me and her clenched fists tremble at her sides. Her chest rises and falls in shallow pants. I take a step toward her. I didn't mean to scare her; I was trying to protect her. I didn't mean to explode like that and put her in more danger. Shaking her head, she backs away from the other girls toward the door. Away from *me*.

"I can't do this." Her voice quivers. "Leo's right, I shouldn't be here."

"Don't say that," says Cancer gently.

Ophelia's throat bobs. "This is a waste of all our time." Her wide blue eyes, deep and clear as the ocean, meet mine, and my stomach drops. "I'm sorry."

"Ophelia, wait," I call, but she's already rushing out the door. I should go after her, but maybe it's better if she's not here. If I hurt her, even accidentally, I'll never forgive myself.

Once she's gone, I press my hand to my chest, hating how it heaves. My limbs are heavy and leaden, every muscle weary from the energy that just poured out of me.

Sagittarius lets out a low whistle. "Looks like Aries might give you a run for your money, Leo." Leo levels her with an icy stare and she holds up her hands. "I'm just saying, the ranking ceremony might actually be fun this time."

"She won't give anyone a run for their money until she learns how to control her chaos," says Leo. "She's going to burn herself out before she even figures out her own magic. She can't handle this. She's too emotional."

Chaos—that's what the power feels like. It ricochets through my chest, unstoppable. I don't know where my heartbeat stops and the electricity begins. It's a swirling tornado of sparks inside with nothing for me to grasp before I get sucked into its whirlpool.

"Niobe assigned you to her," says Sagittarius. "You have to."

"Screw Niobe," Leo spits. "I'm not working with her; I don't even want to look at her."

I flinch. Am I really that difficult? I mean, I know I did nearly set two buildings on fire in the span of two days, but still. I may be useless and reckless, but I didn't think I quite bordered on hopeless yet. But Ophelia ran away from me. She's never run away from me before.

Shame sluices through my veins, cold and slimy. I can't stand here anymore with Leo looking at me like I'm the dirt beneath her shoes.

"Leo," Cancer says. "Doesn't she remind you of someone?"

Leo shifts into that predatory stillness that makes my skin crawl. Her eyes rove across my body, leaving heat and gooseflesh in their wake. "I don't know what you're talking about," she says, but her jaw jumps traitorously.

"Give her a chance," says Cancer. "It's what Niobe gave you, isn't it?"

Leo looks at Cancer, and for the first time, her features soften. For the barest moment, she's not a hardened warrior, or an ice queen, or the only single-digit-ranked witch in the room. For a moment, she's just a girl.

And then the moment passes. She grabs the wooden practice swords from the floor where Sagittarius and Cancer left them. "No magic for the rest of the day," she barks. "You're so out of shape the wind might knock you over. Look at you. You'll never hold up in a fight." When I take the sword, it pulls my arm to the ground, heavy with a solid weight I wasn't expecting. "See? You have the arm strength of wet spaghetti. The Dark Witches will eat you for breakfast, and if you don't get it together, I'll hand you over on a silver platter myself."

So, for the rest of the morning, I don't complain. I let Leo run me through drill after drill with weights, push-ups, sparring, and laps around the training room until I'm dripping with sweat and my muscles can hardly hold me up any longer. When I get back to my room, fully intending to shower and go find Ophelia, I instead collapse into bed for a nap. Even curled up on top of the covers, though, I can't stop the magic from pounding against my veins.

Chaos.

The chaos wants release. *I* want release.

And I can't help but wonder—would unleashing that chaos really be so bad?

9

Ophelia

LEO IS RIGHT—I'M A LIABILITY. THERE'S NO WAY SERENA WILL ever be safe if I'm there beside her, a constant weakness. When she wrapped herself in sparks and flames in the training room, she slipped away from me. It was like she stopped seeing me altogether; she couldn't see anything but power and anger, so hot and terrible that I couldn't help the cold fear sluicing through me. I couldn't reach her when she was deep in the throes of her magic; in mere moments she became someone I no longer recognized. All because she wanted to protect me. If it's that easy to lose her, how long will it be until she's gone entirely?

It's better for both of us if I'm not there, creating more danger for her.

How can the others fling their power around so easily when they know what using it will do to them? They may be content to turn into monsters, but I'm not about to let myself or Serena become one. Nothing is inevitable, I don't care what Niobe and Gemini say. There must be another way, and if no one else is interested in getting answers, I'll find them myself.

There's one place in this Manor that might have information: the library.

I step inside and finally, surrounded by crushing quiet, I can breathe again. There are thousands of books in here; one of them must have more information on the process of becoming a Dark Witch. If there's a cure, word of its existence must be somewhere in the library. I don't care if I have to read every book in the entire collection, I'll find it.

I spend the better part of the morning riffling through the catalog cards at a desk in the middle of the library, deciding on a dozen titles. I half expect someone to come force me out of here and back to the training room, but no one comes. Good. I have enough work to do. There are so many books that it'll take me weeks to uncover everything. I dig through the stacks, struggling to carry the giant tomes with me as I go.

Outside, a bird chirps as it whizzes past the window, tapping on the glass. I can't help but give it a little wave. It probably wants to come inside and be among the books, where everything is so warm and cozy. I find a table in a corner of the library and start in on my pile of books. As I dive into the first one, there's not a lot of actual research to be found.

It's all stories of zodiac witches and their covens. The Isle of Sol has been a home for zodiac witches for centuries, a place for those deemed most powerful to go. While others may form their own covens, there are none that can come close to rivaling the power of those who train here at the Manor. The Twelve. Head witches, like Niobe, have poured magical energy into the citrine crystal in the atrium, forged with old magic by the first head witch, to ward the island from the detection of Dark Witches or the unwanted presence of others.

The next book goes into tales of their powers until they go too far and lose themselves to the magic. That's when their hair begins to turn white. Their teeth grow pointed and their eyes darken. Their skin withers and they grow old, their power eating up all their youth and energy until they have to steal it from others. But worse, their souls rot, unseen to the eye. They maintain energy and youth by stealing it, draining it from zodiac witches in the same way head witches can siphon their own power into the crystal.

The desire to use magic to protect and serve becomes an insatiable need to use it for their own gain. Their emotions slowly fade away until they harm someone and can't stop.

It's like a drug, and unfortunately, Serena has already had her first taste.

I push this book aside and open the next. The pages are thin and fragile. I turn them carefully, my head ducked low over the pages to read the tiny print.

"Hello, Pisces," says a gentle voice.

I whirl, my pulse fluttering in my throat. It's not Gemini this time, though—it's Niobe. My breath catches as I try to mumble my apologies. I shouldn't feel like I've been caught doing something surreptitious, yet I still snap the book quickly shut.

Niobe folds her hands in front of her and they disappear into her flowy emerald dress. "Have you found any literature to your liking?"

"Some," I say too quickly. There was something she wasn't telling us last night at dinner, and now I'm certain she didn't find me here just to say hello.

"I'm glad you're here, you know," says Niobe. Her eyes twinkle and she speaks slowly, like she knows she makes me nervous. "You and your sister both. I've been waiting a long time for you."

"Thank you." Perhaps I should have said that I am glad to be here as well, but the longer I'm here, the less true that becomes. Even now I'm not sure what to say with Niobe watching me. On the outside, she seems warm enough, with her easy stance and wide smile, but there's something else behind it. Like she won't care about me until I break, until my heart cracks open and my powers spill out like Serena's.

Niobe gestures to the table. "May I join you for a moment?"

I nod and she sits, though I'm not sure there's an option for me to say no. She's head of the coven, after all. If I want to stay in this beautiful place with its sunshine and full meals and clean clothes, I suppose I ought to acquiesce to her requests.

"Are you making yourself at home here? If there is anything you need, I hope you will let me know."

"Everything is lovely so far," I say, because it's true. *So far.* I don't know what's next, though, or how long they'll keep me here with no powers.

"That's wonderful to hear." A kind smile crinkles the skin around her eyes. "I came to speak with you because I wish to talk about your powers. I hear your training session didn't go as planned this morning."

I try to sit tall in my seat, my arms resting on the closed book in front of me. I may not have magic, but I refuse to let her think I'm afraid. It's an unfamiliar feeling, but I'm done hiding. If I keep hiding behind Serena and expecting her to protect me, she could get hurt. I'm going to have to fight my own battles. "I don't have any powers."

"Not yet," she says, "but I would advise you to seriously consider what you must do to Awaken your powers. Even without them, it's important that you train and become strong. This coven needs you."

I sputter out an uncomfortable laugh. "You don't need me."

No one needs me. They need Serena: her bravery, her crackling fire. All I've ever managed are a few drops of water. That won't do anyone any good in a fight.

Niobe reaches across the table and covers my hand with her own. "I know you believe that now, but I assure you it isn't true. I've chosen you for a reason."

Maybe I didn't want to be chosen.

I chew on my lower lip. "How do I even get my powers to Awaken?" I ask, letting her think I truly want to know how to do it. If the only choice after Awakening is to turn into a Dark Witch, the best way forward is to never step down that path in the first place. However, I need to know how the Awakening process works if I want to prevent it from happening.

"You let go. That thing deep inside you, you feel it, don't you?" I nod. It's always there, that drop of water. Ebbing and flowing like the tide, locked away behind an invisible floodgate. "Let yourself feel your emotions, *really* feel them. We all have such pain and fear and anger closed away inside us, and all we have to do is let that out. Let the magic wash it away and cleanse it—that's how the Awakening begins. When we feel an emotion too strong for our mortal words to express, too intense for our brains to process, then that power bursts free."

I shake my head. Even if I wanted to, I can't look at those things. I can't take them out of their boxes and turn over each jagged stone because the rip current would wash me away and drown me. I'd rather keep my feet on dry land.

"I know there's something within you, Pisces, a far greater force than you'd like to admit. When you are ready to unleash it, we will be here to help you. All of us. None of us must do this alone."

She pushes her chair back, but I say, "How did you know about us? Me and Serena."

I've wondered since the others said she'd chosen us, and this may be the only time I get a chance to ask. It's not like the orphanage was in a highly trafficked area, where she would have noticed us easily. It doesn't make sense that anyone would know we were there, much less that we're zodiac witches. Leo said the Dark Witches could smell us, but can Niobe? Certainly not before Serena was Awakened, right?

"I've been watching you." She wiggles her ringed fingers and something skitters in the corner, catching my eye. Tiny whiskers, the soft pattering feet, the familiar squeak of a mouse. It's so like the one who used to visit me in the orphanage that my breath catches in my chest.

"That was you?"

My blood runs cold. I was foolish to ever think that little mouse was my friend. It actually was watching me all along, but not in the way I thought.

"Not exactly," she says through a soft laugh. "My animals go where I send them and return to me with reports. I have eyes and ears everywhere."

Her animals. My heart sinks and icy cold washes through my blood until my fingers are shaking and numb. So, this meeting was not by chance, then. I remember the little bird, tapping at the window. That's how she must have known where I was. It must be a useful tool to spy on enemies, but my skin itches at the idea that she might use it to clandestinely watch all of us.

Just as she's been watching me through this mouse. I shouldn't feel betrayed. It was such a little creature. Yet, in those dark, frigid nights, that mouse was my dearest friend, as pathetic as that is to admit.

And it was only ever a spy.

"You saw everything," I say. All that time, I thought we were alone. That no one knew what we were going through, but she knew it all. The pain, the anguish, the nights the hunger was so great I lay doubled over on myself, taking slow, steady breaths like oxygen could fill the hollowness. "You saw everything, and you left us there." My voice cracks. How long did she watch us? A year, five, ten? The rage surprises me and I fight to swallow it back.

Niobe's voice remains calm. "You weren't ready."

"And I'm ready now?" Nothing has changed, at least not for me.

"Your sister is. And from what I've gathered, you're a package deal. I am not cruel enough to separate you simply because your powers have not Awoken. They will, in time."

I clench fingers into fists to hide the shaking. "Did the way we were treated there just not matter to you?"

If she can choose to bring me here now, how is that any different from doing so years ago? She had no right to decide our fate, to decide when was enough or how much torture was too much. At any time, she could have pulled us out of that orphanage and yet she chose not to. She says she was waiting for us, but there was nothing stopping her from retrieving us sooner.

Niobe winces. "It's not so simple. There's more to it than that."

I swallow thickly. "Then explain it to me, please." She spent years watching us suffer in that horrible hellscape. I deserve more than empty excuses and the assumption that I am too small and too stupid to understand. If there's a reasonable explanation, I deserve to hear it myself.

"I am sorry for what you and your sister went through, Pisces, but I cannot pull every girl from her home before she's ready. Do you truly believe that you and your sister are the only witches here who have come from difficult situations?"

"Of course not. But—"

"Every witch in this coven has gone through something difficult: It makes us who we are. It feeds the magic."

"It breaks us."

"It wakes us up," Niobe corrects me. She taps her fingers against the table, gold rings clacking with the motion. "But that doesn't mean it's right. You don't know how it pained me to sit on the sidelines and let all of that happen to you. You must understand, I would much rather have taken you from that awful place and brought you here, but I couldn't."

"Why not?" My pitiful voice breaks, and I long to shove the words back into my mouth until I know how to say them with strength.

"Pisces, I . . ." She sighs and shakes her head. "It's complicated."

I wait for her to explain, but she doesn't offer anything more. "I'm sure it is." I push back my chair, gather my pile of books, and leave her behind.

She doesn't call after me or follow, though I don't expect her to. There's something she's hiding; I know it in my bones, and I'm determined to find out what it is. I'm no one's puppet. I'm not a pawn in her game. If she wants to use me for my powers, I won't give her that satisfaction. If she wants my magic to Awaken, she'll have to try a lot harder than this. The orphanage, the Dark Witch, losing my family and my home—if none of that broke me, nothing will. When I glance down, my palms are pressed with the half-moons of my nails, but my hands are no longer shaking.

10

Serena

AFTER DINNER, I CHANGE INTO THE LONG, FLOWY WHITE dress that's been laid out on my bed. Thin straps leave my arms bare and the soft fabric hugs in at my waist before cascading loose to the floor, where it skims the tops of my shoes. I can't help but twirl in a circle and let the skirts fan out around me. When we were small, other girls at the orphanage dreamed of being princesses, but those dreams were never for me. Tonight, though, in this dress, I feel like a princess. A crown of yellow and white flowers, woven by Virgo with blossoms from her garden, sits on top of my unbound hair.

We all gather in the atrium. In our matching dresses with the citrine crystal overhead glowing in the moonlight, the seven of us might very well be mistaken for fairies. Even Leo has lost some of her harshness. Gold ribbons flutter down from the back of her flower crown and mix with her red hair, making her appear even more like the living embodiment of flame.

I follow the others through the towering glass back doors of the Manor and into the cool night. A path through the meadow and into the woods is marked by floating orbs of flickering golden lights. Fireflies, I realize as I look closer. Ophelia, walking next to me in sullen silence, gives the first half smile I've seen from her all day. "How . . ." she mumbles, as I drift toward the nearest glowing ball. I hold out my hand and the fireflies break formation and flit around me, weaving between my fingers before forming themselves back into a glowing orb.

"Wow," I breathe.

"It's one of Niobe's favorite tricks," says Cancer, smiling when she stops up ahead and notices my fixation. The warm lights from the Manor shine in the darkness behind me and I stop to tip my face to the star-flecked sky. Constellations wheel overhead, too many to make out. I wish I knew more of them and could recognize their shapes. The moon is round and full, casting light down upon us as we cross the meadow and enter the forest.

There were no fireworks tonight at dinner. Sagittarius and Cancer took up spots on either side of me, chatting and laughing, and even Leo didn't shoot any insults my way. I tried talking to Ophelia, who I haven't seen all day, but she sat beside Gemini, silent and sullen. Now she's still too subdued, walking stiffly and stumbling on the hem of her dress. Her arms wrap around her torso like she's trying to hold herself together, and her face is expressionless. Is she dreading where we're headed? The ranking ceremony.

As Cancer peels away from us, walking ahead with Sagittarius and the others, I wriggle my arm through Ophelia's. "What's wrong?"

She shakes her head too fast. "Nothing."

"Bullshit. I know when you're lying, O." Ahead of us, Cancer glances over her shoulder, but I don't care that she can sense our emotions. I lean closer. "Did something happen?" If someone hurt her, I'll find out who. No one hurts her. They'll have to go through me.

"There are things they aren't telling us, things Niobe is hiding. We need to get out of here."

"Ophelia, we talked about this. We decided to stay." Though I never would have admitted it to her or to myself even this morning, I *want* to stay now. After Awakening my magic yesterday and training it today, I want to keep pulling up sparks and see how much power I have inside. Power that tastes like burnt sugar on my tongue, like lightning crackling in my veins, like pure, undiluted rapture. Every second I'm not using it, I ache to be wrapped up in its embrace. When I'm using my magic, there's nothing else. The rest of the world falls away. I've never been so free.

"Please." She pulls me up short when we reach the edge of the forest, letting Cancer and Sagittarius disappear into the twinkling path through the dense trees before she continues. "Niobe is lying to us—I know she is. And between that and all of this talk about Dark Witches and evil and death, we—" She cuts off like she's choking on her words, chest rising and falling rapidly. "I don't think we should be here."

I run my fingers through my hair, lingering on the white streak. The entire lock is leeched of life the way I'll be someday if I let this power bleed me dry. I don't understand how it can turn me into a Dark Witch when using it feels like such bliss, though. "I don't know," I mumble.

Ophelia takes both my hands. "You trust me, don't you?"

"Of course," I say without thinking. "Always."

"Then believe me when I say I can feel Niobe's secrets in my bones, and whatever they are, we need to be far from this place when they come out. And if you never use your magic, you won't have to turn Dark at all."

Am I so selfish that I'd put my magic before my sister? I take a long, slow breath, looking into her pleading eyes. *No.* She comes first. If she says we need to go, then we'll go.

"Tonight, then." I squeeze her hands. "We'll leave tonight."

I doubt Niobe will be happy about it, but I'm sure she'll let us use the ship to get off the island. We aren't prisoners here. We can leave if we want.

"Thank you." Ophelia releases my hands, and we step beneath the forest canopy and into the darkness. Above me, the trees are warped, trunks curved and leaning in toward each other like they're pressing their heads together to create a domed tunnel lit by the firefly orbs. Thick moss blankets the forest floor and cushions my step, a carpet leading us. I make my way across the soft ground and through the cathedral of branches. Everyone has grown silent, and then I hear it: birdsong. It's not the usual twittering and cheeping, but a song. Perched overhead, they sing in unison, a haunting minor melody that sinks into my bones and fills me with anticipation and dread.

We step out of the forest tunnel and into a grove. The open area is ringed by pine trees, the ground coated in moss. The treetops no longer bend and cover us, and I tip my head up to the full moon, huge and round above the ring of trees. The other five witches have already assembled, standing in a circle around a tree in the center. It's different from the other evergreens in the wood, ancient and humming with energy. It's the kind of tree from a fairy tale, with perfectly long limbs that sweep out and up, and wide leaves that rustle in the evening breeze.

My heart pounds faster. Restless energy thrums through me and

I shift from foot to foot, all attention on us as Ophelia and I take our places in the circle between Cancer and Gemini. Gemini's hair is loose tonight, in long spiraling curls that hang to their waist. Across the circle, Leo doesn't look at me, but Virgo offers an encouraging smile. Ophelia slides nervous eyes to me, and I try to nod resolutely.

"Welcome," says Niobe from her place in front of the center tree. A small altar laid with candles and crystals stands before her and her panther lies at her side. Only its golden eyes are visible in the darkness, glowing stars in the night, ever watching.

"Today is one of the most magnificent days I get to share with all of you"—Niobe extends her hands as she addresses us—"Because tonight we welcome not one witch into our sisterhood but two. Aries and Pisces. Sisterhood is a rare gift, and it is even more rare that not only do the two of you share it with us through magic; you share it with each other by birthright. But tonight, through earth, air, fire, and water, all become one. The moment you stepped through those doors, you became family."

My throat constricts. Ophelia is the only family I've had for so long. I take in the faces looking back at me with open yet serious expressions. *Family.* I won't be a part of it, though, not if we leave tonight. I swallow back the heat rising in my throat.

"Now let us commence with the ranking of our new members," says Niobe. "Step forward, Pisces."

I hold my breath as Ophelia walks into the circle and stands across from Niobe at the altar. Her hair cascades around her, tossed lightly by the night breeze. Silence falls over the courtyard and the birdsong stops as Niobe artfully twists her hands.

Niobe lifts a dagger with a jeweled handle from the altar and Ophelia's eyes go wide. I lurch forward, sparks on my fingertips and her name on my lips, but Gemini throws out an arm to stop me. "Wait," they whisper.

"Do not be afraid," Niobe says kindly. She reaches for Ophelia, and though I can see my sister's shaking even from here, she lets the coven leader take her hand and extend her arm between them. I clench my fists hard enough that my nails dig into my palms. Niobe draws the blade across Ophelia's palm. Ophelia hisses as blood blossoms on her pale skin.

With a flick of Niobe's fingers, silver liquid rises from a ceramic bowl on the altar and weaves itself in a long ribbon between each of her fingers. Moonlight glints off its metallic surface. In one swift jab of Niobe's hand, the liquid flies at Ophelia and disappears into the cut.

The courtyard goes so still that Ophelia's gasp echoes like a scream. I fight the impulse to jump forward, to protect her, and this time it's Cancer who reaches out a steadying hand to keep me within the circle. I force myself to stand still, to take a deep breath. Even if Ophelia doesn't, I trust Niobe. Ophelia holds herself still, barely trembling, as veins of silver illuminate her skin from within, the liquid racing through her, glowing as it surges beneath the skin of her arms, her neck, her chest. All at once, her limbs go rigid; her eyes roll back into her head until just the whites are visible. Groaning unintelligibly, she convulses, loses her balance, and falls to her knees. Her crown of flowers topples from her head.

Why is no one helping her?

As if in reply, Ophelia lets out a childlike whimper. Her shaking stops. When she lifts her head, looking up through a curtain of golden hair, she grimaces. Gingerly, she uncurls her wrist from its cradle against her chest and black runes swirl across her skin. They form two half circles back-to-back, bisected by a straight line—marking her as a Pisces. Below that lies a numeral: *CDLXXIX*.

I squint, trying to make sense of it, when Niobe wraps her fingers around Ophelia's wrist. Holding it up for all to see, she says in a seamless voice, "Four hundred and seventy-nine."

Across the circle, Leo lets out a low laugh. I fight back a wince. Of course her rank is low; her powers haven't Awoken. Ophelia staggers back to my side and I try to gauge her reaction, but she drops her gaze.

"Pathetic," Leo says. "Four hundred and seventy-nine? There are five hundred witches in the world. The only ones you're ranked higher than are half-dead."

Ophelia stiffens. "Ignore her," I say. She may have a low ranking, but that doesn't make her weak. Not in the ways that matter.

On her other side, Gemini catches her hand in theirs. At the small, grateful smile that Ophelia passes them, I fight against the lead sinking in my stomach. She's allowed to have other friends. Tomorrow, when we're far from here, it won't matter.

"Leo," Niobe warns.

Leo sets her jaw, but nods. Electricity drips through my veins, preparing to shoot a spark that'll make her apologize, but Niobe is looking at me.

"Aries?" She extends her hand, and I pull my lightning back as I step into the circle.

It's my turn.

My fingers shake. What if I'm ranked so much lower than all the others that Niobe kicks me out of the coven? Ophelia has a reason to be low ranked, but I don't. It's not like I've done anything great with my powers. All I've managed to do is lose my temper, try to electrocute one of my new coven-mates, and nearly burn down the whole Manor.

I force myself not to flinch as the dagger slices deep into my palm. Niobe weaves another strand of silvery liquid through the air. I don't look away as she plunges it into my skin. First, there's the sharp bite of liquid forcing its way into my body, nothing more than a bee sting. Then the thick silver substance enters my veins and floods me with an icy chill. The cold fades, replaced by heat searing the inside of my skin. I grit my teeth against the fire. It's slow at first, creeping, like it's taking stock of what lies within. Within moments, though, it takes off, racing through my veins, infiltrating my bloodstream, devouring me in pure flame.

I double over, hands braced on my knees, as I force myself to keep my feet. Every inch of me, inside and out, is on fire. Silver ripples across the backs of my hands, worming its way through each vein, shifting beneath translucent skin. I want to claw at that skin and peel it off if it means it'll stop the burning. As I fight to hold myself steady, the dull roar transforms into daggers, hundreds of them, wicked and unyielding. They stab at my organs, at every joint and muscle, until I'm certain they're real, ready to burst through my flesh and bone and rip me apart from within. My vision blurs and I can't see anything but wheeling starbursts and complete blackness.

It's going to consume every fiber of my being. It's going to ravage me until there's nothing left and leave me an empty husk here on the forest floor.

I don't feel the ground when it swims up to meet me. My cheek presses into the grass. My vision returns and the pain fades to a dull ache, except for the broken skin on my palm. My wrist prickles and itches, and I know the runes are emerging onto my skin the way they did on Ophelia's. I stay on the forest floor with my eyes closed, in case the magic wants to swallow me whole.

A high-pitched shriek rips through the wood, shaking the leaves on the trees. "No!" Leo screams. "Ten? That's not possible, no!"

She can't possibly see my wrist, and now I don't want to look. As much as I tell Ophelia to ignore Leo, that her opinion means nothing, I can't bear to open my eyes and face her judgment. She'll just ridicule me more for being a coward, though. So I take a breath, count to five, and peel my eyes open to read the number traced in black on my wrist beneath the curving ink of a ram's head sigil.

III—three.

I can't keep back the gasp of shock that bursts out of me. I peel myself off the earth and clamber to my feet amid cheers and applause, my hands trembling in front of me. This can't be real. I blink once, twice, but the number remains the same. I'm ranked third. Higher than five hundred other witches, higher than Ophelia, than most of the coven, than—

I find Leo across the circle, expecting to see the glare I already know so well, but there's no fire in her eyes. Only ice. She fixates on her wrist, unblinking. Her chest rises and falls quickly and her face is beet red.

Ten reads the number on her wrist. No longer a single digit.

"As I expected," Niobe says. She beams at me, and I swear there are tears shining in her eyes. The flickering candles illuminate her ecstatic glow. "Congratulations, Aries." Taking both my hand and Ophelia's, she raises our arms in the air. "Welcome to the Twelve! With these additions to our ranks, we are one step closer to defeating the Dark Twelve and their leader. She may be the highest-ranked witch in the world, but with the second and third in our midst and the power of this incredible coven, we are stronger than we have ever been!"

The others burst into applause—all but one. I won't let her scowling anger take this away from me, though. The universe saw me. It judged me and deemed that there's something inside me worth placing higher than all but two other witches. That number three on my wrist is *mine*. It proves to everyone here that I'm not a helpless orphan or a dangerous child or a worthless girl. I'm the third-most-powerful witch in the whole world and no one, not even Leo, can take that from me.

Niobe releases me and then thin arms wrap around me. Golden hair brushes my cheek as Ophelia squeezes me tightly. "I always knew you were the best," she says. I hug her back, looking anywhere but at Leo over her shoulder. "I'm proud of you."

Proud.

Will she still be proud of me when I tell her that I can't leave tonight? I thought I was all right leaving the Isle of Sol and this coven behind, but I'm not.

I have a place here. I *am* someone here. Maybe it makes me selfish, but I don't want to give that up.

I open my mouth to tell her as much when someone emerges from the forest path on silent feet and slides straight to Niobe's side. It's a porcelain-skinned girl I've never seen before, thin as a reed with stark, straight silver-blond hair that hangs to her waist. The other witches go silent.

"Aquarius," Niobe says. "You've returned."

Scouting, they said she'd been doing while she was away. Aquarius doesn't speak but puts her hand out palm up to Niobe and nods once. Niobe places her hand on Aquarius's and her expression goes slack. She gazes across the clearing, but there's nothing there. Her eyes shift back and forth rapidly, like she's watching something the rest of us can't see.

Niobe's eyes come back into focus and find me. "Aries, Leo, Sagittarius, and Cancer," she calls, voice stern and tight. I snap to attention. "You're needed in my office. Immediately."

Immediately? I avoid looking at Ophelia. She wants to go, but I have to know what's going on. What did Aquarius say that requires immediate attention? We can't leave, not right now. Not when they need me.

Niobe claps her hands once and her panther rises beside her. "Quickly." Her voice is no longer the warm dulcet tone of a mother but an unyielding general commanding her soldiers.

She stalks through the wood back toward the Manor with the panther at her side, Leo first on her heels.

I linger, reaching for Ophelia's hand, but Sagittarius grips my elbow and wrenches me away. "You two can talk later," she says gruffly.

As my hand is ripped from Ophelia's, I give her one last glance over my shoulder. Her mouth hangs open, brows knit together with confusion. I should say I'm not going, that I don't want to know what Niobe wants. Except I do. I want to prove myself. So when Sagittarius opens a portal into Niobe's office, I let her lead me through it.

11

Ophelia

WHEN THE RANKING CEREMONY'S MAGIC RIPPED ITS WAY through my body, it judged me. It scanned every inch of my being and I know deep down that it was displeased with what it found. It raged through me like wildfire, a blaze that couldn't wait to be rid of me. The others seemed to share that sentiment with their pitying looks.

I don't matter here, not the way Serena does. It's yet another reason my bones are screaming at me to run far from this island, though now as I watch Serena's retreating back, I know that's no longer an option. To the coven, Serena is worthy of levels of power and admiration that I will never be able to achieve.

Maybe that's why she walked away from me and left me behind.

Before Aquarius showed up, I knew what Serena wanted to tell me without her needing to say it. She wants to stay here. It's where she belongs, even if I don't. I would have agreed if she'd asked, but instead she just walked through the portal with the others without a word. She went with Niobe without so much as blinking. Without asking if I could come too. She let Sagittarius pull her away, and the moment the portal snaps shut behind her, I feel like we're being torn apart.

Gemini's fingertips brush mine. They bend down to pick up my fallen flower crown and place it gently back on my head. Their hands slide down my shoulders and they twine their fingers with mine, inclining their head toward the Manor. I should step away, but their comforting touch sends butterfly wings flapping in my chest.

"I need a minute," I murmur.

They cock their head, lips parting like they might object, but instead they say, "Of course. Find me later if you want company." Their fingers drift from mine and they loop their arm through Virgo's. The two of them saunter back toward the Manor without giving me another glance.

Alone in the ring of trees, I let my tears spring free.

It's enough that Serena left me behind after promising to leave together, but what's worse is the fear that creeps in and seizes my chest until I can't breathe. She's the third-most-powerful witch in the world—does that mean she will burn out faster? How long do I have with her before she's taken from me forever?

I struggle to catch my breath and sit on the earth before I can lose my feet. I trail my fingers across the mossy forest floor, letting the solidity ground me. Taking a long, deep breath through my nose, I force myself to notice what's around me.

Though Niobe is gone, her fireflies remain. They flit in and out of their orbs of light, creating shapes of flowers and constellations in the air before reforming themselves again and again. The ground is a soft cushion here, dark and rich with soil, begging me to lie down and sink into it. I should go back to the Manor, but I can't bear to step into the halls and face the reality that Serena broke her promise.

She let herself be swept away, leaving me behind. I'm about to lie back in the moss when a voice calls out, *"Pisces."*

I shoot to my feet and swivel in a circle, but no one is there.

"Pisces," the voice says again, a gentle whisper through the leaves.

A shiver goes up my spine, but my heart remains steady, my breath even. Whatever that voice is, real or imagined, I need to find it. I'm not needed in the Manor by Niobe and I'm not needed by Serena either. If Serena won't leave, I'll have to find out the secrets behind Niobe's deception myself. There are lies hidden all over this island, lurking among the greenery, hiding treachery behind each wide leaf, and that must be the way to save her. For once, I can be the one saving *her.*

Instead of following Gemini and Virgo back to the Manor, I let the tug of that call pull me in the right direction. I cross the clearing to a thin dirt path on the other side of the circle. It's dark, but the trees don't bend together here with Niobe's magic, leaving room for moonlight to filter down onto the trail and bright stars to be visible.

The air here smells sweetly of pine. Little white flowers poke their heads out of the forest floor and I try to avoid crushing them beneath my feet as I follow the path into a graveyard. A handful of unassuming headstones, each marked with a name and a sign, are scattered among the trees. I swallow hard at the idea that there were witches just like me and Serena who never left this island. What did they die for? Did they transform into Dark Witches, or did they expire before the Darkness could take them? Shuddering, I move past them, following the path deeper into the trees until the last headstone is out of sight.

It's blissfully quiet here, no sound except the rustling leaves, the crunch of pine needles underfoot, and the forest creatures skittering about. Birds twitter as they flit from tree to tree and squirrels race along tree branches, chittering and chasing each other. The forest is alive, even in the dark of night, and with Niobe distracted, I don't have to worry about spying creatures.

I continue until I spot a glimmer of light, a place where the trees open up into a grove. No, not a grove—a pond. Ringed by evergreens, not big enough to lose oneself in, but big enough that it's likely deep in the middle. The water is calm with light ripples across the glassy, silver surface, a mirror perfectly reflecting the blanket of stars. I crouch at the edge to trail my fingers in the water. It's cool but not too cold, and even from the shore, I can spot fish swimming among swaying kelp fronds beneath the surface. Toward the other edge of the pond, a round stone structure rises out of the water. The water beckons me, and I realize it's been ages since I've had a swim, at least a few years, when the matrons took us on a special trip to a nearby mountain lake. I paddled in the water for hours until they threatened to leave me there alone in the wilderness if I didn't get out and return to the orphanage.

Here, I can swim for as long as I want. I kick off my shoes, place my flower crown on the shore, and approach the water. Gooseflesh pebbles on my arms in the night air, but the moment I step into the water, the little kernel of power that lives deep within my chest unfurls. It yawns, stretches, and sends gentle waves of magic through my body like it's greeting the water.

Cold mud squishes between my toes as I walk deeper into the pond, drawing my arms through the water to get used to the chill. I don't mind the cold, though, not when the tiny waves lapping against my body welcome me like an old friend. The skirt of my long dress billows around me and I flip onto my back to let the water wrap around my body in a cool caress. My hair fans out unbound in the water. I draw my fingers through a silky strand. Time stops as I float, weightless, endless, suspended in tranquility among the stars.

I don't know how long I stay like that, focused on nothing but my slow inhales and exhales and the water's rocking cradle. A light rain begins to fall. Splattering drops brush my cheeks as I close my eyes and let the rain sing to me. It drums against the surface in a steady lull until nothing in the world exists except the rain and the water's embrace from all sides.

"Pisces."

I turn over in the water to see who is calling, scanning the shore. There's no one on the banks, nor in the water with me. After the events of the last few days, I must be so exhausted I'm imagining things. Or perhaps it's the water calling to me through the rain's soft patter.

Something cold and slimy brushes my foot and I twist, gasping. Below me, little fish swim curiously by, and I relax again. How deep is the water? Does anything else live beneath the surface? I duck my head under the water and open my eyes. Serena never understood how I could stand to open my eyes underwater, but it's never bothered me. Perhaps the water knows I'm a friend, or perhaps the sprinkling of magic I have protects my body. I'm fairly certain that's what it's doing now, as I'm not running out of breath the way I ought to be. I go still and let the gentle current inside my veins trickle through me until I feel it enough to reach out an invisible hand. I grasp it, not wanting to force or wake it, but simply asking for its protection and guidance. It must oblige because a bubble of air appears, protecting my mouth and nose until I can breathe freely underwater.

It's not what I thought it would be, the magic. Of course, this is just the small bit of it that naturally exists inside me. While most of my power hasn't Awoken, there are still parts of it I can reach, and being in the water has made those senses pop to life. It's as if on land, my vision is blurry, and the moment the rain hits my skin and my limbs are submerged, the world becomes crystal clear. What would it be if I Awoke? Serena's electricity is sharp and jagged; it slices the air when she uses it and threatens to cleave the world in two. I don't have to be its wielder to feel it in the atmosphere, and I know the others sense it too. It's why Leo looks at her with such fear, disguised as hatred. This, though, is warm and inviting. It's the gentle hug of something welcoming me home.

I peer through the water, now fully able to see the fish swimming. Their glittering scales sparkle in every possible shade, solid and striped, big and small. The grass on the loamy bottom sways, and when it moves, I spot something on the pond's floor.

As I swim deeper, I hear the voice again. *"Pisces."*

It's coming from the water.

I ignore it; it's the magic calling to me. I brush aside some grass to see what it's concealing—the torso of a marble statue, covered in moss and algae. The arms lie to the side and farther, the head. The more I swim, the more of them I come across. Who sculpted them and how did they end up down here?

I swim farther, in search of more, and the pond grows deeper and deeper until I spy a structure in the distance. A small building, moonlight glancing off the pale stones, is submerged beneath the water. How long has this place been here? It must be connected to the stone tower jutting from the surface. I should return to the surface, but curiosity grabs me by the wrist and pulls me forward. This is a freshwater pond with nothing but fish, so I know that I'm safe.

There's no door but I swim until I find a round opening and peer inside. It's a tunnel. Still breathing clean air from my bubble, I push myself inside. Without the light of the moon, the tunnel is pitch-black. I fight back a wave of panic and reach for the walls on either side. The stone is rough beneath the pads of my fingers, and I hold myself in place until my eyes adjust just enough for me to see a few inches ahead of me. The skin of my fingertips tears open on a sharp rock and I wince at the sharp sting of pain.

My heart slams in my chest. But the curiosity, and the pull of that voice, they drag me onward. I move forward through the darkness, half swimming, half pulling myself along by hugging the wall, until I spot a glimmer of light. When I reach it, the water grows too shallow and I scramble to my feet, the bubble disappearing as my head bursts through the surface. There's air in the chamber and I'm standing in a stone circle. The top of the circle extends up out of the water, with thatched metal bars that let in the moonlight. What kinds of ancient rituals were once performed here?

Water slides down my body and drips onto the stones while I cross them and ascend a set of uneven steps leading up to a platform. It's a graveyard of lost things up here, covered in broken desks and dressers, fractured vases, decayed art, more mangled statues.

"Pisces," the voice calls again, louder this time.

I shudder and turn, but I'm still alone.

"Pisces."

I pick my way through shards of broken glass and discarded candlesticks, through tables and water-stained armchairs and piles of tarnished silver until I reach a tall standing mirror, leaning against the wall. My stomach churns and my skin prickles. Something isn't right. I peer at it for a long moment, and then I understand what's wrong—there's no reflection.

I jump backward, my heart flinging itself against my ribs. I step up to the mirror and my mind goes blank. Stretching my hand toward the glass, I wait for some trick of the light to reveal that my reflection was there all along. A hand stretches out opposite mine, but it's too pale, with knotted, bony knuckles. Silver claws extend from the nails. My fingers tremble, but the ones in the mirror remain steady. I force my gaze upward to meet onyx eyes and snow-white hair. Hissing, I jerk my hand away and stumble back.

A Dark Witch watches me in the mirror.

No, not here. She can't be here. I whirl, but there's no one behind me. I can't breathe, my heart is beating so fast. I turn back to the mirror and she's still there. She looks straight at me, stark white hair falling in tangles around her, and she reveals sharp teeth in a sickly smile. I dare a step closer to peek behind the mirror, but there's no one there either.

I turn again, my arms in front of me in a pitiful excuse for self-defense, waiting for her to strike. I wait and wait, but nothing happens. The witch never appears behind me. I step up to the mirror, wincing at the closeness to her image, and press my hand against the glass. It's solid and cold. Real. Though when the Dark Witch moves her hand too and presses her clawed fingers against the glass, I don't feel her touch.

Then I understand—the Dark Witch isn't in the room behind me. She's inside the mirror.

A low laugh skitters through the chamber, bouncing off the stone walls. "Hello, little fish," says the Dark Witch. "I've been waiting for you."

12

Serena

GATHERED IN NIOBE'S OFFICE, WE'RE ALL SOMBER, THOUGH I'm not yet sure why. Cancer stands stock-still with rigid shoulders; Sagittarius shifts from foot to foot; and Leo, sitting in one of the leather chairs in front of Niobe's desk, looks anywhere but at me. The newly arrived girl, Aquarius, wears fitted black pants and muddy boots. Her thigh-length white coat is streaked with dirt and her pale cheeks are flushed. She stands behind the desk at Niobe's shoulder like a shadow and jabs at a spot on the map laid out on the desk.

Niobe's office is covered in books, maps, globes, and stacks of old parchment, as though she spends every moment trying to soak in as much knowledge as possible. A plush white rug cushions my feet, spread across the wood floor. Her huge mahogany desk must be antique with its scrolling legs and well-worn rounded corners. It stands between us, a barrier separating me from my understanding of why I'm needed.

Two birds, one with electric-green plumage and the other orange and blue, perch on the beams overhead. Between pruning their feathers, they stop to watch me the same way I can feel Niobe taking note of every movement I make. From a couch on the other side of the room, her panther's eyes bore into me.

I can't stop the nagging voice in my head telling me that my ranking must be wrong. Even the animals must sense it. There's no way an orphan girl who's spent most of her life powerless and locked away could be so highly ranked. The universe, or the gods, or whoever makes that decision must have been mistaken.

Niobe gives Aquarius a nod and inclines her head toward the rest of us. "Show them."

Aquarius steps around the desk. She still doesn't speak; she simply holds out both hands, palms up. Sagittarius joins hands with Aquarius and Leo, then motions to me to take Aquarius's hand. I slide my fingers onto her frozen palm and Cancer grips my other hand.

The moment my skin touches Aquarius's, I'm no longer in Niobe's office. I'm standing on a mountain pass, towering pine trees lining the path as snowcapped mountains rise on either side of me, piercing the clouds. I swear, trying to wrench away, but Aquarius's unseen hand holds mine tighter.

"Easy," Cancer murmurs. "It's an illusion."

An illusion . . .

I glance around me, realizing that while I can see the scene, I can't feel the frigid air or the breeze ruffling the tree branches. I'm viewing the scene through Aquarius's eyes, experiencing what she saw while scouting. The vision continues, moving through the pass until the trees open up to a valley with a ramshackle building of cracking stones, a crumbling roof, and half-boarded windows. "Greymore Mountain Asylum," reads the sign in front of the building.

Aquarius withdraws her touch and I'm thrown back into reality. I sway and catch myself on the back of Leo's chair. She leans forward, looking at me just to curl her lip in disgust. I clamp down on the urge to whip electric sparks at her.

My stomach lurches. "What was that?"

Niobe leans forward, bracing her elbows on her desk, folding her hands as she regards me with a gaze so serious my breathing calms. My heartbeat slows.

"Our Libra has Awoken. The place Aquarius has shown you is where you will be going," says Niobe. "The four of you are to retrieve Libra as quickly and quietly as possible. The Dark Witches will be able to sense her power, and they can't be allowed to find her first."

"You have to be joking. *She's* coming with us?" Leo snaps, glaring at me. "Aries is completely untrained."

"That's true, but the best way to learn is in the field and we cannot afford not to send her. We've been waiting for power like hers for a long time." She nods toward the black numeral three on my wrist and Leo flinches. Niobe's gaze softens. "We need her just as we need you, Leo, and I trust that you will rely on each other for support in order to find Libra and return home safely."

"What about Ophelia?" I ask. Obviously, the entire coven isn't going; Gemini and Virgo aren't coming, and it seems Aquarius isn't either. Still, I don't like the idea of leaving her behind.

"Your sister will remain here, under the Isle of Sol's protective wards, while you're away."

I can't just leave her, not like this. Not after I walked away from her like that.

"You won't be gone long," says Niobe, as if sensing my hesitation.

"I promise she'll be taken care of—there's no need to worry."

No need to worry? Worrying about Ophelia is my job. It's what I've done since the moment I was born. I take a shuddering breath. Niobe is right: She'll be safe here, safer than I'll be retrieving Libra. I have to do this. She'll understand that, I hope. If I want to live up to the rank on my wrist, I have to earn it. There's no better way to do that than diving in. Head-on. Even if I have no idea what I'm doing.

Gemini talks softly with Cancer on the dock when we arrive, a lantern in their hand casting light onto the wood planks. My heart sinks when Ophelia isn't with them, but why would she be? She's probably too angry at me to say goodbye. I tried to find her before coming to the dock, but she wasn't in her room. I wish I'd been able to search for her, but there was only time to run to my room to change out of my dress and into black pants and a red sweater. Even if I had found her, I'm not sure I could bear to look at her without guilt gnawing me apart.

When Cancer says goodbye to Gemini and boards the ship, I step up to them. "If you see my sister, will you tell her something for me?"

Gemini slides their free hand into their pocket and cocks their head. "You can tell her yourself when you get back."

I shake my head. I'm not worried I won't come back. I'm worried even a day apart without explaining myself will make Ophelia hate me.

"Just tell her I'm sorry." I lean in and wrap my arms around them for a brief hug. "And give her this for me too, will you?"

When I draw back, Gemini nods and presses their lips into a soft smile. "Of course."

Leo stands in the middle of the deck, sharpening one of her daggers. From the firm set of her jaw, the purse of her lips, and the sharp glint in her eye, I know she'd rather I were anywhere other than on this mission. My heart thumps as I step onto the boat under cover of darkness.

Sagittarius flashes Leo a cheeky grin. "I told you Aries was going to give you a challenge."

"Shut up, Sag," says Leo.

Sagittarius tosses her hands up and leans back against the ship's rail from where she lounges on a bench. "Don't blame me. I'm not the one who makes the rankings."

Cancer, standing at the rail by my side, says, "Don't poke the bear, Sag."

"But it's so much fun," she whines.

Leo makes a sweeping motion with her arm and the sails flap, propelling the ship into deeper waters, toward a wall of fog in the darkness beyond. I grapple for the rail to keep my feet as the ship takes off.

Behind me, Sagittarius and Leo still needle each other, but I let the roar of the waves drown them out. The Isle of Sol slips away into the night, taking Ophelia along with it. What will she think when she gets back to the Manor and I'm not there? I promised to protect her, to get her out of this place where she felt so uncomfortable. Where everyone around her is stronger and more powerful than she is. Instead, I left her behind when she was counting on me. The smaller the island grows in the distance, the tighter the invisible tether in my chest pulls. I press the heel of my hand into my sternum like I can rub loose the tautness that never goes away. When I was in the East Wing, that pull was a constant, aching reminder that she was just out of reach. That was when we were rooms away. Now the gulf between us is lengthening, and not in distance alone.

I squeeze my eyes shut, trying to focus on the rocking deck of the ship. Cancer's hand lands on my shoulder, soft yet solid. My back tightens and I slide away from her.

"Don't," I whisper. She'll use her magic on me and mess with my head. I like Cancer and she might be my coven-mate, but that doesn't mean I want her picking apart my emotions and changing them.

Cancer folds her hands behind her back and takes a step sideways with a nod. "Want to talk about it?"

I start to object, but then I take in her open face. There's no judgment or pity there, just quiet interest. She watches me with her head cocked. I swallow hard. "I hate leaving her. I can't stop feeling like something's going to happen to her while we're gone."

"She's safe there. The Isle of Sol is warded, and she isn't alone. She's in good hands—the best hands."

I suppose if anyone can take care of her, it's Niobe. Still, I can't stop the twist in my gut telling me I shouldn't leave her there. "She's my responsibility. If something happens to her and I'm not around—" I choke on the lump in my throat and swallow it back. "I didn't get to say goodbye."

"I'm sorry." Cancer looses a long breath, staring at her hands braced on the rail. "At least you have her, though. Someone to leave behind. Someone to return home to."

Ten years, she said she'd been here. That's a long time to be on this island without family or friends other than the coven. There's a longing in Cancer's hazel eyes, a glassy sheen of tears that makes me ask, "Who did you lose?"

"My mother." She breathes the words like a prayer. "Every day I wish she were still here. I wish that I . . ." She gazes at the tip of the tower, the only bit of the Manor still visible through the fog.

I don't remember my mother well enough to miss her, but the weight of her loss still presses on my chest more often than I'd like it to. What would my life be like if she were still alive? I never would have ended up in that festering orphanage, for one. If Cancer's mother were still alive, where would she be? Somewhere far from here, probably. Safe, rather than being sent on missions and fighting Dark Witches. "I'm so sorry," I say, because I don't have any other words to offer.

She shakes her head, and the grief dissipates from her face, replaced with a soft smile. "Don't be. I loved her, and she loved me. There's no point in wishing for anything more than that. Your sister will be safe, and once we find Libra we'll be back to see her."

My breath has steadied and the pit in my stomach has grown looser and shallower. Cancer is right: She'll be safe. And the more I can build up my powers and learn how to use them effectively, the better equipped I'll be to protect her when we're together.

"How far are we going?" I ask.

"It'll take a while to get to the asylum." Cancer's voice is low and quiet, edged with a deeper calm than I've ever heard from her before, but there's something else beneath it. An asylum. No wonder Niobe sent her for this, with her keen ability to sense emotions. The orphanage was full of suffering; I can't imagine what this will be like. As if reading my mind, Cancer gazes out at the water like it might center her. "Once we get beyond the wards, we'll take Sag as close as possible before we have to portal. The farther the distance, the more energy it takes for her to make a jump."

The Isle of Sol slips away on the waves, and I try not to fixate on it. Ophelia is safe there. Niobe promised she would be, and the Isle of Sol is warded against unwanted visitors. I can't distract myself thinking about her when I need to be focusing my energy on my magic. I'll get to use it for something real this time, something more than shooting at targets and pissing off Leo.

"Will you stop with the knives, already?" Sagittarius groans at Leo. "They're sharp enough. You're just trying to look cool."

Leo glowers. "Is it working, though?"

"It really is, I'll give you that." She laughs and Leo smirks.

Heat floods through my stomach, and I hate the bitter edge that rises inside me and prickles the edges of my electricity. It doesn't matter to me who Leo jokes with. It'll never be me, that's for sure.

Leo catches me looking and flicks her hair over her shoulder. "See something you like?"

My cheeks heat. "Just wondering how it feels to be second best," I retort.

Leo lunges across the deck, fast as a lightning strike. Blood rushes through me with surprise and I'm frozen as she seizes my collar and hauls my chest up against hers. While I struggle to catch my suddenly absent breath, she leans down to snarl in my face. "I'm not second best, and I never will be." I try to squirm free, but her grip is like iron. Her forehead hovers inches from my own, close enough that her rose-scented perfume forces its way into my nose. "This is my coven. Just because you came in two seconds ago and some magical force stamped a number on your wrist doesn't mean you know what you're doing. I told Niobe you're too fresh to come on this mission, but she's so enamored with your bullshit that she made us bring you. One wrong move could blow this whole operation for us, so you'd better know your place and let me take the lead."

With the press of her lithe body so close, I'm too aware of her chest rising and falling against mine in short, agitated breaths. Then Cancer is there between us with weary lines etched on her face, easing Leo back from me. "Walk it off, both of you."

She releases Leo and glides back to sit beside Sagittarius, tipping her head against the rail with her eyes closed.

"Leo." I reach for her arm. I didn't know she would be so easily riled. Why is it that whatever I say, it's not like when the others tease her?

She jerks back like I might burn her. "Don't touch me."

Once Leo is certain the ship is steering us in the right direction, we all move to the cabin Ophelia and I saw when we first boarded the ship. Its cozy warmth makes my eyelids sag, and I stifle a yawn as I remember how long I've been awake.

"Get some rest," says Cancer. "You'll need it."

Leo takes the couch, stretching out her long legs and closing her eyes. Sagittarius curls like a cat in an armchair and I do the same in the one across from her, letting the ship's rocking lull me to sleep.

I'm woken hours later by Cancer's hand shaking my shoulder. I follow her onto the deck in the morning twilight and squint at a foreign shore in the distance. The trees are dusted with snow and the mountaintops disappear into low gray clouds. The air is much colder here than on the Isle of Sol and I tug on the navy quilted jacket I brought, savoring the fleece lining.

Leo lifts her arm like a ballerina, and the ship fully stops despite no one dropping an anchor. "This is as close as we can get without detection."

"This place is in the middle of nowhere," says Sagittarius,

studying a map. All of her gregarious energy is gone, and she stares blankly at the deck in front of us, biting her lip. "I've never portaled this far before. I don't know how long I'll be able to hold it, so go through fast."

When she stands and steps to the center of the deck, we all fall silent.

"You can do this," Cancer says quietly. "Good luck."

I expect her to shoot back a retort about not needing luck, but instead she gives Cancer a grateful half smile. Rolling her neck and bouncing on the balls of her feet, she takes a deep breath and then goes still. Her hands move through the air in sharp rapid bursts. Her fingers cut odd angles too quickly for me to parse each motion until gold shimmers in the air and like a curtain drawing back on another world, the air in front of us splits. Suddenly, I'm not looking at the ship's deck but at the mountain pass I saw in Aquarius's illusion.

"Go," Sagittarius grunts through gritted teeth.

Leo moves first, jumping into the portal with Cancer on her heels. I step through onto solid earth and stumble when Sagittarius comes through so close behind me that she slams into my back. Someone catches my arm and hauls me upright before I can eat dirt.

"Thanks," I mutter before I realize it isn't Cancer who grabbed me but Leo.

She drops my arm like I've stung her. "Keep your feet next time."

I fight to keep my magic from lashing out at her. Grinding my jaw, I say, "Worry about yourself." Leo's russet eyes bore into mine, neither of us willing to blink first.

I tear myself away at the sound of Sagittarius hacking a cough. Doubled over and panting, she braces her hands on her knees. Cancer stands over her with a hand on her back. "This is as close as

I can get," Sagittarius manages to say.

"You did good," says Cancer. "We'll wait until you can continue, and then we go in."

I don't want to wait, though. Not here. We're standing in the middle of a flat pass through the mountains. They rise up like sleeping giants on either side, covered in pine trees and peeking their snow-covered heads out around us. The wind whistles, singing through the valley, and the longer we stand here, the more the fog rolls in and curls the mountains into its grasp. I pull my jacket tighter around me. In the distance, I can make out a crumbling brick building. The asylum. What kinds of horrors has Libra endured that would land her in a place like this? We have no idea what condition she'll be in when we get to her. Or what condition we'll find the other patients in.

The hair on the back of my neck prickles like someone is watching. Every snapping tree branch, every rustling leaf has me swiveling in all directions. What's out there in the darkness, hiding in the fog, waiting beneath cover to come snatch us up?

"N-No," Sagittarius stammers. "We don't have time to wait. It took us long enough to get here and the Dark Witches move fast."

Slowly, like every movement takes effort, she rises and steps forward. Leo gives her a cursory glance and then marches forward toward the asylum, visible in the distant valley. I'm glad to be walking rather than standing like prey in the middle of the forest for whatever predators lurk within.

The closer we get to the asylum, the more I sense Cancer receding from reality. She walks with steady steps and her head held high, but her face pales. She disappears deeper and deeper inside herself, her hands curling into tight fists, her hair growing limp, like she's absorbing all the terror of the asylum ahead.

The sun has just risen when we descend into the valley and reach the asylum. The building looks like it's about to collapse into a pile of rubble at a moment's notice. Stones of all different shades are stained with black. Shutters hang from the windows, tilted and on the verge of falling, like crooked teeth in the mouth of a hellhound. The few lights that are on flicker.

"Do you feel her?" Leo asks Cancer.

"She's terrified." Cancer's voice cracks. I don't envy her powers; my sparks may be volatile and difficult to control, but at least I only have my own emotions to contend with. She shudders and wraps her arms around herself. "Something isn't right, though. There's . . ." Her eyes go distant. "Nothing."

A shiver ricochets up my spine. Nothing? How is that possible when there should be dozens of people inside?

Leo frowns and removes two knives from the holster on her leg. "If we find staff, I'll deal with them. You two get the girl."

"If there's staff, I can help you persuade them to let us in," says Cancer.

Leo shakes her head. "You need to reserve your energy. I have a feeling we'll need it."

Cancer nods. "Someone gets her out, no matter what."

I have to agree. No one should be forced to live in a place like this.

Sagittarius lingers to the side. "I'll stay here," she says, her voice hoarse and weak.

Leo nods and starts toward the door. "Wait," I say. "We can't leave her here." Not when I'm waiting for the forest to swallow her whole at any second. We should stay together, where we can protect each other.

"You can," says Sagittarius. "And if you want me to be able to portal all of us back to the ship you're going to have to."

I have to admit, she doesn't look good. Her chest is heaving, her hair has all but completely fallen from her ponytail, and the sweaty tendrils cling to her face, which has turned so pale I fear she might collapse at any moment. Cancer and Leo exchange tight nods and I know they don't like this plan any more than I do.

"Get some rest, keep watch, and stay out of sight," Leo says solemnly. "We'll be back soon."

Sagittarius forces a grim smile. "Of course you will—you're useless without me."

This is what it means to be in a coven, I realize. Doing what's best for the group, even when it hurts. Even when it means leaving someone behind.

13

Ophelia

I STUMBLE THROUGH THE CAVERN, LOOKING FOR SOME-thing, anything to use as a weapon against the Dark Witch. I grab the head of a small broken bust in shaking fingers. It slips in my sweaty palms. I won't let another Dark Witch hurt me; I won't be a pawn in her game. This time, I won't sit by helplessly.

Pulling my arm back as I stagger away, I'm about to lob it at the mirror when she says, "You haven't Awoken yet, have you, little fish?"

I freeze. She laughs, breathy and soft and muffled, and the glass fogs. Is she truly on the other side of it? I grip the statue tighter but dare a glance around the cavern. She's not in here, and she hasn't stepped through. Is this some kind of trick? The witch cocks her head as her blank eyes rove me up and down. A wave of shame, hot and thick, rises in my throat, threatening to choke me. I don't want to Awaken, so why does it feel like I've failed by not having my powers yet? I don't look at the number inked on my wrist, but I swear I can feel it burning there.

Taking in the cavern, letting my racing mind catch up to my racing heart, I'm now certain she's trapped inside the mirror. I let the bust fall from my fingers and clatter to the stones as I circle the mirror, taking slow, measured steps, trying to slow my breath to match. Her skirt swishes as she sways from side to side, watching me. Deep wrinkles crease her face. She's dressed in a blousy white top and calf-length plaid skirt.

"Who are you?" I ask. She can't have always been a Dark Witch—she must have been someone, once. Did she come to this island to attack the coven? How did she even get on the island, unless she's older than the wards? How long has she been trapped here?

The witch clucks her tongue at me and her black eyes sparkle with amusement. "You don't know?"

I shake my head. There's nothing familiar about her at all. She *feels* different from the Dark Witch at the orphanage. That witch was full of anger and malice and the pure power of storm clouds rolling across the sky to swallow every bit of light in the universe. Maybe it's thanks to whatever power the mirror possesses, trapping her inside and rendering her powerless, but this witch is calmer. She's cold and calculating, rather than bursting with raw aggression.

"If you had Awoken," says the witch, "you would have recognized a fellow Pisces."

My breath catches and I sputter. "How . . . how do you know I'm a Pisces?"

"I can feel it. Just like I can feel that you're afraid."

"I'm not afraid," I lie.

The witch smiles with closed lips, and with her sharp teeth covered, she almost seems human. "Not of me, little fish. Of your powers. Why are you afraid of them?"

"I don't want them." *I don't want to be you*, I almost say. My cheeks heat, but I bite down on my lower lip. I won't be ashamed of wanting to keep my own soul intact.

The Dark Witch's mouth drops open, showing her razor-sharp teeth. "Why wouldn't you want it? You've been given a gift; it would be a shame to let it go to waste."

"A gift," I echo bitterly. This isn't a gift; it's a curse. "What kind of gift turns you into a monster?" The Dark Witch freezes and my hand flies to cover my mouth as I realize what I've said. "I'm sorry, I didn't mean—"

"Yes," she says, stopping me. "Yes, you did mean it; there's no use in lying. You think I'm a monster? Don't worry, you're not the only one. Though I suppose we're all monsters in the end. That's the price we pay. Power isn't free, little fish."

"I don't want it," I repeat. Power means nothing to me. I've never wanted to be powerful. I just want to be free.

The Dark Witch presses her lips into a wistful smile. "You think that now. We *all* thought that once. But when the time comes, you won't have a choice in the matter. One day, when your magic breaks free, you'll be so hungry for it that you won't have any other choice. You'll sit down at that table and eat your fill and when you do, you'll realize you've been starving your entire life."

"Well, it doesn't seem like all that power helped you much, seeing how you're trapped," I say.

The Dark Witch laughs, and again, I'm taken aback by how light and musical it sounds. It's so human. I could close my eyes and imagine it belonged to a very different woman, one made of sunshine and reflective pools of water and unbridled joy. "Don't you want to know who trapped me here?"

"Yes." Although I already know who it must have been. There's one person on this island who knows absolutely everything about it. One person who the fish and the birds and all the little creatures whisper to. One person who must know there's a Dark Pisces down here in the mirror.

"Niobe," says the witch.

My heart skips a beat, although it's the answer I expected. "Why would she do that?" I pick at the skin around my cuticles, trying not to let my face betray how desperately I want to know how much she knows about the coven leader. Niobe said the duty of this coven was to eradicate Dark Witches. So why is she keeping one alive? What is she hiding?

"Our mutual friend likes to mess things up," says the witch.

"What do you mean?"

The witch shrugs. "I mean she has a way of keeping secrets. Important ones."

She's a Dark Witch. Deception and deceit are her bosom friends, so why should I trust a single word that escapes her lips? "You're lying," I say.

"What reason would I have to lie?" She gestures around her at the emptiness in the mirror. What is her side of the mirror like? Is there anything there, or is she simply stuck, hanging suspended in silver nothingness until someone releases her? "I have nothing to gain in this place, and certainly nothing to lose. Niobe will never free me. I only hate to see another Pisces suffer her deceit. As a Pisces yourself, I'm sure you've noticed her lies, have you not?"

I clench my jaw, not wanting to let her know how right she is. "What kind of secrets is she keeping?"

The Dark Witch crosses her arms over her chest, tapping long-nailed fingers on her arm. "Ones I'm certain will interest you and your sister."

I suck in a sharp breath. I force my face into a calm mask, not wanting her to know that mentioning Serena has sent my heart pounding so frantically I can't breathe. "How do you know about my sister?"

"I know far more than you can imagine," she drawls.

Look closer, my instincts scream at me. I take in all the harsh details of her face, her withered skin leathery from time spent without access to the life force of power sucked from young witches. Past the teeth and talons, there's something needling me, some detail I'm missing.

Her clothes. My breath hitches in my throat and my hand presses against my quickening heart. There are rows of blouses just like hers in my wardrobe in the Manor, and that skirt—it's the exact same shade of blue plaid as the ones I've worn for the last two days.

She isn't just any Dark Witch. She was once a witch at the Manor.

14

Serena

"HELLO? ANYBODY HOME?" LEO CALLS AS SHE TURNS THE rusted handle and pushes through the splintered door of the asylum, leading us into the lobby. It's bare, with concrete floors and nothing on the walls. The paint is crumbling and water pools on the floor like no one has bothered to patch the leaks in the ceiling. Like it doesn't matter whether the people here live or die.

Then the smell hits me. It's mold and rot and . . . death. I gag against the stench that forces its way down my throat and into my lungs, as if it might choke every ounce of fresh air from my body forever.

"What is that?" Leo says, clapping a hand over her mouth. Behind her, Cancer's expression is drawn, and she sways on her feet.

Leo stalks to check behind the desk and then gags. I lurch forward to see what's hidden behind the rotting oak antique and freeze.

It's the warden.

Or *was*. Blood streaks the floor beneath his motionless body and spittle is dried on the corner of his mouth. His open eyes stare sightlessly at the ceiling. Bile rises in my throat and saliva coats my mouth. I try to swallow it back but have to double over to vomit behind the desk. I look up, expecting Leo's judgment, but she's just staring at the corpse.

"Did the Dark Witches beat us here?" I ask after I wipe my mouth. I wish I could wash away the sour tang, but there's no time. We may already be too late.

Cancer shakes her head. "This wasn't them." Her voice trembles. "This was *her*. Her Awakening did this."

"Is she . . ."

"She's still here. I can feel her."

Leo drags her hand away from her mouth, paler than I've ever seen her. Her throat bobs as she swallows. "We need to move."

She jerks her head toward the stairs, one knife in her hand, three more floating in the air above her shoulders. I follow close behind her, power gathering like a storm within me. My electricity is ready, just in case.

Suddenly, Leo stops at the top of the stairs, and I barely catch myself before running into her. My feet teeter over the edge of the step. I gasp as I tumble backward, but Cancer catches my elbow to steady me. "What are you doing?" I hiss to Leo.

Instead of walking straight ahead, she hugs the wall, inching into the hallway. With a backward glance, she inclines her head for me to follow. Her face is too cold and emotionless, her back too rigid. When I ascend the remaining stair, I see why.

The hallway is littered with corpses

There are at least a dozen dead, some in uniforms, others in hole-ridden linen outfits. There's so much blood that the floorboards are stained crimson. Streaks of blood coat the walls; splatters and smears and handprints. And the bodies . . . A dozen pairs of eyes stare at the ceiling. Unblinking. Their faces are already turning gray.

This was her, Cancer said. How much horror does someone have to experience to do something like this? I know how it felt when I Awakened—the anger, the confusion. But this? My hands shake, but I refuse to look away. I was sent on this mission for a reason. I can handle this. We can help her. We can save her.

We tiptoe down the hallway, none of us daring to speak, as though the smallest sound might desecrate the dead in this wretched graveyard. I step gingerly, slipping through wet blood and avoiding the bodies.

Footsteps groan behind us and I whirl. A man twice my height lumbers toward us. His face is distorted by purple bruising and his guard uniform is covered in crimson streaks. Is he hurt?

"Leo, don't," says Cancer, but Leo is already moving.

She rushes forward, unbound red hair streaming behind her, and plunges her knife into his chest. He freezes, frowns down at the blade, then rips it out. The silver blade is clean, free of blood. It tips out of his fingers and clatters to the floor. Leo yanks it back through the air and into her hand.

Still, the man keeps shuffling toward us. I stagger backward, sparks crackling at my fingertips. "How is this possible?" I ask.

"He's already dead," whispers Cancer. "They're all dead."

"Damn Libra necromancers," Leo growls. With a screech, she hurls a dagger so fast it's nothing but a blur. With more force than any human should be able to wield, it slices sideways across his neck.

His head topples from his shoulders and rolls across the blood-soaked floorboards. His body crumples in a heap.

I keep breathing through my mouth, stifling the smell of decay, the severed stump of the dead man's neck. Even with his body felled, his hands and feet continue to twitch toward us.

Clothing rustles on the other side of the hall. "Leo," Cancer warns.

One by one, the dead climb to their feet.

They watch us with unseeing eyes, with chests that don't rise and fall and mouths that move wordlessly. Slowly, like each step takes effort, they lumber toward us.

Before I can comprehend what's happening, Leo leaps into motion. She's a whirlwind of fists and steel, cutting through dead men one by one. Cancer pulls a knife from inside her trench coat, longer than one of Leo's, with a curved blade. She drops into a fighting stance, face determined and knees bent. Ready to strike. Her magic won't work on the dead, I realize. There's no mind to influence. Instead, she takes a slow breath, then throws herself into the fray beside Leo.

A woman with a long slice from her temple to her collarbone makes for me. Digging deep, I summon a lightning bolt and throw it. My aim is true. The bolt slams into the dead woman's chest, but all it does is send her staggering back two steps.

She starts toward me again, but Cancer leaps between us. Her knees hit the ground and she slides, curved blade swinging. It cuts through the woman's legs like butter, and she falls. I shudder as she struggles to rise; her mouth gapes open, trying to scream, but no air fills her lungs.

"Aries, go," says Cancer through gritted teeth. "Upstairs, last door."

"I'm not leaving you."

"Go," Cancer insists. I bite my lip, but she's right. My lightning isn't doing anything effective, and I'm not the physical fighter Leo and Cancer are. I'll be more useful finding Libra than trying to hold my own here.

I back away from their fight until I reach the stairs. I take them two at a time, flinging open the door to the upstairs hallway. It's quiet here, no bodies in the halls. I slow, trying to catch my breath. From downstairs, I can hear Leo and Cancer grunting as they fight. The floorboards creak beneath every step, like the asylum itself is wailing. Like the walls are weeping from the horrors they've witnessed. I'm halfway down the hall when I hear her crying.

Her sobs are muffled, withheld. For a moment, I'm not in the asylum anymore. I'm in the orphanage, stuffing my fist into my mouth to stifle any sound the matrons might hear as tears drip down my cheeks.

I shove the memory away as it sends cold licking down my spine and jiggle the handle on the last door. It's locked. I don't have time to try knocking—the sooner I calm this girl, the sooner my coven-mates will be safe—so I focus all my mental energy on the lock and shoot one quick burst of electricity into it. The handle jerks, jumping open at the shock.

Cracking the door, I call, "Hello?"

There's no response except the sobs, growing louder as I get closer. When I slide inside, I don't see anyone. Then a louder whimper echoes in the darkness and I find her in the corner, huddled with her arms wrapped around her knees. She's no more than eight years old. Her deathly white skin is streaked with dirt and tear tracks, and her mousy brown hair is so matted it must be miserably painful. I don't know why I'd assumed she'd be older. I know some of the other witches arrived long before they were my age, and yet I never imagined we'd be here to save a child.

A *child*, in a place like this.

On a thin mattress across the room, there's a pile of clothes, blankets, and patchwork rags so high she must not be able to even get to the bed. The floors, the walls, the windowpanes, every inch of this horrid excuse for a bedroom is covered in dirt. The whole place reeks of not just decay but the rotting stink of death.

Even the orphanage was better.

Lightning burns through me, threatening to pour out of my palms, but I force it back. As much as I long to burn this place to ashes, I can't. Not while my coven-mates are here. Not until I get this little girl as far from this wretched place as possible.

"Hi there." I bend to get on her level the way I would talk to one of the new children at the orphanage. "My name is Serena. What's yours?" She stares blankly, tears falling silently down her round cheeks. I wish Ophelia was here. She'd know what to say. Drawing in a metered breath and trying to push away my anger, I force my voice to be soft and gentle and think of what my sister would say. "It's okay, I'm not going to hurt you."

The skin on the small of my back prickles. I stiffen, waiting for someone to strike me from behind. The girl's silent tears stop falling, and she giggles. The sound is too bright and pure for a place like this. My skin crawls and I whip around, but I can't make sense of the thing lurking behind me.

The pile of blankets isn't a pile of blankets at all—it's a creature. A monstrosity of patchwork fabrics, looming on two feet and standing over a head taller than me.

I turn back to Libra, and the moment I look away, something pounds into my stomach.

I fling out my arms in open air while the world spins, desperate to catch myself as I fly across the room. Every ounce of air in my body whooshes out of me when I slam into the wall and slide to the ground. I'd groan if I could, but no sound comes out. I scramble to my feet, choking as I fight to breathe again.

When I pull myself up against the wall, I realize what hit me. An arm. I squint through the darkness and make out two legs, a pair of arms, and on its head, a poorly sewn jagged mouth and two round ears.

A bear, made of patchwork fabrics and animated by Libra's magic. I'm not sure how she's controlling it, if she's a necromancer like Leo said, but I don't have time to be curious.

I don't dare look away again. Still facing the bear, I search out of the corner of my eye for Libra and find her huddled in the corner. "Is this your bear—"

The patchwork monstrosity lunges for me, and I duck beneath its lumbering arm. Darting behind it, I send a bolt of electricity through the air. It goes wide, pounding into the wall behind and leaving a scorch mark. I try to remember Leo's lessons in aiming. I let my vision focus on my target and will my magic to go where I need it to. I'm in charge. I'm its master.

I exhale and send another bolt shooting for the creature. The edge of its arm catches fire. "No!" Libra shrieks. For a moment, I allow myself to hope, but it flaps wildly and the flames fizzle out.

It's a creature of fabric animated by Libra somehow. How can I kill something that isn't alive?

I fling my arms out and throw every ounce of lightning I have at it. The dark room blazes with bursts of light but still the bear advances. Backing away, I don't let my electricity stop. But my back hits the wall. There's nowhere left to go.

The patchwork bear lifts me off the ground like I'm nothing but a toy doll and tosses me across the room. I hit the ground on my back and the wind rushes from my body. I start to roll to my feet but the creature towers over me. One of its massive legs pins my chest. When I swear, it seems to smile, snout distorting to show an empty maw, no teeth, only darkness. I shoot sparks up at it, but nothing affects it. It shakes its head like my electric shocks are nothing more than flies. Its foot presses down on me and the air squeezes from my lungs until I can't breathe. Is it going to crush me to death? I try to squirm and fight, but I can't get free, can't get a breath. Stars flash in my eyes and all I can think about as the life is pressed out of me is Ophelia. Someone is going to have to tell her how I died.

A dagger flies through the doorway with Leo right behind it. It whistles in the air and rips through the seam of the giant bear's side. The creature stumbles backward and air rushes into my lungs. I pull myself to my hands and knees, trying to breathe, when something pours from the bear's arm.

Dead rats, mice, and a couple of barely recognizable birds fall to the ground in a heap.

The rotten musk in the room grows more potent. The creature was made of hundreds of dead animals. I gag and Leo swears.

"If you vomit again, I'll cut all your hair off in your sleep," Leo says.

Little Libra whimpers. "You hurt my friend." The patchwork creature doesn't seem hurt at all; it advances toward Leo in more pieces this time. "Now I'm going to hurt you," Libra says in a singsong voice that grates at my bones like nails on a chalkboard.

"She's controlling it!" yells Leo.

The bear swings at her again and she barely ducks in time. Her knives whiz through the air in a whirling tornado of metal. Where they rip the seams, more dead rats fall onto the floor. The scent of decay increases until I can hardly breathe. Leo waves an arm, but her telekinesis does nothing to move the bear. It responds to Libra, and only Libra.

"Make her stop!" Leo screams.

I crawl toward Libra. Her arms are wrapped around her knees so tightly that her skin is bone white at the places where she pulls on her own flesh. Her eyes are bloodshot and the look on her face . . . I recognize that look. She's putting on a mask, a brave face, but really, she's a little girl.

I've been that little girl.

"I know you're scared." I keep my voice gentle despite Leo's cursing and grunting behind me as she fends off the demon bear. This time, it's not Ophelia's words coming out of my lips. These are mine. "It's okay to be scared."

As I crawl closer across the disgusting, dirt-coated floor, I realize she's shaking. I sink back onto my knees, staying at arm's length from her. "Look at me," I say, and her gaze comes to land on me.

"It's okay to be scared," I say again. "You have to be scared to be brave. I was in a place like this once, and people were mean to me. They hurt me and my sister. Did the people here hurt you?" She nods, eyes wild and unblinking. "No one is going to hurt you anymore, I promise. I won't let them. If you hurt my friend, she won't be able to help you. We're all here to help you, okay?" She nods, and behind me I hear the fight slow. Leo's breathing steadies.

"I'm scared too," I say, because it's true. "I'm so scared all the time, but we can be brave together. You and me. We can be brave and leave this place and never look back. How does that sound?"

I hold out my hand, and there's a *thunk* behind me as the bear falls to the floor.

"Took you long enough," Leo pants.

I don't look at her, though. I don't dare look away from the terrified little girl in front of me, still shaking. A powerful emotion surges in my chest, because she's just like me. And I saved her. "We're going to get you out of here," I say.

Leo floats her knives back to her and holsters them on her leg again. "We've got to go."

"Don't rush her," I say. I keep reaching for her, but the girl doesn't take my hand. She stares at me, trembling.

Footsteps pound down the hall and I spin to my feet, electricity crackling in blue flames at my fingertips. It's only Cancer, though. Despite her too-pale face, I release a sigh when she slows and enters the room.

"Where the hell have you been?" demands Leo, though her voice is tinged with relief.

Cancer ignores her; her attention goes to Libra. "Let me."

I do, and she slides past me to kneel on the floor and take the girl's hands in her own. I step out of the way, somehow feeling that watching would be invading something private.

"Thanks for saving my ass back there," I say to Leo.

She shrugs. "Death by teddy bear would honestly be the most embarrassing way to go out."

I laugh and Leo shoots me a rare, genuine smile. It lights up her face, and for a moment, my breath catches in my throat. I feel like I've been struck with a rare ray of sunshine in a perpetually gray sky.

Cancer helps the girl to her feet but doesn't let go of her hand. She's calmer now, face less contorted with pain and body steady.

Cancer's magic, at work again.

"Let's get out of here," says Leo. She leads the way out of the asylum and our exit can't come fast enough. I never want to think of this place again. It's going to take me days to scrub the bone-deep stench of death from my body. I drink in a deep breath of fresh mountain air when we step outside, but that longing for freedom is crushed within moments.

A familiar figure is collapsed on the ground in front of the asylum.

Leo breaks into a sprint. "Sag!"

She's fine, I tell myself. Teleporting here took a lot out of her—she probably fainted. She needs rest and then she'll be all right and we can go back to the Manor. Back to Ophelia and the others.

But something cold and oily slides through my gut. The hair on the back of my neck stands on end. Something isn't right.

I go to my knees at Sagittarius's side as Leo turns her over. She gasps and swears.

She's unconscious and Leo shakes her, mumbling her name over and over. When she finally opens her eyes, Leo breathes a sigh, but my heart still throws itself against my ribs. All around me the air itself is screaming that something is wrong. We never should have left her out here.

Sagittarius shakes her head wildly; blood drips from her temple. "No," she whispers, her voice raspy and weak. "It's a trap."

15

Ophelia

I NEED TO GET INTO NIOBE'S OFFICE. IF THE DARK PISCES was a witch here, there must be ledgers or records somewhere, and my guess is Niobe has them. Because Dark Witches wither and grow old at a faster-than-natural rate if they don't consume the magic of witches who haven't turned, it's difficult to tell how old the Dark Pisces is. If Niobe is the one who put her in the mirror, though, that at least narrows a timeline down for me. I wish I knew why Niobe was keeping her there. Is she colluding with her? Or simply keeping her captive? I could ask, but I don't trust her not to lie to me. I need to get all the information I can before showing my hand.

When I step out of my bedroom, the Manor is eerily quiet despite the fact that it's well into the afternoon, until Serena rounds the corner with a wide grin. She's wearing a plaid vest and pants, and her hair is pulled into a slick ponytail.

"What did Niobe want last night?" I ask, but she doesn't answer. Instead, she bursts into a run and races down the hall.

She slams into me, and I catch her, rocking back a step to keep my balance. Her arms wrap around me, but something isn't right. That tug in my chest, the thread between me and Serena, it's still pulled taut. Now, with her hands pressing into my shoulders, her grip is too tight and the scent of jasmine pushes its way into my nose.

"This is from your sister," she says in my ear.

Sister . . .

Realization slams into me. "Gemini?"

I shove them away, every inch of my skin prickling with wrongness. The moment they stumble back from the force of my push, Gemini transforms back into their own face.

I shake my hands out furiously, like I can force the slimy sense of treachery out of my body. "Don't ever, *ever* do that again." I fight back the nausea roiling in my gut. They aren't Serena. How dare they use her face like that and try to trick me.

Their curly hair is still long, swept up into a high ponytail with one white streak through it. The few stray wisps hanging down draw attention to the smattering of freckles across their golden-skinned cheeks. Their brow furrows and they cock their head.

"I'm sorry." They step back from me. "Your sister left on a mission for Niobe and she wanted me to give you a hug. I thought it would be nice if it felt like it came from her, but I was wrong. It won't happen again, I promise."

I barely hear their apology, though. "A mission? Where? When did they leave?" Has she been gone this whole time and I didn't notice? I fell into bed exhausted when I got back to the Manor last night and assumed she must have already been in bed. Warmth leeches from my hands and I pick at the skin around the nails of my numb fingertips.

"Last night," says Gemini, before telling me everything about the plan to recover Libra.

"When will they be back?" I should have gone after her and not let Sagittarius rip her away. What if something happens to her and I didn't get to say goodbye?

"Serena says she's sorry, by the way. She didn't say why, but—"

"I know why." She knew what she was doing when she walked away from me. I still can't get the image of her retreating out of my head, but if she hadn't gone with Niobe, I wouldn't have found the Dark Pisces. I wouldn't be on a path to discovering the truth. If she's going to be out there using her powers, the best thing for me to do is to find a way to stop her from turning Dark. And to do that, I have to find out what Niobe is hiding.

I take a deep breath and force all thoughts of Serena out of my head. She's strong—the third-strongest witch in the world—and she's with Leo and the others. They'll take care of her. I turn my attention back to Gemini. How do they always manage to find me? They stand strong and tall, shoulders back, and their flowy white shirt is cuffed to the elbow beneath their vest, revealing toned forearms. Despite their inappropriate impersonation of Serena, there's something about Gemini that makes the voices in my head go quiet, like the universe is telling me that they're safe. They were only trying to help.

"Where's Niobe's office?" I ask.

They incline their head down the hall. "Why?"

I hesitate, chewing on my lip, and Gemini frowns. "What's wrong?"

"Not here." Not in the hallway where Niobe or anyone else might hear. Not when one of Niobe's spying animals could be just around the corner. Another mouse? A housefly? An ant?

"Come on, then." Gemini tugs me into their bedroom. I've never been in any of the rooms before except for mine and Serena's, which still feel new and pristine, but Gemini's is different. It's been lived in. The walls are purple and flecked with stars and constellations, and above the dresser is a portrait of two androgynous-looking faces with their heads turned away from each other. There are sketches and pages of notes in scribbled ink on the desk, jackets slung over chairs, and a fuzzy blanket across the bedspread. There are piles of library books everywhere—on the nightstand, in the windowsill, on the armchair, stacked in the corners of the room.

Once the door is shut firmly behind us, I peek around, making sure no little mice or crickets lurk in the corners or birds peep through the windows. I exhale a quivering breath and say, "Niobe is keeping secrets."

Their brow furrows. "What kind of secrets?"

"I don't know, but I need to find out." I'm unsure if I should tell Gemini about the Dark Pisces in the pond. I think I can trust them, but the stunt with Serena's face still has me feeling sick to my stomach. There's a little voice nagging in my gut, telling me to keep the Dark Witch to myself for now until I know more about her. "Niobe said she'd been watching me and my sister, but she never took us out of that orphanage. And I have this feeling that something is wrong and I can't shake it. It just keeps eating and eating at me and it won't go away."

I need to know for sure or I'll never be able to rest without the feeling that something on this island isn't right.

Gemini slides their hands into their pockets and eyes me carefully. "What would make it go away?"

"I need to see Niobe's office. Without her there. Maybe there's something about me and my sister that'll tell me what kept her from rescuing us." It's not entirely a lie. I'd like to know those things as well.

I brace myself for them to tell me I need to calm down, to sit and wait until Serena gets home so she can tell me I'm overreacting. But that reaction never comes.

"Let's go." They press their hands against their thighs and stride for the door.

"Wait," I call. "What . . . what are you doing?"

"What does it look like? I'm getting you into Niobe's office."

"How?" Though what I really want to ask is *why*.

"You do realize you're talking to this house's master spy, right?" they say with a smirk. "Niobe's animals have nothing on me."

"You don't think I'm . . . I'm . . ." I can't bring myself to say the words out loud. Since we arrived here, my mind had moved slow, as if through a haze. None of this seems real, and I'm half convinced that at any moment I'll wake up back in my bed at the orphanage, and they'll send me to isolation in the East Wing for my hallucinations about magic and witches and dark creatures of the night lurking beneath enchanted ponds.

"No, I don't think you're crazy." A muscle in their jaw jumps and they look at their shoes for a long moment. "I think we've all been called that too much, right? Also, you're not the only one who thinks something isn't right. I trust Niobe, really, I do. I don't know where I'd be without her. But I also have this nagging feeling that she's keeping something from all of us, and I don't particularly like to operate under murky circumstances. Not if it risks the safety of anyone in this building. So if you're saying something is wrong, it's worth investigating. You're part of this team, and I believe you."

Warmth floods through my chest. Gemini believes me. "But what if—"

Gemini huffs a laugh and shakes their head, making their long ponytail sway. "Are you going to ask questions, or are we doing this?"

I catch myself picking at the skin around my thumbnails and force my hands to my sides. Gemini is right: There's no more time for questions. I need answers.

"We're doing this," I say. "And Gemini . . ." They raise their brows, eyes meeting mine and holding like nothing else exists in the universe. "Thank you."

"Don't thank me until we have your answers."

They lace their fingers with mine again and I don't pull away as they tug me down the hallway and up to the third floor, pressing a finger to their lips as we pass a series of doors.

Gemini slows before one of them, peering into an office and then continuing around a corner, where we stop.

"Wait here. It's the second door on the right back there. Niobe isn't there but Castor is." When I frown, Gemini clarifies, "Her panther."

Before I can ask any more questions, they shift until it isn't Gemini standing in front of me anymore; it's Niobe. They flash Niobe's perfect, bright smile at me and enter the office.

"Come along," Gemini says in Niobe's easy cadence, and clicks their tongue at the panther. "Good boy," they croon, and I peek around the corner to see Gemini and Castor walk down the hall. Gemini drops a quick wink over their shoulder.

I listen as their steps disappear down the stairs, then count to ten for good measure. When I'm certain they're gone, I duck out from around the corner and hurry into the office. I close the door slowly to try to keep it from making too much noise. The office is full of bright sunlight and warmth, with knickknacks and books on every surface. I long to spend hours combing through every one and uncovering their histories. I sneak to the desk on tiptoes, thanking my lucky stars that her colorful birds are resting in their cage with their heads tucked to their chests, asleep. Just to be safe, though, I pull a throw blanket from the back of the sofa by the window and drape it over the cage.

I start with the desk and begin opening drawers. Paper, pens, supply lists, a calendar with meals written on each day, charts with fighting figurations, nothing I wouldn't expect to find in her desk. I work my way down, disappointment growing each time I open a drawer that doesn't contain any school records.

Finding nothing of note in the desk, I move to the bookshelves. I trail my fingers over the spines. It won't be a textbook or a map, so I hunt for things that could be logs or ledgers until I find a series of thin, hardbound books with black covers. I pull the first one from the shelf and open it to the last page. I suck in a sharp breath—there's my name. It's written beside my sign, the current year, my age at entering the Manor, and in newly printed ink, my ranking. Serena's information is written above mine, and before that, the names and ranks of the rest of the coven. I look away without reading much. It somehow feels too intimate to see everyone's given names.

I thumb through the book, unsure what I'm searching for, though the thick black X's beside some of the names—witches who've died or turned Dark—make me shudder. I close the book and move to the next, but when I pull it from the shelf, a stack of photos flutters out from where it was pressed beneath the cover.

I crouch to the floor and gather the grainy photographs. On top is a picture of Niobe sitting on the front steps of the Manor. She's young in this photo, sixteen or seventeen, and her hair hangs long around her in dozens of tiny braids. She's wearing a uniform nearly identical to my own, but her green-and-black plaid skirt hangs longer, brushing against her knee, and her white shirt is blousy. It covers her all the way to the neck and leaves her with very little shape to her thin but tall frame.

In the next photo, she's in the library beside a girl with long, thick curls that frame a round face. The other girl is wearing a blue shirt and I catch a glimpse of a fish tattoo on her wrist where her sleeves are rolled back. There are more of her as I thumb through the stack, though some of the photos have been creased and her face folded to the back. This must be the Dark Pisces from the mirror. She's so ordinary in the photos. Just another girl, full of laughter and wide smiles and innocence. It seems inconceivable that she could become a Dark Witch, that any of us could suffer that fate. Is that why Niobe stuffs the photos inside another book? Is it too difficult to look at her face and see the witch she once was? The friend she lost?

I tuck the photos of Niobe and the girl I think is the Dark Pisces into my pocket and continue looking through the rest. One is of twelve witches, a full coven, posed like a school class picture in two neat rows. Niobe stands beside a blond girl at the center, and when I keep flipping through, the next photo is of the two of them. The ghostly pale girl, also in uniform, stands with an arm around Niobe's shoulders, both of their mouths open wide in laughter. Her eyes are round, clear and blue as sunlit ponds, and her long hair is golden.

My heart stumbles and I peer closer at the picture—that's *me.* No, it can't be, but the girl in the picture could be my twin. I leaf through the remainder of the photos, finding a dozen of Niobe and this girl, smiling with their faces pressed close together, lounging in the meadow, walking on the rocky beach. Who is she? There are more pictures toward the back of the stack of other witches, including one with Niobe in the middle, the Dark Pisces on one side, and the blond girl on the other.

How can she look just like me? I search my memories, but everything is hazy. The woman who slips in and out of fragments of my memory is fuzzy and faded, like I'm gazing at her through foggy glass.

It can't be.

I return to the photo of her and Niobe standing with their arms around each other outside the front doors of the Manor, and turn the photo over. On the back in Niobe's looping scrawl are the words: *"Niobe and Lavinia—first day at the Manor."*

I can't control the sound that *eeks* out of me in a childlike whimper. *Lavinia*—I might not recognize her, but I know that name.

"Did you find anything?" Gemini's voice startles me from the doorway.

Unable to find the words to speak, I hold up the photo. It wobbles from how hard my hand shakes. I swallow back the hot press of tears behind my eyes.

With quick strides, Gemini crosses the room and comes so close I can feel the heat rippling from their body against my shoulder. They frown down at the picture and gingerly grip one of the corners. They lean closer, nose nearly scraping the glossy page. "She looks just like you. It's uncanny."

I can't stop my fingers from shaking anymore and they tremble so hard that the photo slips from my fingers and drifts to the floor. Vaguely, I'm aware of Gemini saying something to me, their brow knit in concern, their hand pressing into my lower back. But I can't hear anything over the roaring in my ears, because that face in the photograph isn't just familiar. It isn't an "uncanny" coincidence that this witch looks like me.

"That's my mother," I whisper.

In these photos she's young and vibrant and alive. She was friends with Niobe.

Gemini picks up the photo from where I dropped it. When they turn it over, their jaw drops. "Lavinia is your mother?" they ask in a low voice. "I thought your mother was dead."

"She is," I say.

Gemini shakes their head slowly. "Lavinia isn't dead."

"Of course she is." She has to be. Why else did I spend ten years in an orphanage? I want to vomit, or run away, or hide beneath a mossy log out in the forest where I could curl myself into a ball and hide forever.

"Ophelia," Gemini says, so gently my heart cracks and I stumble back a step. "Lavinia is alive. She's the leader of the Dark Witches."

16

Serena

"IT'S A TRAP," SAGITTARIUS REPEATS. MY SKIN PRICKLES AS I scan the tree line for any sign of movement.

Leo helps Sagittarius to her feet. "Can you teleport?"

Sagittarius is panting. She screws her face up in concentration and jerks her hand through the air. Gold sparks flicker, but no portal appears. "Sorry," she gasps.

Leo grabs my arm and yanks me to her side. Cancer puts her back to us, and together we keep Sagittarius and Libra between us, shielding them. "Be ready," Leo instructs. "We protect Sag until she can get us out of here."

Protect her from what? I want to ask, but there's movement along the edge of the woods.

Three white-haired women slink out of the forest surrounding the asylum and I'm instantly transported into a memory of another gloomy evening, another dangerous confrontation.

Dark Witches.

Reaching deep inside for my sparks, I position myself in front of Libra. I silently beg Cancer to get her out of here. She's already endured too much.

Leo has her knives out. "They're in the Dark Twelve."

The three witches wear long black robes, with hooded capes slung around their shoulders. Two have pale white skin, one with long thick curls and the other with short-cropped hair that curls around her ears. The other has brown skin with her white hair in tight braids. They each have dark eyes and pointed teeth. Their cloaks are black, with a circular insignia of their zodiac symbol embroidered in silver thread.

"Sagittarius, Capricorn, and Gemini," says Leo. Her voice cracks on the final name and her eyes gutter. "Eighteen, Seven, and Thirteen."

"It seems our reputation precedes us," drawls the Dark Capricorn. Her long white curls form billowing clouds around her face.

My palms are slick with sweat, but I'm determined not to let my fear show.

"There's no need for bloodshed, old friend," the Dark Gemini says in a cold, crackly voice.

Leo stiffens and my heart skips a beat. Leo knew her? "We're not friends," Leo says, voice thick. "Not anymore."

The Dark Gemini simply tosses her braids over a shoulder. "Suit yourself. Hand over Libra and the rest of you will be free to go."

Leo's steely gaze narrows and I can see the gears grinding in her head. Calculating. My stomach sinks—she's about to turn Libra over, isn't she? We can't hand them this little girl so they can drain her of her power and life or force her to join their ranks. I won't allow it.

Instead, she quirks an eyebrow. "You don't want me?"

"We have no need of another Leo," says the Dark Capricorn coolly.

"Your loss." Leo shrugs. "We don't make trades with Dark Witches."

I bounce lightly on the balls of my feet, trying to shield Libra from the Dark Witches' prying view. I wish I could read Leo's and Cancer's minds. My stomach turns as I realize that we have no plan, and no time to sit here and formulate one. All we can do is wait out the clock until Sagittarius has recovered enough to get us out of here.

My only consolation as the Dark Gemini shifts into a burly man twice my height with rippling muscles is that they want at least Libra alive. I want to back away from the Dark Gemini, but I force myself to plant my feet and not cower. She's a witch, not a monster.

"Suit yourself," says the Dark Capricorn. "But you ought to know that your Scorpio and Capricorn have been feeding us well these last few weeks."

Leo snarls a curse, her eyes simmering with rage. When the Dark Capricorn looks at me, my stomach somersaults, but her gaze flits past me and lands on Libra. The lack of visible irises is unnerving, like staring into a black hole and waiting to be sucked inside. Squeezed to death until there's nothing but endless emptiness. "Our leader has big plans for you, little one," she says in a crooning baby voice.

"How big can her plans be if she can't even form her own coven without stealing our witches?" asks Leo.

The Dark Capricorn snarls at her. "Do not pretend to know why we have need of our assets," she says.

Leo snorts. "So, you're saying you don't know. You'll run home to your boss and let her do everything for you?"

The Dark Capricorn reddens and I see what Leo is trying to do. She's riling them.

There's a short burst of white light and the Dark Capricorn transforms. Where she stood moments ago, there's a snow leopard with black eyes and a dappled white-and-gray coat. I blink rapidly. If I hadn't seen her shift, I would have assumed the leopard had come down from the mountains, blending into the snow so similar to her fur. She bares her massive teeth at us and crouches, muscular legs ready to spring. As the Dark Gemini bursts into motion and sprints for Leo, the ground rumbling in the wake of her humongous form, the snow leopard leaps toward Cancer.

Cancer already has her blade out. She dives away from the leopard's snapping jaws and I start to launch myself after them, but the Dark Sagittarius's eyes lock onto me. I send a trail of lightning whipping for her. She blips out of sight long before it can make contact. I whirl, searching for the enemy teleporter, but I don't make it around when a fist slams into my back.

I hit the ground, but not before sending a spray of sparks behind me. She yelps, giving me time to clamber to my feet, but the Dark Sagittarius blinks away again. I lash out again and again with my electricity, but she remains one step ahead of me, always blinking away like the magic costs her nothing.

She stops in front of me, tosses her white hair, and smirks. "Shocking."

I growl and try again, but this time when she moves, it's toward Libra.

My heart lurches into my stomach and I sprint toward the little girl, but Sag appears out of nowhere, grabs Libra, and blips back toward the asylum. Her chest heaves, those few feet likely all she has the energy to move for now, but I'm grateful nonetheless.

"Keep her out of this!" I shout to Sag. Libra wriggles and tries to break free of her grip, but I don't want her anywhere near this. I don't want Sag here either. She's hardly keeping her feet. If we can get free of them, maybe we can escape into the woods to hide until she's strong again.

I shoot lightning at Dark Sagittarius, but trying to hit her is like trying to grab hold of a reflection. She moves through space as easily as most people might swim. Every time I think I have her, she sneaks up behind or beside me with a sharp punch. I thought fighting Dark Witches would be like sparring with Leo or Sagittarius, but it's nothing like that. Every blow has the potential to be deadly. They don't pull their punches or fight with blunted weapons. They're going for the kill.

Nearby, Leo grunts as she struggles to hold off the Dark Gemini. Her sharp knives keep the massive male form at bay until she breaks through and knocks Leo to the ground with one blow. Trying to cover her face, Leo sends small pebbles up from the ground, peppering the Dark Gemini with an assault of stone. The Dark Capricorn is still in snow leopard form and coming at Cancer, but she stumbles. Her ears are pinned flat against her head and her lips are drawn back as she snarls, but when she tries to advance, her limbs are lethargic and slow under Cancer's influence.

I don't realize I've been watching for far too long until the Dark Sagittarius bursts into reality right in front of me and shoves my chest. I slam into the dirt, but electricity bursts from me. It's a squall rather than a single whip. I send a tidal wave of it barreling toward the Dark Sagittarius. It surrounds her.

She squints at me from within her jail of electricity. "Interesting. Our mistress would love to get her hands on you too. So strong, so much more power than the rest of them."

"Your leader will never be allowed to touch me," I growl.

She teleports away but I find her again, wrapping her up in a ball of heat, constantly zapping at her skin. My knees are weak with the effort and sweat dribbles into my eyes, but I don't let up.

Out of the corner of my eye, I see the Dark Gemini dodge out of the path of Leo's onslaught of pebbles and sweep toward Cancer. I try to call out to her, but if I move, my electric cage around the Dark Sagittarius will drop. Cancer turns, fists raised, but one punch to the gut sends her careening into the dirt ten feet away. The snow leopard breaks free of Cancer's control and throws herself into motion toward me.

I dive sideways, narrowly avoiding her teeth, though one of her claws rakes down my arm. Hot pinpricks of blood slide down my skin. Ignoring the cut, I roll just as the snow leopard leaps. Seconds before she can land on top of me, my lightning strike slams into her. She's thrown backward and collapses in the grass with a whine.

For a moment, I can catch my breath, but she hauls herself to her feet, growls, and races off in a blur—heading straight for Sag.

I lash out with my lightning at the same time Leo—in the midst of holding off the Dark Gemini—sends a dagger hurtling end over end for the snow leopard.

Neither of us takes her down in time.

She buries her teeth in Sag's side and Sag goes down with a small, stifled whimper.

A scream rips free of Leo's throat. "Loan!" She roars Sag's real name even as she hurls a second dagger. It sinks into the snow leopard's leg and she falls, clawing at the blade protruding from her leg. I send a bolt of lightning whipping for her that pounds into her and blasts her away from Sag.

She doesn't stay down long, though. Coat dripping with blood, she prowls toward us as the Dark Sagittarius teleports behind us, blocking any way out of the valley. The Dark Capricorn lets out a low laugh and advances. Without Sag, we're trapped here.

Libra screams, high-pitched and earsplitting. She balls her tiny hands into fists.

"Get back!" I yell. She's a kid. She shouldn't have to lose her life to these monsters. But she digs her tiny hands into the soil and lets out a scream so primal, it could only come from a child who hasn't yet learned to suppress her pure, unadulterated rage.

Boom.

A low rumble, like the growl of a great beast, ripples toward us. The ground rocks so hard I lose my balance and the earth swims up to meet me. My palms scrape open on rough rocks and sticky blood prickles on my hands. The Dark Witches are also on their hands and knees, shouting unintelligibly as Leo drags Sag's prone form away from them.

Boom.

The Dark Witches freeze, gaping up at something high overhead. A slow, wild smile grows over Libra's face. Hundreds of birds pour from the trees in a horde of black feathers, a dark cloud blotting out the sun. Their wings beat in time like war drums. They fly in a unit, faster than any creature should be capable of moving, like magic itself is propelling them forward.

Bursting through the door of the asylum is Libra's bear. It stomps forward, swinging at the Dark Witches.

Cancer grabs hold of my hand and yanks me toward the trees where Leo has taken Sag. "Move," she orders.

I lunge for Libra and seize her around her waist, hauling her into the air even as she waves her hands, giggling. Conducting her orchestra of undead fowl.

I brace myself to fight the birds, but they pass over my head and above the other members of my coven as though we aren't there. They're already dead, controlled by Libra. They dive for the Dark Witches, who try to fight them, but there are too many of them. They swoop with razor-sharp claws and ruthless beaks pecking at the Dark Witches' heads and pinning them in place, the bear on one side, birds on the other, until they can't break through.

I release Libra and hit the ground beside Sagittarius. The grass beneath her is already wet with blood, but she groans. I breathe a sigh; she's alive. Blood coats her hands, but she holds them up anyway to draw a shaking circle. Gold sparks spit and fizzle in the air and she grits her teeth. White leeches another strand of her hair and her chest heaves. She's pushing herself too far, I realize, as no portal appears. It's too great a distance, especially when she's hurt.

She staggers to her feet, leaning heavily on Leo's shoulders. I keep one eye on the Dark Witches, sparks at the ready, but they've been overtaken by Libra's army. Their screams pierce the air and all I can see of them are slivers of pure white hair, a taloned hand protruding from the mass of wings and claws, reaching for the moonlight.

When Sagittarius draws another golden circle in the air, an anguished scream tears from her. Like she's being torn in two. The stray front pieces of her jet-black hair drain to white and her fingernails begin to grow in sharp points.

The deck of the ship is visible through the circle, so close.

"Let's go!" Cancer shouts.

"Come on." Libra beckons to her bear, who roars and wheels toward the portal like it means to come with us.

"Stop her!" I yell. If that thing makes it onto the ship, we'll all end up at the bottom of the ocean.

Cancer dashes for Libra and hoists her into the air. The little girl's spindly fingers reach over Cancer's shoulders. "No! My bear!" She screams and kicks, but Cancer drags her through the portal.

"Aries, get out of there!" Cancer calls from the other side of the portal.

A bird breaks free of the mass attacking the Dark Witches and spears toward me. Not one of Libra's birds—the Dark Capricorn. She dives at my face and I run toward the portal as her sharp beak slices at my cheeks. Just as I leap through the portal, though, she shifts into her human form, tackling me onto the deck of the ship.

I scream and shove at her shoulders. Her claws dig into my skin through my clothes. Electricity sparks at my fingertips, burning through her robes. I can't aim with my hands and keep her off me, but I remember Leo's lesson in training. I don't need them. Just as the Dark Capricorn's wicked teeth snap toward me, I send the hottest bolt of lightning I can toward her. It shoots through the space between us and slams into her chest hard enough to knock her off me. She sails backward through the portal and crumples on the ground.

I collapse onto the deck, panting to catch my breath. Still on the other side, Leo seizes Sagittarius beneath the shoulders and hauls her through the portal and onto the deck of the ship. The moment Sagittarius's feet are dragged through, the portal disappears and there's nothing but the sea lapping against the boat and Sagittarius's ragged breathing.

Leo lays Sag down beside me and waves a hand to get the ship moving. I clamber to my knees. The wind roars in my ears, carrying us faster than ever before.

Leo cups Sagittarius's face in her hands. More strands of Sagittarius's inky hair leech of their color. Her darkening eyes roll back in her head. "Stay with me, Sag," Leo whispers fiercely. Sagittarius murmurs something incoherent.

"Is she going to be okay?" I ask. I know there's too much blood. Cancer kneels on the deck to press on the wound in Sagittarius's side, but red still pours through her fingers and seeps into the wood beneath.

"Of course she is. Don't ask stupid questions," says Leo. Her voice cracks, though, betraying the truth. Leo has seen this happen before, I realize, with the Dark Gemini back there who used to be her friend. Sagittarius convulses, body writhing, back arching off the planks. Her eyes roll back in her head.

She's turning.

We need to get her back to the Manor, and fast. Even then, it might already be too late.

17

Ophelia

I CAN'T HEAR PAST THE ROARING IN MY EARS; I CAN'T SEE past the image of the woman standing arm in arm with Niobe.

"I thought your mother was dead," says Gemini, a hand at my back.

"She is." She *has* to be, because the alternative . . .

"If your mother is Lavinia, she's alive. Lavinia is the leader of the Dark Twelve. Believe me, I'd know if she was dead. We all would."

Alive. It can't be. My mother can't have been here. She can't have known Niobe. She certainly can't be the leader of the Dark Twelve, the most powerful witch in the world. She can't be alive.

Thunder cracks outside and rain begins to patter against the windowpanes of Niobe's office, but not even the rain is enough to calm me now. This must be a mistake. There must be other blond women out there, witches who bear a nearly identical resemblance to me. It must be a coincidence. Except for the writing on the back of the photo. I may not remember much about my mother more than a handful of grainy memories, but I know her name. It's written right there in ink.

Is that why Niobe brought me and Serena here, to get back at her former friend? Is that why she left us in the orphanage for so long? Was ensuring our years of torture her way of getting revenge?

I move before I register what I'm doing, not knowing where I'm going, only that I need to get far from here. I'm halfway down the hall when Gemini calls, "Pisces." They jog to catch up but keep their hands clasped behind them when they match my stride, not touching me. I find myself headed downstairs to the second floor, Gemini keeping pace with my furious march.

How could she do this? If she's been alive all this time, how could she leave us behind, trapped in that place? She must have known we were there. How many people knew we'd been sent to the orphanage and did nothing? My whole life, everyone has made decisions for me—my mother, Niobe, the matrons. Even Serena. Is there no part of my life that is my own?

For years, I've thought I was an orphan. That's who I am, it always has been, and it was a lie. How many other pieces of my identity are falsehoods?

"Pisces," Gemini says again. "Stop. We can deal with this. Together."

I shake my head, my hair whipping across my face. A pool of inky black water grows inside my chest, held back by the dam I've built inside myself. A dam that has kept me from looking at that darkness, the hopelessness I felt every night in the orphanage going to bed unable to feel anything but my frozen toes and bone-deep hunger gnawing through the lining of my stomach. Now the flood pushes harder and harder against the gates, yearning to burst free.

She chose power. Over me, over Serena, over our family. Over everything. I refuse to let the levy within me break. Power, and magic, even the swirling darkness buried within—I won't put it before everyone and everything I care about.

Lightning flashes outside and thunder splits the hallway. I'm stopped by the light brush of Gemini's fingertips against my elbow, a feather-soft, hesitant touch that pulls me up short. "Ophelia, please talk to me."

At the sound of my name, my actual name, on their lips, I look at them. A furrowed brow, eyes wide and so heartbreakingly open I want to swim in them.

"How can she be alive?" I say, and then the words come pouring out. "How? All this time, I thought she was dead. I thought I would never get to know her, I *mourned* her. And all for nothing because clearly, she didn't care at all. She left us there. Why didn't she come get us? Did she . . . did she just not want me?"

Tears force their way to the surface until they fall ceaselessly, streaming down my cheeks and blurring my vision. Sobs rack my chest until I can't get enough air down and all that comes out is a feeble whimper. Gemini makes a soothing noise and the next thing I know, they're pulling me in close and tucking me against their chest. Like a helpless child, I cling to them and inhale a deep breath of jasmine from their vest.

"Who wouldn't want you?" they say softly.

They rest their chin on the top of my head, enveloping me in their warmth, and I realize it doesn't matter that there's a Dark Witch on this island or that Niobe is keeping secrets or that my mother is alive somewhere. All that matters is that there's someone in this broken place who thinks I'm worth wanting.

I tip my head back to look up at them, when the front door slams open.

Downstairs, Leo yells, "Virgo!" Her voice is raw and frantic, and Gemini pulls away.

More footsteps and shouting come from the atrium, but above it all is Leo shrieking, "Virgo!" Over and over again until she screams, "*Damn it,* Alicia, I need you!"

Gemini swears. Their face goes deathly pale and they take off sprinting.

I lunge after them, but I'm not as fast and they're bounding down the stairs so quickly they almost fall. When I hit the landing, my stomach turns at the carnage.

Lightning flashes outside and illuminates Sagittarius's body splayed out across the wet marble floor, blood pooling beneath her. She convulses, the whites of her eyes shifting black and then white again. Virgo runs into the room, curls bouncing around her, and falls to her knees. She presses her hands to the wound in Sagittarius's side and murmurs something I can't hear.

I catch up with Gemini and they seize my hand. "What's happening to her?" I ask. It's more than a wound affecting her, draining the color from her hair where her head lies cradled in Leo's lap. Leo's wet hair drips onto the floor; from here I can see her fingers shaking as she brushes them through Sagittarius's hair.

"She's turning." Gemini's voice shakes. Above our heads, the air sparks with small golden circles, pockets that blip in and out, showing glimpses of green grass and stormy seas and snowcapped mountains. Sagittarius's teleportation powers are racing faster than she can control them.

Gemini drags me across the room, past Sagittarius writhing on the floor, and over to Cancer. I hadn't noticed her standing there, pale and covered in blood that I don't think is her own. A little girl with matted hair and a potato sack for a dress huddles behind her. Gemini grabs Cancer's hand too and she nods solemnly.

Where's Serena? Icy fear snakes through my veins, chilling me to the bone. The others are all here; where is she? She should be here. Unless she's hurt too or, worse, wounded so badly they didn't get her back in time. I'm about to ask when she comes pounding into the room with Niobe and Aquarius on her heels. Dried blood crusts small cuts on her face. She rocks into me, throwing her arms around me so hard that my hand rips out of Gemini's. I cling to her rain-soaked jacket despite the reek of blood, dirt, and sweat coating her. *She's here, she's here, she's all right.*

Virgo falls back onto the marble, panting. She runs bloodstained hands across her face. "She'll live," she says. The bleeding has stopped, and Sagittarius's breath has steadied, but the portals still flicker. Her eyes continue to flip to black, and her nails are growing rapidly, sharp at her sides.

"Link up," Niobe orders.

Gemini grabs my hand again. I cling to Serena on the other side and Niobe begins to organize us in a circle around Sagittarius. Virgo and a tearstained Leo join hands until we're all fully connected. Even little Libra wriggles her hand into Serena's, though Serena tries to brush her off and prevent her. The citrine ward crystal hanging overhead catches my eye. It keeps us safe, Cancer said. Nothing feels safe right now, but I gaze at the crystal for a long moment, willing its presence to give me strength. To make me brave.

"Let's bring her back," says Niobe.

A jolt of pure energy shoots through my palms and into my chest. An invisible current hums from Gemini, to me, to Serena, pressing through my palms like magnets, tugging us together. Magic—raw and unadulterated—flows from all of us into the center of the circle. I can't see it, but I can feel it, golden and warm, wrapping its arms around Sagittarius and trying to pull her back into herself.

The pinch of magic I have answers the coven's siren song. Beads of power like shining pearls slip through the blockage inside me, pulled free one by one to flow into Sagittarius. There's no way for me to stop them, though I don't understand how they can be helping. They're a tiny drop in the bucket compared to the gulf of energy radiating from the witches around me.

Bang.

The windows pound open and wind whips through the atrium, whistling in my ears and tearing at my hair. The chill is from more than the stormy gusts, though. It sinks in deep, through skin and bone and into the depths of the soul until I'm shivering. Cancer groans through gritted teeth and Virgo sways on her feet like she might collapse if it weren't for Leo, pressing a shoulder into hers to keep her upright.

My palm, slick with sweat, slides from Gemini's. They catch my fingers before I can lose my grip and hold on tightly. "Don't you dare let go," they say hoarsely. Their long ponytail has receded into short, boyish curls and my heart stumbles as blood drips from their nose and patters onto the marble floor.

Niobe meets my gaze across the circle. "We need you, Pisces!"

The magic trickling through me is already escaping through the cracks in the dam I've built up inside. I'm holding back every last drop of fear that threatens to overcome me and turn my limbs to jelly. If I let it stream out any more, I'll Awaken. I'll have no choice but to give in to the deluge, to risk becoming like Sagittarius, moaning and whimpering on the floor. Her back arches so much her spine must be on the verge of snapping.

I can't.

I won't.

I lock the fear at Sagittarius's fate, the anger at my mother's abandonment, the gut-wrenching sorrow of Serena's betrayal away where I can't see them. To let them out is to let emotion overtake me and allow the magic to spring free. I won't become a Dark Witch like my mother.

"Pisces," Niobe's harsh voice shouts, "we need your energy. You *must* Awaken now."

I grit my teeth and shake my head wildly, but Serena squeezes my hand so hard I think the bones might crack. I cling on tighter.

"Pisces!" Niobe calls again. "Do something!"

What difference could I possibly make? Even if my powers Awaken, we're still not a full coven.

Around the circle are sweaty, pained faces. Faces with clenched teeth and stifled groans and contorted snarls. Blood dribbles from noses and ears onto sweat-soaked skin. Still, Sagittarius thrashes. The portals around us grow larger by the second. This is killing them. Not just Sag, I realize, but my sister and Gemini too. Everyone. Yet they're still standing, pouring everything they have into their sister to pull her back from the brink. How selfish am I that I won't do the same?

"Ophelia . . ." Serena warns, her pained eyes locked onto me. "You don't have to do this."

An earsplitting screech bursts from Sagittarius, inhuman and bloodcurdling. She's almost gone. Beside me, Gemini moans, a breathy sound that cracks my heart in two. These are my friends. My family now. If anything happens to Serena or Gemini or anyone else destroying themselves trying to save Sagittarius, I'll never forgive myself. I can't live my life in fear any longer.

Holding on to Gemini and Serena like an anchor, I unlock the box I've stuffed all my emotions inside. I let my fear for Serena wash through me, let the terror for my friend on the floor fill my veins; it rushes through me, and with it, the knowledge that my mother left me behind in favor of absolute power. It floods me until I can't hold on to another bit of pain. Until I think my heart will crack and shatter into pieces.

The trickle of magic within me races through that emotion, picking up every shard and using the pain as fuel until it becomes a stream, a river, a seething, coursing flood.

I stop holding back the tide, stop trying to contain every little piece of me hiding behind that wall. I won't be afraid of what's inside me anymore. The magic slams up against me, a drumbeat to match my own heartbeat, and all at once, I let it go.

The dam finally breaks.

Magic rushes from every direction. It slams into me so hard that Gemini and Serena are the only things tethering me to reality and keeping me upright as my knees buckle. Magic explodes from me, not in tangible water, but in brilliant white light that joins the others' power, tethering me to them in an unbreakable thread. The magic moves instinctively; it knows inherently how to flow through the other witches and into the center of the circle.

Into Sagittarius.

Raised by phantom hands, her body floats from the ground and hovers in midair. She spins in wild circles. I have no idea if it's the Darkness or our magic or some other cursed force of the universe causing this. All I can feel is the swirling vortex cascading out of me. Crashing waves, high enough to barrel me over until I can't breathe. Sweat drips into my eyes, stinging.

I can't hold on.

My fingers are slipping out of Gemini's again and my head spins until nausea churns in my stomach. I'm about to let go when Sagittarius falls to the ground, motionless.

Gemini releases my hand and the current through the circle breaks. The dizziness consumes me and I don't realize I'm falling until my knees hit hard marble. My whole body shakes at the sudden nakedness, the emptiness of being in my own body and mine alone.

Leo reels forward and half falls, half runs to Sagittarius's side. Aware of Serena kneeling beside me, a hand at my back, I force myself to watch. I fight to catch my breath, waiting. All this magic, my body giving out on me, my whole life changed in one single moment, and now I can do nothing but wait to see if it was all for naught.

Sagittarius coughs, groans, and opens her eyes—they're deep brown, surrounded again by white. "Leo?" she croaks.

With a choking cry, Leo tackles her to the floor in an embrace.

"Nice work, everyone," says Niobe. Her gaze lands on me with a knowing nod.

Serena pulls me to her, hugging me tightly. "It's okay, you're okay." Her voice breaks. "You did it." Kneeling here beside her, the tide subsides to a gentle tug. A quiet lap against the shore of my mind. But it's not that raindrop—and it won't be, ever again.

"You're okay, you're okay," Serena says again, but when she pushes back to hold me at arm's length, looking me up and down like she's assessing me for injuries, there's a glassy edge to her eyes I don't recognize.

Fear.

Strong hands grasp my shoulders and pull me to my feet. I expect it to be Gemini, but it's Niobe who wraps her arms around me. My limbs shake so wildly that I'm hardly able to return the hug, half-heartedly placing my hand on Niobe's back.

"I always knew you could do it," says Niobe, beaming, when she pulls back.

She picks up my wrist, pushes back the sleeve, and turns it over to reveal the number no longer reads 479. Now it's . . . I suck in a sharp breath.

IV.

I ignore the cheers from the rest of the coven, though, as I gaze at that number. My rank doesn't matter. All that matters is that Sagittarius is okay—Awakening was worth it because Sagittarius is okay. It *has* to be worth it. And yet, as I try to recover my shaking breath, I brace myself against a wave of shame that crashes over me and settles like a weight in my stomach. Dragging me down to the bottom of the ocean and leaving me to fend for myself among the creatures of the deep. We may have prevented the inevitable, but it's still inevitable. For Sagittarius, and now for me.

I take another look at Sagittarius, though. She's fine. Not Dark; not a monster. The weight in my chest lifts. She was nearly gone; I thought she was going to turn, but we brought her back. Our magic did that. If we could stop her from turning, could we stop other witches? Could we prevent the turning altogether? Maybe Niobe is wrong and turning isn't inevitable, not if I can stop it, for my sister and for myself. For every witch in this room. Suddenly, the magic in my veins doesn't feel like poison. It feels like hope.

18

Serena

I USED TO DREAM OF NIGHTS LIKE TONIGHT. A NIGHT FULL of friends, sitting around a bonfire at the edge of the woods beneath a blanket of stars smattered across the indigo sky. Everyone took the afternoon to clean up, change out of their grimy clothes, and rest, and we're now sitting outside under the stars. Celebrating. At least, I think we're celebrating, though I'm not sure Ophelia feels that way. She's hardly spoken since her Awakening, but I don't want to push her. Not when I know she didn't want to Awaken. Now that she has, how can I protect her? There's no stopping her from turning and becoming a creature she so vehemently doesn't want to be. There's nothing I can do. I may be ranked third, I may have power surging through my veins, but against this? Against total Darkness? I'm powerless.

I sit as close to the fire as I can without my eyes watering from the stinging smoke. I could watch the flames forever, leaping higher and higher, enchanting me with their dance, weaving and twining together, twisting and swaying with the wind. Heat washes over me, but I relish the warmth against the crisp air. The fire kisses my skin, a fond friend whose touch is gentle and soothing.

Beside my chair, Castor is curled on the grass with his massive head resting on his paws. I stroke my hand across the silken fur between his ears. He huffs and I jerk my fingers away, but then I realize he's purring. I run my hand along his back in slow, methodical strokes, letting the vibrations reverberate through me.

In the past few hours, color has returned to Sagittarius's face. Her hair is more than half white now, a reminder of what she went through tonight and of how close the light and dark are to one another. A reminder to all of us of how easy it is to cross to the other side. Leo sits in front of her, leaning against her chair. Her head tips back, eyes closed, as Sagittarius absently braids her hair with a quiet familiarity that makes my heart ache.

Virgo slips out of the building and approaches with a tray of goblets full of candy-pink liquid and Gemini perks up.

"Whatcha got there?" they ask, like they're trying to be casual.

A sly smile spreads across Virgo's face. "Little something I've been cooking up," she says sweetly.

Gemini pumps their fist and the others cheer in delight.

"What is it?" I ask. Virgo extends a goblet to me and I accept, the cold glass biting into my palm as I wrap my hand around it. Virgo hands a glass to everyone except Libra, who doesn't seem to mind. The little girl sits cross-legged in the grass in front of the fire in fresh clothes as Cancer works on brushing out the mats in her hair. With the dirt scrubbed from her face, it's even more apparent how hollow and gaunt her cheeks are. She gazes into the flames, swaying back and forth like she's dancing along with them. Niobe brought her out here, led a brief ranking ceremony, and got the fire started, but slipped away back to her office a few minutes ago. For someone so small, Libra is powerful. Ranked thirteenth. The tattoo on her wrist is stark against her pale skin.

"Okay, newbies." Gemini raises a glass of Virgo's pink concoction. "This is Mystic Mead and it's the greatest thing Virgo has ever invented." They down half their drink in one gulp and then slump back in their chair.

"Careful." Virgo laughs.

"I refuse to use moderation when it comes to Mystic Mead."

Sagittarius clears her throat and sits up straighter in her seat. "To my sisters!" she says, raising her glass. "If it weren't for all of you, I wouldn't be here. I owe each of you my life." She turns to Ophelia, whose shoulders curve inward at the attention. "Especially you, Pisces. I know how difficult that was for you, so thank you. I will never forget this sacrifice." Her seriousness fades to a wry smirk. "And who knew you'd rank high enough to make Leo drop again!" She nudges Leo with her knee. "What are you, in the twenties now, Leo?" Leo rolls her eyes and flicks Sagittarius's leg. Sagittarius just grins. "To Pisces!" Sagittarius declares, and takes a swig of her drink.

"And to everyone who helped rescue the newest member of our coven!" adds Cancer, grinning at Libra. "We'll get Capricorn and Scorpio back. We'll save our friends, complete the Twelve, and take down the Dark Witches!"

The circle erupts with cheers and clinking glasses.

Cancer takes Libra by the hands and spins her in a circle until the little girl giggles madly. Virgo and Aquarius join them, and together they skip around the fire, dancing with flailing limbs and wild smiles.

I take a ginger sip of the pink liquid. It's sweet, pomegranate I think, with a touch of bitterness cutting it that might be grapefruit and something herbal. Rosemary, maybe. Fizzy warmth trickles into my stomach and loosens the knots in my shoulders and the middle of my back. The edges of my vision blur, softening the world's fringes. I hold on to the arm of my chair. If I let go, I might drift away up through the smoke and let it carry me, weightless, toward the stars. Maybe I'd get stuck up there, floating forever. Tiny yet shining. Dazzling. Forever.

Ophelia clinks glasses with Gemini, their fingers brushing together as they both redden. The dancing girls slow to a stop, panting, and return to their seats. Virgo pulls her yarn from beneath her chair and starts to crochet. Her hands work quickly yet deftly, maneuvering her hook through the thick purple yarn.

"I wish I knew how to do that," I find myself saying. I don't have any skills like that, ones that create things. Sometimes I wish I grew up differently. That I'd had time to grow vegetables or paint or knit. I wish I'd been allowed the luxury of softness.

"If you want, I can teach you," she says.

"If she likes you enough, she'll make you a scarf for your birthday," says Sagittarius.

"I like all of you," says Virgo.

"Yeah, but some of us had to wait more birthdays than others," says Gemini.

Virgo sticks her tongue out at Gemini, who tosses her a rude gesture and a wink.

"How did you learn to do that?" I ask, nodding at the yarn in her hands.

"My mom and I used to crochet together when I was a kid. She owned a plant nursery, but she'd also sell scarves and hats and other crafts there." Virgo's hands stop and her eyes go glassy. "I miss her," she whispers. "This helps me feel close to her, though."

Cancer squeezes Virgo's forearm, getting a grateful nod in return.

"Come to the med wing sometime." Virgo smiles softly at me. "We can have a lesson—you'll pick it up in no time."

"Can I come too?" asks Gemini.

Virgo levels them with a mock-serious glare. "You know you're not allowed in there. Your thumb is so black, it's a miracle it hasn't rotted off."

"If it did, you'd put it back on for me, so why does it matter?"

She clicks her tongue. "Because my plants don't deserve to suffer because of you."

Gemini laughs and rests their fingertips on Ophelia's knee. She leans toward them with an ease I can't help but envy. I've never had that with anyone. I don't want to be upset with her. It isn't her fault that someone likes her, or that she floats through the world with a gentle serenity that makes everyone melt before her. Back at the orphanage, no one locked her up in the East Wing because she was dangerous.

She's easy to want to protect. She's easy to love.

I'm no such thing.

But now that she's Awoken, how can I protect her from becoming the exact thing she doesn't want to be? We should have left when she wanted to and this never would have happened. It's my fault for not keeping my word.

Libra sits on the ground in front of me. She rests her head in my lap. "What's wrong, sissy?" she asks.

"Nothing." But Libra gazes up at me with wild eyes the rich hue of freshly tilled earth. Are my emotions that obvious? I run a hand across her hair, clean chestnut locks now soft beneath my touch. "Look at you all cleaned up," I muse.

Libra scrambles onto her knees and cups my face between her two tiny hands. "It's gonna be okay, sissy. That's what Daddy always tells me when I'm scared, and Daddy is always right."

"Where's your daddy now?"

"He's dead." She rocks back onto her heels with a shrug. "So is Mommy."

The others have stopped their conversations now and watch Libra intently. There are no tears in her eyes, no sorrow in her voice. As a Libra, maybe her constant communing with the dead has made her immune to the permanence of death. Or maybe this is what it looks like when sorrow goes too deep at such a young age.

"Will you tell us about your parents?" I ask gently.

Libra's face lights up with a brilliant smile, dimpling her cheeks. "My daddy was the biggest, strongest, bravest man in the whole wide world! He could climb trees faster than a squirrel and shoot straighter than anyone. Mommy had the prettiest singing voice. It echoed through the trees like magic. When it stormed, she'd hum songs to me so I wouldn't be scared." She pauses, smile wavering. "We lived in a little cabin with creaky floors and a red door. I helped Daddy collect firewood, and Mommy taught me which mushrooms didn't bite back. We were happy." Her voice softens and her eyes grow distant, like she's slipping through a memory. "One day, we were out looking for tracks when I saw the biggest squirrel I've ever seen! I ran after it to see where it lived, but it was too fast. When I stopped, I couldn't find Daddy anymore."

The bonfire crackles, and Libra's eyes gleam in the firelight.

"Then the bear came. A great big brown bear with paws the size of soup pots. I was really still, just like Daddy taught me. But Mommy must have come looking for me, because I heard her scream. She always screamed my name when she was scared." Her small hands curl in her lap. "Daddy found me. He shot at the bear and it got mad. It . . . it got him. Mommy told me to run away. She told me not to look back."

I hold my breath as she falls silent. So much pain and death for such a little girl to endure. When she speaks again, though, her voice is airy and bright. "But it's okay. I wasn't alone for long. I went back to our cabin and I cried for days, I missed them. I kept talking to them every night, even when they didn't answer. And then one day . . . they did. They didn't say much anymore. Mommy would hum the same note over and over, like she forgot the tune. Daddy still tucked me in, but his hands were always cold." Libra blinks slowly. "Then people came. They said they saw smoke from our chimney." Her voice wavers for the first time. "They dragged me out of the cabin. I screamed. I told them I wasn't alone. I tried to tell them that my parents were still inside, but they didn't believe me. They thought I'd gone mad."

Leo watches Libra with her mouth agape, shaking her head. Cancer comes to kneel in front of Libra. She places her hands on the little girl's shoulders and says in a serious voice, "Well, aren't you the bravest little witch I've ever met."

Libra beams. "I know." She bares all her teeth in a sharp grin. Cancer jerks backward, pretending to be scared, and Libra throws her head back in a wild laugh. Like someone who may have survived the forest but left pieces of herself behind.

"What about you, Cancer?" I ask when Cancer settles herself

back in the chair beside me and picks up her drink. "How did you get here?" Her face clouds and she stares into the pink liquid. I remember the wave of sadness that came over her on the boat when she mentioned her mother. My palms go slick with sweat. I shouldn't have asked. "You don't have to share if you don't want," I mumble quickly.

She offers me a small smile that doesn't reach her eyes. "No, I don't mind sharing. It was a long time ago, ten years. I was twelve, living with my mother and my stepfather. You know, we talk all the time here about witches turning Dark, but there are other kinds of darkness out there too. My stepfather had that darkness in him when he drank. He'd get a little alcohol, and he just became a different person. He could never have just one: He had to keep going and going until he got this mean look in his eyes. Once that happened, there was no getting through to him. At first it was a couple nights a month, then a few a week, until it was every day. And the more he drank, the meaner he got, and the meaner he got, the more he . . ."

She takes a shuddering breath and Leo puts a hand on her knee until she's ready to continue. "He would hurt my mother. And the older I got, the more abusive he became, and there was nothing I could do. I was always trying to just stay out of his way. If he didn't notice me, he couldn't be angry with me, so I tried so hard to be a perfect, good girl so he couldn't take out his anger at me on my mother. She always protected me, you see, even when she couldn't protect herself. She was the sweetest, most loving person in the entire world. No one deserves the kind of pain that man could inflict, but least of all her. One night, things got so bad that she'd had enough. She finally got up the courage to leave, so after he passed out, she came into my room and we packed a few things to take. I didn't care that we couldn't take much or that we had no idea where we were going, only that we were finally, *finally* going to be free.

"But he woke up. He tried to block the door, tried to stop us leaving, and he was so big that there was nothing my mother could do against him. He was huge compared to her, and when he put his hands around her neck and started to strangle her, all I could think was that she was too small. He was going to kill her. I just stood there, helpless, watching the light leave her eyes, and everything that I'd held inside, all the fear and pain and anger I'd bottled up and kept him from seeing, hit me all at once. I didn't know then that I had powers, but they Awakened in that moment. All I wanted was for him to die, instead of her. *He deserved* to die instead of her. I just kept repeating 'Die, die, die,' in my mind, over and over, until he let go of my mother's body, took a kitchen knife, and stabbed himself in the eye.

"I was too late, though—she was already gone, and I was left all alone there. Just me, a newly Awoken witch, alone, with my heart completely shattered. It wasn't long until Niobe and a little redheaded girl showed up." She gives Leo a nod and Leo squeezes her knee again. "I've been here ever since, and even though I miss my mother every single day, I'm so grateful to have sisters like you all. This is my family now."

Silence falls heavily over us. Our circle is full of glassy eyes, shining in the firelight. Still sitting on the grass, Libra nuzzles into Cancer's knee, but the light doesn't return to Cancer's expression.

Across the fire, Ophelia looks back at me. Tears stream down her face, but she doesn't wipe them away.

"Thank you, Cancer," I say. "For sharing."

Ophelia rises and retreats toward the trees, swiping at her

cheeks as she goes. I abandon my place by the fire and rush after her. "Ophelia, wait!" I call. The others watch as I get up and follow her, tripping over Castor as I go.

She stops a few steps into the woods, the branches swaying in the evening breeze casting shadows like tiger stripes across her face. She looks like a wraith. So pale, with her golden hair marred with one white streak.

"Ophelia, what's going on? Are you okay?"

She shakes her head and brushes away the last of her tears. "Of course I'm not."

I run my fingers through my hair, not sure how to begin apologizing for leaving and breaking my promise. If we'd left like she wanted, she never would have had to Awaken. "I'm sorry, I just . . . I thought . . ."

"You thought what? You thought you'd go on a dangerous mission without telling me after we agreed to leave?"

Guilt twinges in my stomach, but I say, "Niobe needed me."

"*I* needed you."

"You're just mad because you don't trust Niobe."

"For good reason," says Ophelia. "She's keeping secrets from us."

"Like what?"

Ophelia holds out a photograph. "Like this."

She waves it at me and I pinch the corner between two fingers, careful not to smudge it. There are two women in the photo. One is clearly Niobe and the other . . . She's young and fresh-faced, and I mistake her for Ophelia until I look closer. It's not Ophelia. That face drifts back to me, tugging at forlorn corners of my memory.

"What is this?" I ask, hating how my voice shakes.

"Turn it over."

The name written on the back hits me like a punch to the stomach. I can't breathe as every fuzzy memory comes careening back in full focus.

"Our mother is alive," Ophelia says.

I freeze. It must be the Mystic Mead I drank making me hear things. "What did you say?"

My own voice sounds garbled in my ears, like I've been plunged underwater.

Then she tells me everything. I really must have had too much to drink. Or she has. "No."

I shake my head fiercely. "No, that can't be true."

She can't be alive. Alive *and* the leader of the Dark Twelve.

My body is suddenly not my body, as if I'm floating somewhere outside myself, trying desperately to bring myself back to the earth. Breathe in, breathe out. Swallow the thick saliva in my throat. Focus on my heart banging on the inside of my ribs. Feel the ground beneath my feet.

Remember that this is real.

Ten years, we were left to rot in that orphanage. Ten years of being beaten and starved and tormented. Not because our mother was dead—because she left us there.

Hot tears creep their way onto my cheeks and I blink them back before I start crying in earnest. I won't cry over this woman. I clearly meant nothing to her, so I won't give her the satisfaction of my tears. I've grieved for her enough over the years, and yet somehow, knowing she's alive creates a stabbing ache beneath my sternum more painful than mourning her death ever was.

"Don't you see what this means, though?" Ophelia takes my hand. The anger in her face has faded and her breathing has steadied. Her eyes glimmer, but not with anger. With hope. "We stopped Sagittarius from turning tonight. We pulled her back from the edge. If there's a way to reverse the turning, if there's a cure, we can save Mother. We can be a family again."

"A family?" I spit the word through a laugh. "That woman is not my family. Family doesn't leave without a trace for a decade. Family doesn't abandon each other."

"I've been thinking, though. What if she only abandoned us because she became a Dark Witch? Do you really think she would have left if she hadn't turned Dark?"

"You don't know that! What I do know is that it doesn't matter why she wasn't there; it matters that she wasn't. She's the leader of the Dark Twelve. She doesn't care about us, so why should we try to save her?"

And Niobe.

Niobe has done nothing but lie since the moment we walked in the door. She knew we were at the orphanage; she knew who our mother was this whole time. Maybe Ophelia was right to say we shouldn't trust her. I've been running around doing her bidding like a good little lapdog, and all this time she's been keeping things from me.

No.

Not anymore.

I start to stalk out of the trees and up to the Manor. I don't care that it's late, or that I've portaled halfway across the world and back, or that I've expended nearly every ounce of my energy.

"Where are you going?" Ophelia calls, hurrying after me.

"I'm going to Niobe's office," I snarl. "I'm going to make her explain everything. Who does she think she is to keep this from us? She doesn't have the right."

Ophelia catches my arm and whirls me back around. "Stop, Serena."

"No!" I wrench my arm away. "She lied to us. Doesn't that matter to you?"

"Of course it matters."

"It's our lives!" I choke on a sob. "She's playing with our lives like we're pawns on her chessboard."

Ophelia says in a low, calm voice, "I've been trying to tell you since last night that she's lying to us, but we have to do this the right way. If we march in there tonight and start yelling at her, she'll just say we're being too emotional. She'll never tell us anything."

"We deserve the truth."

She reaches for my hand and this time I let her take it. She wraps both of her hands around mine and squeezes. "Please, Serena. It's late. We'll talk to her tomorrow; we'll get the truth. Let's get it in the light of day, though, when we're rested and ready."

"Tomorrow," I say slowly. "Promise?"

She nods. "Promise."

19

Ophelia

THE AIR IN THE GARDENS BEHIND THE MANOR SMELLS sweetly of gardenias, and fat bumblebees buzz around their delicate petals. Cancer brought me to a burbling fountain in the center of the rows of hedges and flowers in full bloom and has been explaining how to harness my newly Awakened powers. My plan to confront Niobe will have to wait until the afternoon. At the back of the Manor, I can make out Virgo walking through a giant greenhouse. The morning sun is warm and bright; it glitters on the greenhouse's glass windows.

A figure of a woman stands at the top of the two-tiered bronze fountain. Her hair is unbound and her arms are upraised, holding a sun in one hand and a moon in the other. Water streams from her hands and cascades down into the basin, where lily pads float. I draw water from it, weaving it into ribbons.

Magic ebbs and flows beneath my skin, requesting release. There's so much more of it than that small drop I used to feel, more than I ever could have imagined. I didn't realize it would be quite so easy. The water responds to me like an old friend. I shape it into little animals, sending squirrels and chipmunks made of water racing down the garden paths. Libra giggles and claps her hands in delight. They zip around as Libra chases them and return to me before diving into the fountain and disappearing.

Control is key, Cancer said—not pushing myself too far, beyond the scope of my abilities, the way Sagittarius did, and not losing myself to my emotions, the way she says Serena often does. Cancer watches me for a while. "You're a natural," she says. I don't expect the swell of pride that fills me.

Cancer leaves me to practice on my own. I focus on my magic, directing the drifting current through my body and out through the tips of my fingers as she instructed. She keeps half an eye on me while she spends most of the time sitting cross-legged in a nearby gazebo with Libra, teaching her how to breathe and control the barrage of emotions that no doubt cascade through her tiny body.

What could I be if I had known when I was Libra's age what I know now and let the seed of power unfurl when I was small? Would I have turned Dark already, or would I have learned to control it better with a mind so young and pliable?

Weaving ribbons of water through the air makes my anger fade, though, like the cool liquid is washing it all away. I thought the magic would feel overwhelming and harsh, but the more I use it, the calmer I become. Every bit of power begs me to use more and wrap myself in it like armor. For the first time in my life, I feel capable. Strong. Why was I ever afraid of Awakening?

I keep pulling clear, fresh coils of water from the fountain. I let them intertwine and braid themselves together and dance through the air until I lose myself to the steady beat of the water's music.

Until the rest of the world falls away and there's nothing but me and the water and the thrum of magic like a drum, showing me which way to march. Reminding me how to keep moving forward, whatever it takes.

Cancer leaves the garden and instructs Libra and me to keep working for another hour until lunch. I'm impatient to talk to Serena, though, so after thirty minutes I take Libra by the hand and lead her back to her room. I drag myself down the hall with my limbs loose and relaxed yet depleted like a used dishrag that's been rung dry and left in a crumpled pile in the bottom of the sink.

As much as I want to go to my room and take a long nap, I go to Serena. When I find her in her room still passed out, I don't wake her. After the mission to retrieve Libra and saving Sagittarius last night, she needs to rest and recover, so I go instead to the library. Now that Serena and I have both Awoken, it's more important than ever to figure out how to stop the process of turning Dark. Or at least slow it. After seeing the agony Sagittarius was in last night, I never want that to happen to me or my sister, but she was almost gone. She was on the brink of turning, and our power pulled her back, and if that's possible, I'd bet anything that curing a Dark Witch is possible. If we're going to confront Niobe about her lies, I need as much information as I can possibly get my hands on.

When I've gathered a stack of books, I set myself up at a table in the corner and get to work flipping through them, searching for any information on the creation of Dark Witches. I flip through page after page, scribbling notes on a stack of blank pages I brought along with me. Each year, one witch is born per sign, and though it's likely that the children of witches will have powers, it's not a guarantee. Just like some of the witches here, power can turn up without magic in the bloodline. What every text acknowledges, though, is the fact that losing control and burning out by using too much power at once is the fastest way to turn into a Dark Witch. The more members of a coven there are to lean on, the more likely the process is to slow—a few tomes even describe the power sharing we did last night, although it's hard to capture the feeling in words and all of theirs fall short.

But no . . . I peer closer at the text.

Zodiac witches are stronger together, but it's not just that the turning process slows with more witches. With a full coven of twelve zodiac witches, they become strong enough as a unit that the turning can be delayed. The text says that with a full coven comes the power to do the impossible. Hope quickens my pulse.

There's a story about a full coven, the first ever full coven. The original Twelve. They were able to harness their power and keep witches from turning Dark. While they reigned, there was nothing but peace and prosperity. Zodiac witches thrived and lived long, full lives. It was only when one of them died and their ranks were broken that the Dark Witches started gaining power and became the force they are today.

We don't have a full coven yet, but if we can get Scorpio and Capricorn back from the Dark Witches, we could complete the Twelve. I think of what we did last night, bringing Sag back from turning. I didn't know that was possible, but the force of that power, the strength we had together with ten witches, how much stronger could we be if we had a full coven? Together, maybe we can keep each other from *ever* turning. I take a deep breath and force my hope back down. I still need a way to turn Lavinia back. If something happens and Serena turns before we find the other two witches, I need a way to turn her back too.

I keep making headway through the pile of books until I reach an old crumbling one with a faded cover. It's not very long, maybe only a hundred pages, each of which is lined with gold trim.

Zodiac: The Birth of a Coven.

At a glance, it's a dry history on the origin of witches, no different from the other dozen I've just combed through. But I leaf through the pages, squinting at the small print until my eyes ache. In the middle of the book I pause on a section full of colorful, albeit faded, illustrations.

The chapter title reads, "*Zodiac Demons: Deadly Magical Patrons.*"

There's a section for each sign with a paragraph of text beneath and a small image of twisted creatures. I jump to the last image—Pisces. The picture is of a woman with tangled red hair, skin bare except for metallic scales that cover her in patches. Her lips, pulled back into a vicious snarl, reveal sharp teeth like a shark's and her feet and hands are webbed. It's her eyes, though, that draw me. Soulless and black. A creature of the murkiest bowels of the ocean.

I scan the text until I catch the words—"T*he first and future witches.*"

First. I think I understand as I read on. We're descended from these creatures. Is that why we're destined to become monsters? Is it simply so ingrained in our nature, in our origins, that there's no use in fighting it? It's the *future* bit that I don't quite understand. I scan the brief paragraph beside each sign, but there isn't much there. Each one has a description of the demon's physical form and the type of powers they grant to witches under their classification. I need more information.

I peruse the images, unsure if they're premonitions of what's to come or reminders of what lurks beneath our skin. I need answers, but I don't trust Niobe enough to ask her for them. She's lied about so many things, how can I trust her to tell me the truth about this? There's someone else, though, who I might be able to ask, so I take the book back to my room and head out into the forest to ask her.

20

Serena

THE AFTERNOON BRINGS A SHARP RAP ON MY BEDROOM door. I rush to it, expecting to find Ophelia back from training, but it's Cancer instead.

"Niobe needs to see you in her office," she says.

My shoulders stiffen. "Why?" Does she know that Ophelia discovered the truth about Lavinia? I'd hoped we could confront her about it on our own terms, but if she already knows, she'll have the upper hand.

"She just wants to check in after yesterday's mission."

"Where's Ophelia?" I shouldn't do this without her, not after we promised to talk to Niobe together.

"I don't know. She left training early and I haven't seen her since."

"I have to find her first."

Cancer shakes her head, short hair skimming against her collarbones. "This won't take long, and Niobe doesn't like to be kept waiting. Let's go."

I take a long, slow breath through my nose and fight back the heat rising in my gut. I can stay calm and just talk about the mission. I can save talking about our mother until later, when Ophelia is with me. When we can be a team.

I follow Cancer to Niobe's office and the door already hangs ajar. Niobe sits at her desk, her perfect, smooth skin glowing in the bright sunlight, and there's not a single wrinkle in her silk blouse. Gemini stands beside her, talking in hushed tones with their heads bent close together. I try not to look at the little birds sleeping, the door to their cage cracked open. My blood burns hot in my veins at the contradiction, but I bite my tongue. If I'm a bird, my cage is locked with lies.

Niobe swivels toward the door. "Ah, thank you, Cancer," she says. "How was Pisces's training this morning?"

"She did well. Although she left earlier than I instructed—I'm not sure where she went."

Niobe gives Gemini a long look and a nod, and Gemini slides their hands into their pockets. "I'll get out of your hair," they say, leaving the room with Cancer following after.

"Thank you for coming, Aries," says Niobe with a soft, kind smile once the door snicks shut after Gemini. She gestures toward the armchair in front of her desk, but I don't want to sit. Electricity hums through my bones, buzzing in my ears. She has sat there for days, smiling in my face, lying to me. Still, she has the audacity to act like everything is normal, like nothing is wrong. I shouldn't say anything, but accusations force themselves into my mind, and it's getting harder and harder to keep them pressed behind my lips. Niobe continues, "I wanted to check in to see how things were going, and—"

"You knew," I blurt.

Niobe furrows her brow. "Knew what?"

"Don't play games with me." I lurch toward her desk. My palms hit the dark wood and I lean in toward her face, twisted in false confusion. "You knew our mother is alive. You knew she's the leader of the Dark Witches, and you didn't tell us. We've been here for days! You've had chance after chance to tell the truth, and you've sat here and lied to my face!"

The office lights flicker and I clench my hands into fists, trying to rein in the sparks threatening to flare at my fingertips.

Niobe folds her hands on the desk in front of me, her expression never wavering. "And for that I apologize, Aries." I flinch at the still unfamiliar name. She gestures toward the chair again. "Please, take a seat and I swear to you, I will explain everything."

My breaths come in short, ragged bursts. She could lie again, but there's something like sorrow etched in the fine lines around her eyes, so I sit. Something heavy presses onto my thigh. Castor has dropped his head into my lap, gazing up at me. I place my hand between his fuzzy ears and let the weight of his skull press me down into the chair and ground me.

"She was a student here," I say. "With you."

"She was." Niobe stands and goes to a table set against the wall where steam curls in slow tendrils from a teapot. She pours tea into a porcelain cup and places it on saucer in front of me. The bright scent of mint wafts upward along with the steam, etching a tiny bit of clarity into my mind.

"Forgive me for not telling you the truth sooner," says Niobe as she sits, adjusting her emerald skirts around her. "I did not wish to overwhelm you and your sister. You had just Awoken and arrived in a new place. It seemed like too much to throw at you at once."

"What we can handle isn't for you to decide." We're not children. We don't need her to make choices for us.

Niobe folds her hands on the desk and looks down at her rings for a long moment. "Lavinia and I lived at the Manor together, and from the moment I met her, we were inseparable. We were the first- and second-ranked witches, and even though we spent every moment trying to best one another, the competition made us both stronger. She's the most powerful witch I've ever known. Every time I learned a new skill with my magic, or mastered a new maneuver, she was right there with something even more impressive to show." Her lips press together. "I got close, but I could never quite keep up."

"And you just let her turn Dark?"

Niobe's throat bobs. "Lavinia had a theory, that there was a way to reverse the change after becoming a Dark Witch and return to a healthy state. She thought of it like a sickness, something that could be cured. All she wanted was to improve the race of witches so we could be strong."

My breath hitches in my throat. Maybe Ophelia is right. Maybe there really is a cure.

"I believed her, for a time," Niobe continues. "There was so much we planned to do together, but no matter how hard we tried, we couldn't find a way to stop witches from turning. When she had the two of you, things changed. She became more desperate to find an answer once she realized you both had power as well. She was terrified of letting you Awaken."

I snort bitterly. "Because that worked out so well."

"She couldn't protect the two of you and herself. The Dark Witches figured out what she was working on and still, she wouldn't stop. She was trying every bit of taboo Dark magic, reading every book, looking into every legend. Eventually, the Dark Witches feared she might succeed. Her ranking was enough to keep them scared to go near her, but once you were born, she was terrified they would target you and Ophelia to get to her. She couldn't keep them at bay forever. So, over the years, she slowed her magic use. She couldn't afford to risk expending all her energy and turning Dark, not when she had you both to defend. And when you were around five years old, it happened. They came. I was with her and we sensed their presence, but it was too late."

"How? You were the two highest-ranked witches in the world. You seriously expect me to believe you couldn't hold off some Dark Witches?"

"Power isn't everything." Niobe's eyes go glassy and there's the barest twitch at the corner of her lips "They were more prepared than we were. We thought we were safe, but even if we'd been ready, they brought two dozen Dark Witches with them. It didn't matter that we were the two strongest there—we couldn't fight all of them at once. By the time we realized what was happening, we didn't have much time. Our priority was to get you and your sister out safely, and your mother, Lavinia . . ." She lets out a shuddering sigh and pinches the bridge of her nose between her thumb and forefinger. After a moment, she releases her hand and looks back up at me, her face a stoic, emotionless mask. "Lavinia did what she had to do to protect you girls. She sacrificed herself even though turning was the last thing in the world she wanted to do. To hold the Dark Witches off long enough to give me time to get you both out."

"You let her," I whisper. Snippets of memory flash before me, things I'd left untouched, gathering cobwebs in the back of my mind: a dark night, my mother rushing around the house, harsh words on her lips and fear in her eyes. A tight, teary embrace, Ophelia weeping, a woman shushing her as we step out into the cold. I was so small that I'm not sure whether those visions are real or imagined, but they careen into me like a freight train. I grip the arms of my chair as though the physical contact can keep me from descending deeper into the foggy recollection. Castor presses against my leg and huffs a warm breath onto my fingertips.

"I tried to convince her to leave with me, but she was a stubborn woman, your mother," says Niobe. "I told her we could hide, but she knew the Dark Witches would never stop hunting her. Or you, so long as she was with you. Even though she knew it would take every drop of her power and turn her to hold them off for a few minutes, she insisted. So she made me promise to keep the two of you safe, and I—"

"And you ran away," I finish. "Like a coward."

She flinches like I've slapped her. "Yes," she says hoarsely. "And if you don't think I ask myself every day if I made the right decision, you'd be wrong. But your mother did what had to be done. She fought them off while I ran with you both. I didn't know for certain what happened until word of her turning began to spread. The Darkness made her more powerful than before and I knew that she would soon come for me too. You weren't safe with me, even here. I knew she would stop at nothing to figure out how to break the wards and get to you. I took you to the orphanage and told you it was a camp, a place to stay for a while until your mother returned, even though I . . . I hoped she would never find you." She braces her head in her hands. "I can still see your little faces, so small, standing in the window watching me leave. I wish I could have kept you with me, but she would have known I had you. Without your powers yet, you were impossible to trace. I kept an eye on you so that the moment you Awoke, I could be the one to get to you before Lavinia or her coven could."

I grip the chair harder, fighting the shaking in my arms. Our mother sacrificed everything for us, turned Dark to save us, and now . . . now we're the ones who have to fight her. And no one even had the decency to tell us.

"You left us there. You should have gotten us to Awaken back then, before we ever could have gone to that place."

"Serena—"

"No!" I spit. "Do you have any idea what we went through there? Don't sit here and tell me it was for my own good, because there was nothing, absolutely *nothing,* good about that hellhole."

"You would have risked turning faster."

"I don't care!" I leap from my seat, slamming my hands onto the desk. The light hanging overhead flickers and whirs until it goes out with a sharp crackle.

Niobe rises and Castor climbs to his feet, snarling at me. "Do not presume to understand things you have no idea about. If Lavinia is allowed to fill her coven, there will be consequences far worse than you can possibly imagine."

"Then explain it to me," I bite back.

Niobe slowly glances between me and the chair, waiting. I grip the edge of the desk until my knuckles go white and my breathing slows and I sit back down.

Niobe returns to her seat and Castor reclines again, though his golden eyes remain trained on me. "Lavinia is building a coven, the Dark Twelve, some of whom you've already met face-to-face. She wants to build the most powerful coven in the world."

"That's why you're building our coven. To rival hers."

"Yes. Because while Lavinia never discovered a cure, she did learn something else." She pauses for a long moment, eyeing me warily, like she's considering not telling me despite all her promises of truth. I brace myself to leave before she can tell me any further lies, but she sighs and says, "Your mother learned that there's a second turning, after becoming a Dark Witch."

I choke on my sharp intake of breath. Something after becoming Dark? As if the Dark Witches aren't grotesque enough, there's something more? "What else could there possibly be?"

"I'm not entirely sure," says Niobe. "It's not been done, at least not for centuries, but Lavinia thinks this is the natural life cycle. We go from witches to Dark Witches to demons."

"Demons aren't real." Demons are myths, legends, not actual creatures. They're not something I could potentially become.

"Lavinia believes they are. She believes they exist somewhere between the human and supernatural, and that if she pushes her Dark Witches hard enough, she can achieve that second turning. With a full Dark coven, she believes it's possible."

"Is it?"

Niobe presses her lips together. "I don't know," she admits. "I've never seen it, but there are ancient accounts of it. I don't particularly want to give her the opportunity to find out one way or another, and the only way to stop her and rid the world of Dark Witches once and for all is with the best possible coven I can assemble. And with you on our side, I think we might be able to do it."

Niobe almost had the full coven, I realize, until the others were kidnapped.

"I'm sorry, for everything that transpired that night," says Niobe.

"I'm sorry for leaving you there, but everything I've done has been to protect you. That doesn't stop now." She takes my hands in her warm, calloused fingers. "I will protect you, Serena, no matter what it takes. You and Ophelia both." She squeezes firmly. "I swear it."

I jerk my hand out of her grasp and stride for the door. It doesn't matter what she swears, or what my mother and her Dark Witches are planning, I don't know who I can trust anymore. They left me behind—both of them.

I have never been enough. Not for the matrons at the orphanage. Not for Niobe. Not for my own mother. It doesn't matter what I am—zodiac witch, Dark Witch, demon. I will never be enough.

21

Ophelia

WATER DRIPS OFF MY LEGS AND SLIDES DOWN TO POOL ON uneven stones. After cutting through the pond's murky water with fast strokes, my arms slicing the waves like they're sun-warmed butter, I gulp the stone alcove's musty air. This time, I was quick finding the crypt and the alcove where the Dark Witch remains trapped. I don't waste time and instead march through the trove and straight up to the mirror.

The Dark Pisces smiles through closed lips. "You're finally Awake," she says. "Congratulations, little fish." I fight back a wince. I've heard that word constantly lately—*congratulations*—yet I don't feel joyful when it comes. I haven't achieved anything but betraying the one thing I promised myself I would never do. "Ranking fourth is a great honor."

I squirm beneath the witch's hard gaze, but I'm not here to discuss my rank. "What do you know about the zodiac demons?"

Her eyes narrow. "Why?" she asks slowly.

"I want to know about our origins. To find a way to stop us from turning Dark."

"Why would you want to do that, dear?" The Dark Witch cocks her head. "You don't try to stop the leaves from falling from the trees or the spring from thawing the frost. It's simply nature running its course. You can freeze the flower buds to keep them dormant for a few weeks, but you can't stop them blooming forever."

"Maybe I don't want to bloom," I say.

Maybe I wish to remain a small green shoot forever.

"You say that now. But you don't know the truth. It's not a scary thing, no matter what Niobe might tell you. It's freedom. You get to shed your skin, burst out of your cocoon, and spread your wings. You won't be held down by silly things like humanity any longer." She frowns, her expression growing sad. "You're like me, little fish. It's our way; our fate is written in the stars. You feel things deeply—too deeply. If you let go of those feelings, you would make an incredible Dark Witch."

I stiffen. "Like my mother?" The witch hums absently but says nothing. "Tell me about my mother. I know you were her friend. I know you were friends with Niobe too."

I'm sick of lies. I want the truth.

"I did know your mother, you're right," she says. "I knew Niobe too. They both came here a year before I did, but once I arrived the three of us were thick as thieves. We were friends for a decade." She sits inside the mirror, crossing her legs in front of her. She motions to me with an open hand and I sit in front of the mirror. The stones are cold and damp. I loop my arms around my knees.

She gazes through the mirror over my shoulder, lips twisting wistfully. "Many years ago, I wasn't so different from you. I lived here, I trained, I had friends. I convinced myself, as we all do, that I would never turn. But nature finds a way. I was on a mission with

Niobe and she was wounded. It took everything in my power to get her home alive, and she lived, but I went too far. The coven tried to stop me, but they couldn't and I didn't want them to. There's so much more power to be had if you let go."

"So why did she lock you in here? You saved her life."

"And it's for that reason I believe she was too weak to kill me outright. We had a pact, you see. Before your mother and I came into our full power, the three of us agreed that if and when any of us became Dark Witches, the others would put them down. Lavinia had already turned and Niobe was too softhearted to kill me, so she used Dark magic to bind me in here. Niobe was too weak to kill your mother too. She let her get away and now she'd rather send little girls after the most powerful witch in the world, rather than face her herself."

I shudder. Could I kill Serena if she turned into a Dark Witch? Would she want me to? There has to be a cure, a way to stop the transformation before it takes hold.

"My mother," I say. "How do I stop her?"

"You don't. You're better off joining her because there's no force in the world great enough to take her down."

"That can't be true." She's a Dark Witch, but she's still mortal. She can still be stopped. Despite everything she is, I shiver at the idea of having to kill her. If there's a cure, a way to stop the turning process, maybe there's also a way to reverse it and return to the light.

"Niobe would be proud of you, little fish. Not twenty-four hours into Awakening and you're already scheming against your own flesh and blood. She may act like she wants to protect you, but she'll push you as far as she needs to push you to get what she wants. Even if you go Dark in the process."

"What do you mean?"

"Who do you think made your mother turn?" She shakes her head, white hair swaying too slowly within the mirror's magic. "I was close with Niobe, but nowhere near as close as she was with Lavinia. They were best friends, two powerful witches with the potential to conquer the world together. Until Niobe became jealous when Lavinia surpassed her in the rankings. She tried to kill Lavinia when she was pregnant with the two of you, because she never cared about your mother's friendship. Eventually, she pushed her too far, but Lavinia didn't die. She snapped."

My blood turns to ice, but there's something deeper, an anger that spins like a whirlpool in my chest. "Why would Niobe do that?"

"Look around," says the Dark Pisces. "She trains innocent witches to fight battles she doesn't go into herself, hoarding the most powerful like collectors' items so she can wield you like pawns on a chessboard. You think what she's doing is righteous, but she's no better than the Dark Twelve. She had me fooled for years, but she's selfish. She's using you for her own personal gain, sending you into harm's way to meet her own agenda because she's too much of a coward to go herself."

My palms are slick not just with water now but with sweat. I hug my arms tighter around my knees. I've known for days that Niobe can't be trusted, and this confirms it. If she actually cared about our well-being, she would have taken us out of that orphanage years ago, but instead she left us there to suffer. To break us so we could be more powerful before she would deign to deal with us. How long did Niobe know about Libra's whereabouts? Leaving that little girl in a dirty asylum was nothing but cruel, and then she sent Serena and the others to retrieve her and sat in her cozy office while they fought and nearly died for her.

"Is there a way to reverse turning Dark?" I ask.

The Dark Pisces winces. "You truly are just like your mother."

I sit up straighter. "What do you mean?"

If I can show Niobe that there's a cure, she can release the Dark Pisces from the mirror. She can be free, go back to being who she was when she was a young witch with Niobe. Why would Niobe try to hide that information?

"There's a book." The Dark Pisces cocks her head, surveying me like a hawk. "Your mother and I found it, many years ago, but Niobe didn't like us using it, so we hid it from her."

A book. I knew it. My heart jumps into my throat. "Why did she disapprove of it?"

"We were using it to search for a reversal of the turning, but Niobe claimed it was Dark magic. She thought it too powerful."

What does she mean by *powerful*? Is Niobe afraid whoever uses it will be stronger than her, or worried the use of it will be too much and turn us Dark? Or worse, does she believe it has answers she doesn't want us to have? Either way, I deserve to see it for myself. I deserve to make my own decisions, to not have things concealed from me.

"There are more ways to do magic than Niobe can teach you," says the Dark Pisces.

My hands curl into fists so hard that my nails bite into my palms. Secrets upon secrets, they grate at me, gnawing ceaselessly, begging me to find them. "Where is it hidden?"

"Search the Pisces bedroom. Look for the sea and you'll find it."

Secrets upon secrets, and I'll uncover them all, even if it kills me.

22

Serena

I DON'T KNOW IF IT'S FROM FIGHTING THE DARK WITCHES, my conversation with Niobe, or getting clobbered by a giant necromantic bear, but I feel like I got hit by a train. My limbs are heavy and rubbery, my shoulders ache, and my stomach is mottled with blotchy blue bruises where the bear's arm struck me. Worse than the physical soreness, though, is the throb inside my chest. Pouring all that power into Sagittarius, draining it from myself to save her, sapped my energy.

I storm into the training room, ready to practice. I have to get better, stronger. The next time we meet Dark Witches, I'll be ready. I'll be ready for my mother to be with them. Alone in the training room, I set up targets and get to work. I want to use the lightning to ground myself. I want to delve so deep into my power I can't think of anything else.

I work steadily, channeling the electricity through me until I can hit the center of the bullseye over and over and over. Until I can hit two at once, across the room from one another.

Until I'm certain I won't miss.

Footsteps on the hard floor pull my attention from my electricity. Leo leans on the doorframe, spinning a dagger in one hand. Her skirt is impeccably pressed, her hair flowing free across her shoulders. "Oh good, you're here." She twirls the end of her white strand of hair between her fingers. "I need a sparring partner."

"Not now, Leo," I grumble through gritted teeth. She's the last person I want to deal with today.

"It wasn't a request."

My skin prickles. "Yeah, well, who outranks who?"

A dagger whizzes through the air. It whistles as it passes too close to my ear and arcs to the floor. The blade sinks into the crash pad behind me, slicing into the thick material.

I balk. It's a real dagger, not a training prop or a blunted blade.

"What are you thinking?" I bark at her.

She shoots me a wicked smile and another dagger sails for me. I duck, heat burning through my entire body. I don't have the patience to deal with her needling today. I wanted to train by myself. Why can't she leave me alone?

"Screw you," I spit. I strike with my lightning, intentionally aiming just beside her. I want her to leave, but I don't want to burn her to a crisp. I sink into the magic, letting it rush through me but not letting it take over. I won't lose myself to it again.

For every dagger she throws at me, I'm already spearing lightning to meet it. I spin and twirl. Steel flashes in the beams of sunlight streaming through the windows above us.

"Is that all you've got?" She laughs. "You're weak!"

She's wilder than usual, all control thrown out the window. Her feet lift off the ground and she rises high into the air, her hair floating around her as she spins until she levitates above my head. She dives faster than I can call on my lightning and her heels pound into my chest, kicking the air from my lungs. My feet fly out from under me and I slam into the floor. Hardwood bites into my elbows, and I hate the high whine of pain that tumbles out of my lips.

Leo cackles, feet on the ground again, but I don't bother trying to stand. I roll as sweat drips into my eyes, and fling electricity at her, but not in a bolt. The short burst shoots through the air and I will it to shape itself into circlets around Leo's wrists.

"I'm as strong as you and I haven't had to train for ten years to get there," I say, dragging myself upright.

She yelps in pain when her skin brushes the makeshift electric handcuffs. They hover above her skin and move with her as she tries to pull her hands through. It doesn't stop her from telekinetically yanking a round shield from the wall and hurling it at my head, but at least it keeps her from trying to punch me. I send a shock of lightning at the wooden shield and it clatters to the ground, a scorch mark marring the center.

I'm so focused on the shield that I don't see her move. Her body slams into mine so hard I rock backward into the wall and drop my hold on her electric handcuffs. With her newly freed left forearm, she pins my chest to the wall, feet braced against mine. With her right, she presses the cold flat of her dagger against my throat.

Her nose is barely inches from mine. The scent of rose chokes its way into my throat. I squirm to get free, but every part of me is touching her, trapped between her body and solid stone. I barely dare breathe for fear I'll slice my skin open on the sharp steel. She laughs in my face, breathy and hysterical.

"What the hell is wrong with you?" I pant.

"Everything," Leo hisses, her breath a whisper against my cheek.

I send a surge of sparks from my fingertips into her thigh and she jerks back with a curse. The moment her body shifts, I duck out from beneath her arm, but she wastes no time. Weapons sail from the walls.

Wooden prop swords, blunted knives and axes, shields, a bow and a dozen arrows, ropes—they swirl around me like dancers in a hellish routine. I dig down into the pit of flames in my stomach and draw out my own tornado of lightning to match.

I shove my hands forward and it explodes, like it's coming straight out of my chest. Flashing tendrils of light spin around me, so close their heat licks at my skin. I squint against the bright, burning light. In a raging pulse, it propels outward and sends Leo's weapons scattering.

We both hit the ground as they rain down around us. I throw my hands over my head, but I don't need to. There's a buzzing, electric barrier in a humming sphere around my body. Protecting me.

I take a shuddering breath, crouched among the debris.

A dagger pounds into the wall behind me and wobbles where it sticks. Red-faced, fists balled, vein protruding from her neck, Leo lets out a primal scream.

I freeze, but sparks still dance on my fingertips. Waiting in case she strikes again, ready to match her if she needs to work out whatever this is with force.

Her blow never comes.

Instead, she slides to the ground and slumps onto the mats. She loops her arms around her knees in a hug, and suddenly, she seems fragile, like if she squeezes herself too tightly, all that anger will shatter her. Her cheeks are hollow and violet bruises kiss the skin beneath her eyes. Did she manage to sleep at all last night, or did she lie awake, worried about Sagittarius? I release my force field, drop onto the mat beside her, and cross my legs. Waiting. We sit side by side, the room silent except for our ragged breathing.

"You okay?" I ask after a while.

"Do I look okay to you?"

"No, you look like shit."

She cuts her eyes to me. "Who needs Cancer when you're so good at comforting me?"

"Is comfort what you want? Because it looks like you want to murder me."

"I find murder very comforting."

I can't help the chuckle that bursts out of me. "Has anyone ever told you you're an extremely confusing human being?" One moment she's trying to rip my head off, the next she's sitting here making jokes.

"All the time," she says, failing to hide a slight wince. Last night, Cancer said Leo was with Niobe when she was brought to the Manor, which means Leo has been here for more than a decade. People probably do find her confusing after so much time here on this island. Leo's thumb grazes over the tattoo on her wrist. "When I first got here, I was ranked twentieth."

She says the number in a small voice, staring down at her hands.

"You were just a kid." There's no reason to be ashamed. Especially for a kid, twenty is impressive. I imagine her like Libra, small and scared, and my heart breaks.

"I don't think I've ever really been a kid," she says with a sad smile. "Niobe had me in training the moment I arrived. I used to look at that rank every single day and I swore to myself that I would get it into the single digits. I mean, obviously it changed as I aged and got more powerful, but I trained for years. I *earned* it."

She scrubs her hands across her face, and when she looks up at me, I feel like I'm seeing her for the first time. A girl without a family, raised to be a vessel for magic. A girl without a home, just like me.

Leo shakes her head and the white strand in her hair falls forward to cover her right eye. "You show up here with a single-digit ranking like it's nothing, and it gets to me. Things come easily to other people, and I have to work my ass off for them. And now other than Niobe, I'm the senior member of this coven. I've seen everyone else die or go Dark or both. If I'm still here . . . it's up to me to prove that my rank isn't for nothing. Everyone else looks at me to be the best, to take the lead, and I owe it to them to take care of them."

I stiffen. It's a sentiment I know well—not wanting to protect someone, but *needing* to. Thinking that deep in your bones you're only worth something if you can shield them from the whole world.

The words are easier to say to Leo than they are to myself: "You don't owe anyone anything."

"But I should be able to protect them. I'm supposed to be a leader and bring everyone home, but instead I couldn't stop them from taking my friends, I couldn't stop them from attacking us, and because of me, Sag . . . Sag almost—"

She stifles a sob and buries her face in her hands. I scoot closer to her and, without thinking, put my arm around her shoulders. They're thin, but I can feel the muscles in her upper arm, built from years of trying to be strong for everyone else. I wait for her to push me away, but she doesn't. Instead, she leans in closer.

"When I was nine years old, a member of our coven turned. The Dark Gemini we fought at the asylum, it was her, and I was terrified with no idea what was happening. I looked up to her—she was so strong—and then in an instant, it was like I didn't know her anymore. One day she was my friend, my big sister, and then she was my enemy. And Sag has made me promise if she ever . . ." She shudders and squeezes her eyes closed. "We've promised each other we'll end things for the other person if it comes to that, but yesterday when I thought it was happening, I knew I wouldn't be able to do it. She's my best friend, and I failed her."

"You didn't fail her. You got her home," I say. "You can't do anything more than that."

"It's not just her, though. I was there the day they were taken, Capricorn and Scorpio. There were too many Dark Witches—it was all I could do just to get away alive. If I had tried harder to save them, maybe they'd still be here, maybe—"

"There's no use in rehashing what could have been, Leo. You did the best you could."

"You weren't there."

"No. But I don't need to have been there to know that."

Leo doesn't know how to half-ass anything. She wouldn't want to. Not when there are lives on the line, people she cares about. I don't need to know the details of that mission. I only need to know Leo.

"What good is my best if everyone I love dies?" she whispers.

My thoughts spin—Sagittarius is alive. Capricorn and Scorpio are still alive, wherever they are, as well as Niobe and everyone else in the coven. "Who, Leo?" I ask.

She hangs her head. "My mom."

Oh. I don't press. I wait, watching her quietly, an invitation but not a demand. She accepts. "My mom was a witch too, an Aries," she says. "She was always off on missions hunting Dark Witches. But then she started to change. I'd never seen a Dark Witch before, so I thought she was just sick and it was getting worse and worse. One night I woke up when she came home from a mission and she was screaming in the kitchen, writhing around in pain. I ran in to try to help her and she zapped me. She screamed at me to run, but I didn't listen. I kept yelling for her, trying to help her, but then she fully turned and started attacking me. She was throwing sparks, trying to chase me to feed off me, and I didn't know what was happening—I just saw my mom becoming this . . . this monster." Her voice cracks on the last word. "I was so sure she was going to kill me. She didn't care if she hurt me, my own mother. That's when my powers were Awoken. I didn't know what was happening, but this power rose up inside me and I had to stop her. I was waving my arms, trying to get her to stop, when a knife flew out of the kitchen. I didn't mean to hit her, but it went right into her chest. There was blood . . . so much blood. . . ."

Her gaze is so hollow that I want to squeeze her tighter.

"I killed her," she says. "I was only six years old, but I still see that day in flashes like it was yesterday. I have nightmares of it. The knife, my mom on the floor, blood . . . everywhere." A shudder racks her body. "And then Niobe showed up and carried me out."

I swallow hard. Was that before or after she'd left me and Ophelia at the orphanage? If I'd grown up here alongside Leo and Cancer, how different would my life have been? The four of us could have been the best of friends, training and laughing and playing together in the meadow outside the Manor. For a moment, I can believe that it was real. Too quickly, it slips away. There's no use grieving what might have been.

"I'm sorry, Leo," I say. "But it's not your fault. You were protecting yourself."

"I know. That doesn't mean I feel any less guilty, though."

"My mother turned Dark too. Until I came here, I didn't know what happened. I thought that she was dead, but she's not." I take a deep, shaking breath and force myself not to look away. "She's the leader of the Dark Twelve."

Leo sucks in a sharp breath. "Lavinia is your mother?" She rakes her fingers through her hair. "That explains why you and your sister are so high ranked." She chews her lip like she's considering something, then asks slowly, "What's she like?"

"I don't know. I was so little when we were . . . separated from her." The words are hard to form after all these years thinking she died. "I remember reading with her, baking cookies. She was just . . . my mom. But now I don't know what she's like. If we meet her face-to-face, I don't know if I'll recognize the woman that I see in my memories."

Leo nods grimly. "It changes people. The Darkness."

"What if that's what's going to happen to me?" I hadn't been afraid of turning Dark before, but after what Niobe told me, it seems inevitable. Even with the best intentions, the desire to protect, my mother still became Dark. She went from protecting me and Ophelia with her life to trying to capture us. To killing innocent people. People we care about.

"No." Leo shifts to sit cross-legged and grasps my knee. "That won't happen to you."

"How do you know?"

"Because I do. Screw Lavinia. Who cares if she's ranked first? She doesn't matter; *you* do. You're powerful. What you did against the Dark Witches at the asylum with hardly any training? That was damn impressive." She flinches as the words come out, but my heart still swells at the compliment. "We can beat them."

For the first time in too long, I start to believe it: We can beat them, and I'm going to have to. She's my mother—if anyone is going to put an end to her it's going to be me. But to take down the Dark Twelve, I need this coven.

"Together," I say, holding a hand out to Leo.

She rolls her eyes, but takes my hand, her grip iron as she shakes mine. "Together," she agrees.

Sunlight slants through the roof of the training room and lights up Leo's eyes so I can see all the glorious shades of red and orange and brown melding in her russet irises. She's a living flame. I'm struck with the desire to ask her name, but I hold myself back. Leo doesn't give anything freely. It's something I'll have to earn. I'm not sure I can imagine her as any other name, though. *Leo.* It suits her. She's a lioness defending her pride. Today she let me into the icy exterior to see the fire that burns beneath the surface. Hidden, like she's afraid someone will snuff it out. As if anyone could steal that force from her.

Then she blinks and all her softness disappears. She straightens and shrugs out from beneath my arm. "If you tell anyone I've gone soft, I'll kill you," she says.

I bite back a smile. "Your secret's safe with me."

23

Ophelia

I TEAR APART MY BEDROOM, SEARCHING FOR ANY PLACE A book might be hidden. I go through the shelves checking every book, though I doubt the Dark Pisces would be so obvious, and yank open every drawer. When I'm convinced there are no secret panels or hidden compartments in the dresser or wardrobe, I shove the bed out from the wall and press my fingers into any grooves on the wall, hoping a door will spring free, and do the same on the wall behind the fish tank. I check each of the floorboards, but none of them are loose, so I go to move the dresser out from the wall and find it stuck to the wall behind it

Strange—nothing else in the room is mounted to the floor or walls. The bed, chairs, and wardrobe moved easily. I push aside the things I've left there, a hairbrush and hair band, a pair of socks, and focus on the items that were already here. The various seashells are nothing but decorative, so I move to the mermaid statue. At the bottom of the rock she's perched on a tiny symbol of a fish is etched so small I would have missed it had my face not been mere inches from it.

I try to pick it up, but like the dresser, it's secured to the surface of the wood. With both hands, I tug at it, hoping it'll pop off or twist to reveal a secret. The Dark Pisces knew about the book's hiding place, though, and said Niobe didn't. Does that mean it's somewhere only a Pisces can find?

I raise my hands and call water droplets out of the air, concentrating as Cancer showed me until I'm weaving a thin ribbon around each hand. Biting my lip and focusing my vision on the figurine, I draw the water ribbons toward it. Just as I used my hands a moment ago to twist, I wrap one ribbon of water around the mermaid's torso, the other around the rock beneath her, and send the ribbons in a spiral.

The statue rotates ninety degrees and I withdraw the water.

With a click and a high-pitched creak, the dresser swings out, connected to a panel of wall behind it that opens like a door. My breath catches and I rush to lock my bedroom door from inside, my blood pumping too fast through my veins. Crouching, I peer into the opening, but there's no book concealed there. Instead, there's a passageway, a few feet leading to a stairway down. I stick my head through carefully and find that though the entrance is short, the tunnel has plenty of room to stand inside. I crawl through the doorway and into the blackness of a musty stone tunnel. Should I have brought a lantern? The dresser groans, and I lunge for it with a gasp, but the door slams shut. The last thing I want is to get sealed in the dark by mistake, but I force myself to take long, slow breaths until my eyes adjust. It's not pitch-black; there's a glimmer of light at the end.

I head toward the light shining from the bottom of the stairs, trailing my fingers along the damp stone wall to keep from tripping on the uneven steps as I descend. My heart thunders in my chest. I'm not sure how many levels I go down, but I continue until I'm certain I must be underground. The deeper I go, the more humid the air becomes until it feels like I'm slogging through water and sweat beads on my skin. When I reach the sliver of light at the bottom of the stairs, I find another door. Through a barred window at the top of the door, I catch a glimpse of a grotto.

The door is locked, though. I try calling on the water like I did upstairs, but weaving around the bars, shooting it into the lock, nothing works. I turn a slow circle in the dim light—there must be a key somewhere. There's nothing down here but bare brick walls. I scan the walls, letting my eyes flit over the bricks until they stop on one that's slightly different. Pale gray rather than black, it's in the wall across from the door, just over my head.

I stand on my tiptoes, fingers scrabbling and scraping against the rough stones. The brick is loose, so I wedge my fingertips into the space separating the brick from the others. Gritting my teeth, I wiggle it back and forth until it slips forward just enough that I can pull it out of the wall.

Dirt crumbles onto my hand, but there's nothing in the hole where the brick once was. Though disappointment sinks in my stomach like a stone, I trace the nooks and crannies of the brick. A thick layer of dried mud coats the back. I try to scrape it off with my nails, but it's too caked on. Pulling water from the humid air, I douse the brick until the dirt softens and washes to the floor.

An iron key clatters to the ground from where it was pressed between the mud and the brick. It fits perfectly in the lock on the door, and I open it, stepping into the grotto.

There are empty fish tanks along the uneven stone walls, dirty with old algae clinging to the glass, and chests full of colorful pebbles and seashells. In the center is an empty fountain, long dried up. The fluted stone is topped with an open-mouthed, blue-scaled fish.

Maybe this was once a place for a former Pisces to practice water magic, a secret passed from Pisces to Pisces over time. On the other side of the fountain is an arch carved into the wall, an alcove where a statue or a vase might sit, but instead, it's there: the book. Like it's waiting for me. The black cover is cracking, veined with gold, with thin gilded pages. My heart stumbles.

Pisces, it seems to sing to me.

Like the tide, it pulls me. There must be something in here that'll keep me and everyone else from turning.

Gingerly, afraid the binding might fall apart if I touch it too roughly, I reach for it. A solid shield of air stops my fingers an inch from the cover.

I draw water from the damp air around me and will it into a stream. It flows in a long ribbon, which I weave in and out of my fingers and send toward the book. It passes through the shield with a flicker of blue light, wraps around the book, and knocks it off the shelf.

I rush to it and shake the few droplets of water from the cover, though they slide away with ease. For a moment, I clutch it to my chest, waiting for an alarm to go off or a trap to snap down around me. When nothing happens, I tuck the book beneath my arm and carry it out of the grotto and back up the stairs. When I reach the closed door to my bedroom, it opens for me like it senses who I am, and I crawl through, making sure to close it behind me.

In the refuge of my room, I throw myself onto the bed and open the book. Leafing through it, I see nothing on the surface about a cure. There's not much information at all; it's a book of spells. Each page has a title, a small pen sketch at the top, and an incantation. I've never seen any of the witches here use an incantation. They use raw magic, which every book I read in the library says is the most natural form, shaping our powers with our minds and bodies as we've been training to do. Spells are more complex. They take more energy but can yield greater effects. Is that the trick to not turning? Using spells rather than raw magic? Or maybe there's a spell in here that can reverse the Darkness? But to do that, I need to first learn how to use spell work. I need to experiment.

I sit cross-legged on my bed and leaf through the spells. Each one has a heading with a title and a description of the spell, followed by the spell itself written in a language I can sound out but don't recognize.

At the back of the book there are spells that require one of each zodiac witch. Did the Dark Pisces know about those? Is that why she told me about the book? Maybe one of them can help keep witches from turning, like the stories say the original Twelve were able to do.

The spells toward the beginning of the book, though, seem small and simple, a few words each. I open to one of the first pages, a dehydration spell, and grab a red apple from my desk that I'd swiped from breakfast.

The spell is five words I say carefully, hoping I'm pronouncing each one correctly. When nothing happens, I let myself feel for the current running through me and will it to bend itself around each syllable. I say the words again, and every drop of water in the apple flies out of it. The new moisture hangs in the air as the apple itself shrivels to nothing but a wrinkled dark husk barely recognizable as a fruit.

The words, an ancient language with an abundance of vowels and soft consonants, cling to my lips. I swear I can see them shining there before me, just as pure light dances through my body. I feel good. I feel strong and in control. I need to try another.

I go into the bathroom, plug the tub, and turn on the tap as hot as it will go. When it contains several inches of scalding water, steam rising in curling tendrils from it, I speak a freezing spell. Sharp cracking sounds reverberate off the bathroom tiles, and then the bathtub is completely iced over. When I pound my fist on the surface, it doesn't break.

I spin in giddy circles, bouncing on the balls of my feet. If I can do all this, what else can I do?

I melt the ice with another spell, then flip the page and say a spell to form a shield. Water droplets pull themselves out of thin air and form a perfectly round disk of water that hovers just over my knuckles like an extension of my hand. I might be able to do this without the book, with weeks of practice and constant concentration funneling into the shield, but using the spell, I don't have to think about it. It's solid until I decide to let it drop. I wield it with my left hand; then with my right I form little daggers of water in my usual way. One by one, I fling them at the mirror, letting them bounce back so I can practice deflecting them with my shield before they can strike me. I block dagger after dagger of water until they've all fallen and created puddles at my feet and I let the shield drop. It dissipates back into the air, evaporating like it was never there.

My chest heaves, but with excitement rather than effort. If this is what magic is, I don't know why I was ever afraid. It sets my heart racing and my blood pumping like I've eaten too much sugar or drank more coffee than usual. I want to dance and jump and scream my delight to the whole island.

I flip the next page—blood control. Of course, I don't know why I've never thought of it.

Blood is 90 percent water. If I can pull water out of the moisture in the air, why shouldn't I be able to meld the water in blood to my will as well?

I look around for something to try it with, as I don't dare attempt it with another person yet. The fish. I approach the fish tank, watching them swim lazily through the water, blissfully unaware of anything outside the walls of their tank. I focus on the fish nearest me and intone the words of the spell, and the moment they're out of my mouth, I gasp, jerking back. I can feel it, the slow pulsating of blood through its body in my grasp. I flick my fingers and it stops moving. Another flick and it spins itself in one circle, then another, until I stop it again. The water in its blood responds to my every whim. One by one, I take hold of each fish in the tank until I can move them through the water like marionettes, fins moving when and where I command.

Blood rushes in my ears, pounding in excitement. So much of this world is water—if I can bend the blood of other creatures to my will, what else can I control? The ocean? The clouds? The weather itself? The whole universe is at my fingertips and my blood is singing, thumping in my veins, drumming as it begs me to tug more at the threads of every drop of moisture I can grasp.

I flip the page to the next spell—a storm. I glance out the window at the blue sky without a cloud in sight. Could I create a storm from nothing? The magic flowing through me pounds, begging me to *try, try, try*. I've hardly dared think about the number inked on my wrist and what it means. It means I'm strong. Powerful. With my strength and the spells in this book, I can beat anyone. I can keep the Darkness at bay. I have to know if I can do it.

I pick up the book and rush out of my room, out of the Manor, and into the meadow. The sun warms my cheeks as I start through the tall grass toward the cliff, drawn without a second thought to the ocean. I stop when I get closer to the bluffs and open the book to the page I've saved with one finger.

It seems innocuous: a little water, a little wind, a small manipulation of nature for a few minutes. It can't be that much different from controlling the water present in the atmosphere to create the water ribbons I made earlier.

I take a deep breath, exhaling slow and steady, and recite the words of the spell in a low monotone. Once. Twice. Three times.

I let the magic flow out of me, filling the words until the magic is a rush. It takes hold of every drop of water in the atmosphere on the island. The air crackles with power, and for a moment, I flash outside of my own body like I'm holding the entire rocky crop of land in the palm of my hand. It's mine to control: the sky and the water, every drop of moisture I taste on my tongue. I imagine it twisting and bending, writhing, warping itself to my will.

The sunshine fades and darkness creeps across the Isle of Sol. Thunder claps and raindrops pelt my skin. A laugh burbles from my lips. I turn my palm up, collecting water in my cupped hand. Water, where there weren't clouds even a minute ago, spills from a sky suddenly laden with heavy gray clouds and rolls down my skin until my clothes and hair are soaked. I don't mind, though. This rain is *mine.* It pounds into me, and I can't think past the dizzying, cloying sense of power coursing through me.

Of course I'm supposed to have this book. The very earth is mine to command but it's not ripping power from me—it's giving it to me, pouring it ounce by ounce into my body until I can't stop it from flowing back out and feeding the rain.

I find myself moving toward the edge of the cliff, toward the water. The book tumbles from my hands and into the wet grass, but I don't need it anymore. The storm is coming from within me, and for once, I don't want to stop it. I was so afraid when my magic broke loose the first time, like it was going to consume me and strip my flesh from my bones. Now, though, I'm not afraid. My bones call to the storm, longing to let it drench me in its waters.

Lightning splits the sky in a jagged burst over the ocean waves. The water crashes and crests against the jagged rocks in a symphony playing a slow crescendo, a tune for my ears alone, its conductor. The rain comes down harder and harder until I can hardly see through it. I stop at the edge of the cliff, watching it pound into the sea. The tide rises higher. The sucking surf surges and falls, massive whitecaps spraying high into the air. The sky darkens and thunder rumbles.

I step closer to the edge and lightning flashes again, illuminating the darkness.

My head spins with dizzying excitement until I feel weightless, swaying on my feet. I can bend the waves, shape them until they reveal their secrets. Until I'm unstoppable. I could tumble from this ledge right now, fall into the waves and discover everything hidden beneath them. I could control the sea itself. No one would be able to stop me.

I take another step.

"Ophelia, stop!" someone calls behind me, barely audible over the pounding rain.

Gemini's white shirt is drenched. It clings to their chest, exposing every muscle and plane. I swallow against my thrumming heartbeat in my throat. At the sight of them, I feel the phantom touch of their fingers, brushing lightly on the bare skin above my knee at the bonfire, sending tendrils of heat up my leg. I see the shadow of flames dancing across their face, the soft, reassuring smile that made the rest of the world fall away. My pulse quickens and I burst into a run toward them. They step back, though, away from me, with one hand extended like I'm some rabid animal. Water sluices from their hair, plastering it to their head and running in steady streams down their cheeks.

"What are you doing out here?" Their brows knit together and I long to take a finger and press that tension away, to wipe the water from their face with my fingers, but the tug of the ocean behind me is too strong.

"I have to feel it." I take two steps backward, toward the cliff's edge, but Gemini seizes my wrist. Their grip is firm and tight, holding me in place, but not so strong that it hurts.

They hold up the spell book. "You shouldn't have this."

"It's mine." I reach for it, but they hold it away from me. Why don't they want me to have it?

"It's Dark magic," says Gemini, squeezing my wrist harder. They wave the book in the air. "Look at this, it shouldn't be possible. It's too much."

I slide my wrist from their grasp. "Too much?" The magic dances in my veins, singing and sparkling like a chandelier lit with a thousand candles. "It's not too much, Gemini—it's perfect. It's mine!" The book, the magic, the rain, the wind, all of it is mine and mine alone. "There are spells in here for the whole coven, though," I say. "Don't you want to know what we can do, all of us together?"

Thunder cracks, louder and closer this time. The wind rips at my hair. It howls like a rabid wolf, hungry to devour me. Gemini grips me by both shoulders, forehead hovering close to mine. "Ophelia, look at me," they say. My magic calls the rain and makes it come down harder. "You have to stop this before you burn out!"

"No!" I jerk away from their touch. They reach for me again, but I don't want them to touch me. They want to stop me. A bolt of lightning blazes between us, heat blasting onto my skin and scorching the earth. Gemini leaps backward, cursing.

The rain's drumming beat fizzes in my veins like Virgo's Magic Mead did, warm and sweet and beckoning me to sink into warm oblivion. I want my skin to be so slick I no longer know which molecules are mine and which are the rain's. I want to be one with the water.

"Ophelia, look at me!" Gemini screams over the droning rain. "You have to let go."

"I can't!" I insist. This is the most freedom I've felt in years, maybe in my entire life. I would be a fool to give it up, even if I could.

"Let go, Ophelia." They surge toward me and thread shaking fingers through my hair to hold multiple strands of pure white up to my eyes. "You're going to turn, and I won't be able to stop it."

That can't be. I'm not turning, am I? I shove at their chest, pushing them away again. This can't be what Darkness feels like. Darkness ought to be frightening, a curse, but this shimmering light inside me isn't a curse. It's the power of the entire universe, lightning and thunder, rain, and wind at my fingertips. Never again will I be a terrified little mouse, hiding powerless beneath the covers while the world rages around me.

I am the storm now.

Wind howls and sends the rain slanting sideways, pushing Gemini farther from me. "Please stop," they beg.

"I can't." I don't know how. I don't know if I want to.

Determination sparks in their eyes, and they take off sprinting toward the edge of the cliff. My breath catches in my throat as they fling themself over the precipice. For a moment, their body hangs suspended as a bolt of lightning washes the scene. My heart stops—all of time stops. And then they plummet.

"Gemini!" I scream.

The storm still rages, the sea below a churning mass of waves against jagged rocks, and my body moves of its own accord. Without looking back, I throw myself off the cliff after Gemini and let my body free-fall into the icy water.

24

Serena

OPHELIA DOESN'T RESPOND TO MY KNOCK ON HER BEDROOM door, but maybe the sound was drowned out by the pounding rain and rumbling thunder. I need to talk to her about Niobe and hope she'll forgive me for confronting her on my own. I knock again, but when she still doesn't answer, I crack the door open. Her room is empty.

"Ophelia?" I step inside, peeking to see if she's in the bathroom. It's empty too, though. The bed is made but the comforter is rumpled. She must have been here recently. I turn to leave, but then I see the fish tank against the wall. Every single fish in the tank is still. Suspended in the water, motionless. All their mouths are moving, their eyes still alert. They're alive; they're just . . . stuck.

I press my hand to the cool glass. How is this possible? Lightning flashes outside and I wince at the brightness. My skin tingles the more I look at the fish. Something isn't right; I can feel it in my bones. I need to find Ophelia.

I rush down the hallway, checking Gemini's room first, but they're not there either. Voices echo from the sitting room and I poke my head in, hoping it's her. Instead, it's Niobe, Cancer, Aquarius, and Leo standing around a table laid with maps. Niobe and Cancer stand stiffly as Aquarius drags her finger across the surface of one of the pages. Leo leans against the wall with her arms crossed tightly over her chest.

"What's going on?" I ask from the doorway.

Cancer opens her mouth to answer, but shuts it quickly until Niobe gives her a nod.

"Aquarius found the location of the Dark Witches' sanctum while she was scouting yesterday," says Cancer. "She was able to track one of the Dark Twelve there."

I rush into the room, all thoughts of Ophelia ripped from my mind. Going on the offensive is the real way to protect her—to protect all of us. "Where?" I demand.

Cancer and Aquarius part, letting me come between them to view the map. Aquarius points to a small cluster of islands in the middle of the ocean, one of which is circled.

"Is Sag well enough yet to get us there?" I ask. "Is the sanctum warded? When are we attacking?"

"Slow down, Aries," says Niobe coolly. "We need to plan this carefully and not be hotheaded."

I ball my hands into fists. "I'm not being hotheaded. They don't know we have this information, do they?" Aquarius shakes her head. "Then we need to strike now, before they realize we're onto them."

Cancer shakes her head. "I don't like it. It's too easy." Aquarius's mouth twists in a grimace and Cancer amends, "I know it hasn't been easy for you getting this information. I just mean, it feels like a trap."

"So we go expecting a trap," I say.

"Not everything is so simple," says Niobe. "I will not put the lives of any more of you at risk unless we have every bit of information.

There's too much we don't know. We aren't aware of their numbers or their defenses. I will not send you all on a suicide mission for the sake of your personal vendetta. Is that clear?"

I flinch backward, hating how Cancer's and Aquarius's questioning gazes bore into me. "Lavinia is my mother," I explain.

Aquarius's eyes go wide and Cancer squeaks, "What? I thought your mother was dead, Aries—"

I wave them off, not wanting to explain right now. "This isn't about her. They have members of our coven held captive. Are we really just going to leave them there?"

"Aries is right," says Leo, bracing her hands on the table. I glance over at her in surprise. Leo, agreeing with me? That's a first. She gives me a nod and carries on studying the map. "We have the element of surprise. We need to take it. They have Capricorn and Scorpio. We can't afford to wait any longer."

"What are the Dark Witches doing to them?" I ask.

"Draining them of energy and power," says Cancer. "It's how the Dark Witches sustain themselves. They feed on us until we're . . ." She trails off, wincing at a sharp glower from Leo.

Rain pelts harder against the windows. The wind roars, forcing tree branches to scrape against the glass. The storm reminds me of another dark, stormy night not long ago.

"What if we lure them out?" I say. "They can sense power; it's why the Dark Gemini was there in the orphanage waiting to feed on me and Ophelia, and why they showed up to the asylum with Libra, right?" Cancer winces, looking away quickly. "So I'm presuming they want as many of us as possible, either to join their coven or to use as a power source. Why not have some of us lay a trap and draw as many out as we can? Then their defenses will be down and the rest of us can sneak in and grab Capricorn and Scorpio."

Niobe nods slowly. "It could work."

"Where, though?" asks Leo. "We can't do it here because of the wards."

"We can't take the wards down?" I say. "Not even for a short period? If they could sense us here on the island, they'd definitely come."

Niobe drums her fingers thoughtfully on the tabletop. "The wards are old magic. Generations of head witches before me have funneled energy into the crystal in the entryway to keep them running. There's no way for me to empty it without destroying the crystal outright, and even if I could, it would be too risky."

A shrill scream rips through the hallway and we all turn toward the sound, a knife already in Leo's hand.

Libra stumbles into the room with her arms wrapped around herself.

Niobe lunges toward her, going to her knees in front of the child. "What's wrong?"

Sparks fizz at my fingertips as I scan her body, searching for anything that might have hurt her, but there's nothing. She's physically fine.

Libra whimpers, and Niobe gently shakes her shoulders. "Tell me what's the matter."

"Someone's dead."

I exchange glances with Leo, who is still poised with her weapons out, ready to defend. "Who?" I ask.

The sky opens up, thunder cracks, and rain rushes down in torrents, pounding against the windows.

"One of us," says Libra.

25

Ophelia

MY STOMACH TWISTS, WIND AND RAIN BATTERING MY FACE as I plummet through the air. Icy water hits me and I twist and roll to avoid hitting a rock. The waves batter me, even below the surface, but the moment I'm submerged, the storm clouds in my mind begin to part. The water washes my skin clean of the magical drunkenness until all I'm left with is cool clarity and the knowledge that I have to find Gemini.

What were they thinking, jumping like that? I fight my way to the surface, but they're nowhere to be found. With a deep breath of briny sea air, I dive back down. The salt doesn't sting my eyes when I open them; the water embraces me like an old friend and points me toward Gemini. They're unconscious, drifting beneath the surface, limp limbs buffeted by the fast-moving water.

Please be alive, I beg the water silently. *Please.*

I cut my way through the waves, swimming deeper and deeper until I reach them. Grabbing hold of them around the waist, I kick us to the surface, my legs burning as I propel us faster. It's a miracle they didn't hit any of the jagged rocks. Their head lolls against my shoulder when I break through the surface.

Around us, the storm has calmed. There's nothing but a light drizzle and the sun pokes its head out of the sky. The waves are calmer now, a loving lap against my shoulders that makes staying afloat simple. The water wraps me in its arms and all of the tumult and torrent that was both inside me and outside has receded. Clinging to Gemini's waist, I cut through the water one armed. It pushes my back, speeding me quickly to shore.

I haul Gemini onto dry land and fall to my knees beside them. When their chest rises shallowly, I collapse onto my heels in relief. I pull the water from their lungs and throat until it spews out and they cough and sputter, spitting water everywhere. When they try to sit up, I shove them back down.

"Are you insane?" I hiss.

"Probably." Gemini smiles weakly and my stomach somersaults. Water plasters their dark hair to their head and drips in rivulets down the golden column of their neck. "But I've kind of always wanted to do that."

A sob bursts out of me. "Well, next time, wait to try your dangerous ideas until we're not in the middle of a torrential storm!"

"My dangerous ideas?" they ask sharply. They pull themselves into a seated position, one hand gripping my shoulder to steady themself. "I wasn't the one practicing Dark magic! You shouldn't have been messing with things like that. It's risky for even the most experienced witches. Where did the hell did you find that book?"

Dark magic? "I didn't know," I mumble. "They were just spells."

Gemini rakes both hands through their sopping curls, shaking their head. "What do you think spells are?"

"I just thought—"

"No!" they practically shout. "You didn't think, did you?"

"That's none of your business."

"It *is* my business when you're trying to drown the entire island. It's my business when you're about to burn out and turn yourself Dark. How could you do something like that?"

"How could *you* throw yourself off a cliff?"

"Because it was the only way I could think to snap you out of it! It's like you weren't really there and I didn't know how else to reach you. I just knew the water would bring you back."

"I don't care!" I smack their shoulder with a wet slap against hard muscle. "You could have died. If something happened to you—" I choke on the words. "It doesn't matter if I was out of control, or turning Dark, why would you risk your life for me?"

"Because I—" Gemini's chest heaves. Salt water glistens on their cheekbones; their bright eyes bore into mine. "Because I care about you." They brush the wet white strands of hair from my face, leaving a ripple of gooseflesh in their wake. "And I'd jump off that cliff a thousand times over if it meant protecting you. Even from yourself."

"I don't need—"

I don't finish the sentence before they close the space between us, lips crashing into mine. A small, surprised sound escapes my lips but I cling to Gemini's shoulders. Their arms wrap solidly around my waist and pull me into their lap. They nip at my bottom lip with a low growl and I plunge my hands into their curls the way I've longed to.

We press together in a tangle of lips, teeth, and tongues until Gemini is on top of me, pressing me into the sand. I don't care that sand sticks to my skin and finds its way into my hair; all that matters is Gemini and their hands on me. Their kisses are hungry now, hot and pressing, and still, it's not enough. I want to be closer, feel more, until I stop knowing where my body ends and theirs begins. Gemini's hands find their way beneath my sopping sweater and trace fiery circles on my stomach.

They pull back an inch and pause, pressing their forehead to mine. "There's something I want to share with you, Ophelia." They breathe my name like a whispered prayer and my heart stumbles. "My name is Reyes."

Reyes. It feels right somehow, like it fits them. Gemini does as well, two names, two sides of the same charming, kind, gentle, caring person. "Nice to officially meet you, Reyes."

Their name on my lips draws a smile larger than I've ever seen from them, sunshine bursting from their freckled skin and washing over me. I lean up and kiss them again, that smile against my lips. I don't know how long we lie there wrapped in each other's arms, kissing until my lips are raw and Gemini has somehow lost their wet shirt in the process.

I press kisses to velvety swathes of golden skin, my hands raking up and down their solid shoulder blades until Gemini stops abruptly. They pull their lips roughly from mine and a chill washes over me. At the absence of their kiss, I'm too aware of us, out here in plain sight on the beach. Why did they stop? They hover over me on their hands, staring at something in the distance. I long to touch their face and brush their hair away, but I don't let myself.

"Are you . . . Did I do something wrong?"

Gemini whips their gaze back to me, brows knitting together. "No, not a thing." They brush their lips against mine, softer this time, a whisper of affection. "There's something over there, though."

Easing off me, they help me to my feet and then I see it too. Something has been washed up on the shore, and it doesn't look like a log. "Maybe it's a turtle," I say, but Gemini is already moving, racing down the beach. I sprint to keep up, but as we get closer, I have the slithering feeling in my gut that it's no turtle.

Her shape becomes more apparent—it's a girl, around my age. She's spread out, unmoving in the sand, one of her legs splayed at an unnatural angle. Her long waves of wet black hair fan out around her head and her skin is a deep brown peeking out beneath the layer of sand coating her.

"Capricorn?" Gemini swears and falls to their knees beside the unmoving girl, sand spraying in their wake. They shake the girl by her shoulders but she doesn't stir.

Capricorn? She's one of the girls the Dark Witches kidnapped. "Did she escape?" I ask. But Gemini is bent over her, one hand looped around her wrist as their face hovers against her blue lips. "Gem?" I ask when they don't respond.

Gemini's stricken eyes meet mine. "She's dead."

26

Serena

I'M TOO LATE.

I'm always, always, *always* too late. There's no time for tears, though, as Libra says, "I told you," pointing down at Ophelia and Gemini in the atrium beneath the turning metal gyroscope in the light of the ward crystal.

Standing over a dead body.

I scan the girl once, twice, three times, making sure I don't know her. Then I look at my sister and fight back all the questions leaping into my mind: Where did they find this girl, why is she soaking wet and covered in sand, arm in arm with a shirtless Gemini, and more importantly, why are there two more white streaks in Ophelia's hair?

There isn't time for those questions now, though.

Leo shoves me aside as she hurtles down the stairs. "Capricorn!" She tries to pull the girl to her feet, but her body can't hold itself up. "We have to get her to Virgo."

Gemini reaches for Leo's shoulder. "Leo, she's—"

"Do it!" Desperation is thick in her voice. I know we're both reliving what happened in this very room, not long ago. Sagittarius writhing and pale, blood slicking the floor, white hair and black eyes. We got lucky then.

I rush to them and take one of Capricorn's too-limp arms beneath my shoulders. Her arms are covered in lesions and bruises, some yellowing and faded, others violet and new. Her weight threatens to push me to the floor, but I grit my teeth and draw on every ounce of strength in my arms and core. Gemini leads the way, Ophelia close on their heels.

"Come on, Cap," Leo mutters as we carry her between us. "Don't do this."

I don't have the heart to tell her I'm certain Capricorn can no longer hear her pleas.

The med wing is a giant greenhouse with plants interspersed among shelves of perfectly organized vials of herbs and tinctures. The rain has almost stopped, but the few falling drops are thunderous on the glass roof. Virgo is already waiting with an apron and goggles on, alongside Niobe, Cancer, and Aquarius, who rushed straight to her after Libra found us.

"Cap?" Virgo exclaims. "What happened?"

"We don't know. She just washed up onshore like this," says Gemini.

"Get her up here." We lift her onto a large wooden table in the center of the greenhouse and Virgo examines her, with her hands and with her magic, while Leo paces back and forth like a tiger in a cage. I can sense Virgo's healing power hovering over Capricorn's body, scanning every muscle, every bone. The more Virgo scans, the more her face blanches. "Leo, I don't . . ."

Leo moans pitifully. She falls to her knees beside Capricorn with her elbows braced on the table, and her head in her hands. "No, no," she cries. "Please, there must be something you can do."

Virgo kneels beside her and pries her hands from her face. "I'll try. She's our sister. I swear, I'll try."

Leo takes a long shuddering breath and rises. I go to her side and we watch as Virgo runs her hands through the air over Capricorn's body again. Footsteps echo down the hall and Sagittarius rushes in to complete our circle around Capricorn's body. The back of my hand brushes against Leo's. She doesn't look at me, but I swear her fingers linger. I want to break through that icy stare and let her know that I see the tears threatening to fall from her eyes. She doesn't have to bear all of this on her own.

"Don't waste your energy, Virgo," says Niobe. "She's beyond our help now."

"No," Leo says fiercely.

Niobe speaks in a low, firm voice. "The best thing for us to do right now is find out how this happened and get justice for our sister. There's no use in burning ourselves out trying to revive the dead."

Her voice is strong and commanding, but I see the way her mouth twists and her forehead wrinkles. I see the way she won't look at Capricorn's body for more than a moment. One of her witches has died. This isn't any easier for her than it is for Leo, but she doesn't have the luxury of breaking down.

"There has to be something we can do," says Ophelia. There's a pool of water beneath her feet from her dripping hair and clothes.

Libra pushes out from behind Cancer, who was trying her best to keep the little girl from seeing the broken body on the table. "There is."

"No," Sagittarius says quickly.

Ophelia's lips part in confusion. "What is she talking about?"

Even though I understand, the idea makes my stomach twist. "Necromancy," I say. "She wants to bring her back."

"Do it," says Leo. "Bring her back."

"No way," says Gemini, and I have to agree with them. Bringing rodents and birds back to life for a few minutes is one thing, but bringing a person back from death? It isn't feasible. She'd be a shell of herself, like the corpses in the asylum.

"It could get us more information," says Niobe. "I don't think she's been dead long; she might be able to remain lucid for a few minutes to tell us more about the Dark Witches' sanctum. But it'll only be for a short time. Even the best necromancers can't bring back consciousness for more than a few moments."

"It's cruel." Sagittarius shakes her head. "She's suffered enough."

"You don't know she won't be able to come back," says Leo. "Maybe Libra can do it. Forever."

"She can't," argues Sagittarius.

"That's not true," says Libra in her small, high voice. "I can make the puppets do what I want, but I can bring people back other ways too. Really back, to talk and everything."

I can't be the only one nauseated at the idea. Sagittarius is right, she's suffered enough at the hands of the Dark Witches. We should leave her to rest in peace.

"I think we should do it." Cancer's voice cuts through the rising argument. The room goes quiet. Of all the people in this room, Cancer is the last person I'd expect to agree to this. The emotions of someone brought back from the dead, even for a few moments, would be devastating. "It's what she would want. She would want us to have answers, to be able to save the others and avenge her death."

We all look to Niobe, who nods. "Go ahead and try," she tells Libra.

Libra's face scrunches and her hands bunch into fists. Her chest rises and falls shallowly until she places one hand on Capricorn's abdomen. I don't see the magic flowing from her into Capricorn's body, but I feel it. It floats through the room like a warm summer breeze, beckoning everything from darkness to light. From death to life.

She grabs Cancer's hand, starting a chain of linked hands around the circle. A kernel of my power slips from my body and I don't try to hold it back. From the grit of Leo's teeth and the press of her fingers in mine, I know it's happening to her too. It's worth it, this little bit of giving, though it scrapes and slides, yearning to crawl back into my body. A few moments of my body burning from the inside out. I bite my lip against it for a few seconds until it dissipates.

Capricorn's body lurches and Leo squeezes my hand so hard the small muscles in my wrist scream. On the table, my coven-mate's bloodshot eyes fly open.

And then she starts screaming.

Her back arches off the table. Her limbs thrash in every direction.

"Hold her down!" shouts Niobe. Taking hold of Capricorn's shoulders, she forces her back against the table as Leo and I leap forward. She bucks and kicks, but I pin her leg down.

"No! Don't touch me! No!" screams Capricorn, the only intelligible words she gets out. The rest is guttural, primal. It's the terrified shrieks of a girl who's seen Darkness face-to-face.

Cancer touches her fingers to Capricorn's temples, keeping her from banging her head back against the table. "Shh, shh, it's okay."

She strokes the undead girl's hair. "You're home."

Cancer holds Capricorn's head, murmuring more soothing words and calming her. Capricorn stops screaming; her arms stop flailing and she lies still.

Everyone releases her and steps back. Guided by Cancer's hands on her back, she struggles to sit up. Leo surges forward and wraps shaking arms around her. Capricorn grips Leo's shoulder. "What happened? I shouldn't . . . I . . . Did I die?"

Leo lets her go and asks, "What do you remember?"

Capricorn's face goes slack and her lower lip quivers. "I . . . I don't know. . . . Everything is so fuzzy." She presses the heel of her hand against her forehead like it might unlock some memory.

Niobe slides closer to her. "I know it's difficult," she says, her hand on Capricorn's knee. "But is there anything you can tell us about the Dark Witches? What are their numbers? What are they planning?"

Capricorn shakes her head. "I don't know how many there were. More than just the Dark Twelve, though." She squints at Niobe and presses her hand harder into her skull. I can't watch her, the suffering and pain etched on every inch of her face. I look away and find Ophelia tucked into Gemini's side with their arm wrapped around her. Cancer sways beside them. She catches herself on the wall before she can lose her balance, but from the green tint of her face I don't think it'll be long before the contents of her lunch end up on the greenhouse floor. "They want our power. They're draining us. . . ." Capricorn gasps like she's remembered something. "She gave me a message, though. For you."

Her eyes land on me and cold shivers lick up my spine. "She wants her daughters back." My breath hitches in my throat. She knows.

She knows our powers have Awoken; she knows we're here.

"Aries was recognized at the asylum, and now Lavinia wants Aries and Pisces to complete her coven," Capricorn continues. "She found another Libra, they're the only two she still needs. She has a ship waiting just beyond the wards and she has a way onto the island. If they don't surrender themselves within the hour, Scorpio is going to wash up next and the Dark Witches are going to attack."

Everyone looks to Niobe, who shakes her head firmly. "No, there's no way for Lavinia or any Dark Witch to get to this Manor. The wards are secure." She turns sharp eyes to Capricorn. "What's their plan to get onto the island?"

Capricorn shakes her head. "I . . . I don't know."

My attention snags on Libra. She's gone too pale. Her hands are balled into fists and her chest rises and falls too quickly. She's barely holding the connection.

"Think, Capricorn," says Niobe. "What is the exact location of their ship? Which side of the island are they on?"

"I don't know anything, I swear," she cries.

Sweat drips from Libra's brow and her eyes are glassy. She sways on her feet. Cancer grips her shoulder. "Niobe, we have to stop," says Cancer.

"Not yet," says Niobe without turning her attention from Capricorn. "Do they have a way to get past the wards?"

"This is too much for her," says Cancer. She shakes Libra's shoulders like she's trying to make her stop her magic, but Libra looks to Niobe.

Niobe ignores her. "How many Dark Witches are on their ship? Is Lavinia among them?"

"I don't know, I don't know!" Capricorn screams. She presses her hands to her face like she can hide behind them. She falls back onto the table and her body starts to convulse.

Libra lets out a small whimper that cracks something in my chest.

"Niobe," Cancer snaps. "Let her go!"

Horror passes over Niobe's face as she finally turns from Capricorn and looks at Libra, shaking and struggling to keep her feet. Her throat bobs. "Sever the connection, Libra."

"Wait!" Leo flings herself over the table at Libra, but I grab her by the waist and haul her back, flailing and snapping at me like a wild animal. "I'm so sorry, Cap," she sobs. "I'm sorry I couldn't save you, but I'll get Scorpio back, I swear."

Libra stumbles into Cancer who grabs her before she can fall and wraps her in her arms. Capricorn goes motionless.

Leo rocks into me with a scream that threatens to rip me in two. All I can do is hold her, kneeling on the hard floor as she sobs into my shoulder. I fold my arms around her, trying to hold the broken pieces of her together, even though I know they've already shattered beyond repair.

"I'll do it," I say. "I'll give myself up." Maybe I can convince Lavinia to take just me and leave Ophelia out of this. She can get another Pisces, someone else. Once she sees I'm ranked third, I might be able to persuade her to take me alone. It'll get me into the sanctum. It'll get me close enough to face Lavinia and end this once and for all. No one else needs to get hurt. Leo kneels beside the table, holding Capricorn's lifeless hand and weeping into her shoulder. I can't let anyone else suffer this fate. No one else in this coven will mourn like this if I have anything to say about it.

Leo jerks her head up. "You will not."

The whole coven begins speaking at once.

"Absolutely not," says Sagittarius.

"You're not expendable," says Virgo.

"There's no need for such rashness," says Niobe. "Lavinia may know now that you're on this island, she may be waiting nearby, but she cannot get to us here. These wards have stood for centuries; no Dark Witch has ever set foot . . ."

Her face blanches, and for the first time, there's genuine fear in Niobe's eyes. "Where is Pisces?" she asks.

I whirl, searching for Ophelia, but she's no longer in the circle. Gemini turns with a surprised gasp to the empty place beside them where Ophelia stood only minutes ago. The door to the med wing is wide open, and my sister is nowhere to be found.

27

Ophelia

"BACK SO SOON, LITTLE FISH?" ASKS THE DARK PISCES.

The moment Capricorn said Lavinia wanted me and Serena or she'll kill Scorpio and attack the coven, I raced to the pond. I need answers and I need them now, so I can give myself over to the Dark Witches and see my mother. If I can just figure out what the Dark Witch meant, if one of the rituals in the book can really reverse the turning process, I can save her. I can turn her back and put an end to all of this.

"Tell me what you know," I say. She's not telling the whole truth. Before, I thought I had time to find it for myself, but now I have to do this before Serena can give herself up.

"You found the book," says the Dark Pisces, but I have no interest in playing her games. Not today.

I cross my arms over my chest. "Do you miss it?"

"Miss what?"

"Magic," I demand. "Life." She's been trapped in a mirror for over a decade. She has nothing in there, no food or water or scenery.

No one to talk to. No life.

"Of course I miss it," she says hoarsely. "I miss it every single day. I want to run in the grass and eat a delicious meal and dance and do any number of things I can't do in this nothingness."

"Then tell me what you and my mother knew. Tell me what's in that book, and I'll speak to Niobe about freeing you from this mirror. You do want to be free, don't you?"

The Dark Pisces stares at me unblinking for a long moment and hot frustration burbles in my chest until I want to scream. Finally, she says, "Swear it. Swear you'll have me freed from this mirror."

"I swear it," I say, and I mean it. If I can cure the Darkness, there's no reason to leave her trapped. She can return to her former life.

The Dark Pisces nods. "Do you want to know why Niobe is collecting the most powerful young witches she can find? She wants your power. To siphon even a few drops of power from a lesser witch, they'd quickly see a difference. But a powerful witch? A few drops stolen here and there? You'll hardly notice it."

"Like the Dark Twelve are doing. Like the Dark Gemini in the orphanage wanted to do to me and Serena." But Niobe is more powerful than any of us. She doesn't need our strength.

"She's storing it." The Dark Pisces holds her clawed hands up. "In the crystal in the atrium."

"The others said the crystal helps maintain the wards."

"That's what she wants you to think. Just as Dark Witches use the power of others to stay young and strong, Niobe uses it to keep herself from turning. It was her plan for years: Even before she was head of this coven, she and your mother were plotting a way to do such a thing. How do you think she's kept from turning for so long? The crystal isn't a ward. It's a vessel for power."

A shudder goes down my spine. Of course Niobe would have lied about that. But how does that help me? "What does that have to do with the book?"

"Niobe is a hypocrite. She didn't want your mother and me using that book, but she used its Dark magic to store energy in the crystal. You've seen it yourself now that the energy and power of zodiac witches can stall the process of turning, but enough of it in a highly concentrated dose? There's enough power in that crystal for a Dark Witch to absorb—enough to bring them back."

My head spins and I hug my arms tighter around my knees. If Niobe has all that power, she could use it to find Scorpio, or to get rid of the Dark Twelve for good. Instead, she sends us to do her bidding and leaves witches, witches she recruited and claimed she would protect, to die, all to keep herself from turning. After all, the Dark Pisces is right. Niobe is the oldest witch I know who hasn't turned.

"This isn't right," I say, jumping to my feet, righteous anger flowing through me. How many teenagers—kids, really, all of us—have died so she could save herself? "How can she do this?"

The Dark Pisces rises as well, her motions smooth and fluid like she's moving through water. "She's not who she makes herself out to be."

I take a shaking breath. All I have to do is steal the crystal, give myself up, and shatter it to release my mother from the hold the Darkness has on her. Without a leader, the Dark Witches will scatter. They'll be nothing when faced with her strength and power when she's no longer Dark. For once, Serena won't have to protect me. I can be the one to take care of her.

I rise and start toward the water, ready to swim back to shore. If I'm going to confront Niobe, I can't afford to wait any longer. I won't allow anyone else to die because she's too proud to deal with her messes herself.

"Aren't you forgetting something?" The unusual edge to the Dark Pisces's voice pulls me up short. She's too still, her face a mask of pure calm. Her lips split in a fanged grin. "You swore to free me."

My heart skips a beat. "I can't. I don't know how." I promised to get Niobe to let her out, not to do it myself.

"But you do. You only have to try."

"That's not what I agreed to," I say firmly. "I swore to have you freed, not to free you myself."

"I've helped you, little fish, and you'd leave me trapped here? We're free spirits, you and me. We're meant to swim, not be caged like Niobe's sad little birds. Now free me."

Do I owe her this? I pull at the skin around my thumbnail so hard I know it will bleed. Serena would say it's reckless, but she isn't here. The Dark Pisces has helped me, and all her claims have been true. She understands me. Why shouldn't I free her? I'll be able to help her turn back soon enough. No one deserves to spend their whole lives trapped, frozen behind glass.

"Free me," she insists, desperation in her voice. "I can't be stuck here any longer. I've helped you learn the truth about Niobe. Now it's your turn to help me get free of her bonds."

My heart thunders in my ears. I look at the Dark Pisces in the mirror, this person who has helped me so greatly since I came to this island, but her black eyes only remind me of her rotted, decaying soul. Can I let such a creature roam free?

"Please," she insists.

I squeeze my eyes shut like I might find an answer stamped on the back of my eyelids, but there's nothing.

"Ophelia?" a small, familiar voice says behind me.

No. They can't be here—how did they find this place? I turn slowly, holding my breath, and my heart stumbles to a halt when I see them.

Gemini is standing at the top of the steps.

28

Serena

I'M STILL SHAKING, BLOOD ROARING IN MY EARS. I DON'T know why I expected Lavinia wouldn't remember us or care that we're here. She's a Dark Witch. She's devoid of emotion and nostalgia, so I know she doesn't want to see us for a family reunion, a decade overdue. Somewhere, deep down, I knew she hadn't forgotten that Ophelia and I exist. Yet that would have been easier to bear.

Niobe gathers me, Leo, Cancer, and Sagittarius in the sitting room, while Virgo and Aquarius take care of Capricorn's body. Libra remains with them, too calm as she lingers near Capricorn's unmoving form. It's as if her proximity to the dead subdues all her wild energy. Gemini runs off to find Ophelia, and as much as I want to rush after her too, Niobe insists I'm needed here, gathered back around the table of maps and battle formations. She's probably just gone to be alone and clear her head, something she's been doing a lot lately.

"She'll be okay," Cancer murmurs beside me, low enough that the others can't hear.

Physically, yes, she'll be okay. I need to see her, though. I need to take her hands in mine and remind her that I'm her protector. It's been my duty since the moment we came into this world, and it's my duty still. I need to make sure she knows that I'll take care of this. I'll be the one to give myself over to Lavinia. I'll end this.

There's no reason for her to be afraid.

I loose a long breath and nod, rubbing at my sternum where some invisible weight presses on my chest.

"We don't have time to lose, girls," says Niobe.

Leo braces her hands on the table, hair cascading down on one side of her tearstained face. Sagittarius and I dragged her out of Virgo's med wing, away from Capricorn's body, as she wept. The lioness, broken, all her fire extinguished.

Capricorn is yet another person Leo has lost, another death to add to the roster of people she holds herself accountable for. No matter that there was nothing she could have done. Her eyes are red rimmed and puffy, but her jaw is set firmly. She's a commander, falling back into her role. Ready to lead. Ready to assume responsibility again, and again, and again.

"What's the plan?" she says in a gravelly voice.

Niobe, standing tall at the head of the table, slides her gaze to me. "If she wants Aries, we give her Aries."

I swallow hard and nod. Lavinia is my mother—this is my fight. Not theirs.

"No," says Sagittarius. "Aries is one of us. We don't give our sisters up to Dark Witches, no matter who they are." She gives me a short nod and my heart swells. I've grown so accustomed to only having Ophelia. I never thought I'd have friends like these, sisters ready to fight for me. I don't deserve them.

"Lavinia is wickedly smart, but she's arrogant," says Niobe. "If we send Aries in first, she'll think we're coming to the table. She'll think she's got the upper hand. She won't be looking for any further threats, and that's when we strike."

"We can't take on all of them at once," says Cancer.

"We treat their forces like a snake," says Niobe smoothly. "Cut off the head to kill the body."

She catches my eye without blinking and holds my gaze for a long moment, waiting for me to object to her threat against my mother, but I don't. Ophelia isn't here to protest with all her grand ideas of cures and happy returns to our past.

I give Niobe a sharp nod and she turns to the plans in front of her. "My birds are searching for their ship now. We'll meet them at sea and let them think Aries is giving herself up. While they're distracted here, the rest of us will infiltrate the Dark Witches' sanctum. I know Lavinia and there is no way she's on that ship, but I'm betting she sent the best of her Dark Twelve, which means their forces will be split. She won't be expecting our arrival and with her most trusted sentinels out of reach, we'll have a better chance at eliminating her."

When I understand the plan, I retreat from the table and leave Leo and Sagittarius to discuss the details of their attack. Cancer sinks onto the cushions beside me. "How're you holding up?" she asks.

"I'm fine," I mumble. Her eyebrows lift, but she simply leans her elbows on her knees, waiting. "Why was it easier to mourn her death than to learn she's alive?" I finally ask. "Why couldn't she stop using her powers? Were Ophelia and I not enough for her? What does she want with us now?" The questions pour out of me and I ball my hands into fists, stuffing them into my lap to stop them from shaking. "I wish I could turn it off and stop the emotions altogether." I wince as the words leave my mouth. Shutting off all my emotions would make me no better than a Dark Witch.

"Emotions aren't simple," says Cancer. "They get wrapped up in each other, the pain and fear and grief, until they're hard to separate. But she's your mother; you're allowed to feel however you feel."

"She's not my mother anymore," I snap. Cancer nods slowly. "What?" I groan.

"I know you think your mother left you, but she didn't." I protest, but Cancer holds up a hand. "Your mother, your *actual* mother, not the Dark Witch, didn't choose to leave you. She gave everything she had to protect you. She became something she never wanted to be because of how much she loved you."

"So I'm supposed to just forgive her?"

"No. You don't have to forgive her, but if you take all this anger with you into the Dark Witches' sanctum, you run a real risk of not coming out again. I think you need to look within yourself and realize that your mother did not throw you away."

She pauses, looking at Niobe for a long moment with narrowed eyes. "There's something you should know, Serena, about that night at the orphanage," she whispers, but Niobe's gaze snaps to her and she falls silent.

"What is it?" I ask.

She shakes her head quickly and Niobe turns away again. "Never mind, it's nothing. I just want you to understand, *really* understand, that you, Serena, are not inherently leavable. Look around," she instructs, and I do. I take in Niobe, poring over the plans. I take in Sagittarius and Leo with their heads bent, talking through fight moves. And then I look at Cancer, who could have easily been doing anything else to prepare herself, and yet is here at my side. She squeezes my knee. "We're not leaving you behind, do you hear me?"

I swallow hard against the lump in my throat. "I hear you."

29

Ophelia

"OPHELIA, WHAT'S GOING ON HERE?" GEMINI'S VOICE IS TOO low and calm, like all their charm has been washed away. They scratch their head, brows knit together and lips parted. They take one step toward me, water spiraling out of their hair and dripping from their clothes.

"How did you get here?" I ask. I hate the way my voice trembles.

"When I saw you headed out here alone, I thought you might need help, but this . . ." They tug their fingers through their curls and step closer to the mirror. The Dark Witch says nothing. She clasps her taloned hands behind her back and gives Gemini a closed-lipped smirk. "What the hell is this?"

"Niobe put her here a long time ago," I say.

"That doesn't explain why you're talking to her. Is this what everything is about? Feeling like Niobe is doing something wrong, snooping in her office, the book?"

"Niobe *is* doing something wrong. She's siphoning our power, like the Dark Witches. She could use all that power to turn Dark

Witches back, but she's keeping it all for herself."

Gemini gestures wildly to the Dark Witch. "She's lying to you!"

"I trust her—"

"And I trusted *you*," says Gemini, raised voice ringing in the small space. "But now I see that I shouldn't have. The other times you came here, I thought you just liked the pond. It's why I jumped in the water today—I thought it would calm you—but if I'd known you were talking to this—this *thing* all this time, I—"

"The other times?" My blood runs cold. "If this is the first time you've followed me here, how do you know I've been here before?"

Gemini stiffens and their face goes slack. "Ophelia . . ."

I stagger a step back. Gemini wouldn't be spying on me; they're my friend. I thought they were *more* than my friend, but all the times I ran into them in the hallway or in the library, on the cliff yesterday, even right now, I thought it was because they were trying to be kind to me. I thought they were trying to make me feel at home and include me as a member of this coven.

"Have you been following me?"

"I saw you go for a swim a few times. I just . . . I—"

"Answer the question," I snarl.

"Yes," Gemini admits. "I've been keeping an eye on you since you got here. Niobe asked me to."

My hand flies to my chest and presses down, trying to slow my cracking heart as it punches against my ribs. "I thought you were my friend."

"I *am* your friend, Ophelia." They step toward me, extending a hand, but I push it aside.

"No! If the only reason you were ever spending time with me

was so you could report everything I was doing to Niobe, you're a spy, not a friend."

"I'm not a spy. I was following orders."

"Not a spy?" I sputter. "What did you tell her? Did you report everything I've been doing, everything *we've* been doing?"

"Yes," Gemini breathes.

"That's spying, Reyes!"

"You don't get to call me that right now," they say sharply, and I flinch. Gemini winces, tugging their fingers through their hair. "I'm sorry, I really am, but just because this started as an assignment from Niobe doesn't mean it didn't become something else. I didn't keep spending time with you because Niobe told me to. I spent time with you because I wanted to. You're smart and kind and caring, and I kept seeking you out because I want to be with you."

"Why did you follow me out here today? As my friend or to 'keep an eye on me'?"

"Because you were upset! Because I was worried about you. Because I didn't want you to face everything alone." Their shining eyes meet mine. "Because I love you."

The words threaten to crack my heart. I must have misheard them. I can't remember anyone but Serena ever saying those words to me. As much as I want them to be true, how can I trust them now?

"Please, Ophelia, I *need* you to believe me. Please, let's go back to the Manor and I can explain everything, I swear."

They try to take my hands but I tear away from them like their skin burns to the touch. "There's nothing to explain. You lied to me—you've been lying since the moment I met you!"

"All right, then, if you won't let me explain, how about you explain how you were about to let that Dark Witch out?"

I flinch. "I wasn't."

Gemini glares at me, the hard expression out of place on their soft features. "Yes, you were. I heard you talking with her."

"And what would be so wrong with that?"

"She's a Dark Witch. We can't have a Dark Witch loose on this island—she'll destroy all of us."

"She wouldn't do that." I look to the Dark Pisces for confirmation, but she's gone stock-still.

Gemini's bark of indignant laughter echoes across the stones. "You have no idea what she will or won't do. She doesn't feel emotions. She's a monster. We have to get rid of her."

"Niobe knows she's here. If she wanted to get rid of her, she could have done it years ago. Why is your leader keeping a Dark Witch on this island? She's the second-highest-ranked witch in the world. If she's devoted to taking out the Dark Witches, why isn't she out there hunting them herself?"

"I don't care about Niobe. This witch can't be here. I'm putting an end to this." Gemini seizes the head of a marble bust and pulls their arm back.

"Don't!" I scream, reaching for their arm, but my magic takes hold of their blood before my hands can. Gemini's limbs lock, the bust still clenched in their upraised fist. Their blood pounds as the water in it stops answering them and instead responds to me and only me.

My chest heaves and I know I should feel guilty for taking control from them, but they've been lying to me. They've taken control away from me since the moment I got here.

Gemini's body is frozen but their face crumples in a mask of shock. Their eyes go wide in terror, and something in me answers that. For once, I'm not the weak one, the one stripped of agency and power.

Buzzing fills my ears until I can't hear around the blood rushing and the burning, pulsing desire to squeeze the invisible fist clutching Gemini's blood until it yields to me entirely. Until it can't flow any longer.

"That's it," the Dark Pisces drawls from behind me.

"Shut up," I growl.

"This is what you want to give yourself over to the Dark Witches for? This coven doesn't care about you. If they did, they would have rescued you years ago. They would have told you the truth about the crystal."

"Don't listen to her," says Gemini.

"They've been manipulating you, little fish. Is there anyone in this Manor who hasn't lied to you from the second you arrived? You know how to stop the lies, don't you? You stop them at the source."

"The source," I echo. I can feel Gemini's blood pulsing faster now. It would be so easy to stop it. So, so easy to show them that I'm stronger than they think. I'm not a helpless little girl, needing everyone to conceal the truth from me. I don't need anyone to spy on me or keep an eye on me. I'm the fourth-most-powerful witch in the world. Isn't it time I proved it?

"She's manipulating you," says Gemini.

"Shut up!" I say. "Stop trying to convince me. Everyone is manipulating me!" Blood drips down my palms now from the half-moon cuts made by my nails. I want to clamp my hands over my ears and press and press until I can't hear anything anymore. The Dark Pisces is right: All anyone has done is feed me falsehoods. Niobe and the others talk about sisterhood, but if this is what sisterhood is, I don't want it. For a moment, I can almost feel Gemini's lips pressed to mine on that beach, their body settled on top of mine in the sand. Why couldn't I see that they never cared about me at all? It was all an act. Power surges through me, threatening to spill out and drown Gemini and the Dark Pisces. To devour this entire island.

"So stop it," the Dark Pisces says. "End the lies. End the manipulation. End *them*."

I yank water from the air and freeze it into a dozen razor-sharp daggers of ice. They hang poised in the air around me. My hands pull back and I meet Gemini's warm eyes, wide with fear. They're afraid of *me*. This person I trusted—this person I loved.

"Ophelia, *please*." Gemini's voice cracks.

My hands are already moving. I shriek, trying to pull the ice daggers back, but all I can do is turn. Icicles shoot in a wave, not for Gemini, but for the Dark Pisces. They crash into the mirror and it shatters. Shards of glass splinter apart and slide from the frame and onto the ground.

The Dark Pisces is gone.

I drop my control over Gemini's blood and struggle to catch my breath. It's like I've been doused in a bucket of ice water. I let the Dark Pisces worm her way into my head with her slimy words and her encouragement of Dark magic. Gemini's gaze is bruised; their lips part in disbelief. The bust clatters out of their hand, now released from my grip. What have I done? My hands shake so violently I can't control them any longer.

"Gemini," I breathe. "I'm so sorry, I—"

"Stay away from me." Their voice breaks. Hands upraised, they stumble back. "It's over. She's gone. Keep your Dark magic if you want, and your secrets, and your conspiracies—but don't expect to keep them with me."

"Gemini, please." *Don't leave me,* I want to beg. *Tell me it was all a lie, that you weren't playing me like a fool, that you don't hate me,* but there's not a spark of affection in those honey eyes. No trace of anything but hurt and betrayal.

Gemini stalks down the stairs and into the water. As they go, they shift into a barrel-chested man, with more room in their lungs for air, no doubt. They don't give me so much as a glance back as they plunge into the waves and disappear.

I sink to the ground among the bits of destroyed mirror. For a moment, I swear I see the Dark Pisces's reflection in a sliver of glass, but it's gone as soon as I look twice. A crushing weight presses on my heart, threatening to bury me beneath the stones below me. I should have listened to Serena the day we arrived and run as far away as I could. Before I could get hurt. Before my heart could cleave into a thousand pieces. I don't care that blood pricks on my skin where my knees sink into bits of broken glass. I sob, wrapping my arms around myself, desperately trying to hold tight to whatever scrap of me is left, when a clear voice says from above me, "Thank you for keeping your word, little fish."

30

Serena

OPHELIA STREAKS INTO THE SITTING ROOM WITH DRIPPING-wet hair, panting. Her eyes are wide and wild, frantically searching until they land on me. I leap up from the couch, scanning her to see if she's been harmed, but she seems unhurt. She presses a palm to her heaving chest to slow her breath as I lurch toward her, Cancer on my heels.

"I messed up," she sobs before I can ask what's wrong, and launches into a rambling explanation of everything—Dark Witches and spell books and ponds. Why didn't she tell me any of this? I don't have time to feel betrayed now, though, as the others gather around her, weapons drawn.

There's an intruder on this island.

"I'm so, so sorry, Serena. I just wanted to get rid of her. I didn't know breaking the mirror would let her out, but I don't—I don't—" She breathes in and out too quickly, unable to catch her breath.

I squeeze her shoulders. "Don't panic," I say, as much to myself as to her. "It's okay. We're going to handle this." All thoughts of giving myself up to Lavinia and setting out for the Dark Witches' sanctum leave my mind. We have to find the Dark Pisces, before she can harm anyone.

Niobe sweeps across the room toward us. "You released her?" she asks in a too-steady voice. Her face is grave but unafraid.

"Niobe." Ophelia shrinks into my side as her shoulders cave in. "I . . ."

"Where has she gone?"

Ophelia rubs at her temples. "I don't know, it all happened so fast. She was there one second and gone the next. I'm sorry, I—"

Niobe wastes no time with apologies, though; instead she takes charge. Her shoulders straighten and her mouth presses into a firm line. With one resounding clap of her hands, the other witches snap to attention. "There's been a change of plans. Gather the rest of the coven. Find her."

Leo is already in motion. She lurches out the door and down the hall in one direction, motioning to Sagittarius and Cancer to take the other direction. Their shouts ring through the Manor.

"You two, with me," Niobe orders, and strides out of the room. I hurry after her down the hall and to the front staircase, Ophelia rushing behind us.

"Where will she go?" I huff as I struggle to keep up with Niobe's long, steady steps.

"The atrium," says Niobe without looking at me.

Crash.

Niobe curses and bursts into a run, streaking down the hall faster than I knew she could move. She skids to a halt at the top of the stairs and I pull up short. A choked sound tumbles from my lips when I behold the atrium below.

A Dark Witch wearing a uniform nearly identical to ours stands at the bottom of the steps with her arms upraised toward the ceiling. The citrine ward crystal that once hung suspended above is in a thousand shattered pieces on the dark marble floor. Irreparably broken.

Silence falls over the Manor, heavy and thick. The wards are broken.

I thought I would be able to feel the wards like a phantom film coating the island, but there's no difference in the air now that they're gone and there's nothing keeping any other Dark Witches from waltzing right in and taking what they want.

"She lied," Ophelia whispers in a small, broken voice.

"You shouldn't be here," Niobe says to the Dark Pisces, too evenly, like she's reining her power in. She descends the stairs slowly, attention trained on the Dark Witch.

The Dark Pisces grins and nods to Ophelia, half concealed behind me. Ophelia's skin is tinged with green, her lips pressed so thin they're white. "When you locked me away, Niobe, you forgot one important thing. I had nothing in there but time—time to plan exactly what I wanted to do to you when I escaped."

Before she has time to elaborate, however, Niobe flicks her hand and hundreds of thorns from the roses outside the open windows fly toward the Dark Pisces. She blocks most of them with a shield of ice. Though a handful of thorns graze her skin, blood sliding down her cheek like a deadly tear, she smiles with sharp teeth. She levitates an orb of water over one hand with a contented sigh. "I'd forgotten how good that feels," the Dark Pisces drawls.

With a flick of her wrist, the orb shoots toward Niobe. It presses against her mouth, forcing water down her throat. Ophelia gasps and reaches for Niobe, trying to use her own power to pull the water away as Niobe claws at her face. Despite choking and sputtering, Niobe extends a hand toward the Dark Pisces and the trees outside bend their branches. Before they can touch her, though, the Dark Pisces wraps herself in a cloak of water, folding herself away from view until the water ripples and forms a wall. It nearly obscures her from sight, though I can make out her figure spearing toward the back door of the atrium, headed out onto the lawn. The energy she absorbed from the crystal has made her far faster than any person should move. I fling electricity at the water and steam hisses through the air, blocking my vision further, but the wall doesn't give way.

"You'll regret the day you locked me up, Niobe." The Dark Witch's voice grows more distant by the second. Then the wall of water drops, the bubble around Niobe's mouth along with it, and the Dark Pisces is gone, plunging into the forest beyond the Manor.

Niobe gasps for breath, hands on her throat. She brushes Ophelia aside with a murmured assurance. When her jagged breaths steady, her jaw tightens and she surveys us. Small footsteps patter into the atrium and Libra pounds into the foyer with Aquarius and Virgo on her heels, both armed and stony faced. Libra's small hand slides into mine. "Don't be scared, big sis. We can fight." I squeeze her hand, wishing I could somehow infuse all her fire and bravery into my own body.

Leo and the others return and gather in a circle around the shattered remnants of the crystal.

"If the Dark Witches really are outside the wards, they'll sense the wards are down. They will come for us," Niobe says. "Prepare yourselves to defend this house and each other. We'll split up—Pisces, Libra, Virgo, and Aquarius, you're with me. We can't have the Dark Pisces loose on this island. The rest of you, hold your positions here."

I nod, though my head spins. Libra's hand slides out of mine and for a moment, I feel like the world is about to tip out from beneath my feet. There are Dark Witches coming here, to this island. This place that's supposed to be impenetrable. Ophelia meets my gaze as the others follow after Niobe out the back door. She opens her mouth like she means to say something, but Niobe orders, "Now, Pisces!"

Ophelia winces but follows Niobe out the back door and into the forest. The moment she's gone, cold washes over me. This isn't a training exercise. There are no more plans or schemes. We were supposed to go into their territory on our own terms, but now that's all gone out the window. Every person in this Manor, every person I care about, is at risk. All because my sister didn't trust me enough to come to me. What have I done to lose that trust?

"Outside, let's go," Leo says. Her voice is steady as she takes over for Niobe and leads us outside and into the meadow beyond the front doors. She scans the gray horizon like she can see the Dark Witches approaching. "This is our home. No Dark Witch has ever breached this island, but we are not defenseless. We protect this place, and we protect each other, is that clear?" We all nod. "Protect Aries and Pisces. They're the last two remaining witches she needs to complete the Dark Twelve and she cannot be allowed to take them."

Leo waits with one foot in front of the other, daggers out and poised at her sides. Gemini and Sagittarius strategize with their heads bent together, Sagittarius bouncing on the balls of her feet.

Silently, Cancer comes to my side. I ready my sparks. I can't see or hear anything but my own too-shallow breathing and the thumping of my heart. "You can face this, Serena," Cancer says. "We're with you."

Sweat beads on my palms. It's deathly quiet and my skin tingles with anticipation.

Golden sparks burst in the lush meadow before us.

A portal opens and six Dark Witches step out: Aquarius, Cancer, Taurus, Leo, Capricorn, and Sagittarius. I expect them to make demands like they did at the asylum, and I step forward to offer myself to them.

Instead, they burst into motion.

A metal throwing star whips from the Dark Leo's hand before she moves. I'm barely able to dodge it as we all scatter. The Dark Leo chases me, another sharp star whizzing around her head. It moves too fast, like she's trying to distract me by watching it instead of her. I race across the grass, ducking and dodging as metal zips around me. My force field of electricity keeps the throwing stars from getting too close.

I wheel around to face her and bend showers of sparks to my will until nothing exists but me and the burning current of pure power flowing around me. The lightning acts as my hands, grabbing anything and everything the Dark Leo hurls at me and flinging it away. I lash out at her with a bolt, cracking it into her shoulder. She yelps and goes flying across the grass, struggling to rise.

There's nothing but sweat and blood and shouting as people whirl and weave through the fray. I lash lightning in every direction, hitting every Dark Witch I can possibly strike. Gemini has made themself massive, towering like a giant more than double the height of an ordinary person. They swipe at the Dark Taurus, despite being slowed by the piles of rocks the Dark Taurus builds around their feet to keep Gemini from being able to lift their massive legs.

On one side of the meadow, Cancer faces her Dark counterpart. They stand opposite each other, unmoving, a mess of contorted faces and rapidly changing expressions. On the other, Sagittarius and her counterpart are locked in a nimble teleportation match. One winks out of sight and reappears to strike the other with a fist, only to swing and miss. Round and round they go, jumping away and back, faster than I can parse.

Castor snarls and snaps, swiping with his claws and teeth at the Dark Capricorn, who fights him in the form of a tiger.

Leo shouts and grunts, trying to free herself from a thick jungle of weeds. It surrounds her like a cage and crawls inward, grabbing onto her legs as she squirms and struggles. On the outside of it, the Dark Aquarius stands watching. Motionless.

It's an illusion, I realize, one of the Dark Aquarius's tricks. I send a lightning strike barreling toward Leo. It ripples into the illusion and the image breaks apart. Leo blinks gratefully at me before starting in on the Dark Aquarius with her knives drawn. She sends one whizzing for the Dark Aquarius, but shouts, "Aries, behind you!" as she levitates another high into the air.

My body moves instinctively and I send a burst of lightning before I have time to turn to face whatever is behind me. The bolt ricochets off the blade of Leo's knife and shoots backward. I whirl around in time to see the deflected lightning bolt strike the Dark Leo in the chest and blast her backward. The force of the blow lifts her feet from the ground and she flips end over end before collapsing in the grass.

"Go help Gem!" Leo shouts. "I've got this!"

Gemini fights at the cliffside, backing the Dark Taurus up to the edge of the cliffs. A flock of black birds swirls around them at the Dark Taurus's command, careening out of the forest in a cloud of wings and shrieks. They dive-bomb Gemini in a squawking horde, clawing at their face. Gemini swipes at the birds with long talons that have grown out of their knuckles.

"Gem, get down!" I shout as I race across the field. Gemini throws themself to the ground as I lash a lightning bolt that goes whizzing over their head. The twisting mass of birds cleaves in two, breaking formation as my lightning bursts through their ranks. They scatter back to the cover of the forest and the Dark Taurus twists, managing to avoid the strike, but falls from the edge of the cliff and into the water below.

I breathe a sigh of relief. One down, at least until she can get herself back up the hill. I run to Gemini and pull them to their feet. Their face is flecked with shallow cuts from beaks and claws. "Thanks," they pant.

My relief is quelled too quickly, though, as the hair on the back of my neck prickles.

I whirl, sparks ready, but it's not a Dark Witch behind me. It's Ophelia, weaving water into intricate shapes at her fingertips and glaring at me. Where are Niobe and the others?

"What's wrong?" I start toward her, but a whip of water streaks for me and goes wide.

"What are you doing?"

Her answer is a spear of ice, the length of my arm, hurtling toward me. The shrill cry that bursts from her lips is so unlike any sound I've heard from her that I nearly don't respond in time. My lightning bolt meets her spear in midair and it evaporates in a burst of steam.

"Ophelia, stop!" Why is she fighting me? I don't have time for this, not when Leo is fighting for her life and Cancer is trapped between her counterpart and the Dark Sagittarius

Still, Ophelia comes for me and my head spins. She moves faster than I've ever seen her, limbs jerky and erratic as they summon wave after wave of water. I form a shield of electricity around myself. Steam fills the air, obscuring her from my view.

"No wonder Mom left us!" Ophelia shouts. "Why would she want a mess like you?"

She raises her arms again and a wave of water as tall as the nearby trees barrels toward me. I throw myself sideways and a burst of lightning streaks from me. It slams into the center of Ophelia's chest.

Her eyes go wide, panicked, and suddenly I can't breathe. *No, no, no.* What have I done? I was only trying to make her stop. "Ophelia!" I scream. I lunge for her as she falls, but as my hands go out to grab her, she slips through my fingers.

Her body disappears like smoke.

I reach hopelessly for empty air where she fell. The Dark Aquarius stands a few feet away, smirking at me. "Not so much better than us, are you?" she asks.

I struggle to catch my breath. It was all an illusion. Ophelia didn't really say all those things. I didn't really try to kill her. She's not even here.

I grab hold of the current of my power and the air around me erupts with sparks. They surround me, each one blazing like a supernova as they spray into the Dark Aquarius. The force knocks her off her feet and flings her backward into the Manor's stone wall. She whimpers in pain and falls to the earth without getting back up.

I should check to see if she's still alive, but I have to help the others. I spent too much time stuck inside the illusion. Gemini and Sagittarius hold off the Dark Taurus, who is soaking wet after being knocked from the cliff and retrieved by the Dark Sagittarius, while Leo and the Dark Leo are a whirlwind of steel.

Cancer, however, is trapped between the Dark Cancer and the Dark Sagittarius, doing her best with her fists and a single dagger. Her chest heaves like she's exhausted most of her magic, and though the Dark Cancer moves like she's walking through molasses, the Dark Sagittarius blinks in and out of view. She appears and disappears on one side of Cancer, then the other, boxing her in so quickly that Cancer can't move her arms, much less land a blow.

I sprint for her, but the Dark Sagittarius appears in front of me. A portal opens a step ahead of me and I nearly fall onto the deck of the Dark Witches' ship when someone slams into me and knocks me to the grass.

Cancer.

I roll over and blast the Dark Cancer and Dark Sagittarius back with lightning and throw up a barrier of electricity between us.

"Thanks," I pant, clutching Cancer's hand as she helps me to my feet.

Her chest heaves and her shoulders sag, but a weary smile blooms across her face. "Of course, I—"

The whistle of steel cuts the air.

Cancer's eyes go wide. Her mouth gapes open, but no sound escapes. Slowly, her shocked expression flickers from confusion to pain to understanding. Her gaze finds mine and holds. I reach for her, but she staggers back.

Then I see it. The hilt of a dagger buried between her shoulder blades. A perfect shot, clean through her heart.

Dark Leo's work.

"No!" Leo's scream rips through the battlefield behind me as Cancer falls. It happens too slowly: Her short hair flies behind her, her arms grasp at thin air.

No. No, this can't be happening. I should have seen the Dark Leo's attack—I should have stopped it.

I catch her as she collapses, her body limp in my arms, and lower her to the grass. Blood, far too much blood, seeps through my shirt, staining my hands crimson. "Cancer, please, stay with me," I whisper into her hair. We have to get Virgo. She can fix this.

Cancer's magic surges. It courses through me, pressing into my chest in a flood of warmth, of love, of everything left unsaid. It blankets the battlefield and the fighting stops. Comforting silence falls over the island.

There is no blaze of glory, no grand display of skill. Only a final, impossible act of love, emotion strong enough to rewrite fear into peace, even as death takes her.

And then she's gone.

31

Ophelia

THE FOREST IS TOO QUIET. ALL THE TWITTERING BIRDS, THE humming cicadas, the chattering squirrels have fallen silent, like they can sense the predator in their midst. A predator I let out of her cage to hunt everyone I care about.

I creep through the woods, still bright with shafts of evening sun filtering through the branches overhead. The Dark Pisces could hide in here for ages without being found. Niobe's magic helps us blend into the forest. She softens the earth to muffle our steps and brushes aside twigs and leaves that might rustle underfoot. She walks with a thick wooden staff, ready to use as a weapon, if the need arises. Libra keeps to my side with her hand in mine, not because she needs my reassurance, but because if I let go, I'm certain she'll bound off into the trees and give away our position.

"Niobe," I say, but she presses one finger to her lips in warning.

I just need to talk to her and explain that this was all a big mistake. I didn't mean to let the Dark Pisces out and I certainly don't mean for anyone to get hurt.

Niobe gestures to Virgo and Aquarius, walking behind us, each with a dagger drawn. "Eyes out," she says.

We make our way deeper and deeper into the forest as we scan the trees for the Dark Pisces. My breathing is shallow and my heart thunders. I grip Libra's hand tighter, afraid it'll slip from my sweaty grasp.

She spent more than a decade trapped in nothing but the dark emptiness of that mirror. What does that do to a person? Would she even want the cure I've been trying to find? She lied about the crystal, I know that now. It was never anything but a ward.

"Little fish," a voice croons through the trees, and all of us straighten, peer through the foliage, alert. "Come out, come out, and play with me."

I slow my steps, searching for her voice, but I can't tell which direction it's coming from.

"She's toying with us," says Niobe in a cool, even tone. "Don't let her frighten you."

If only it were that easy. If only I were as brave as Serena. I should have told her about the Dark Pisces the moment I'd learned of her. She would have known what to do. She never would have let things get so out of hand.

"Who's the frightened one?" the Dark Pisces says sweetly. She's definitely behind us now as we move into the small graveyard, picking our way through the headstones. "I'd say it was you, Niobe, frightened enough of a little Dark Witch to lock me up in a mirror with no one to play with."

"I do not have to explain my actions to you," Niobe says.

Virgo signs something to Aquarius, who creeps off to flank us on one side while Virgo takes the other. The trees are more open here, among the gravestones. We're more exposed. I scan the tree line, searching for white hair, for silver talons.

"Why don't you explain your actions to your young charges, then?" The Dark Pisces's voice shifts to the left now. "Explain to them how you would abandon them, lock them away if they turned."

"That was a long time ago," says Niobe. She flicks her fingers, a signal to Aquarius, and I'm no longer in the forest. I'm in my bedroom. It's messy: The bed is unmade and clothes I've never seen before are strewn across the floor.

Three girls lounge across the bed in their uniforms, resting back in the mountain of pillows with their legs tangled up in one another's. The girl with long braids and ebony skin must be Niobe, and beside her, Lavinia. In the middle is the girl with curly onyx hair and pale skin from Niobe's photos. The Dark Pisces. They're all smiling, leaning on each other. A half-eaten box of chocolates rests between them.

A reminder to the Dark Pisces of who she used to be.

Suddenly, a tidal wave crashes into us. The water barrels into me and knocks me off my feet, ripping Libra's hand out of my own. Aquarius's illusion is washed away and the Dark Pisces emerges from the trees and towers over us. Frigid water invades my nose, my mouth, my throat, and shoves me onto my back. I sputter and cough, trying to get fresh air into my lungs, vaguely aware of the others on the ground nearby.

Niobe sweeps her staff out and knocks the Dark Pisces's feet out from beneath her. When she hits the ground, the water stops forcing itself into my throat. I choke up the last of it, spitting it onto the ground. The Dark Pisces is down for only a moment, though. Water shoots for Niobe and wrenches the staff out of her hands. Niobe pulls herself to her knees. She digs her hands into the earth and the ground beneath the Dark Pisces crumbles, sending her falling into a hole that nearly devours her. With an enraged shriek, she fills it with water and buoys herself back up to the surface. Heat kisses my skin and a surge of boiling water pounds into Niobe. She shrieks at its scalding touch and it washes her backward, out of the graveyard and into the trees.

I climb to my feet and send streams of my water to meet hers, icy cold to match her boiling hot. Steam pours through the trees, clouding my vision, but I shoot spears of ice toward the Dark Pisces.

The distraction is enough that the Dark Pisces stops her onslaught of the others, focusing her full attention on me. I fling one of my ice spears. It pierces her shoulder, and Virgo uses the Dark Pisces's shocked pause to leap at her with fists and dagger. Virgo manages to get one swipe across the Dark Pisces's upper arm, where she's already been injured by my ice, before she's batted away easily by a blast of water. She crashes into a tree and slides down to the earth with a soft moan.

Aquarius hurtles for the Dark Pisces and two massive mountain lions race alongside her. The Dark Pisces doesn't balk at the illusion, though. She bends a whip of water upward and lashes it around a jagged tree branch. With a sharp tug, she yanks it down and sends it careening into Aquarius's stomach.

The force of the blow knocks Aquarius off her feet and she tumbles through the air. She lands too hard, her leg hitting a gravestone at a painful angle.

A snap reverberates through the trees.

Aquarius tries to rise, but her leg crumples beneath her and she hits the ground. Bone protrudes from the wound where her pants are torn and bloody. She opens her mouth but no sound comes out.

"No!" Libra screams. She raises her arms and the ground rumbles. Dirt shifts across the small graveyard, and one by one, hands claw up out of the soil and reach toward the sky.

I fight against the burst of nausea at the sight of the dozen corpses. They climb out of their own graves and drag their bodies out onto the grass. Most are so old that the flesh has rotted from their bodies, leaving nothing but bare bones that clink and rattle with movement. Niobe, drenched and standing at the edge of the graveyard, stops. She stares at one of the corpses like she's seen a ghost.

Capricorn.

The girl climbs out of her grave, freshly dug this afternoon, looking for all the world like she could be alive and fighting alongside us. Virgo's skin is tinged with green and she sways like she might be sick, but she rushes to Aquarius. Her hands work quickly, knitting flesh and bone back together where blood pours out of the wound.

Niobe blinks and swallows hard, before turning back to the Dark Pisces.

Libra waves her arms and the dead witches march forward in sequence. The Dark Pisces's eyes go wide. She shoots water at them, but there's no choking the air from the dead when she tries to force water down their throats. They surround her on all sides until she's backed into a tree. Their hands reach for her, but Niobe says to Libra, "Don't let them kill her yet."

The tree groans and shakes, and its branches wrap around the Dark Pisces's torso, holding her captive against the trunk.

It's not Niobe the Dark Pisces glares at, though. It's me. "I knew you were nothing but your master's lapdog in the end."

"Better a lapdog than a liar," I say. "You tricked me."

Shame washes over me, hot and pressing. Gemini was right: I never should have trusted the Dark Pisces. I never should have gone into that pond in the first place. I've put this whole island at risk, all to satisfy my own curiosity. Libra approaches my side and wraps her arms around my waist. I rest a hand on her shoulder and squeeze once.

The Dark Pisces's sharp gaze slides to Niobe. "Still too soft to kill me? Why haven't you?"

"You were my friend," says Niobe. Her knuckles are white where she grips her staff.

"Yes, and we had a deal. As my friend, didn't you owe it to me to see your promise through?"

"I cared for you. I didn't wish to see your life ended."

The Dark Pisces spits into the pine needles at her feet. "So you cursed me with a fate worse than death?"

Niobe shakes her head. "I hoped someday I could free you. *Cure* you."

"And we could all be together again?" The Dark Pisces rolls her eyes. "We can hold hands and skip and eat sweets like when we were teenagers? Be realistic, Niobe. You know better than that."

"I'll not stand here and apologize for sparing my friend's life," says Niobe. She searches the Dark Pisces's face like she's hunting for any scrap of the girl from the photos I found in her office. Would I recognize one of my coven-mates if they were turned? Would I see their familiar expressions in the withered, wrinkled face of a Dark Witch? Would I recognize my own mother?

I don't have time to ponder those answers, though. A ripple of power reverberates through my chest.

"They're here," says Niobe. "We need to finish this." She waves a hand at Virgo.

"Get Aquarius and Libra back inside." Virgo doesn't wait for further instruction. She hauls Aquarius up from the ground and slides an arm beneath her shoulders. Libra helps as much as she can on the other side, and together, they help the injured illusionist hobble off into the trees.

Niobe approaches the Dark Pisces, pushing through Libra's corpses, who stand unnervingly still. "You want to hold hands and relive our glory days?" Niobe asks. "Then let's reunite you with an old friend."

Before the Dark Pisces can respond, Niobe brings her staff up and slams it into the Dark Pisces's temple.

32

Serena

ROARING FILLS MY EARS. BUZZING PRESSES IN ON ME, though the battle has gone still from Cancer's final display. The Dark Witches have stopped their attack for a moment and stand reeling, but I know it won't be for long. I need to get up and ready myself for what's next.

Before I can rise, though, Niobe emerges from the forest, Ophelia on her heels, dragging the Dark Pisces by her shirt collar. I scan Ophelia, who seems unharmed save for a cut on her arm. Niobe's eyes widen when she takes in the scene: Cancer in my arms, Gemini dripping in sweat and barely keeping their feet, Leo screaming as she explodes in grief and rage, Sagittarius with tears streaking her cheeks.

I hate to leave Cancer, but I slide her from my lap and onto the bloodstained grass. I run to my sister and pull her into a hug, mumbling a stream of apologies.

Niobe pounds a wooden staff into the ground and it ripples, knocking the Dark Witches from their feet.

"Stop!" Niobe booms.

Leo and the others retreat, breathing heavily as they stumble to join me and Ophelia. Together, we form ourselves into a small unit to wait for the next attack. Castor stands half-crouched at my side with blood dripping from his maw. His golden eyes are trained on Niobe, like he's awaiting instruction to leap into the fray once more. Leo's shoulder brushes mine, and I dare a look at her pale face. A trickle of blood dribbles from her temple, but I resist the urge to wipe it away.

Niobe leans on her staff as the Dark Witches clamber upright. Seven pairs of black eyes glare at her. "You dare come into my territory—my *home*—and attack my witches?" asks Niobe in a firm, steady voice. "No. If you have a score to settle, you settle it with me."

Niobe only makes it two steps before the Dark Leo is on her. She strikes hard and true at the Dark Leo. Plants and roots shoot up from the ground, and rocks sail through the air, pelting at the Dark Witches who all surge toward her. Her staff is a brutal weapon. It twirls and spins, knocking into witch after witch with one end and then the other. Where her staff misses, her powers don't. She's slowing too fast, though. Sweat slips down her brow and a low moan slips out of her. With the crystal broken and her power weakened, how long will she be able to last?

Roots rip up from beneath the grass. They claw out of the earth and pluck up each of the Dark Witches like small children.

Niobe corrals the Dark Witches and tosses the Dark Pisces among them. They struggle against the roots wrapped around them like vipers, squeezing until their faces are bright red with pain. Green plants and vines rise from the ground and circle the Dark Witches. They lattice together in a thick barricade.

Fencing them in.

Shutting us out.

Niobe steps into the circle. "Enough!" she declares. "Lavinia wants a prize? Then take me and leave my coven unharmed."

"Don't." I try to shout the word, but it comes out a hoarse whisper.

Niobe ignores me. Her eyes dart to Cancer, too still in the grass behind us.

"That was not the agreement," hisses the Dark Leo. "It's Aries and Pisces she wants."

Niobe lifts a brow. "You expect me to believe Lavinia would forgive you for leaving me here when I've offered myself freely to you? We both know she's wanted me as a prize for years."

The Dark Witches share hesitant glances. One by one, they nod their agreement. "Very well," says the Dark Leo. "You have our word. Come with us and we'll leave your witches be."

Niobe holds her arms out wide and drops her staff in the dirt. Her lattice of vines collapses. "Then we have a deal."

The Dark Witches grin with razor-sharp teeth, inhuman expressions that send shivers down my spine. There's a flurry of movement, witches moving faster than I can make out, and Niobe hits the ground.

Leo screams and lurches forward, daggers drawn.

"No!" Niobe shouts. She throws a hand out toward Leo, who stops short. "Stand down, all of you. That's an order, Leo!"

Leo's whole body trembles with restraint, but she obeys. Niobe can't do this. She can't give herself up, not for us. I'm vaguely aware of Ophelia at my side, of Sagittarius's fingers twitching as she calculates the risk of teleporting into the midst of the Dark Witches, of Gemini gripping Ophelia's elbow. Beside me, Castor growls but doesn't move, like Niobe's orders have forced him to stay where he is.

The Dark Sagittarius makes a portal, and I spy rugged dark cliffs through the opening. "Our mistress will be glad to see you after all these years, Niobe." Her rough laugh skates along my bones and my blood runs ice cold.

This can't happen. We need Niobe. This is my fight, my mother who needs to be dealt with. I should do it myself. I push toward Niobe, to offer myself up, starting to shout that they should take me instead. A hand clamps over my mouth and drags me backward. Sagittarius hauls me against her. "Don't even think about it."

The Dark Witches yank Niobe to her feet and I beg her silently to fight, but she lets them pull her toward the portal.

Just as she is about to be dragged through, the Dark Taurus turns with a deadly smile. Her eyes lock onto mine. With a flick of her wrist, a twisting mass of thorny vines shoots for me. They wrap around my arms, binding me. Sharp thorns burrow into my flesh. I thrash as blood prickles on my skin and Sagittarius tries to drag me back, away from the Dark Taurus's grasp. Every motion only makes the vines wrap tighter, squeezing like a python.

"You gave your word," Niobe hisses at the Dark Witches.

"You should know better than to trust the word of a Dark Witch," the Dark Leo cackles.

Leo roars, slashing at the vines with her knife, but they're too thick for her to cut through. Sagittarius holds on to my waist, and I try to dig my heels into the ground, but I'm pulled forward, toward the Dark Witches and their portal.

There's a flash of movement, and a jagged blade of ice slashes down through the branches, severing them. Blood rushes into my arms and I stumble backward, only Sagittarius's grip keeping me upright. Ophelia leaps in front of me, shielding me from the second barrage of branches the Dark Taurus sends for me.

I grab for her hand, but the Dark Taurus's branches wrap around her chest. She gasps as they squeeze the air from her lungs.

"Ophelia, no!" I cry.

Her eyes meet mine. "I'm sorry," she murmurs.

The Dark Taurus rips her away. My fingers slide through hers and she's pulled off her feet and into the midst of the Dark Witches. The Dark Pisces surges toward Ophelia and slams an elbow into her temple. Ophelia crumples, and the Dark Pisces tosses her over a shoulder.

A battle cry on my lips, I try to charge after her, but Sagittarius pulls me back again. "No! Let go!" I shout. I thrash against Sagittarius, but she's too strong.

"Lavinia can't have both of you," she says in my ear.

Arms grab at Niobe from every side until she's surrounded by a wall of inky dark robes. I catch one last glimpse of her defiant eyes, her hand reaching through the mass of bodies and toward me, as a Dark Witch wraps her arms around Niobe's chest and both Niobe and Ophelia are dragged through the portal.

"Ophelia!" I scream.

She disappears, and it's as though every ounce of air is sucked out of the world. The portal shuts. Niobe's staff lies discarded in the center of the circle.

It's over.

Ophelia is gone.

The world around me grows too silent, too heavy. Choking on

a sob, I wrench free of Sagittarius, shoving her so roughly that she stumbles. Castor yowls, a mournful cry that splits the storm-laden air and cleaves my heart in two. Now released from Niobe's orders, he runs to where she last stood. I try to gulp down normal breaths.

The stillness lasts only a moment before Leo wails.

I stand there for what feels like a lifetime, unable to bring myself to move, but the others go to Cancer and I have to be with them. I have to witness this, no matter how much it aches. My feet are like blocks of cement being dragged across the grass, like they don't really belong to me, and my vision is fuzzy. None of this is real, *please* let none of it be real. My heart pounds wildly and I pray desperately that Cancer is alive, though I know somewhere deep down it's a fool's hope. My hands are itchy and crusted with her blood.

Those hazel eyes that were once so full of warmth and love are dull and unseeing. Leo pulls Cancer into her arms and cradles her like a child, weeping into her hair.

There's nothing left to be done. She's already gone.

I am always, *always* too late.

33

Ophelia

I COME TO ENVELOPED IN WARMTH AND SOFTNESS. I'M cocooned in silken sheets with a fluffy pillow tucked beneath my head. I don't dare open my eyes. For a moment, I think I must be back in my bed at the Manor, safe in my room. But the last thing I remember is the Dark Pisces's bared teeth and the sharp crack of her elbow into my skull as she dragged me into darkness. Did they kill me? My head throbs, though. My head wouldn't hurt if I were dead, would it? I crack open my eyes.

I'm lying in a massive bed with a mountain of pillows at my back. I expected many things of the Dark Witches' sanctum, but I thought I'd be thrown in a dungeon to rot, not allowed to sleep in a beautifully furnished guest room. Violet velvet curtains cover the window, though watery daylight seeps through the crack between them.

I push back the covers and climb out of bed. Cold hardwood floors bite into the soles of my bare feet. I draw back the velvet curtains for a view of the sea. The waves are rough, crashing against jagged rocks, spreading all the way to the horizon. Gulls screech, wheeling in lazy circles over the whitecaps. It's daylight, but the sun is obscured by steely clouds. How long have I been asleep?

There's a sharp rap on the door and I whirl, a dagger of ice materializing in my fist.

The door creaks open.

"Hello, little fish," says the Dark Pisces, sliding into the room.

I fling my ice dagger at her but she brings up an ice shield to bat it away. "*You*," I hiss. She tricked me. She destroyed the wards. She allowed an army of Dark Witches onto our island, and Cancer is dead because of her.

I wince.

No, not because of her. Because of *me*.

I whip twin ribbons of water, intending to choke the air from her lungs, to make her pay for what she did to me and my coven. She meets them easily with her own until water pools on the floor.

A burst of cold water strikes my face and I blink against the frigid droplets.

"Easy there, little fish," the Dark Pisces drawls. "I'm not here to hurt you."

"Not here to hurt me? Why should I believe you when all you've done is lie to me?"

The Dark Pisces wraps ropes of water around me before I can stop them, binding my arms to my sides and squeezing until I struggle to breathe. She snarls with pointed teeth. "I told you the truth about the book. I told you the truth about your mother."

I squirm against her bonds. "You lied about Niobe! I trusted you!"

"I did what I had to do to free myself and I will not apologize for that. Until you've spent years trapped in nothingness, unable to speak to anyone or breathe fresh air, you can't begin to understand." Her hold on me drops, water splashing to the floor. "Now, if you've had enough of this, you've been invited to dinner."

I suck down a full breath of air. There's nothing I can do to fix it now. Cancer is dead. The wards are broken. It's my own fault for trusting this Dark Witch, and she's right. I don't know what I'd do in her shoes, with no emotions left and nothing to keep me from losing my mind inside that mirror. I can't waste my energy fighting her, not when I don't know what awaits me beyond that bedroom door.

"Dinner?" I ask. When they dragged me through the portal, I thought they were taking me prisoner. This room doesn't seem like a prison cell, though, and I doubt prisoners get invitations to dinner. My stomach grumbles at the thought of food and the Dark Pisces gives me a knowing smirk.

"With your mother," she explains. "She's been looking forward to seeing you."

I may have not expected dinner, but to meet my mother? That's exactly what I'm here for. I have to see how far gone she is, if there's anything left within her of the woman I remember. I have to know if there's anything left to save.

The Dark Pisces nods toward the wardrobe and the dress hanging there. She slips out and I change my dirty, wet clothes. My new black dress has long sleeves that cuff at the wrist, a row of three silver buttons leading to a round collar, and falls to mid-thigh. I find my shoes, which have been cleaned of mud and left by the door.

When I'm dressed and have detangled my hair with a comb that's been left on the dresser, I follow the Dark Pisces out into the hall. My shoes echo on the inky black marble, veined with ribbons of white. We don't go far before the Dark Pisces opens a door and holds it open for me.

"Right this way, princess," she says.

My skin prickles at the title: princess. Is that what I am to them, or is this some kind of mind game Lavinia wants to play with me?

When I enter the dining room, though, it takes my breath away. There's not a single room in the Manor that holds a candle to this place. This is a lavish hall fit for royalty, for grand banquets and multicourse meals that leave you confused about which fork to use. The polished marble floors reflect the light of the crystal chandeliers. Most of the room is taken up by a large rectangular table, big enough to seat twenty people at least, and ornately carved with flowers scrolling along the sides and down the legs.

The Dark Pisces pulls a high-backed chair out for me and I sit. The table is laid with candles all the way down, but only two places are set. One at the head of the table, clearly meant for Lavinia, and one to her right, where I currently sit. Between fluted columns along the wall, the windows overlook the sea. The sky is so stark and gray against the stormy waves, I can no longer tell water from air. How far beyond that horizon is Serena? Is she searching for me? Or are she and the others buried too deeply in their grief for Cancer to worry about me? A pang of sadness shoots through me; I should be there with them, laying her to rest. Comforting one another.

Before I can dwell too much more on the absence of Cancer and her steady presence in this world, the dining room doors open and a Dark Witch sweeps into the room. The air grows heavy in her wake. Her long, ice-white hair is pin straight and hangs unbound to her waist. The way she moves, like she's floating through the air, is as familiar to me as my own heartbeat. It doesn't matter that her appearance has changed. I would know her anywhere simply from the steady drumbeat in my soul chanting, *it's her, it's her, it's her.*

My mother.

The other Dark Witches I've seen have appeared older, but Lavinia's porcelain skin is youthful and unmarked. How much power has she drained from Capricorn, Scorpio, and countless other young witches to look so young and fresh? Still, her face is not the one I remember. There's something familiar in the full lips, the round shape of the eyes, the gentle slant of her eyebrows. But she holds herself with none of the softness she once did. This woman, this Dark Witch, is a queen.

"My sweet Ophelia," she says. I suck in a strangled breath as she steps closer, speaking my name like a half-forgotten spell. "You're magnificent. Just as I knew you would be."

She reaches for me, and I flinch back, but the touch of sharp nails across my cheek is featherlight and her arms are gentle as she draws me into an embrace. Every ounce of tension melts away from my body when I'm enveloped in her arms, as if my muscles instinctively know who she is. Her cool breath brushes my ear as she whispers, "Welcome home."

She may be a Dark Witch, but that voice . . . that voice haunts my dreams. My memories. I close my eyes and for a moment, I can imagine that voice coming out of someone entirely different. Someone soft, who smelled of cinnamon and vanilla, whose cheeks were flushed with warmth and affection, who twirled in long floral skirts in our summer garden.

I thought she would be unrecognizable. I thought she would be a cruel, unfeeling monster. I was wrong. While she may be physically transformed, she sounds the same. She *feels* the same. For the first time in ten years, my mother is holding me. I blink back the hot tears pressing against my eyes. She may be trapped in an icy shell, a prisoner of the Darkness consuming her, but she's still in there. I can feel it.

I can save her.

She pulls back and delicately brushes one strand of hair back with a claw-tipped hand. "Sit, sit," she says. She slides gracefully into a seat and I return to mine. "You've been out like a light all afternoon. You must be starving."

She clears her throat. "You're dismissed," she orders, and the Dark Pisces slips from the room, leaving me alone with my mother.

"You have no idea how good it is to finally see you," says Lavinia. "I trust you slept well, if only for a few hours?"

I nod, struggling to find my voice. Who is this woman? I expected an unfeeling Dark Witch, and instead, she's sitting here looking at me like she might actually care about me.

"Why . . . why am I here?" I ask after a moment.

"You're my guest, of course. It's been a decade since I last saw you and I'd like us to spend some time together after all these years apart." She leans forward and rests her elbows on the table. She props her chin on top of her folded hands in a gesture far more ordinary and human than anything I expected from her. "The truth is, Ophelia, I want you to join me. I want you as a member of my Twelve so we'll never have to be apart again. So consider this an official invitation. Turn. Accept your full power and rule the world at my side."

I bite my lip so hard I taste iron in my mouth. "What about Serena?" I ask carefully. I can't say no yet, not outright. If I do, I have no way of knowing if she'll keep me alive or free from her dungeons. It all sounds harmless enough, were it not for that one little word: turn.

"Serena will join us soon enough, but today is about you." Lavinia smiles softly. "Now, I know you've been taught by Niobe that things are black and white. You all are good, and Dark Witches like me and my coven are evil, but it's not so simple. Magic isn't just Dark or light; there are nuances and shades to it."

I think of Gemini, insisting that the spell book, the storm, my blood control, was all wrong. It didn't feel wrong, though. Is it wrong to be strong? To be so powerful that nothing can stop you? Or is it just that wielding that much strength frightens everyone else?

Lavinia continues, "I do what's right for me. For my coven. And if you wanted to do what's right for you, you would know that your emotions are rotting you from the inside out. I know you feel them in everyone else, the water in the blood singing to you. Doesn't its song hurt your ears? Aren't you exhausted from trying to pick out every note in the chord to find out what's really going on?"

I have to admit she's right on that account at least. From the moment I've stepped in here, she's told me nothing but the truth. Her emotions are crystal clear. It's refreshing, speaking to someone who says exactly what they mean.

"With Niobe, you will always be treated as second to Serena. Inferior, simply because of that number on your wrist." Lavinia nods toward my tattoo and I instinctively pull my sleeve down to cover it. "With me, you won't be a number. You won't live in your sister's shadow. You'll be a member of my Twelve, the first coven in history to explore the final evolution. With the power of twelve witches, a full coven, we will possess power like this world has never seen. We can find depths to magic that have never been found, miracles of nature that witches like Niobe say are impossible. Together, we can make history, you and I."

My breath hitches in my throat and it takes everything in me not to let her see how good that sounds. I don't want to turn Dark, at least I think I don't, but I've convinced myself for so long that I'm all right being the afterthought. My sister is strong and powerful and brave, and I'm a pitiful little bird, too afraid to fly. What if I didn't have to be afraid? What if I could spread my wings and become the powerful one for once?

The doors open again and Lavinia sits back in her seat. "Ah, here we are!" She beckons to a girl around my age who slips into the room carrying two plates full of food. "Hurry up now, we don't want to keep my lovely daughter waiting."

The girl's thin arms shake beneath the weight of the tray as she approaches slowly. Her plain black jacket and pants hang from her emaciated body, and as I take in her gaunt face, the bags under her eyes, the tattoo peeking out from beneath her sleeve, I realize she's not just any serving girl.

She's Scorpio.

34

Serena

THE IMAGE OF OPHELIA BEING DRAGGED THROUGH THE portal by the Dark Pisces plays over and over again in my mind as I pace back and forth in the sitting room. She gave herself up. How could she think she was so expendable? Is this her way of trying to atone for releasing the Dark Pisces?

"We have to go get her," I say for the thousandth time, but no one is listening to me. My hands, clenched into fists at my sides, shake uncontrollably. Why is everyone just sitting around? We know where the Dark Witches' sanctum is—we should be moving.

Virgo took charge quickly once the Dark Witches were gone to heal Aquarius, who is now resting but is badly wounded. Then she had Cancer's body moved to the med wing to prepare it for burial. I couldn't follow her and continue looking at Cancer's unseeing eyes.

I failed her.

I keep pushing the memory of her falling from my head because there's nothing I can do about it right now. I can't lose myself to grief when there's still one person left I stand a chance of not failing again, and that's Ophelia. The longer I wait, the more chance there is something has happened to her. That is, if she's still alive at all.

No—Ophelia isn't dead. I would know. I don't know how, but somehow, I would feel it. The tether in my chest that connects me to her would have broken. A piece of my soul would be extinguished. It's broken and bruised, battered and torn to pieces right now, half buried beside Cancer, but it's still intact. Ophelia is alive and I have to get to her before that changes.

Leo, Sagittarius, and Gemini have changed into black pants and shirts, and Libra sits cross-legged on the floor, watching us with eerie calm. Leo hasn't spoken a word since the Dark Witches left the island. She sits motionless in an armchair. Her hair hangs limply around her face and her eyes are hollow and sunken.

"Leo, please," I say again, stopping my pacing to brace my palms on the table. "We have to go after them." I want to scream at her to answer me, to look at me, to say *something*, but she doesn't respond.

Leo stares blankly, just as she has for the last two hours. Her unnerving stillness makes my stomach churn. I wish she would insult me, yell at me, do anything to show me that her fire hasn't been extinguished.

"I told you already," Sagittarius snaps from where she leans against the mantel, "your sister made her choice. If they took Niobe, none of us stands a chance."

"So we give up?" No matter the odds, I won't leave Ophelia there. It's been excuse after excuse: Sag can't jump that far after the fight, we need to take care of Aquarius, we need to replenish our energy. I'm sick of hearing reasons we shouldn't go.

Sagittarius glares, red-hot ire in her usually cool tone. "This is what Leo has been saying since the moment you got here, and I should have listened to her. You're too reckless and hotheaded. We can't just walk into a den of Dark Witches without a plan, especially not when we're drained."

"You don't have to walk in, then. I'll go myself."

"How? Have you somehow developed your own teleportation powers?"

I grit my teeth. "I just need you to open a portal and send me through. You don't have to come too."

"And then what? You take on Lavinia and the Dark Twelve on your own? You'll never survive it, and even if you do, you won't be able to get yourself back."

"What do you care?"

"I care that I don't want to lose any more of my sisters tonight!" Sagittarius lurches across the room to glower in my face. "I want to get Niobe and Pisces and Scorpio back as much as anyone else, but I need to be sure that you're not going to fly off the handle."

"That's not fair." I can take care of myself. I've proven that to this coven.

"It's your fault this happened in the first place! If you'd stopped her, she and Niobe would still be here and Cancer would still be alive."

I flinch. "I didn't know," I say softly. "Believe me, I wish I had." If I'd seen what was going on, maybe I could have talked some sense into her before things got so horribly out of control.

Sagittarius scoffs. "How could you not have known? She's your twin!"

"If there's anyone you should be yelling at right now, it's Gemini." I whirl, pointing at Gemini, who slumps on the couch with their head in their hands, fingers pulled tight through their short curls.

"They knew Ophelia was sneaking around in the pond and didn't tell anyone."

Gemini's head jerks up. Their eyes are red rimmed. "How was I supposed to know there was a Dark Witch in that pond?'

"You knew she was using Dark magic and you didn't tell anyone."

"And *you* were too self-absorbed to notice anything was wrong in the first place!"

My chest is too tight; my breathing grows shallow. How did I not realize what Ophelia was doing? Was she really so lonely and scared and hurt that she would turn to Dark magic and trust a Dark Witch more than me? We're supposed to tell each other everything, and she was lying to me. I should have known something wasn't right.

"You're right." I return to my pacing until there must be a trail worn in the carpet from my steps. I look at Leo again, still unmoving, barely blinking. "Ophelia wanted to leave after the ranking ceremony, and I should have listened. I should never have gone on the mission to get Libra. If I hadn't left her here all alone, she would never have found the Dark Witch. We could be far from here by now and none of you would have to be in danger because of us."

Every memory of the last few days comes pouring back into me, every mistake, every conversation with Ophelia where I was too bullheaded to listen. It's my fault she thought no one would care if she gave herself up to the Dark Witches. I should have made sure she knew that none of this matters—the Manor, the magic, the coven—none of it matters to me if she isn't here. I tear my hands through my hair, pulling hard at the ends until my scalp burns with pain. "This *is* all my fault. Cancer's dead, they took Niobe and Ophelia, and now everyone else is in danger because the wards are down, and if I had just stopped for one second and listened to what she was saying to me, if I hadn't been so damned selfish, none of this would have happened. But I have to go and fix this. I need your help, *please.* What happened to sisterhood? To being a coven? Doesn't that mean anything to you?"

Leo stands and I freeze. Finally, she's going to say we should go; she's going to jump into action as the commander I know her to be. But she doesn't look at me. Head down, gazing at the floor, she slowly approaches.

"Leo, I—"

Crack.

She slaps me across the face. My head rocks sideways with the force of the blow. Pain lances across my cheekbone.

"Pull yourself together," she orders, jolting me back to reality. I blink at her in surprise. Sagittarius and Gemini have gone still, gaping at Leo.

Libra leaps to her feet with a shriek. "Leave her alone!" She starts to charge at Leo, but I shake my head.

"It's okay," I say despite my stinging cheek and Leo shuddering with rage in front of me. Libra stops, her little hands balled into fists and her face screwed up in confusion.

Leo grabs my shoulders and shakes me. "How dare you stand here and act like you're the only one upset right now! You don't get to make demands and freak out and act like no one else is in pain. You think I don't care about this coven? Cancer is dead. *Dead!* My sister is gone, and you don't get to tell us what we have to do. You don't get to tell us how to feel."

"Leo, I—"

"No!" she screams. Her breath comes in jagged, shallow pants and her nails dig into my arms through my shirt. "There's nothing more for you to say right now. You want Pisces back? Then get your head on straight and stop acting like you're the only one who's lost someone."

"You're right," I say, my voice breaking. "You're right, I'm sorry." Leo releases my arms. I force myself to take long breaths, slowing my racing heart. I was so focused on getting to Ophelia that I didn't stop to think about anyone else. They're all suffering. Grieving. Especially Leo, who knew Cancer best.

Sagittarius's face goes slack. She falls into an armchair and sinks her head in her hands. "I'm sorry too, Serena," she says. "I just . . ."

"Don't apologize. I have to get my sister back, and Niobe too, but I can do it myself. I don't want anyone else to get hurt."

"No," Leo says firmly.

"Please, Leo, she's my sister," I beg. I know she's hurting right now, but Leo knows as well as I do what it's like to have people relying on you. People you can't bear to let down. "I promised to protect her. I can't just abandon her."

A muscle in Leo's jaw jumps. She's still quiet, but her eyes have regained their bright ferocity. She twines her fingers through her hair, braiding it, then exchanges a long look with Sagittarius like they're having a silent conversation. Finally, Leo nods. "Fine. But Sag and I are going too."

"I can't ask you to do that." I was being unfair. She should be allowed to grieve, not feel like she has to jump back into action to help me.

"You're not asking. She's a member of this coven—you're not the only one who cares about her. And Niobe is my family. I owe it to her to get her back." Leo swallows hard, throat bobbing. "It's what Cancer would do."

I raise my eyebrow at Sagittarius and she makes an attempt at a wry smirk. "Somebody has to get you dumbasses home in one piece."

I turn to Gemini. "What about you?"

Gemini nods. Their face is tinged green, eyes bruised and haunted, like they're seeing Ophelia instead of me. "Of course I'm coming."

Libra runs to my side and wraps her arms around my waist. "Me too," she says. "I can fight too."

"No," I say. I can't justify bringing her on this mission, though, with so much danger and uncertainty. She whines and I kneel beside her. "Aquarius is hurt and Virgo isn't a fighter like you are. They need someone to take care of them and keep them safe. Do you think you can do that?"

Libra nods solemnly. "I'll protect them."

I tuck a long piece of chestnut hair behind her ear. "Brave girl," I say. She throws her arms around my shoulders and I hug her tightly.

"Meet back here in one hour," says Leo. "Rest, get something to eat, and grab your weapons. It's time to end this."

35

Ophelia

I GAPE AT SCORPIO AS LAVINIA BECKONS HER CLOSER. SHE'S holding two plates of food, but I don't look at them. I'm too busy scanning every inch of her for injuries. There are none visible. She's walking fine, her face is gaunt and thin but doesn't have any signs of scars or bruising more than light purple circles of exhaustion beneath her eyes. With her long black jacket, buttoned to the collar, there's nothing visible aside from the smooth, unblemished skin of her hands and wrists. Her dirty-blond hair is unevenly cropped above her shoulders, like someone cut it carelessly, and her brown eyes watch me warily.

"Scorpio, my darling," says Lavinia kindly. "This is my daughter Ophelia."

"Lovely to meet you." Scorpio dips her head and I return the gesture.

"Scorpio is one of our honored guests here," says Lavinia.

"She's not . . ." I pause, unable to come up with a judicious way to ask why Scorpio isn't in chains, rotting away in a dungeon somewhere.

"A prisoner?" Lavinia offers with a wry twist of her mouth. "No, contrary to what Niobe may have told you, Scorpio is here of her own free will. Isn't that right, dear?"

Scorpio nods once, lips just barely lifting at the corners. She approaches the table and places the plates on it, but when she pulls her hand back, it catches on my crystal goblet of water. The glass topples from the table and hits the floor, shattering.

Scorpio hisses a sharp breath. "I'm sorry." She drops to her knees to pick up glass shards with her bare hands. "I'm sorry, I'm sorry, I'm sorry," she whispers.

"It's okay," I say. I push my chair back and join her on the floor, picking up one of the largest shards. Sharp glass pricks my finger and I drop the shard with a hiss of pain.

Blood blooms on the tip of my forefinger.

Lavinia is beside me before I can register the pain. She pushes Scorpio out of the way with her hip and nudges me back into my seat. With the touch of her finger, the nick knits itself together. Lavinia lifts my finger to her lips and kisses it.

"No harm done," she says, and returns to her seat. I flex my fingers. There's no blood, no scar, no sign of a wound at all. "Eat, eat! We need you to regain your strength. No daughter of mine is going to walk around hungry and weak."

For a moment, I'm five years old again, back in our cottage. I can see my mother the way she once was, standing at the stove, stirring a pot of stew with a wooden spoon and urging me to eat more. Maybe she hasn't changed so much. Niobe always told us the Dark Witches were evil, emotionless, but Lavinia doesn't seem that way. What if we've been wrong about the Dark Witches this whole time?

Scorpio cleans up the remainder of the glass and then stands in the corner by the window, waiting. We eat in silence and I realize how hungry I am after being out for so long. Dinner is full of delicious roasted vegetables, salmon with a lemony cream sauce, and buttery potatoes, each bite richer than the last.

"Our Capricorn," I say carefully. "What happened to her?"

"A tragedy," sighs Lavinia, shaking her head. "She was impossible to reason with, poisoned against us. She was so fueled by Niobe's lies that she attacked members of my coven." A vicious shadow passes over her porcelain face. "I will always protect my coven."

I force myself to swallow a bite of my roll and nod. "Of course," I murmur.

"Do you know why you and Serena were left to rot in that hideous orphanage for all those years? Hidden from a living mother who would have come for you, cared for you, loved you in any form?" I suck in a shaking breath, each word hitting me like daggers to the chest. "She kept you from me, Ophelia. My own daughters. All so she could use you as pawns against me and twist a mother's love into a weapon." Her voice is venomous, laced with cold fury. "Did she ever tell you why?"

Wordlessly, I shake my head.

"Well," she says softly, "why don't we ask her now?"

She pushes her chair back and rises in one fluid motion. She extends her elbow to me, and when I rise, I tentatively loop my arm through hers. If I close my eyes, I can pretend we're just mother and daughter walking down the street together, visiting shops and running errands. As much as I know that's not reality, there's a tiny piece of my heart, a piece that has spent years longing for warm hearths and family dinners, that yearns to believe it could be true. Somewhere inside is the piece of a little girl who just wants to be a regular family again, no matter how impossible it may be.

As soon as Lavinia is out of her seat, servants rush forward to begin clearing the table and I expect Scorpio to follow suit, but Lavinia snaps her fingers and Scorpio falls into step behind us. Lavinia leads me down the hall and I let her steer around the corner until we reach a towering set of oak double doors.

"This is the throne room." Lavinia pauses at the entryway.

The doors glide open like they know who stands before them, and we step into a room that might once have been a cathedral, with the high vaulted ceiling and arched windows that stain the floors with shafts of evening sunlight, illuminating crimson and white veins in the marble. Twin rows of columns line the sides of the room, leading the way to a raised dais topped with a black throne. A sun, a moon, and stars made of sculpted metal protrude from the top of the throne, like whoever sat in that chair would wear the celestial bodies like a crown.

In the center of the room, a wheel is carved into the ground, but instead of numbers like a clock, it's marked with zodiac symbols, like the floor of the Manor. Each symbol and the lines connecting them are filled with deep red liquid.

Blood.

My stomach turns at the sight of so much crimson and where it must have come from.

Someone moans. A figure lies in a heap, unconscious but still breathing, at the center of the wheel. *Niobe.* Blood streaks across her face and arms, and a small pool of it has formed beneath her, flowing into the carved zodiac wheel on the floor. I can't contain my horrified gasp and Niobe's eyes flicker open at the sound.

"Ophelia?" Niobe murmurs in a gravelly voice. "Don't . . . don't listen to her."

Slowly, I back away from Lavinia. "What have you done to her?" I demand.

"Nothing more than she deserves," says Lavinia. She crosses the room slowly and comes to stand in front of Niobe with her hands clasped gracefully before her. "She kept us apart, Ophelia."

"Let the girl go." Niobe sways as she pulls herself to her knees. Her gaze lands on Scorpio, still standing behind Lavinia, quiet and docile as a mouse. "Let them both go, and I'll stop getting in your way. I'll turn a blind eye on you and the rest of your coven. Just let them go."

Lavinia purses her lips like she's considering it, then grins. "That's a generous offer, but no, thank you." She scans Niobe, whose face is twisted into a disgusted scowl. "Don't give me your self-righteousness. You're no better than me, collecting your menagerie of witches, training them to be players in your game."

"I never asked for this," says Niobe. "It needn't have come to this if you hadn't been so desperate to achieve a second turning."

Niobe gives a bitter laugh. Legs shaking, she rises to her feet to face Lavinia fully, but before she can approach the Dark Witch, Lavinia bends down. In one swift motion, she pulls out a dagger, draws it through the blood on the throne room floor, and licks the blade.

Niobe's body stops as still as a statue, just like when I harnessed the water in Gemini's blood.

Blood magic.

Niobe's eyes are wide and panicked as they land on me, but I don't know how to help her. I can't release her from Lavinia's grasp.

"I'm not desperate, old friend," says Lavinia. "I'm simply curious. I want to know what this world could be, rather than accepting it for all its apparent limitations. Limitations you're content to pretend don't exist. It's pathetic the way you've convinced these girls that there's a way out, that they're not just delaying the inevitable." She looks to me. "We're meant to turn, Ophelia. There's no need to be frightened of the transformation as you've been taught to be. We're not soft and small like ordinary humans. We're meant to use our power. To evolve."

"You're sucking witches dry or forcing them to turn," says Niobe. Lavinia must be allowing her to speak, though she can't move her body. "You're trying to make them into demons you don't even know truly exist. Explain to me how that constitutes natural evolution."

"It's just as natural as Awakening." Lavinia cocks her head with a twisting smirk that sends a chill up my spine. "It's far more different than what you did to Serena."

Niobe's eyes snap to me, her mouth parting as anguish ripples from her. "That was different."

Cold slithers through my body at the deceit in Niobe's words. "What is she talking about?" I ask. What did she do to Serena?

Lavinia seizes Niobe beneath her jaw. "Tell her!" Lavinia orders. "Tell my daughter how you could have retrieved her from that orphanage and kept her safe, but instead, you sent a rogue Dark Witch to force her sister to Awaken."

My blood runs cold. I'm thrust back into a memory, of Cancer scrying into the Dark Gemini's eyeball. She lied about what she saw in it. To protect Niobe. All this time, she knew what Niobe had done. She forced Serena's Awakening, all so she could get us here. To use us.

I swallow back the hot lump rising in my throat. "Tell me that's not true," I say. Have I spent my entire life being manipulated? Niobe left us at the orphanage, the matrons treated us like less than the dirt beneath their shoes; how long would we have gone without Awakening if Niobe had just left well enough alone? We might never have needed to know about the full extent of our powers. I would never have had to worry about becoming a monster.

Niobe's face shutters into the mask of an unfeeling general. "I'm sorry, Ophelia, but it had to be done. We needed you and Serena to Awaken. It was for the sake of the coven."

Lavinia's cold laugh rings out again, echoing through the throne room. "For the sake of your army of manipulated children, you mean. Your precious Manor, where you could finally be the most powerful of them all. Do you see, Ophelia? Do you see how she twists the truth and uses others for her own gain? She's always been like this, since we were girls." Her clawed grip on Niobe's face tightens, forcing Niobe up to her knees. "You were jealous of me. Don't deny it. You were so desperate for a taste of my power, desperate to stop me from becoming more powerful, desperate to control my daughters the way you could never control me."

"I was desperate to save them," Niobe says in a pained whisper, "because I failed to save *you*."

Lavinia releases Niobe and stalks up the dais. She sinks into her throne, gazing down at Niobe's frozen form with savage satisfaction. Scorpio takes up a place standing beside her, ever attentive.

"I'm afraid you won't be saving anyone now, Niobe," Lavinia croons. "Not even yourself."

"I've spent decades without turning, Lavinia," says Niobe. "Trust me, I will not be giving in now."

Lavinia shrugs. "Pity. You do realize that if you turn, you won't have to live with this guilt any longer. What you've done to these girls, what you've done to our friend, what you didn't do for me." She lifts an eyebrow. "You were supposed to kill me, weren't you? The moment I went Dark, and yet here I am." She holds her arms out and turns in a slow circle, baring sharp teeth in a wolflike grin. "Yours for the taking, and still you can't bear to put an end to me, can you? So turn. Turn, and we never have to be apart again. We can rule this world together."

"The girl I once knew," says Niobe, "the girl who was my best friend in the entire world, would never want that. You once believed that we didn't have to turn, that there was a way to not lose control of our power and burn out. You fought for that, Lavinia, don't you remember? For your daughters not to have to live the life you're currently living. Don't you want more for them?"

"Of course I do," says Lavinia. "I want them to be part of the first coven in history to make the final evolution. What could you possibly dream of that's more than that? We will achieve things no witch has ever done before. Ophelia, everything Niobe told you, everything she taught you, was a lie. You see it now, don't you? This is what it truly means to be Awakened. To have your eyes opened to core truths of the world." She extends her arm, offering me her hand. "The entire universe is at your fingertips now, my darling. Waiting to be shaped. Transformed." Her smile widens. "All I've even wanted is for us to transform it together."

"She's deceiving you, Ophelia," Niobe hisses. "Her words are poison."

Poison? I laugh at the word. All Niobe has done since the moment I arrived on the Isle of Sol is manipulate me. She's done it since the moment she sent little mice to spy on me in the orphanage and a Dark Witch to try to force me to Awaken. If anyone has been spewing poison, it's her. I can feel it in my bones.

"The only person in this room who has been lying to me, Niobe, is you."

36

Serena

THE MOMENT I STEP THROUGH THE PORTAL AND ONTO THE beach, the rot and decay seep into my skin. It's not a scent or anything in the air itself. It's the way it feels. Like this fortress is dying from the inside out. The cold is sharp and stabbing as knives. We're on an island, but it couldn't be more different from the Isle of Sol. A black fortress sits on a rocky shore, sharp towers piercing the sky laden with thick, dark clouds. Even from here, I hear the waves crashing against the shore. Gulls screech, and the ocean sings to me as it breaks against the rocks and sprays droplets of frigid water onto my arms.

When the four of us are through, Sagittarius closes the portal. Now that she's rested, she was able to portal us farther than she's ever gone before. Getting so close to turning has only made her stronger, her magic more powerful. The number on her wrist has changed from fifteen to twelve. Looking at her half-white hair, I wonder how I'll find Ophelia. Has Lavinia forced her to turn? Will I find my sister unrecognizable and white-haired? Or will she be half-dead, drained of all her energy?

"Lead the way," says Leo. I step to the front of our group, a position I've never held before, and feel for the tether in my chest. It's not as taut as it was at the Manor, but it's still pulled tight. I follow that thread, creeping across the beach. We have to get out of the open before we're spotted.

I lead us away from the ocean and toward the fortress. Sagittarius and Leo form a solid unit behind me as Gemini guards our back. I move around the base of the fortress and keep following the thread like it will lead me straight to Ophelia. As I walk, the tug grows stronger, yanking on that thread and pulling me toward the fortress, but I don't see a way in. I hold up a hand and the others stop behind me. I run my hands along the stone walls until I find a long groove in the stone the height of a door.

"Here," I say. If it is a door, though, I can't get it free. I push and pull at the rock but it doesn't budge. The others join me in trying, but nothing moves.

"Let me try something," says Gemini.

Their features flicker and they shrink until I can't see them anymore. I raise an eyebrow at Sagittarius, but she shakes her head. She didn't teleport them. When pebbles and grass at my feet rustle, I squint to make out a tiny figure moving. They've made themself the size of a bug, small enough to slide through the minuscule gap between the ground and the door.

After a moment, a portion of the stone wall eases open and Gemini stands behind it, their usual size, with their fingers on a rusty metal handle.

I creep across the threshold into a long tunnel. The damp smell of earth clogs my nose and water drips from the ceiling. Leo hands

Gemini their weapons and closes the door, plunging us into pitch dark. I form a ball of electricity that hovers above my palm. Its glow is enough to light our way as we pick through the muddy ground. I don't know how far we walk silently in the darkness, brushing aside cobwebs and dead rodent carcasses, but eventually we reach a door. It's too polished for this dank tunnel, made of gleaming black wood.

Leo twists her fingers, the bolt slides free, and we step into the fortress.

I let my ball of electricity disappear and move slowly into the hallway, trying to keep my steps quiet on the hard floors. Chandeliers hanging overhead are reflected in the black marble, and the arched windows let in the few traces of afternoon sunlight that escape the gloomy clouds over the sea beyond. The sanctum's walls ooze unease and Darkness, but somewhere within the black fog is that tug. Ophelia is here.

I let electrical current flow through me, ready to use the moment I need to call on it. I follow the pull of my bond to Ophelia down the hallway and around the corner. The halls are dim, the lights in the chandeliers and wall sconces kept low.

We clear one hallway, then another. Silence hangs heavy over us, perforated only by our careful footfalls and steady breaths. As we approach another corner, steady footsteps click on stone.

Leo's body goes loose in a fighting stance. She hands Sagittarius a knife. "Lights out?" she asks.

I squint in confusion but Sagittarius nods. "On it."

She blinks out of sight just as Leo moves her hands and the curtains draw themselves over the windows as the sconces tear out of the walls. The hallway is thrown into blackness just as a Dark Witch rounds the corner. There's a flash of light, Sagittarius appearing behind her, and then a squelch, a grunt of pain, and a thud.

Leo relights the one sconce she's left intact. It illuminates Sagittarius, standing flushed-faced over the dead witch. Leo steps over the body and bumps her knuckles against Sagittarius's.

"Works every time," she says.

We continue until voices float toward us. I strain my ears, hoping one of them is Ophelia's, but none of them are familiar. Leo presses a finger to her lips and we slow, listening.

A low voice echoes around the corner. "She wants to do it tonight," says the first voice.

"How?" hisses another. "She only has one girl. They can't complete the ritual without both of them."

"The other will come," says the first voice.

A new voice laughs. "Or so she says. Wishful thinking if you ask me."

"Good thing no one asked you then. I—" Their conversation stops abruptly as we round the corner, but we don't give the six Dark Witches time to react before we strike.

Sagittarius and Leo move as a unit. Showing that they are two people who have trained and fought side by side so much that they read each other's bodies enough to need only a word or two between them. Where Leo leaves an opening, Sagittarius appears before a Dark Witch can strike her. When Sagittarius blinks into a new position and doesn't see the enemy blade heading for her, Leo knocks it out of the air. And the witches they miss find themselves face-to-face with Gemini and me. I spin sparks at them, slamming into their chests and leaving them unmoving on the ground. Gemini takes on most of them with nothing but a blade, though they've made themself taller with muscles that ripple beneath their shirtsleeves.

Leo slams the last Dark Witch against the wall, pinning her there with her power. "Where's Lavinia?" The Dark Witch curses, but Leo presses the flat of her blade against her throat.

Over Leo's shoulder, the Dark Witch's eyes land on me. "It's you," she gasps. "She's in the throne room."

"Want to give us a map?" drawls Sagittarius.

The Dark Witch doesn't answer, but Leo presses the dagger hard enough that blood blooms on her pale neck. "One floor up, last door at the end of the hall."

Without so much as a thank you, Leo slashes her knife across the Dark Witch's throat and she slumps to the ground, gargling as bright red blood pours onto the white-veined marble.

Leo wipes her knife clean on her pants. "Let's go," she says.

The path is clear as we move down the hallway and toward the stairs at the end of the hall. This place must be three times the size of the Manor. It's a maze. Every ounce of warmth seems to be sucked away, pulling life from my bones with each second I remain here.

We're halfway up the staircase when the hair on the back of my neck prickles. I start to tell Leo I think we're being watched when someone behind us calls, "Stop!"

We freeze. Eight Dark Witches stand in formation at the other end of the hall with razor-sharp smiles and claws out. The Dark Witch who spoke glares at us. "We don't tolerate intruders in our home."

I stand taller, preparing myself for a fight. We held off nearly this many before, but we were fresher.

Leo steps in front of me.

"Aries," she says slowly. "Find your sister. We'll hold them off."

She rolls her shoulders as the witches slowly approach down the hallway, a solid unit of long swishing robes and sickly smiles. They take their time, like they know we'll be easy to pick off. Gemini and Sagittarius close ranks in front of me.

"Leo," I breathe. I can't leave them here.

They don't turn back to me. Leo's knuckles are bone white on the hilt of her dagger. "That's an order," she says. "Go. And don't get caught."

I want to retort that I don't take orders from her, but she's right. I'm no good to anyone if all of us die in this hallway. So I run. I take off toward the throne room and the pull I feel in Ophelia's direction, and even when I hear the sounds of steel clashing and muffled grunts behind me, I don't look back.

I run as fast as my legs will carry me, taking the stairs two at a time. My thighs scream at me to stop, but I keep pushing, following that feeling and nothing else. I pound down the last hallway until I reach a humongous set of double doors. My senses pound at me, shouting that she's there. She's just beyond that door. I slow to a walk and breathe deeply to calm my racing heart until it stops feeling like it's about to explode out of my chest.

When I push open the door to the throne room, my breath sticks in my throat.

Ophelia is in the center of the throne room, but she's not in irons. She's not on her knees, not writhing in pain, not bloody and tortured. She's standing in front of a Dark Witch who sits on a throne. Ophelia's hands are clasped behind her back and her head is cocked inquisitively. She's wearing a clean black dress with no visible signs of injury. I don't let relief and confusion take over yet, though, because the throne room floor is slick with blood. It fills the carvings of a zodiac wheel carved into the floor. Each of the carved symbols and the ring connecting them are full of crimson liquid.

And it's not any Dark Witch sitting at the front of the room.

That's my mother.

Another girl I don't recognize stands meekly at Lavinia's side. She's not a Dark Witch, and her black jacket and pants that hang too loose make her look like a servant. There are purple bags beneath her eyes and her cheeks are gaunt. Her choppy blond hair is stringy and limp.

Niobe stands near Ophelia, but she's far too still. She's bruised and her shoulders are hunched in exhaustion.

I ignore Lavinia, though. My feet move of their own accord and I run to Ophelia, pulling her into my arms. When she hugs me back, I say in her ear, "Let's get you out of here."

Ophelia jerks out of my embrace. I grab her hand, ready to pull her away.

Lavinia rises and descends the steps. My instincts scream at me to run from this predator, but I hold my ground.

"Hello, Serena," she says. My heartbeat stutters at the sound of the lilting voice that's haunted my dreams for the last ten years. She opens her arms like she means to hug me, but I step away from her and she instead folds her hands in front of her. Her sharp nails gleam in the light of the chandeliers. "You girls have no idea how long I've been looking forward to this day, to have both of you back at my side so we can be a family."

"Family?" I spit the word. "You don't know the meaning of family. You abandoned us. She's my family," I say, gripping Ophelia's hand tighter. "Not you."

Lavinia nods slowly. "I know you believe that now, but things will be different once you both join me. We can all be together again."

"I didn't come for you," I spit, tightening my grip on Ophelia's hand. "I'm taking Ophelia, and I'll die before I let you stop me."

"Such blazing ferocity," Lavinia says, eyeing me with detached fascination. "Such strength of will." Her words drip with satisfaction and her hungry eyes linger possessively on me. "You truly are your mother's daughter."

I am no such thing.

My mother deserted me, and the matrons locked me away, but there's one person—*one*—who has never once abandoned me. She can't be under Lavinia's spell, not really. She must have a plan.

"Ophelia, what's going on?" I ask.

Ophelia gives a half smile, but it's not reassuring enough. "Just listen to what she has to say."

Listen? How can she ask me to listen? We should be fighting Lavinia, not standing around listening to her poison our minds. She's not our mother anymore. "I'm not turning Dark," I say.

Lavinia circles us like wolf sizing up its next meal. I hold my chin high and assess her as she assesses me. Why is Ophelia just standing there? There's no fear in her face or in her steady stance.

Lavinia stops in front of me. I cringe back as she brushes a strand of white hair from my eyes. "Oh, my dear Serena, I'm so sorry you have so much hardness in your heart. So much emotion poisoning you. If Niobe hadn't taken you from me, everything would have been so different. I could have kept you here with me. Safe."

"Emotions aren't poison," I say. "I love Ophelia; I love my friends. I loved *you*."

"I loved you too," she says with far more gentleness than I thought a Dark Witch could muster. "I loved both of you more than anything in this entire world. This is all her fault." She nods toward

Niobe. "She stole you from me, and now she's done nothing but lie to you and turn you against your own mother.

"Look at her," says Lavinia, and I do. Though she can't move, is staring at me like she's trying to tell me something. Lavinia's words are lies. I have to get us out of here before she can spew any more of them. "After all these years, she's still jealous of my powers. She—"

I can't contain it anymore. Lightning surges through me, crackling out of my hands in two long lightning bolts that wrap around Lavinia's chest like pythons, cutting off her words. Her eyes flash and her lips pale. I lash the lightning to the side, throwing her off her throne and to the ground.

The surprise is enough that her concentration drops and her hold on Niobe's blood releases. "Get out of here, girls!" Niobe shouts.

Glass shatters on marble and a thick tree branch punches its way through the window. It collides with Lavinia and sends her flying sideways. "I should have killed you long ago," Niobe rasps.

Lavinia is up in an instant, though, knife drawn, but she doesn't advance on Niobe with steel. She advances with blood. Daggers of blood, like thin, razor-sharp arrowheads, rise from the blood in the zodiac wheel and whiz through the air at her command.

I don't wait to see if they land; I'm getting Ophelia out of here right now. I grab her hand and pull, but she doesn't budge.

"What are you doing?" I yell, but when I whirl to face her, her eyes are wide with fear.

"I . . . I can't move." Her voice breaks. "Serena, why can't I move?"

Niobe and Lavinia are spinning and grunting around us, a whirlwind of blood and earth. I search past them, though, for Scorpio, rushing toward us. "Explain," I demand.

"She has your blood," Scorpio says in a small voice. "She's had it this whole time." I want to scream at Scorpio to fight back and help us, but then I catch a glimpse of the tattoo on her wrist. *CDLII*. They've taken everything from her, nearly every drop of magic and energy. It's a miracle she's alive and standing.

I grip Ophelia's forearms and try to move her again, but it's no use. She's locked in place.

"How?"

"I don't know, I . . ." She sucks in a sharp breath. "Oh God, she did it at dinner, didn't she?" Scorpio ducks her head and nods, cheeks growing pink.

I want to explode out of my body. "Somebody tell me what the hell is going on, right now. Did she hurt you?"

"At dinner I pricked my finger on a broken glass. Lavinia . . . she healed it but . . ." Ophelia's eyes finally shine with the clear brightness I know so well.

"She only took a little," says Scorpio. "So she won't be able to keep her hold on you for more than a few hours unless her concentration is broken. Then she'll need more blood to get control again."

"You have to go, Serena," says Ophelia. "Before she can get to you too."

"Absolutely not."

If Ophelia is trapped, I'm trapped. I'm not leaving this place without her.

37

Ophelia

MY BODY IS NO LONGER MY OWN. MY LEGS ARE LOCKED IN place and I can't so much as twitch my fingers. I try to wriggle against the invisible bonds, but nothing moves. I can't even reach for magic, as if my blood itself is frozen within my body. If this is how Gemini felt when I took control of their blood, I'll beg forgiveness on my knees the next time I see them. If there's a next time.

Lavinia was planning this from the start, I realize. From the moment I pricked my finger at dinner. Scorpio has jolted to a stop, restrained by Lavinia, and was probably under Lavinia's control this entire time. Was she directed to knock the glass over so I would hurt myself? This whole time, I thought I had free will when she could have seized control of my body at any moment.

I see everything clearly now. Lavinia doesn't care about us as her daughters; I can't believe I let myself think for so much as a second that she might want to reunite our family. She cares about us only as pieces on her chessboard, two missing links in the chain to complete her Dark Twelve. We're nothing to her.

"Please just go, Serena," I beg again.

Lavinia can't complete her plans unless she has both of us. But Serena remains at my side, attention fixated on Scorpio. She lunges for the girl and shoves the sleeve of her jacket up. Bruises, some fresh and violet, others old and yellowing, mottle her skin, just as they had Capricorn's. The tattoo on her wrist shows her rank—452. Serena swears. They've taken everything from her, nearly every drop of magic and energy, leaving just enough to keep her alive and standing.

On the other side of the throne room, Niobe ducks and dodges out of Lavinia's grasp, sending vines up through the cracks in the floor to wrap around Lavinia's ankles. Niobe is already sweating and panting, though, too drained from fighting the Dark Witches at the Manor, and Lavinia frees herself from the snares quickly. The blood daggers nick Niobe's skin until her face and arms are peppered with tiny cuts. She undulates her hands and a round shield woven from fallen branches and leaves forms on her arm. Sticks and bark pelt toward Lavinia to rival her daggers.

"Enough of this," Lavinia growls.

She flies at Niobe, daggers of blood sailing through the air one after another until the white veins in the floor are stained crimson. One blood dagger sails for Niobe's chest, which she blocks with her shield, but she doesn't see the second dagger Lavinia aims for her legs. She twists, trying to evade it, but it slices through both of her calves.

I scream as blood spurts and Niobe falls onto her back, struggling to rise. Lavinia towers over her, her foot grinding into Niobe's chest. "You can't win against me, Niobe," says Lavinia. "You never could." Blood rises around her, forming a long sword poised above

Niobe's heart. A slow, deadly smile grows across Lavinia's face. "I think it's time to promote my daughters in the ranks."

"No!" Serena screams. She flings herself across the room, blasting Lavinia backward.

Marble tiles crack beneath Niobe as she struggles to her feet. She staggers, barely holding herself upright. Still, she sends jagged shards of marble whirling toward Lavinia. Where they gash Lavinia's skin, though, the wounds heal instantly and she's on her feet again. Blood rises from the moat on the floor and wraps around Niobe's hands, forcing her shield to drop. Serena shoots lightning for Lavinia, but Lavinia's ribbons of blood intercept it and steam hisses through the room.

Lavinia advances on Niobe, but Serena leaps into her path, sparks at her fingertips. Lavinia is faster, though. Her open hand cracks across Serena's cheek. Serena's head slams to the side and she falls to her knees. Blood trickles down the side of her face where Lavinia's claws have split skin.

Lavinia caresses Serena's bleeding cheek. "My brave little warrior," says Lavinia. "My sparkling girl. You've forgotten who gave you those powers." Her tongue darts out to lick at the blood and Serena's body locks with a strangled gasp. My heart sinks. She should have listened to me and run when she had the chance.

Her hands still tied with blood, Niobe manages to re-form her shield. Her chest heaves as more marble tiles explode and the ground ripples, forcing Lavinia to stumble. She loses her footing and falls, but her gaze snags on something in the doorway. Her jaw goes slack and she gasps.

My own chest constricts with hope—the others have come—as Niobe pauses and turns to look. At nothing. The doorway is empty.

It's just long enough for Lavinia to surge for Niobe.

She swipes a sharp nail across Niobe's arm. Her silk robe slices like butter. Lavinia's claws come away bloody and she licks the ruby liquid.

Her otherworldly laugh curdles my blood. "So easy." She curls her fingers into a fist and Niobe's knees hit the ground as she stifles a grunt of pain. "We've always been the same, you and I, and we still are."

She unfurls her fingers and Niobe gags like she might be sick. "Not anymore," Niobe says. "You've changed. You once preferred death to this Darkness inside you. You once would have sacrificed everything to prevent someone from hurting your daughters the way you're hurting them now. I know you remember, Lavinia."

"Oh, I remember." Lavinia leans inches from Niobe's face. "I remember being weak. I remember being unable to fight back. I remember being chased across every corner of creation without rest. Above all else, I remember running from my true self. But I don't have to run any longer. Not even from you."

She clenches her fist, and Niobe's arm lifts into the air at Lavinia's bidding. It twists behind her back, farther than anyone should be able to bend. At the sickening snap of bone, Niobe screams. Her arm drops to her side limply. Our eyes meet, tears streaming down my face, and I hope she knows I'm sorry—for releasing the Dark Pisces, for believing Lavinia instead of her, for doubting her determination to fight for us. But it doesn't matter how sorry I am.

We're all at Lavinia's mercy now.

I reach invisible hands for my magic, willing it to take control of Lavinia's blood the way I took hold of Gemini's. Power strains within me, but like my water, her constraints bind my magic too.

Lavinia steps toward me, the scent of lavender so incongruous with the iron stench of blood. She draws her fingers through a strand on my hair with a soft smile, and I wish more than anything that I could pull away from her touch. "I'm sorry to do this to you, my darling." She gestures at my frozen body. "I thought it best you see who your beloved leader truly is. True leaders do not control and coerce. They do not put their charges in danger or force them into situations without the whole truth."

Crack.

I don't know where Lavinia strikes, only that Niobe is screaming and the sound shreds my insides.

Crack.

Sweat drips from Niobe's brow and now I see the blood, sliding down the back of her hand. Coating her fingers. Pattering to the floor. She tries to hold back another scream and it comes out in a repressed moan.

"Please, don't do this to her," I say. She may have forced Serena to Awaken and put both of our lives in danger, but she didn't do it with malice in her heart. As betrayed as I feel, I know that to be true. I could feel it in her words. She doesn't deserve this kind of torment.

"Don't you want the truth? Become a member of this coven, Ophelia, and I swear to you, I will never stand between you and the truth." She extends her hand toward me once again. "What do you say? Will you join me?"

"No. Not like this."

Lavinia grins, blood still staining the corner of her lips, but her glee fades when footsteps echo down the hall. There's a flash of red hair, and for a second, I let relief cascade through me at the sight of Leo, until I see who drags her in by the elbow. A Dark Witch. The witch's black robes are tugged up over her head, only her white hair visible beneath her hood.

Red hair spills out of Leo's braid and clings to her sweaty cheeks. Her arms are nicked with cuts and blood trails in thin streams down her pale skin. Her eyes dart between me, Serena, Scorpio, and Niobe, and hopelessness surges in my gut.

Lavinia cocks her head. "Oh dear, what do we have here?"

"We've apprehended an intruder," says the Dark Witch.

Lavinia beckons her forward. "Bring her to me."

Leo spits, pulling against the Dark Witch, but she can't get free.

The Dark Witch drags Leo to the front of the throne room and Lavinia looks her up and down. "I wasn't aware I was expecting another guest," she drawls. "But I suppose we can always make room."

She raises her clawed hands, tipping Leo's chin with one talon. To her credit, Leo doesn't look away. She stares Lavinia dead in the eye.

Lavinia inclines her head to the Dark Witch holding Leo. "Add her to the others."

Just as she starts to turn away, a dagger slips from Leo's sleeve and into her hand.

With one solid motion, she sinks it into Lavinia's side. I gasp, waiting for the Dark Witch to stop her, but she pulls back her hood and her facial features shift, skin going from pale to golden, eyes black to honey, white hair to chestnut curls, and my heart stumbles to a stop at the face that appears.

That's no Dark Witch—it's Gemini.

38

Serena

RELIEF COURSES THROUGH ME AT THE SIGHT OF GEMINI beneath the Dark Witch's hood at Leo's side.

I try to push against Lavinia's bonds over my body to run to Leo, but I can't move so much as my pinky finger. Lavinia doubles over, pressing her fingers against her wound, as Leo backs away across the throne room, chest heaving.

Leo raises another dagger, but Lavinia straightens. Without flinching, Lavinia pulls the blade out of her side and inspects it. Blood seeps from the wound but stops within moments.

"Oh, I like *you*," she says to Leo. She slides me an amused grin. "I can see why Serena does too."

Two daggers float from Leo's belt and into her hands. I wish I were helping her but I can do nothing but watch her run across the room, unleashing all her daggers at once. They whirl in a tornado of deadly sharp metal straight for Lavinia, but she dodges as though her magic controls her whole body, allowing her to move faster than any human should be able to.

She slashes her knife for Leo, but Sagittarius teleports beside Leo, knife drawn, and blocks the blow. Before Lavinia can strike again, Sag grabs Leo's hand and jumps them both to the other side of the room.

Sagittarius pops into reality at Lavinia's back. Lavinia whirls to face her, and while Sag teleports in and out of view faster than I can parse, slashing with her knife and evading Lavinia's grasp, Leo transforms herself into a tornado of deadly metal. While they hold her off, Gemini runs to Ophelia.

"I'm sorry, I'm so sorry," Ophelia sobs when Gemini falls to their knees in front of her, brow knit in concern. They try to pull her to her feet, but like Niobe, she can't be moved.

Gemini takes her face in trembling hands and presses their forehead to hers. "No, I'm sorry," they say. "I should never have lied to you. I was wrong."

"I should have told you about the Dark Witch, I—"

Gemini stops her with a soothing noise. "It's okay. It's all okay. Let's just get out of here."

"I'm sorry I didn't trust you," Ophelia whispers.

"I'm sorry I didn't make you feel like you could." They press a kiss against Ophelia's lips, but a pained cry from Sagittarius grabs their attention.

Sagittarius has her blade upraised, but Lavinia is too quick. She slices Sagittarius across the cheek and licks the knife, and then Sag is paralyzed.

Screaming, Leo charges Lavinia, tackling her to the ground. They writhe on the floor, Leo grappling to stay on top of her. Lavinia smiles a sharp, bloody grin and brings her talons up to claw at Leo's face.

Blood drips from the cuts and weeps down onto Lavinia. She sticks out her tongue and lets Leo's blood fall into her mouth. She swallows and Leo's limbs lock. She falls off Lavinia and curls in on herself with an anguished groan.

Crack.

Leo's arm falls limp at an unnatural angle, her cry wrenching at my heart. "No!" I scream. Not Leo too. "Leave her alone!"

Leo hovers off the ground, Lavinia's magic hoisting her in the air. She bucks and kicks, but it's no use. Her blood is under Lavinia's control.

Lavinia flicks her fingers like she's brushing away a fly and Leo careens through the air. She crashes into a pillar with a sickening crunch and slides to the ground. Tears stream down my face and I can't help the shriek that rips from me. Is she still breathing? I can't tell from here, and there's too much blood already on the floor for me to tell if any of it is hers. She has to be okay. I can't lose anyone else.

With a furious cry of indignation, Gemini leaps up and runs at Lavinia. Lavinia intercepts them with an elbow to their temple and a slice to their shoulder. Ophelia screams their name when they hit the floor, groaning, unable to move. Their eyes shutter, etched with confusion and panic.

Lavinia laughs as she surveys all of us, the sound making my blood grow hotter. It shouldn't be possible, all of us here powerless, unable to so much as lift a finger against her.

This is why she's the most powerful witch in the world. No one should be able to wield such power over another person's body, let alone six at once, and yet here she is, with all of us clenched in her fist.

"There's no use fighting, girls," she says lightly, inspecting her bloodstained nails. "Surrender now, and no one else has to get hurt."

I look to Niobe, immobilized on the blood-drenched marble floor. She gives a faint, almost imperceptible shake of her head despite the tears streaking her cheeks.

Lavinia notices my gaze. She rolls her eyes at Niobe. "I suppose you'd tell me to let them go. That it's you I'm after, is that it?"

Niobe's eyes glitter with hatred, a silent affirmation.

"You flatter yourself, Niobe," says Lavinia. "I have no interest in washed-up narcissists. My daughters will turn and complete my coven. Whether they want to or not."

Lavinia has every one of us locked in her grasp, kneeling on the floor ready to be controlled. Leo lies unconscious in a heap and all I know is that Lavinia can't be allowed near her. She can't touch one hair on her head. I try to move my arm, my leg, my fingers, but I don't budge. Lavinia's magic is too strong. I can't escape it, not even to check if Leo is still breathing.

"I'll ask you both one last time," says Lavinia, standing between me and Ophelia. "Will you turn willingly and help me complete this coven?"

I hold my breath, waiting for Ophelia to answer. What would my answer be if she gives in? We're meant to be together, no matter what. If she turns, would I go along with her?

"Never," Ophelia spits, and my chest swells with pride.

Lavinia rolls her eyes and her gaze lands on me. "And you?"

"Not a chance in hell," I growl.

"Then let's finish this."

Lavinia claps her hands twice and the doors to the throne room bang open. Nine Dark Witches sweep into the room—the rest of the Dark Twelve. Or at least, there will be twelve of them soon, if

Lavinia has her way with Ophelia and me.

"Since you girls aren't willing to join on your own, I fear it's time to take matters into my own hands." Lavinia steps toward Ophelia and brushes a clawed hand through her golden hair.

"Don't touch her," I snarl.

Lavinia clicks her tongue and shakes her head. "I wish it didn't have to be this way, but you've left me with no choice."

With a wave of her hands, my feet lift off the ground. I struggle, but I can't move as she levitates the two of us high into the air above the throne room. I hang helpless, knowing that even the smallest whim from Lavinia could send me crashing to my death. My stomach twists at the dizzying drop and Ophelia lets out a small whimper.

"Be strong," I whisper, not sure if the words are for me or for her.

"It's time to complete our coven!" Lavinia declares. She looks up at me. "Aries first."

The Dark Twelve gather in a circle below us. They link hands, just as we did to save Sagittarius on that horrible night that now feels so long ago. The moment their circle links, my body seizes like it's been squeezed in an invisible fist. The Dark Witches begin to chant. Their voices are otherworldly, half singing, half shouting in guttural tones that scrape against my bones.

They're draining my energy, my power. Sparks pop and fizz out of my fingertips, pulled by their magic. They burst through the room until they hit a Dark Witch. She yelps but doesn't leave the ring of Dark Witches. Still, the sparks come. I can't stop them or aim them away from my friends below or from Ophelia, hovering a mere foot from me. Her eyes are pleading, tears spilling over and rolling down her cheeks.

Another bolt of lightning spears out of me and I jolt, unable to control my own body.

Power swirls and sloshes inside my head, too fast to grab hold of. Everyone I love is in this room, powerless. I grit my teeth against the burning pit of rage in my stomach, growing and growing with nowhere to go. I have to get control. I can't let it consume me. They're already stealing my power too fast; the more I let out, the quicker I'll turn Dark. I try to breathe, to establish the calm that settled over me like a blanket at Cancer's command back in training. I wish she were here. She would know how to help me.

"I'm sorry," Ophelia says, voice cracking.

She scans something above my eyes. Is my hair is turning white? "I don't want it," I moan.

I try to stay calm, to take long, slow breaths and unspool this knot of rage within me, but every breath fuels the rampaging electrical storm. I try to imagine tamping the power down, pressing it deep into the rich soil of my body and burying it in the earth. It's too hot, though, and the Dark Twelve's magic wraps a fist around my power and yanks. My skin feels like it's on fire, burning from the inside. Sweat drips down my brow and into my eyes. The harder I try to push the power away, the more the heat grows until it burns. I can feel the blood inside my body, burning lava coursing through me.

A scream bursts from my lips, echoing through the room and bouncing back in the voice of someone I don't recognize. I no longer know if the hot liquid on my cheeks is sweat or my own furious tears. The shaking takes over my whole body now and I convulse in midair, unable to control my own body thanks to the iron grip of Lavinia's power.

A wave of electrical current ripples out of my body. Sparks shoot uncontrollably out of all ten of my fingers, spraying in every direction. Emotion is poison and the venom is spreading through my veins. It's pumping through my blood, nearly to my heart, and all I can see is red fuzzing the corners of my vision.

I can't hold on.

It's over.

Burning tears at my nail beds. My cuticles rip open and sharp nails shoot out of them, itching and ripping until I want to climb out of my own skin. Until I'm so dizzy I have to squeeze my eyes shut and bile burns my throat. Still, electricity splits every cell in my body, so great that the only thing tethering me to this moment is Ophelia's voice.

"This is my fault, Serena, I'm so sorry," she cries.

Each word from the Dark Twelve gathered below draws more and more energy from my body. Sparks explode from me and singe my skin. Their sting is nothing compared to the Dark Twelve's power, pulling me apart from within.

"It's Lavinia's fault. Not yours," I say, gritting my teeth against the pain. I refuse to let Lavinia hear me scream. She's the one whose magic is tearing me to shreds from the inside out, like she's squeezing power from my body, forcing me to give everything. Once she's done with me, she'll turn to Ophelia next. We'll become monsters, just like her.

I can't fight this. It comes from somewhere too deep, a well that keeps going down and down and down. I don't want to become Dark. I won't be like my mother, an emotionless shell of the person I once was. Making the people I love suffer at my hands.

I'd rather die.

"Ophelia," I croak. Nausea roils through my stomach. "You have to do it."

She has to do this now, while Lavinia and her Dark Twelve are too busy chanting and trying to complete their spell.

"Don't say that," she says through her tears. "You can hold on, I know you can."

"Please," I beg. "I can't."

"You have to. Fight it, Serena!"

"I don't want you to get hurt. I don't want to be the one who hurts you." I'm supposed to protect her. No matter what. My mother may have been the one to give me that charge, but it's mine and mine alone.

That's my destiny, not this Darkness.

"It's too late for that," she sobs. "I'm already hurt. *This* is hurting me. You have to fight this."

"I wouldn't ask you unless I had to. Unless I knew you could." I cling to her image like she's the last life raft on a sinking ship. I was foolish to ever doubt her. She's strong and brave and powerful, and though I hate asking her to do this, it's the only choice.

"No," she says again, but her voice is weaker this time. "I can't do it. I'm not strong like you."

"Me?" I swallow back the hot lump rising in my throat, even as my limbs feel like they're being ripped apart in every direction. "I'm not the strong one; you are. You've always been the strong one. You can do anything."

It's true. It's always been true. Our entire lives, Ophelia has been the strong one, the one who keeps fighting, the one who never gives up. She snuck through the orphanage in the middle of the night to get to me, she Awoke her powers even though she didn't want to just to save Sagittarius and our coven, she never once gave up on the idea of finding a cure for us. It's too late for me. She'll have to find that cure on her own now, but if anyone can do it, if anyone can stop the Dark Witches for good, it's her. My sister. The strongest person I know.

"There has to be another way," Ophelia sobs, and I wish I could comfort her. I hate asking her to do this, but every inch of my body is on fire. Sweat drips from my skin and each breath sears through my body, failing to fill my lungs.

"There's not," I moan. I wish there was, but there isn't. This is the only way to keep Lavinia from completing the Dark Twelve so Ophelia and the others can stop her. There's not much time left. "They can't have both of us, Ophelia. *Please.* I can't hold on any longer. You have to kill me before I lose my humanity and turn. We both know how this ends."

"I love you," she sputters.

Tears stream down her face and I allow myself this one moment to let everything else fall away. To pretend it's just me and her, the way it was always meant to be.

One last time.

"I love you too."

39

Ophelia

MY SISTER IS MY WHOLE WORLD. SHE IS MY LIGHT IN THE darkness, my protector, my best friend. Suspended above the throne room, though, red-faced and shaking, with talons protruding from her fingers and her hair bursting in strips of white, I don't know her anymore. The tether between us is too taut; it strains in my chest, ready to snap at any moment.

"We both know how this ends."

This isn't how things are supposed to end, though, not for us. I can't do this to her. I don't want to be like my mother, falling prey to the easiest choice, but I can't see another option. If she turns Dark, she's going to send this whole room up in flames and all of us with it and Lavinia will be one step closer to having a full coven. If our roles were reversed, she would do this for me. She would know how to do the hard things, even if it broke her heart.

I don't dare look down at the Dark Twelve circled below us, their chanting growing louder and louder. On the outside of their circle, Sagittarius screams while Gemini bellows curse after curse at Lavinia and her Dark Witches. I have to do this before Lavinia notices. If she stops me, Serena will never forgive me. It has to be now. I take one last look at the deep green eyes I love as they roll back into her head for the last time and turn black.

I let myself listen to the song of the water in my blood—our blood. If I can take hold of the water in everyone else's blood, shouldn't I be able to control my own? I reach for the water in my blood and will it to give itself back over to my control. I let it wash away Lavinia's hold, cleaning my veins with its sweet freshness. I reach for Lavinia next. If I can take hold of her blood and stop her, I can put an end to this. But with her grip still on me, I can't project my power to any blood but my own.

And Serena's.

Her blood is my blood; her heart is my heart.

Identical.

I follow the tether between us from my chest to hers and take hold of the water in her blood, pulsing slow and steady through her body. There's nothing else I can do. Nothing but free her from Lavinia's hold on her body and silently sing the water in her blood a lullaby, willing it to sleep.

Her heart thumps erratically, that vital organ I love with all of my own still-beating heart, and I will it to slow until each beat grows farther apart than the last. For a fraction of a moment, Serena lifts her chin. Her face is no longer contorted in pain. Her clear eyes shine with gratitude and her lips part soundlessly. Before she can speak, though, her heart gives one last pump and stops.

Snap.

The tether between us breaks and my heart skips a beat. I can't breathe as the force of that fracture ricochets into me.

Serena's chin slumps onto her chest, all light extinguished from her eyes.

Tears stream down my cheeks and I bite my lip to keep from screaming, hard enough to draw blood.

The Dark Twelve's singing comes to an abrupt stop.

"You," Lavinia hisses, eyes wide in shock.

The scream I've been holding back bursts from my lips and cleaves through the room. I clutch at my chest, like that will help me gulp down more air. There's a gap in me, somewhere in the slot between my two lowest ribs. A place another soul should curl against mine and now there's nothing but emptiness. No thread, no pull, no connection. No Serena.

She's dead.

Golden light shoots from her limp form, still hanging suspended across from me. It rushes out of her in a glimmering ribbon and courses across the space between us. Blinding, white-hot pain shoots through me as the golden thread spears into my chest, connecting us, and for a moment, I think our plan has backfired. For a split second, I allow myself the hope that my sister and I are so deeply intertwined that the universe won't permit us to exist separately and will force me out of this world along with her.

As the last of her golden thread sinks into my chest, the pain fades and all I'm left with is heat, rippling in waves through my arms and legs.

White light explodes from me. The force of it blasts the Dark Witches off their feet and tosses them against the walls. Their magic releases its hold on me. My stomach rockets into my throat as I free-fall, throwing out a wave of water that sweeps beneath me and cushions my fall. My knees bark in pain as I hit the hard marble,

Serena landing unmoving at my side.

I scramble across the floor to my sister. She stares, unblinking, at the ceiling. My fingers on her wrist don't find a pulse. Tears stream down my cheeks and patter onto her body. I wail, not holding them back as I cradle her to my chest and bury my face in her hair.

"No!" Lavinia screeches. "Foolish girl! What have you done?"

I lower Serena to the ground, tugging at the foreign power building inside me. Lightning ripples out of me in a sharp burst. Heat crackles at my fingertips, fizzing out of me. It's expansive, full of something headstrong and protecting and loving.

Serena.

Sparks stream from my left hand, water from my right.

Somehow, impossibly, her magic left her body and shot into mine. It burns through me, scraping and tearing and ripping until every inch of my skin is burning. I want to claw it out and I scream, trying to release the pain that's eating me alive. Power threatens to swallow me from within.

Lavinia steps toward me, shocked eyes wide, but I pull myself to my feet wielding electricity in one hand and water in the other. How is this happening? No witch can have two zodiac powers; it shouldn't be possible.

"What did you do?" I demand.

Lavinia stares at me for a long moment, white lips pressed together tightly, and then laughs. She actually *laughs*. She stands there like she doesn't care that her daughter is dead on the ground mere feet from her. My vision blurs at the edges, tinted with red. Nothing will ever be the same again. There's no coming back from this, no redemption for me if my sister isn't in this world. There's a lump like a hot coal in my throat, choking me. This world was too cruel to her, to both of us, from the day we were born. It isn't fair that we were left behind and made warriors for a cause we never chose.

It happens too fast, as if I've lost my footing on a stair. The momentum pulls me backward before I can catch myself and suddenly, I'm slipping, unable to stop, sliding and sliding with no end in sight. Waves of water, rushes of electrical current, all crash together and threaten to electrocute me.

One phrase pounds a rhythm in my head: *Serena is dead, Serena is dead, Serena is dead.*

And I'll make every one of them pay.

Lightning leaps up my arm and flies out of my fingertips and strikes Lavinia's side and flings her to the ground. Her head cracks against the marble, knocking her unconscious, collapsed in a pool of blood. With her grip on them broken, Gemini leaps to their feet, screaming my name. They start toward me, but I throw up a fence of electricity, locking them out. Locking the Dark Twelve and Lavinia in. This is my fight now, my vengeance.

"Get out of here, Gem!" I shout.

They let out a brutal scream that echoes into my bones, but I don't turn back to them because the Dark Twelve are on their feet again, surging for me. I take hold of the water in the river of blood in the floor, forming it into a crimson wave of water twice my height. It barrels toward the closest Dark Witch. The moment it crashes over her, I strike with Serena's lightning, frying her where she stands. Her body jolts and lands with a splash in the blood pooling beneath her.

"Pisces!" screams Sagittarius. But I strike again at the next witch and the next, water and electricity together, taking them down one by one until nearly all of the Dark Twelve are on the ground, kneeling in the blood and water coating the marble floor. It's too easy, batting them aside like a cat does a mouse, with Serena's powers and my own at my fingertips. I bury myself deeper and deeper inside the magic, begging it to make me limitless.

"Ophelia, stop!" cries Niobe.

Why should I stop? We're supposed to destroy them—isn't that what Niobe and Gemini and Leo and all the rest of them want? They deserve it after what they've done to us. They've taken everything from me. My mother, my sister, my friends, taking and taking and taking until there's nothing left inside me but a mangled shell. Half of myself is missing, lying dead and extinguished forever.

I will never be whole again.

My limbs stop being my own. They're conduits for magic and nothing more. The lights from the chandelier sputter until they burst, raining glass down. Someone screams as shards fall, but they don't touch me. Water and flame slam into each other to form a wall of steam, rising in billowing curtains until it's too thick to see through. Until power flows out of every inch of me, pure and undiluted, cocooning me in its flame and flood. Panicked screams rebound through the hall and someone shouts for a retreat, but they're trapped, fenced in by electricity and flame.

Good.

It's about time someone was afraid of me.

My arms and legs shake as the magic rushes out of me, a storm in every direction.

"Ophelia!" Gemini yells, still fighting for me, though they should have given up long ago. They're still at the edge of the electrical field, pounding their fists against the impenetrable wall, even as they hiss at the burns scalding their hands and arms. "You have to fight this!"

They've done nothing but tell me to stop using my power since the moment I Awoke. Why should I fight this? I've never felt more alive. What's the use of stopping and living my life afraid and alone? There's no life left to live without Serena; there's nothing at all worth having. Instead, I throw myself into her power. If this power, this vengeance, is the last piece of her I still possess, I'll cloak myself in it and use every drop. Warmth wraps itself around me in a loving caress of power and I never want to leave its embrace. In its arms, I don't have to think about Serena and the aching hole in my chest where that tether was. I don't have to think about anything other than the sweet siren song of magic. Lavinia is right: Only a fool would give that up. It comes easily, naturally. Like breathing.

"Do what nature has ordained," said Lavinia.

Nature ordained me and Serena to be together forever. We came into this world together, and if we cannot go out of it together, I don't care what happens to me any longer. I let my vision blur. I let my limbs lift of their own accord and the cloying drumbeat of Serena's electricity and my water take over as they pound themselves together.

One by one, I seize hold of the water in the blood of each of the Dark Twelve until they're on their knees before me, circled around me and Serena. All except Lavinia, who struggles to rise with blood dripping from her temple.

"Ophelia, please!" Gemini begs, but Sagittarius is already making a portal and dragging an unconscious Leo toward it.

"It's too late," Niobe says grimly. "We have to leave her."

Sagittarius blinks into existence before me and scoops Serena's unmoving body into her arms. Her eyes linger on mine. "Please, Ophelia. Come with us."

I shake my head. I can't leave. I can't go back to the Manor and pretend that everything is the same. Nothing will ever be the same again. I have to finish this, for Serena and for myself.

With a pop, Sagittarius leaps back to the other side of my circle of electricity. Niobe shoves Scorpio through the portal ahead of her, then hefts Leo into her arms and steps through. Sagittarius calls for Gemini, who looks back, lips forming my name, before Sagittarius shoves them through the portal and disappears with Serena in her arms.

They're gone. *Serena* is gone. The absence of her body slams into my chest and threatens to cleave me in two.

Light explodes out of me, burning my eyes, but I don't close them. Serena's magic coursing through me is the opposite of everything my magic is. Hot and certain and fierce. It melds with mine, steaming as fire and water meet, and bursts from every inch of my skin, fizzing and sparking like she's here. With me. Fueling me. My hair whips at my face, pure white like snow, as my nails grow and grow. The well of power inside me deepens until I can't feel the bottom anymore. I dig down, but there's no stopping it, tunneling into the core of myself, of the earth, of the universe.

My breathing eases. My thoughts stop racing. It's like I've been dropped into a cool pond, the water sweet and luxurious. Like the weight pressing on my chest has been lifted, and I no longer know why I was so upset in the first place. Everything is still. My mind feels like a frozen lake in the dead of winter, glassy and calm.

This isn't Darkness—how could anything so weightless be Dark? It's light. It's magic and power and life and *freedom*.

In the pool of blood on the throne room floor, a flicker of

movement draws my eye. My reflection stares back at me, but I don't recognize myself. Golden hair has been replaced by white, blue eyes by black, and the expression on my face is blank. My breath catches as I take in the monster, but the fear doesn't come. The Dark Witch in my reflection is strong. She's someone I was always meant to become; why couldn't I see that before? For the first time in sixteen years, I see everything with perfect clarity. This is where and who I'm meant to be. I raise my arms, fingers splayed wide, and the number on my wrist changes.

I.

A hoarse laugh spills out of me, one I hardly recognize as my own. I'm the most powerful witch in the world. Not my mother, not Niobe, not Serena.

Me.

I will not be a simpering, scared little girl anymore, hiding behind my sister's skirts.

I will never be powerless again.

Lavinia, back on her feet, steps unsteadily over the Dark Twelve, all held captive. A slow smile grows across her face. "You understand now, don't you?" she says. "Now that you've tasted real power."

I lift my chin and lock eyes with Lavinia across the blood-soaked throne room, knowing deep in my bones that I could defeat her now, if I tried. Knowing I don't care to. There is no power in this world that matters anymore when all I can feel is the cavernous emptiness on the other end of the tether in my chest.

In a cold, hard voice I hardly recognize, I say, "Tell me how to bring my sister back."

My words don't shake. They're not a plea, not a question, not a thunderous roar.

They're a command.

Lavinia watches me, silent, but I don't look away. This is all I have left. Blood. Power. Grief that hollows me out and lights something merciless in its wake.

I killed Serena to save her. Now I'll burn the world down to get her back.

EPILOGUE

Lavinia

Rain patters lightly on the cottage windowpanes, the soft lullaby of sweet summer nights. Pale pink clouds mingle with gray, candles flickering, illuminating my two perfect girls at my feet before the fireplace. On nights like these, I want nothing more than to bottle the deep scent of cinnamon, the slant of sunlight through the window, so rare on rainy evenings. A light in the darkness, just like my girls have been for their six years on this earth. I want to freeze the image of them forever in my mind. Ophelia golden-haired, my mirror. Serena dark, her opposite. Two sides to one coin. The same, yet different. A walking contradiction.

With a silver needle, I prick each of them on the forefinger. Ophelia winces and averts her gaze from the drop of blood blossoming on her skin. Serena, though, doesn't look away from me. She watches me carefully as I swirl my fingers, drawing twin droplets of blood into the air. I mutter the spell under my breath like a whispered prayer. A promise. A mother's quiet hope.

I don't know how long it will be until they find me, or how much longer I can protect the girls. This is the one thing I can give them that will last a lifetime. The drops of blood spin. They chase each other through the air between the girls until they meld into one, hovering. No one speaks. A breeze floats through the room, despite the closed doors and windows.

"Hold out your hands," I tell them.

They follow instructions, holding their palms up, fingertips grazing in the space between them. I let the blood release. A drop splashes onto each of their skin, leaving one glowing patch of skin in the center of their palms. With wide eyes full of wonder, they press their palms together as the glow fades.

I slide to the ground between them and wrap my arms around them. They crowd into the hug, pressing their sweet faces into my shoulders. I breathe in the scent of them; herbs and lemon soap and the clean scent of childhood clinging to them like fresh linen.

The spell is complete.

"You must protect each other," I tell them. "No matter what happens."

When I am gone. They'll have each other, always. Should the worst happen to one of them, their magic will fill the other. They'll live on through each other.

Always.

There is no force on this earth strong enough to contain their magic—not even death.

ACKNOWLEDGMENTS

This book is filled with strong, fearless women, and it wouldn't exist without the incredible women in my life whose love, wisdom, and unwavering belief helped me bring this story to life. Every page carries a piece of their magic, and I am endlessly grateful for the ways they lifted me, guided me, and believed in what I could create.

Kirsten—you were there from the very beginning, helping me find the perfect vessel that would hold this story. Your trust is the bedrock on which this whole book stands.

Mackenzie—working with you has been pure magic. You helped me give these characters their voices and this world its life, and I can't thank you enough for all the heart and energy you poured into it.

Sara S—thank you for letting me rewrite again and again until the story finally felt right. You never let me settle, and your guidance helped *The Twelve* become everything I wanted it to be.

Whitney—my sister witch, from day one you've always believed in my imagination, even when I doubted it. You help me see the light when I'm stuck and always remind me to trust my instincts. Your presence in my life is a kind of magic I'll always carry with me.

Sarah N—from the invisible ties that have always bound us since we were kids to every bit of advice and insight you've shared, your guidance has helped me see this story more clearly. I'm so grateful for you.

HarperCollins—thank you for believing in the magic of this story and helping it take flight into the world.

Finally, thank you to my readers—for stepping into this world, for believing in magic. Every page you turned, every heartbeat you shared with these characters, has made this story alive in a way I never could have done alone. The coven's doors are always open to you.